BLOOD MOON

BLOOD MOON

A CAPTIVE'S TALE

RUTH HULL CHATLIEN

Ruth Hull Chatlien

BOOKS BY RUTH HULL CHATLIEN

Blood Moon: A Captive's Tale

The Ambitious Madame Bonaparte
AMIKA PRESS

Modern American Indian Leaders
MASON CREST PUBLISHERS

Blood Moon: A Captive's Tale © Copyright 2017, Ruth Hull Chatlien
First Edition   ISBN 13: 978-1-937484-46-0
AMIKA PRESS   466 Central AVE #23 Northfield IL 60093   847 920 8084
info@amikapress.com   Available for purchase on amikapress.com
Edited by Jay Amberg and Ann Wambach. Cover art and design by Lane Brown. Map illustration by Deirdre Jennings. Author photography by Richard Mack. Designed and typeset by Sarah Koz. Body in Ronaldson, designed by Alexander Kay in 1884, digitized by Rebecca Alaccari and Patrick Griffin of Canada Type in 2006–2008. Titles in Handserif, designed by Gerhard Grossmann in 2008. Thanks to Nathan Matteson.

*To the memory
of Sarah and Chaska*

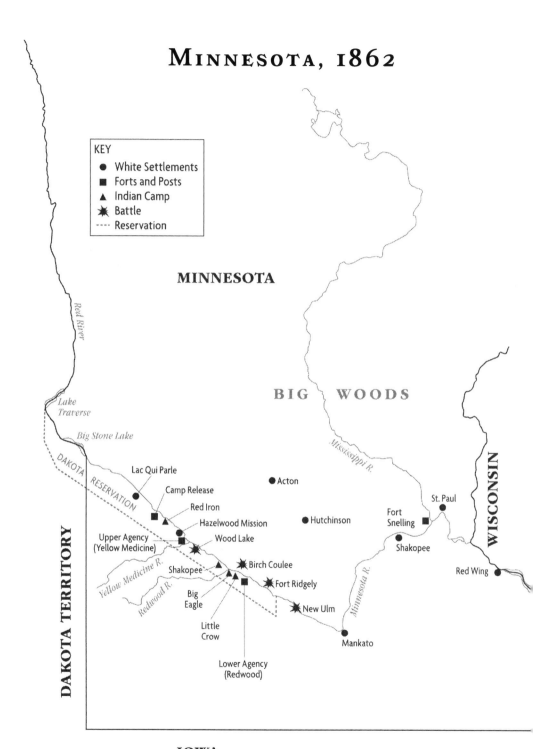

MINNESOTA, 1862

KEY
● White Settlements
■ Forts and Posts
▲ Indian Camp
✸ Battle
---- Reservation

MINNESOTA

BIG WOODS

Red River

Lake Traverse

Big Stone Lake

DAKOTA RESERVATION

Lac Qui Parle

Camp Release

Red Iron

Hazelwood Mission

Upper Agency (Yellow Medicine)

Wood Lake

Shakopee

Big Eagle

Little Crow

Lower Agency (Redwood)

Yellow Medicine R.

Redwood R.

Birch Coulee

Fort Ridgely

New Ulm

Acton

Hutchinson

Fort Snelling

St. Paul

Shakopee

Red Wing

Mississippi R.

Minnesota R.

Mankato

DAKOTA TERRITORY

WISCONSIN

IOWA

A NOTE ABOUT NATIVE NAMES
AND THE DAKOTA LANGUAGE

During the 1800s, the native people who went to war against the settlers of Minnesota were widely known as the Sioux. This is not their proper name; the term was derived from an insulting label placed on them by their enemies the Chippewa (now called the Ojibwa). The correct term for the Eastern Sioux is Dakota. Sarah Wakefield, however, was a woman of her time and called them Sioux in both the title and text of her captivity narrative. Since I have chosen to write this novel in an approximation of her voice, I have followed her practice. I use Dakota for the language and Sioux for the people.

Similarly, like Sarah, I use the names Chaska and Hapa for two of the main characters, even though I know the current preferred spellings for those names are Caske and Hepaŋ. These names refer to birth order, with Chaska meaning firstborn son and Hapa meaning second-born son. Whenever I used Chaska's personal name, however, I used the current spelling Wicaŋhpi Wastedaŋpi in all places except where I am quoting from primary sources. Sarah rarely used the name Wicaŋhpi Wastedaŋpi, which some translate as "Good Little Stars," so I felt I had more flexibility in using the spelling I preferred.

Finally, I have attempted to reproduce some of the Dakota language in dialogue, after studying beginning materials on websites and in books. I considered having these phrases and sentences reviewed by a native Dakota speaker but ultimately decided against it. Sarah Wakefield was not a native speaker, and although she eventually acquired a fair amount of proficiency, it is unlikely that she spoke the language with complete fluency. If there are any errors in the use of Dakota, they are my own, but they represent mistakes that a beginning student of the language would make—and therefore seem a better representation of the way a white captive might speak and record the language than perfectly executed sentences would.

CHAPTER

1

JUNE 1862

THE SOUND OF FRETFUL CRYING SEEPS THROUGH COTTONY LAYERS OF sleep and tickles my mind into wakefulness. I open heavy eyes. Next to me, my husband mutters, "Shut her up, will you?"

John is a doctor who spent all day yesterday attending a woman going through a prolonged and dangerous labor. When he came home after ten, he refused supper, downed several shots of whiskey, and fell into bed.

I rise and go to our children, who lie in the eastern half of our sleeping loft. The two "bedrooms" are separated by only a curtain, which does little to block noise. As a mother, I take comfort in knowing that I will hear if my children are in distress, but John resents any disruptions to his sleep.

First, I determine that our four-year-old son slumbers soundly. Then I reach into the cradle and feel my seventeen-month-old daughter's forehead. It is warm but not alarmingly so. I put a finger into her mouth to rub her lower back gums and detect hard bumps beneath the surface. *At last.* Her first set of molars is coming in. For days, Nellie has been drooling more than usual, so I've been expecting this.

I put a towel over my shoulder, lean my girl against it, and proceed to pace up and down the room, rubbing her back. Her sobs subside to whimpers.

The attic is stifling. Heat rises during summer days and lingers into the night. The curtain that John insists upon drawing for marital privacy blocks any cross breeze that might flow between the windows on the gable ends of the house.

I walk to the eastern window, hoping for fresh air and a glimpse of sky. When I went out to the privy before retiring, the moon was rising above the treetops—large and full, a glowing ivory orb that resembled a lustrous pearl nestled in black velvet. Its beauty made me glad to be living out here on the Minnesota prairie where we have such a fine view of the heavens.

Now, however, when I glance outside, only a thin crescent moon rides in the sky. My chest squeezes with dismay. How is this possible? Leaning out the open window, I notice that the interior curve of the crescent is blurry. Then I see the faint circular outline of a shadowy full moon against the black sky. *An eclipse.* I exhale in relief. I've read about lunar eclipses but never seen one. How wonderful to witness such an unusual event.

The shadow creeps so slowly across the face of the moon that its movement is impossible to discern, yet as the minutes pass, the area of darkness grows and the crescent shrinks to a glowing sliver. When Nellie falls back to sleep, I put her in her cradle but do not return to my own bed.

The heavens declare God's glory, I think and wonder what our neighbors make of this celestial event. John is one of two government-appointed physicians on the Sioux reservation in southern Minnesota, and Indian villages surround the Upper Sioux Agency where we live. I doubt that the Indians have enough scientific learning to account for this phenomenon. No doubt their medicine men have an explanation, most likely one that will increase their hold over the poor, superstitious people.

The still-changing satellite mesmerizes me. At the very instant the last threadlike arc of light disappears, the moon turns the color of rust. The entire orb becomes visible once again, so that a red-orange disk dominates the sky. I clasp my hand over my mouth to keep from crying out. Shadowy areas pulsate across the surface. Sometimes the moon grows darker, but then the angry color reappears.

Is it the end of the world? Some warning phrase pokes at my memory, but I cannot call it to mind.

Thoroughly frightened, I retreat to our bedroom and shake John by the shoulder. He grunts and rolls away from me. I jostle him again.

"Wha...? Is...there emergency?"

"Come look out the window," I whisper. "The moon has turned to blood."

"Oh, Sarah!" John groans. He rubs his face, dragging his hands from his eyes down to his chin and back up again.

"Please," I beseech him.

He rises, looking like a specter in his loose white nightshirt, and follows me through the curtain and across the children's room. When he reaches the window, he observes the moon for a few seconds and then says in a dangerously tight voice, "Was it like this when you got up?"

"No, there was an eclipse, but as soon as all the light disappeared, the moon turned red just as you see."

"Stupid cow." John wheels away from the window, grabs my earlobe, and twists it. I gasp. He speaks in a low tone. "There's a perfectly logical scientific explanation that has to do with earth's atmosphere and refracted light, but you wouldn't know about that, would you?" He leans in closer. "Don't ever wake me up for such a foolish reason."

Squeezing my eyes shut so I won't see his scorn, I whisper, "I'm sorry. I won't do it again."

John jerks away and lumbers back to bed.

As soon as he passes through the curtain, I lean against the windowsill, panting from pain and humiliation. Tears ooze from my eyes as I recall the words *stupid cow.* This isn't the first time that John has disparaged my ignorance. Coming from a farm family, I have fewer years of formal schooling than his sisters, but I've always been an avid reader, and when we first married he told me he was proud of my attempts to improve myself. *He doesn't really think you're stupid. He's tired and irritable. You shouldn't disturb him after such a difficult day.*

I still find the ruddy moon unnerving despite John's insistence that there is a scientific explanation. Suddenly, I remember the prophecy that nagged at me earlier: When the Bible describes the end times, it says, "The sun shall be turned into darkness, and the moon into blood."

3

But if it's a sign, what does it mean? Can it be that the red nation surrounding us is about to go on the warpath?

No, I tell myself. I conjure up the image of the women I visit in nearby villages—their friendly faces, their warm greetings. The Sioux have lived at peace with white settlers here in Minnesota for more than 200 years. The blood moon is just as John said, a natural phenomenon and nothing more.

Repeating that over to myself, I make my way back to bed.

CHAPTER

2

"Mama, mama, come look!"

The voice of my son breaks into the conversation I am having with my hired girl. Jimmy races into the kitchen and stops so abruptly that he nearly topples over. He gazes up at me, his blue eyes as wide as I have ever seen them. "Mama, a b-big war party is riding past."

My heart lurches as I remember last month's ominous sign, but mindful of my son, I place a hand on my chest to calm the palpitations. Although I am by nature a fearful woman, I must appear calm for the child's sake. "Past the agency?" I ask. "They are not stopping here?"

"No. They are riding to the ford. Very fast."

I expel my breath, yet my nerves remain as taut as freshly tuned piano wires. The Sioux have been restive this summer, so I dare not dismiss the possibility of danger. Jimmy grasps my hand and pulls me toward the parlor. I resist, saying, "Wait, let me think."

My servant speaks up, "Mrs. Wakefield, I think I know what is happening."

I glance back at the raven-haired girl, and for a moment, God help me, I wonder if I can believe her. Because Mary is Sioux. The name she was given at birth was Makawee, but the Reverend Mr. William-son renamed her when she enrolled in his mission school. For a second, I stare at her. Although she is clad in a blouse and skirt like a settler, all I can see is the bronze skin and high cheekbones that mark

5

her as a different race from me. Then I remember how tenderly this girl has helped nurse my children through their illnesses, and I tell myself I can trust her.

"Go on."

"I heard that the Chippewa killed two of my people on the 22nd. This party must be going to take revenge."

So they are not going after whites. My knees go so weak with relief that I brace my hand upon the table. During my years in Minnesota, I have learned a thing or two about the enmity between the Chippewa and the Sioux. In 1858, when John and I were living in Shakopee, the two tribes fought a battle so near the community that many townspeople went out to watch as though it were a wrestling match at a county fair. After the fight ended, John treated the wounded Sioux, and I assisted him as much as I was able, given my lack of medical training.

Now Jimmy leads me out the front door. We leave our fenced-in yard, cross the path that bisects the cluster of agency buildings, and climb the slight rise of land on which the warehouse stands. Once we reach that building, we halt and gaze at the government road that runs past the agency and curves toward the ford just west of the place where the Yellow Medicine River empties into the Minnesota.

The war party that gallops before us is large indeed. Even though I delayed coming outside for at least a minute, a steady stream of riders still passes our settlement. They travel so quickly that clouds of dust rise as high as the horses' flanks. Judging from the direction they are headed, I conclude that Mary must be right. The party seems to be heading toward the Big Woods to fight the Chippewa.

Most of the warriors are bare-chested above their breechcloths and leggings, and despite the dust and the speed with which they travel, I see streaks of red and yellow war paint on their faces and chests. Some wear eagle feathers in their hair. Their yells of rage send shivers down my spine.

As the last rider disappears from sight, I put a hand on my son's shoulder and gently turn him around. "Let's go back in the house."

"But I want to see Father." Jimmy gestures toward the brick warehouse beside us where my husband has his office. "I want to tell him about the war party."

6

"Don't be silly. He is probably closeted with a patient. Besides, you know the building looks out on the road. I am certain he must be as aware of it as we are."

Jimmy pushes out his lip mutinously, but I laugh and tousle his white-blond hair. Now that I know my family is safe, I want to dance across the prairie with my little boy in my arms. The position of the sun tells me that it is nearly noon. "Let's get something to eat. How about a nice glass of milk and a jam sandwich?"

About nine o'clock that night, I retire to the second floor. First, I check on my children, tucked in their beds under the eaves. Eighteen-month-old Lucy Ellen, nicknamed Nellie, lies on her back with her arms spread as wide as the cradle will allow. In contrast to her tow-headed brother, she has her father's dark brown hair and my mother's swarthy skin. In the crib next to her, Jimmy lies curled on his side, clutching his favorite carved horse. As I gaze at them, I say a silent prayer of thanksgiving that the terror I felt earlier today was naught but a false alarm.

Then I draw the curtain that separates their section of the sleeping area from ours. I sit at my dressing table, pull out my hairpins, and begin my brushing ritual. Because I have always wished for more beautiful hair—mine is a dull, medium brown—I brush it every night to give it more gloss.

John enters the room carrying a cut glass tumbler filled with whiskey. I bend at the waist to brush the underside of my hair so I can pretend not to notice. Although I dislike it when he drinks heavily, I know from experience that his mood will only worsen if I protest.

After a minute, I sit up and resume brushing the normal way. "I don't think I have ever seen as bloodcurdling a sight as the war party this morning," I remark, relieved that I no longer have to maintain a calm demeanor for the children.

"You don't say." He sets the half-full tumbler on the marble-topped bureau and removes his frock coat. "Did you faint or merely wail in terror?"

Tears sting my eyes. I lay down my hairbrush and gaze at his reflection in the mirror on my dressing table. "On the contrary, I main-

7

tained my composure quite well. You can ask Jimmy if you will not believe me."

John shakes his head, rubs his eyes with the heels of his hands, and after swallowing the last of his drink, sits on the side of our bed. He rubs at a scratch in the heavily carved footboard. "No need, Sarah," he mutters. "You would hardly be the first woman to quail at the sight of Indians on the warpath."

That comment is likely to be as close to an apology as I will receive. My husband is swift to ridicule and loath to admit that his wit can be hurtful. Turning on my backless stool, I face him. "Mary said the warriors went to fight the Chippewa."

Pensively, he scratches his bushy side-whiskers. "That is what I heard too. But it could just as easily have been us. The Sioux have been grumbling a great deal about the late annuity payment."

Icy fear grips my stomach, but I want to prove that I can be rational even in the face of danger, so I say, "I would grumble too if my children were starving. Why don't the traders extend credit so the Sioux can buy some food? The gold shipment will get here eventually."

"Yes, but Myrick and the others have heard the annuity is going to be paid in greenbacks this year, and you know how their value is falling. Besides, the traders don't trust Galbraith to renew their licenses after this season, and if they extend too much credit, they may not see those debts paid before their tenure expires." John rests his right foot on the opposite knee, pulls off his boot, and drops it on the carpeted floor. He groans and rubs his toes. "Sarah, I wonder if I made a mistake bringing you and the children out here."

So that explains his gloom. John obtained the post of agency doctor a year ago through the influence of his younger brother James, a lawyer and former state legislator. As soon as President Lincoln took office, all of Buchanan's Democratic appointees were turned out of their patronage jobs and replaced with people who had contacts in the Republican Party. "You only wanted to gain a post with a steady salary instead of a practice where the patients could not pay half the time."

John pulls off his remaining boot and rises to stand before me. Lifting my chin, he asks, "And will you say the same if the Sioux go on the warpath?"

I swallow hard and nod. He bends down to kiss me. His lips are wet, and the alcohol fumes on his breath are overpowering. His fingers fumble at the buttons on the front of my dress. Grasping his arms, I pull myself up and embrace him. My husband is a man with a voracious appetite for physical pleasures: beer and oysters, whiskey and cigars, and the comforts of our marriage bed. It does not surprise me that this is how he chooses to assuage whatever anxiety remains from the day.

Days pass, and my sense of alarm subsides into a dull uneasiness, like the faint sensitivity that sometimes lingers after a toothache. I tend my children, harvest crops from our garden, and make pickled onions to spice up John's meals during the long, dull winter. As July comes to a close, I eagerly await the first ears of corn and check every day to see if silk has started to show. Last year we had a drought, and my vegetable patch did not bear well. This summer has also been dry, but John set up a crude wooden gutter and a rain barrel at the back of our house, which has collected enough water to keep our garden going.

Early in the morning on the first day of August, I knock on Mary's door to make sure she's awake and then go out to gather eggs. The Upper Sioux Agency is built on a bluff overlooking the Minnesota River. As I cross our backyard, consisting of prairie grasses that John must scythe every week, heavy dew soaks the hem of my dress. To the north, where the bluff drops away to the valley, a few tendrils of mist rise from the river like fingers waving a greeting to the morn. The breeze carries a faint scent of mint, and a nearby meadowlark calls: three piercing whistles followed by a warble.

I duck my six-foot frame to enter the chicken coop and search for eggs. We have forty-odd Plymouth Rock hens, so I usually gather enough to sell to other agency employees. John allows me to use my egg money to buy clothing patterns and fabric. Today is a good day: thirty eggs.

When I exit the coop, I notice two middle-aged Sioux men talking behind the warehouse on the ridge. They are not farmer Indians; that much is obvious from their long hair and traditional dress. I suspect they might be chiefs waiting to ask the agent, Thomas Galbraith, if the gold is here. For the past several weeks, various bands have been

9

setting up camp in the valleys along the banks of the Minnesota and Yellow Medicine rivers even though Galbraith instructed them not to come in to the agency until he sent word. He has told John that the Sioux's annuity—their annual gold payment for the lands they ceded —is late this year on account of the War of the Rebellion. However, by mid-summer, many of the Sioux were starving, so they disregarded Galbraith's instructions and began to arrive.

One of the men glances my way, and instinctively, I lower my egg basket to hide the bounty I have gathered. I know such a reaction is foolish since neither man shows a trace of hostility. In fact, I think I recognize one of them as someone who attends Dr. Williamson's Dakota church. I nod in greeting.

John calls me too sentimental, but I cannot help but feel guilty that we have so much food stored up for the coming winter when I know how desperate the Sioux are. They are no longer allowed to go hunting off the reservation, and the growing numbers of settlers in southern Minnesota have so stripped the region of game that hardly any animals wander onto the ten-mile-wide ribbon of land where the Sioux are supposed to stay. Although it is their custom to share their food with any of their people in need, the few Indians who have become farmers cannot grow enough to feed the multitude that have so far refused to take up the plow.

Recent conditions have worsened matters. The last two summers drought shriveled the corn, and last year, a plague of cutworms mowed down much of what did grow. Then, we had a brutally long winter, which delayed the spring hunting. The Sioux have had barely enough food for months. I have seen them desperately forage for wild turnips and the tuberous roots of marsh grasses.

Yet I know that John is right. Even if we were to turn over the almost 300 pounds of ham, salt pork, dried beef, and salted cod in our larder, how far would that go toward feeding 5,000 famished people? I am not Christ, able to perform a miracle with a few loaves and fishes. All our carefully gathered provisions would provide less than a single meal for the Sioux masses, and in the end, my own family would starve this winter because of my misdirected generosity. Still, it grieves me to see the Indians' hunger. Reentering my house, I pray that the gold arrives soon so they can obtain supplies and return to their winter camps.

After Mary comes in with a full pail from milking our cow, she and I make a large breakfast of eggs, bacon, and biscuits, and by the time everything is ready, John and the children have gathered at the table. My canaries—five birds divided between two cages in the dining room—are trilling cheerfully at the shaft of light that streams through our eastern window. I pour John's coffee, then sit opposite him, and feed bites of egg to Nellie. She has already nursed upstairs, but I am trying to coax her into eating more solid food. As I smile into her bright-eyed face, I remind myself that I have many blessings to be grateful for.

Among them is the beauty of this sun-filled room with its potted ferns, sheer curtains, tulip-patterned wallpaper, and substantial mahogany sideboard. In the year we have lived here, I have turned our little frame house into an elegant abode. A few months ago, John hired a traveling photographer to take pictures of the interior of our home, which he mailed to his older sister Lucy in Connecticut. The letter of astonished praise we received in return was gratifying to my chafed pride. Lucy's correspondence with me has always been cool, as though she doubts that any woman bold enough to travel to Minnesota on her own could be refined enough to make a proper doctor's wife, whereas the Wakefields are a fine old New England family. John's father was a doctor and state legislator, while his grandfather fought in the Revolutionary War.

John spreads wild strawberry jam thickly upon a biscuit and asks, "What are you going to do this morning?"

"The usual chores. And probably mend that shirt you tore last week."

"I have some socks that need darning too."

I nod and decide to ask Mary to search through the dirty laundry for them.

"You also need to finish the household accounts for July so I can look over them tonight, and you still haven't answered Julia's last letter. And I want you to make a complete inventory of everything we have in the larder."

"Yes, John," I say, digging my nails into my palms to keep from betraying my resentment. Talking to John feels like knocking at a door, not knowing whether it will be answered by the witty, protective man I fell in love with or a caustic stranger who may turn violent over the smallest offense. Because of his volatile temper, I police my behavior to keep from enraging him; even so, I sometimes fail to predict what will set him off.

Fleetingly, I wonder if he wants the inventory to make sure I don't defy his recent ban on giving food to any Indians who come begging, an issue we have argued about many times. John downs the last of his coffee and leaves without another word. I turn my attention to making sure the children finish their breakfast.

An hour later finds me sitting in the parlor with Nellie on the floor at my feet. She babbles nonsense as she plays with a battered set of tin cups that John used to carry when he practiced medicine among the coarse miners of the California goldfields. I am looking through the June issue of *Godey's Lady's Book,* which arrives by mail every month. If I must toil at thankless tasks all day, then I want to do something I enjoy first. I always love studying the hand-tinted fashion plate at the front of *Godey's,* and today's offering is no exception. The dress at the center of the image enchants me. It is made of rose-and-white gingham with a fringed rose sash about the waist and ruched rose fabric decorating the square neckline and the lower part of the skirt. I wonder if I would look ridiculous in such a gown. Would the sash draw too much attention to my stout figure? Perhaps if I were to make it in a darker color, it would be more suitable for a woman of my height and girth. Yet that shade of rose is so lovely.

Sometimes I wish we still lived in town where I could wear pretty clothes to ladies' clubs and the occasional concert. But the truth is, I might not do those things even if we lived in the city of St. Paul. I have never had many friends. Although life out here on the agency is rough and sometimes lonely, I have more freedom than I had growing up in Rhode Island or living in town the first years of our marriage.

A harsh screeching erupts in the dining room, and I jump up, afraid that one of the cats from the stable next door has sneaked through the open window to hunt my canaries. When I rush through the doorway, however, I see my son standing on a dining room chair and poking a stick into one of the birdcages.

"James Orin Wakefield, stop that at once."

As I come around the table and lunge for him, he eludes my grasp by jumping off the other side of the chair and crawling under the table. The scamp knows very well that I will have a hard time squeezing my bulk under there.

After pulling up the corner of the tablecloth, I press my hand against the table and bend down, trying to catch sight of my son crouched among the chair legs. "How dare you torment those sweet birds? You know I cannot abide cruelty."

"I wasn't being mean," he declares, his voice muffled. "I was trying to make them sing."

"I don't believe you. Yesterday you said they make your ears hurt." I yank John's armchair away from the head of the table. "Now come out of there at once. Your punishment will be worse if I have to get down on the floor to get you."

"No, Mama. Don't spank me. You know my father doesn't like it when you hit his little boy."

Jimmy has always been verbally precocious, but today his odd third-person speech stops me cold. Evidently, my son has finally figured out that John disapproves of my reliance on corporal punishment. My husband will spank the children himself if he thinks they deserve it—and more than once, he has struck me in a rage—but he says such methods of discipline are a man's prerogative, not a woman's. My fingers fairly tremble with the urge to strike Jimmy, but I restrain myself. Instead, I wipe my moist palms on my skirt. "I will not spank you if you say you're sorry and promise not to do that again."

"I promise, Mama." He crawls to a point where I can see him—but where he can still duck back if he wants to. "I'm sorry."

I step away from the table and say, "Come on out of there."

Despite my best intentions, something in my tone causes Jimmy to retreat back under the table like a tortoise into its shell. He begins to cry.

At that moment, Nellie crawls to the doorway between the dining room and parlor and repeatedly calls, "Mama!" My son is wailing, and Mary is clattering pans and singing hymns in the kitchen. Although the canaries have stopped squawking, I feel as though I am barely keeping afloat in a swirling eddy of chaos.

Abruptly, I march into the kitchen and tell Mary that I am going out and she should watch the children. Then I leave the house through the front door, exit our yard, shut the gate behind me, and walk to the community stable.

As my eyes adjust to the barn's dim interior, I see Ben, the stable boy, mucking out the nearest stall. I pass him on my way to our mare, and he asks, "You taking her out today, Miz Wakefield?"

"I might." The thought of riding away from the pandemonium at home is nearly irresistible. When I reach our stall, Lady extends her head over the gate. I stroke the side of her neck, put my face at the end of her nose, and blow into her nostrils. Lady returns the greeting. She is an eight-year-old bay Morgan with a white star on her face and one white sock on her right hind leg. John bought her as a filly shortly after our wedding, and I have never known a gentler horse. She nickers softly and I answer, "Sorry, girl. I forgot to bring you a treat."

I keep my face close to the mare's and close my eyes as I continue to stroke her neck. Lady smells of hay, dust, and sweat, and her scent brings back the memory of the many outings we have taken together. Often on Sundays if the weather allows, I will harness her so Jimmy and I can ride bareback to Dr. Williamson's mission—or even farther north to Dr. Samuel Riggs's mission at Hazelwood, located on the banks of Rush Brook. John is a Freemason and does not care for going to church, so I am free to attend the congregation of my own choosing.

I have never seen more beautiful country than the land near Rush Brook. Hills surround it on every side, lending a majesty to the scene that lifts my spirits every time I ride there. Just as at the agency, the lands adjacent to the brook rise high above the streambed, so high that when I emerge from the trees that tower above the brook and gaze down upon the Indian town below, I imagine I am staring at a doll's village such as Nellie might play with.

To reach this stream on my journey to or from the mission, I must carefully start Lady down a steep path that, if it has recently rained, might be slick with mud. That horse is as sure-footed a mare as ever existed and picks her way delicately among the stones and tree roots we encounter on the trail. In the meantime, I hug my boy tightly to make sure he doesn't tumble off during the descent.

Until the unrest of these last few weeks, whatever anxiety I experienced on those journeys was due to the rigors of the trail rather than the fear of going among the Indians. I confess, when we first moved to the agency last year, I felt tremors for days, imagining that every night noise was the precursor to an attack. Only a short time here, however, sufficed to teach me that the Sioux are a kindly, pleasant folk. Even now, with so much discontent among the Indians, I have faith that the wisest elders will prevail and we will come through this uneasy time without violence.

On our weekly Sabbath excursions, as my son and I head home through the Indian camp on the banks of Rush Brook, we usually see women sitting at their cook fires preparing the evening meal. More often than not, one of them will call greetings to me using the name they gave me last summer— *Taŋka-Winohiŋca Waŝte,* meaning "large, good woman."

As soon as I dismount, one will ask, *"To'ked yauŋ he?"*—"How are you?"—while another might offer me her pipe. The older women love to smoke, but they can do so only when they are resting or working at sedentary tasks such as baking bread. Their pipes, which they call *ca'ŋnuŋpa,* have T-shaped bowls fashioned of red pipestone, which they rest upon the ground as they smoke through two-foot-long ash stems, carved and decorated with beading. Many an evening, I have spent a pleasant hour smoking and gossiping with them before returning to my house. In this way, my son and I both have gained a basic competency with the Dakota language.

Today, smarting from the way John assigned me a list of onerous chores as though I were a servant, I stroke Lady and imagine riding away from our settlement to visit my friends among the Sioux. I could bring them some flour from our larder (since I have not yet done my inventory, John will never know) and offer to help with their cooking or sewing.

Doing so would make me feel like a truant from school. Oh, what a delicious sense of freedom it would bring. But how would I explain my dereliction of the household duties to John? Especially now when he is so uneasy about the mood of the Indians. With the anger in the Indian camps, I do not know for a certainty that the women would welcome me. And since I am a mother of young children, how can I risk my safety for such a flimsy reason? Can I take the chance of leaving my precious babes motherless for the sake of a mere holiday?

No, I cannot. Nor will I risk enraging John. Sighing, I kiss Lady upon her velvety nose and then go back toward the house.

CHAPTER

3

I JUDGED CORRECTLY IN ASSUMING THAT JOHN WOULD NOT WISH ME TO go riding in the present unsettled circumstances. When Sunday comes, he forbids me to attend church. All morning as I go about my household chores, I repeatedly glance out our windows to see groups of Indians walking around the agency, talking among themselves, and gesticulating at the brick warehouse.

The August sun is scorching, the air is as heavy as a wet towel, and by afternoon, the children whine peevishly. Nellie suffers from heat rash, while Jimmy pouts because I require him to remain in the house while his father scythes the grass. John had intended to walk the quarter mile to sub-agent Nelson Givens's house after that chore was done, but given the unusual number of Indians in the settlement, he changes his mind.

Instead, John challenges our son to a checkers tournament. They remove to the outdoors, carrying two dining room chairs into the backyard and setting up the game board on an overturned barrel. The high squeals of triumph that come through the open window tell me that my husband is allowing Jimmy to win. I bring them a plate of sugar cookies and return to my sewing in the parlor.

In the late afternoon as I water the drooping zinnias by our front doorstep, a middle-aged Sioux comes to the gate and asks if he may have a drink of water. *"Hay,"* I answer, which is "yes" in his language, and go into the house. When I return, I hand him a tin cup of water and three sugar cookies. He holds them in his palm and stares at them before taking a cautious bite. Then he smiles broadly. "No ice cream?"

I laugh. Last year, only a month after we came to this place, we had a scare on the morning of July 4th. A friendly Sioux warned us that angry Indians were coming to make mischief. We and the other agency employees hid in the jail most of the day until a second messenger came to say the attack had been called off. So we held our Independence Day dance that evening as planned. In addition to the mission people, we had invited local chiefs, and I tried to create goodwill by giving them portions of all our refreshments, including the unfamiliar ice cream. "No ice cream today," I answer the man at my gate. "Only when we have a feast day."

"O.K." He eats the last cookie. "Thank you. Sweet crackers are good."

That simple human exchange makes me ashamed of the worry I have been nursing. As the man strides off toward the Indian encampments, I wonder if our fear of these people is not itself part of the problem. I suspect that we would be in very little danger if only the settlers and traders would treat the Sioux justly.

As I prepare supper, my heart is lighter than it has been all day, and I describe the encounter to John and the children as we eat. Jimmy laughs at the phrase *sweet crackers,* and the baby giggles when she hears her brother's merriment. After the meal is done, John pushes back his chair. "Things have quieted down, so I think I'll go see Givens after all. He promised to show me some fossilized shark's teeth he found up at Big Stone Lake."

I scrape the children's leftovers onto my own plate. "Shark's teeth? Here in Minnesota, so far from the ocean?" As my gaze falls upon the chicken bones, an exciting idea takes hold of me. "Could this be proof of Noah's flood?"

John snorts and pulls on his frock coat. "More like the evidence of a geologic cataclysm. At any rate, it should provide more scientific interest than I usually find in this godforsaken place."

I gaze at him, wondering at his sour attitude. In town, he raged against petty-minded people and the constraints of conventionality, but now that we live close to the frontier, he scoffs at our neighbors' rough ways and lack of education. John is a discontented man who doesn't seem to know exactly what he wants, and for the life of me, I don't know how to help him sort it out.

He kisses the children, tells them to mind me, and grabs a cigar from the case on his desk. Then he leaves, whistling as he walks out into the still-bright evening.

Perhaps because I am already in a reflective mood, the sound of the merry dance tune carries me back six years to the night we first met. John whistled then too as he left me.

I came to Minnesota at the age of twenty-six to escape ignominy at home. Events beyond my control had irretrievably blackened my reputation, although I swear before God that I did not deserve the censure. I had been foolish and gullible, not sinful, but no one was willing to believe me—least of all those who should have protected my honor. God answered my prayers for redemption by providing a way for me to go west.

Relatives of one of the few schoolmates who still deigned to acknowledge me had moved to the Minnesota Territory in 1855 and settled in the new town of Shakopee. Not four months after their arrival, a runaway team overturned a wagon, killing both my friend's cousin and his wife. The couple had three adolescent sons, all of them old enough to hire out as laborers, but that left no one to care for their elderly grandparents. So the Rhode Island branch of the Phelan family engaged me to travel to Shakopee to be the old couple's housekeeper. The pay was low, but I had room and board, a few hours each day to dedicate to my own pursuits, and best of all, the chance to make a fresh start.

My first season there, Mrs. Phelan fell and twisted her ankle. As she lay sunk in melancholy over her son's death, she caught first a summer cold and then pneumonia. Repeated applications of mustard plaster failed to bring her relief, so I sent for the town's physician, Dr. Wakefield. When he rapped on the door, I opened it to find a man in his early thirties, with wavy brown hair combed from a side part. His deep-set blue eyes swept my figure, and his lips twitched upward. I flushed, certain he was amused by my plain face and mannish size. After a curt nod of greeting, I led him to the upstairs bedroom where Mrs. Phelan lay coughing.

Hours later as I sat sewing in the parlor, I heard a heavy tread on the stairs. Automatically, I rose to light the doctor's way out. Lifting my kerosene lamp, I was shocked to see the weariness etched upon his face. "How is—"

He shook his head. "I gave her tartar of antimony to induce vomiting and mercury to purge her intestines, but the congestion in her lungs is no better. I fear that she may not make it."

My heart throbbed with pain for the old couple. "Does Mr. Phelan know?"

Dr. Wakefield nodded. "I spoke to him quietly in the hallway because I didn't want to distress his wife. He's sitting with her, watching as she sleeps."

Sympathy for the doctor overrode my earlier hurt feelings. "You look all done in. Let me bring you some hot coffee."

He checked his pocket watch. "It's late. I shouldn't keep you from your bed."

"I don't mind. I made pie this afternoon. Would you like a piece?"

Dr. Wakefield raised his eyebrows. "What kind of pie?"

"Custard."

He held up his hands in a gesture of surrender. "How can a man say no to that?"

I nodded to the parlor door. "Have a seat in there, and I'll bring you the food."

"Thank you, Miss..."

"Brown. Sarah Brown."

A few minutes later, I set a mug of black coffee on the table beside the sofa and handed him a plate with a quarter of the pie. John forked up a large bite, closed his eyes as he chewed, and sighed in contentment. "Miss Brown, you are a prodigious cook."

Blushing, I bent low over my sewing. I was trimming the edge of a cuff with a fine-pleated ruffle, a task that requires precision.

"The Phelans keep you at your work very long hours," he observed after a minute of silence.

"Oh no, not at all. This bit of sewing isn't for them. I fear the position with the Phelans may not last long." I glanced up to see if he understood that I was referring to their age, and he nodded. "I have always wanted to set up my own shop as a dressmaker, so I started taking orders from the ladies in town to see if I can gain enough customers to support myself once I must live on my own."

He used his fork to scrape up the last crumbs of pie. "With your skills at cooking and plying the needle, I would think you more likely to marry than to go into business."

I rose to take his plate. Stung by the fear that he was mocking me, I blurted, "Surely you must have noticed that I lack other qualities men desire in a wife."

He gazed at me thoughtfully. When he stood, I realized that he was my equal in height. "I see only that you're a fine figure of a woman, Sarah Brown." My mouth dropped open in disbelief, and he laughed. "You can take that as my considered medical opinion."

Dr. Wakefield walked to the hallway, where he put on his hat and picked up the medical bag he had left there. Then he whistled a tune as he went out into the night.

The memory causes me to sigh as I stand there still holding a dirty plate. Mary comes into the dining room to help clear the table, and I turn to my children. "What would you like me to read to you tonight?"

Early Monday morning I wake to the sound of distant shouting. As I try to decipher the origin of the commotion, I gaze at the boards a few feet above my face. The ceiling of our second floor slants with the roof, and the headboard of our bed is pushed beneath the eave. I rise, being careful not to bump my head, and go to the window in the western gable end of our room.

The sky has begun to lighten, but the sun hasn't risen completely, so in this direction the heavens are still more sapphire than cerulean. Looking past the clustered agency buildings—two employee duplexes, the jail, and the shell of the burned-out school for manual labor—I gradually discern that the top of the hill to the west is filled with dark figures, both standing and on horseback.

"John," I call in a low voice, not wanting to wake the children. He doesn't stir. He was drunk when he arrived home last night, so now he is sunk into heavy sleep.

I move to his side of the bed, shake him, and quickly step back out of reach. "Damn it!" he roars and flails his arm wildly. "Can't you let a man be?"

"It's the Sioux," I whisper. "They are gathering on the hill above the agency. There must be scores of them."

John sits up and presses his forehead. "By gad, Sarah, don't exaggerate."

Without a word, I walk to my side of the bed and pour a glass of water from the carafe I keep on the nightstand. I hand it to John and wait until he drinks it down before I ask, "Don't you hear them hollering?"

He grunts in response. Then he rises and steps behind the screen where we keep the chamber pot. He groans loudly, but I still hear the plinking sound of his stream hitting the container.

After he finishes, he goes to the window. The sky is lighter now, and when I join him, I can see that if anything, I have vastly underestimated the number of warriors who are gathering. John lets out a low whistle. "Tarnation."

He turns away, kneels before the trunk set beneath the eaves, and rummages through it to find the field glasses he used years ago when he and his brother rode the countryside looking for tracts to acquire for a land speculation scheme. Lifting the glasses to his eyes, he scans the horizon again. As he does, the shouting ceases and is immediately replaced by singing. The high jingling of bells and deep pounding of drums accompanies the rhythmic chanting.

"I can't tell what's going on," John murmurs. "They might be gathering for a ceremonial dance. They're dressed in their finery, and I don't see a lot of guns."

"What if you're wrong? What if they attack?"

After setting the glasses on the windowsill, he looks at me, eyes dark with dread. "What can we do? The only way the four of us could get away would be to take our wagon, and with just the one horse, we would never outrun them. All we can do is stay here and hope for the best."

As he dresses, I think, *This cannot be happening.* I remember the friendly Indian I spoke to yesterday. "John, we have friends among the agency Indians. And you've traveled around the reservation helping so many others. We're not like the traders who cheat and insult them. They won't hurt us."

John cups the side of my face with his hand. "These are savages you're talking about. They don't think the way we do. If they're angry with one white person, they don't care how they take their revenge. Any white victim will do."

"I don't believe that," I answer, although his certainty has shaken my confidence. "The man I gave water to yesterday knew me. He remembered the kindnesses I have done for his people."

Shaking his head, John sits on the edge of the bed near the footboard and pulls on his boots. "I don't have time for breakfast. I have to get to the agency and see what plans Galbraith and Lieutenant Sheehan have made for our defense."

"I'll bring you something to eat after I feed the children."

"No. I want you to stay inside." John starts for the staircase but stops and returns to squat before the still-open trunk. He pulls out a box, removes a pistol from it, and loads the gun with bullets. "You know how to shoot this, don't you?"

Guns make me uneasy, but at a time like this, what can I say? I nod, and he lays it atop the dresser. "Don't let Jimmy know it's there."

As he passes me, he kisses me on the forehead.

Suddenly weak, I sink on our bed. What could John mean by leaving me the pistol? I can't possibly fight off hundreds of warriors with only five bullets. Does he expect me to kill the children and myself rather than be taken? The idea is too horrific. "Dear God," I cry, "please don't let things come to that."

After letting out a deep, shuddering breath, I rise and put on my clothes. Not a sound comes from the children on the other side of the curtain, and I wonder if they can possibly still be asleep despite the increasing uproar outside.

As I pin up my hair, a noise like a stampede commences, and the singing grows louder and more fervent. Through the window, I see a mass of Sioux rushing down the hill toward the agency, those on horseback leading the way. There must be more than five hundred altogether.

Turning from the window, I go to the head of the stairs and call down, "Mary! Mary, are you up?"

"Yes, Mrs. Wakefield." She comes to the foot of the staircase and gazes up at me. Even in the dim light of the hallway, fear is visible on her face, and this terrifies me more than anything else.

"Go outside and fasten the gate. You're Sioux; they won't hurt you. Then come back inside, lock all the doors, and latch the windows."

She nods and hurries away. I enter the children's part of our sleeping room. Nellie is sitting with her knees pulled up to her chest. When she sees me, she climbs out of her cradle, scampers over to me, pulls at the front of my dress, and cries, "Noo noo"—a sign that she wants to nurse.

"Not now," I say. "Let me see what is happening outside." She cries in outrage as I walk away from her.

Jimmy, still in his nightshirt, is standing at the east window. He has pressed the side of his face against the left window frame to get the best view possible of the combined warehouse and headquarters, which is positioned across from the front of our house. I stand beside him to look in the same direction.

"I saw Father walk over there, but I don't see him anymore," he said, and my heart aches to hear the fear in his voice.

"Your father is fine." I lay a comforting hand upon his shoulder. "Don't forget we have a company of soldiers stationed here," I say, even though from my vantage point, not a single blue uniform is visible. All I can see is a multitude of Indians surrounding the warehouse. They sing, shout, flap their blankets, charge the building, and then retreat, waving lances, rifles, and war clubs menacingly.

The agent Thomas Galbraith rounds the corner of the building and takes a position before the warehouse door. Galbraith is a slight man in his late thirties, with red hair, a receding hairline, and a short beard whose scraggly whiskers reach high up on his cheeks. He crosses his arms and shakes his head emphatically. Afraid that we might be about to witness a scalping, I pull my young son from the window. "Go put your clothes on, Jimmy. You don't want people to see you dressed in your nightshirt like a baby."

Galbraith makes a vehement horizontal gesture with both hands, pushes his way through the milling Sioux, and returns to the front of the building—no doubt to lock himself inside. The crowd of Indians continues to grow. I've closed the upstairs windows, and as the sun climbs in the sky, the second-story room grows warm. My throat tightens with panic as I imagine the Indians setting fire to the house—

the only wooden building at the agency—and roasting us alive. Pressing my face against the glass, I look straight down and see that Sioux have entered our fenced-in yard. Already, they surround the house and more keep coming.

Violent knocking at the door below causes me to jump. Jimmy starts toward the staircase, but I grab him by the shoulder. "You sit right there on the bed and watch your sister. Do not come downstairs until either your father or I call for you."

Then I duck into the other section of the room, snatch up John's pistol, and put it in my pocket. Even though I may not be able to save my own life with such a weapon, I will do what I can to keep the warriors from my children. The sound of shooting may bring soldiers to the house in time to defend Jimmy and Nellie.

As I descend the staircase, I see Mary grasping the newel post at the bottom. Again, fists pound upon the door, and both of us jump. "Go upstairs and sit with the children," I say in a low voice. "I will deal with this."

"No, ma'am, you should let me talk to them."

I shake my head. "Be a good girl now and do as I say."

After taking a deep breath and asking God for protection, I put my right hand in the pocket holding the pistol and open the door with my left. Half a dozen warriors crowd around my front step with dozens more milling about the yard. "What do you want?"

One of the younger men at the back shouts, *"Mazaoŋspe oŋg 'e uŋciŋpi!"* I recognize only the words for "we want" and shake my head to indicate my lack of comprehension. The warrior at the front, a very tall man with a creased face, raises his hand to quiet the others. "We want axes. Give us all you have."

The warrior's voice is grim, and his statement is a demand, not a request. The word *axes* fills my mind with images of tomahawked bodies, and a wave of nausea passes through me, but I dare not let them see me quaver. The thought of my babies cowering upstairs injects steel into my spine. Inching my hand deeper into the pocket, I curl my three lower fingers around the grip of the pistol and put my index finger on the trigger. "Come with me," I say, certain they will kill me as soon as I give them what they want. If I can, I will try to shoot two or three of them first.

I walk through the dining room, trailed by all six warriors. One of them laughs when he sees my canaries and says something in Dakota to his companions. In the kitchen, I pick up the small hatchet leaning against the side of the fireplace. We use it to chop kindling. When I hand it to the warrior who leads this foraging party, he glares at me. "Axes," he repeats, but he keeps the hatchet all the same.

When we go out the back door, the garden is filled with Indians, and I think it odd that they did not break open our shed and take what they wanted. As I cross the yard, they stand silently watching me. Once in the shed, I look around the dim interior until I see the axes hanging on the wall. I cross to them and hand over John's six-pound felling axe and his pride and joy, the two-and-a-half-pound splitting axe that he recently ordered from the East. John claims it is one of the first axes on the Minnesota frontier with the newly designed double-bit head. "These are all we have," I say and slip my hand back into my pocket to grasp the pistol.

The leader stares into my face until he is satisfied that I have told the truth. He signals to his companions, and they file silently back to the warehouse without laying a hand on me or even stealing food from my kitchen. As I step out into the sunny yard, I glance at my chicken coop and see that it appears unmolested.

My intestines roil and I duck into the outhouse just in time to relieve myself. Then I return to my house. Instead of going upstairs immediately, I stand at the parlor window and watch as two warriors wield our axes against the thick wooden door of the warehouse. Within ten minutes, they break their way inside and commence carrying out bags of flour and piling them in a wagon. Through my front door, which the Sioux left ajar, I hear their shouts of triumph.

Galbraith does not appear, but a new set of voices reaches my ears. Young Lieutenant Timothy Sheehan is leading his force of 100 men toward the warehouse, each of them with a revolver at his side and a rifle held diagonally across his chest. As the troops deploy around the building, one of the Sioux lunges for a private's rifle, which fires into the air. Enraged, the warrior grabs the private's hair, unsheathes a knife, and lifts it to his scalp. The private drops his rifle and grabs the Indian's wrists, but he can't free himself. "Sweet Mother of God," he shrieks.

"Wait!" Sheehan shouts. He and the warrior with the knife stare at each other with the intensity of men about to duel. "Stand back, men, weapons at the ready," Sheehan orders in his Irish brogue. The soldiers retreat a few steps, and the warrior releases the terrified private, who sinks to his knees and retches onto the grass.

A lumbering sound comes from the right, and several soldiers, led by baby-faced Lieutenant Thomas Gere, wheel a short-barreled artillery piece into position and aim it at the warehouse door. The Indians loitering outside sullenly move out of the line of fire.

Sheehan, his face pale but steely, shouts, "Leave the building, or I'll blow you all to hell." He gives a sergeant an order, and a dozen or more soldiers jostle their way toward the warehouse.

I raise a hand to my mouth and watch in terror as several fistfights break out. Miraculously, none of the soldiers resort to firing their weapons, and within a short time, they drive all the Sioux from the brick structure. Although I can hear much angry murmuring, the crisis appears to be over.

Sheehan looks to the warehouse expectantly, but when none of the agency employees show themselves, the lieutenant sends a sergeant to the front door. A couple of minutes pass. When Galbraith, escorted by the officer, emerges around the corner of the building, he looks and sounds as though he has been drinking. "All ri', boys," he calls. "The fun is over. Put the supplies back."

A howl of rage rises from the Sioux, and Sheehan takes Galbraith by the arm and pulls him into our yard to get him away from the mob. Galbraith exclaims in a high voice, "Make 'em return that flour!"

"No," Sheehan replies. "I'm more concerned with preventing bloodshed than I am with protecting your damned stores. The Sioux may take what's in that wagon and welcome."

"I can't allow that!"

Sheehan releases his arm and walks away. "Then you stop them!"

With that, the Sioux in the driver's seat of the wagon flicks the reins to start the horses moving, and the other warriors disperse. Exhausted by the tumult of the morning, I close my front door and walk upstairs to see how my children have fared.

CHAPTER

4

"The wives of Galbraith and some other agency employees are leaving for the Lower Agency tomorrow," John says without preamble when he comes home for his midday dinner. "I'm sending you and the children with them."

I set a plate of corn bread on the table and place my hands upon my hips. "What do you mean you're sending us? Don't I have a say?"

John places his fists upon the table and leans over it. His eyes flash, and I step backward, instantly regretting my saucy tongue.

"What the Sam Hill is wrong with you, woman? You saw what happened this morning. Do you mean to stand there and tell me that you don't want to take my children to safety?"

The accusation is too much to bear, and I cannot resist speaking my mind even if he slaps me for it. "I saw the riot better than you did, John Wakefield, locked away in your fine brick office. Half a dozen of those enraged savages forced their way into this very house, and all I had for protection was a single pistol." He flushes dark red at the imputation that he failed me, and I forge ahead, despite fearing that I have gone too far. "Of course, I don't object to transporting the children to safety. What I mind is leaving you behind when the situation is so explosive. I have no desire to be a widow."

"Oh, Sarah." He pulls back from his aggressive stance and sinks into his chair at the head of the table. "I am a government employee. I cannot leave my post."

I sit catty-corner from him. "Not even if we're in danger? Surely, the position of agency doctor does not require you to sacrifice your life."

"Don't you see? If I cut and run over a skirmish that resulted in no bloodshed, I'll be branded a coward. I would never get another patronage job as long as I live."

"Would that be so terrible?" I reach for his hand. "You're a fine doctor, John. You don't need a government post to make a living."

He lifts his chin stubbornly. "You remember what it was like in Shakopee. With this post, the pay is steady."

"Unlike the Indians' annuity," I say.

"That isn't our doing, Sarah. The riot this morning made it clear that the Sioux's rage will not subside until they have their gold in hand, and if the money comes in greenbacks, God help us. That's why I want you and the children to go down to Redwood until the payment comes."

Sitting back in my chair, I press my lips together to keep from arguing further and reigniting his wrath. When I married John, I thought I had at last found permanence and respectability as the wife of the town's physician. I imagined him treating the people of Shakopee for decades and retiring as a much-loved pillar of the community. Little did I know then that my husband has no interest in the kind of methodical, selfless service that builds such a reputation. His restless spirit is too easily drawn to the promise of adventure, such as the California Gold Rush, or easy money, like his failed land-speculation scheme. I made the mistake of berating him too sharply after the latter debacle, enraging John so much that he beat me in the street in sight of all our neighbors. His medical practice fell off after that public display of temper, a second, unacknowledged reason why John relocated our family out here on the far end of an Indian reservation.

"How long do you think we'll have to be gone?"

He shakes his head. "I don't know. I don't think you should return until the threat of an uprising has passed."

"I need to know how many clothes to take."

John rubs his brow, and I notice deeply etched crow's-feet at the corners of his eyes. The dapper young doctor I married six years ago looks middle-aged now. "Pack for a week," he says. "If you have to stay longer, you can launder your things."

I nod. "You will have Mary to do the housework here."

He wrinkles up his nose. "That won't be necessary. I can get by eating cheese, crackers, and sardines, and I'm perfectly capable of rinsing out my own shirts."

His answer doesn't surprise me. Although John has always treated the Sioux cordially in his professional capacity, like so many of the people here, he views the Indians as little better than animals. He tolerates having a Sioux servant because it makes it easier for me to maintain his home the way he likes it, but he does not want to be alone with her.

I spend the rest of the day making sure that we have enough clean clothes for a week and folding them into our trunk. Jimmy is excited because he is old enough to remember last year's journey to the agency, but Nellie follows me around the house in consternation, sucking her thumb and trailing her rag doll. Every time she sees me pick up something that belongs to her, she says plaintively, "Mine, Mama." She refuses to lie down for a nap. Finally, in the late afternoon, I sit in the rocking chair in the children's bedroom and nurse her till she falls asleep.

The next morning a small convoy of wagons gathers to travel to the Lower Agency. Nervously, I notice a group of Sioux off to the side watching us. They stand with their arms folded across their chests and impassive expressions on their faces.

John lifts our children into the wagon seat and then takes hold of both my hands. In a low voice, he says, "When you return, all this trouble will be over and life at the agency won't be so trying. Things should get better for us."

"I would like that." I smile tremulously, hoping that he is talking about our marriage too, not just relations with the Indians. "Please, keep yourself safe. Remember that your wife and children love you."

His eyebrows shoot up in the expression of sardonic surprise he employs so often. Leaning toward me, he kisses my cheek and then helps me into the wagon. I press my lips together and blink back tears when I realize that John is going to send me away without reassurances of his love.

A commotion occurs near the head of the convoy. Craning my neck, I see that Agent Galbraith has climbed into the same wagon as his family. Several Sioux warriors move to the middle of the road and one holds out his hand, palm toward the wagons. In a stentorian voice, he shouts, "Women can go, but agent stays here."

Galbraith stands up and blusters, "I will not. I have business at the other agency I must attend to."

"You have business here," the warrior says, and the men who stand on either side of him display knives and tomahawks.

I clutch Nellie to my breast so she won't see any violence, and I look for John, who—thinking we were about to leave—has stepped back from the wagon. He stands at the side of the road, watching Galbraith with an expression of rage. As John moves forward to intervene, Lieutenant Sheehan rides past and pulls up his horse between Galbraith's wagon and the Sioux.

"Get down from there, man. I thought we agreed 'twas only the women and children who'd be leaving this morning."

Galbraith attempts to continue his bluff: "That was before I remembered some urgent business at Redwood."

Sheehan stares at him a long moment, scratching one cheek as he does so. "I daresay it will keep. Now get down, so these good people can be on their way."

Grumbling, Galbraith jumps down, and the Sioux step aside to open the road. As the lead wagon sets off, I look to John again. He stares at me with a solemn expression. After a moment, he places his right hand on his heart and bows his head to me, and I understand that he is communicating love after all.

Once our wagon starts to roll, I rearrange Nellie so that she can gaze out at the passing scenery. She leans against my bosom with her thumb in her mouth. Jimmy has already clambered up to the front seat so he can talk to the driver.

We are soon out in open country. On either side of the road bloom yellow black-eyed Susans, purple coneflowers and blazing stars, and pale lavender asters, rising above the green and gold waves of rippling grass. When I first came to Minnesota, I had no idea how much I would come to love this wide-open land with its vast prairies and crystalline lakes. I would be happy here if only John and I could learn to live more harmoniously.

The problem is we married too soon, I think, as the wagon jounces down the government road. Yet, given my reputation at the time, I'm not sure what other choice I had in that long-ago autumn.

As John had predicted, Mrs. Phelan died soon after his first visit, although he had returned every day in a valiant effort to save her. The grandsons came to town for the funeral, and I made a luncheon of sandwiches and cake for those who attended the service. Seventy-four-year-old Jacob Phelan bent beneath the burden of the losses he'd suffered in the past twelvemonth, but he did not weep. The next day the boys had to return to their jobs on various farms about the county, but before they departed, the oldest, seventeen-year-old Jake, said he would be pleased if I would stay on to care for his grandfather.

At first, I thought things would be well. I cooked delicacies and coaxed the old man to eat so he wouldn't waste away as his poor wife had. To my delight, John Wakefield began to take me for buggy rides on Sunday afternoons if he didn't have an emergency. We would drive to the river, where I would serve him picnic lunches that left him groaning about a too-full stomach. As we ate, John would tell me stories about wild times in San Francisco or about the nearby prehistoric Indian mounds. I would talk about my childhood, dwelling mostly on my happy memories of my father and, as much as possible, avoiding mention of my stepfather, Pitt Vaughn.

One rainy September Sunday, when John came to take tea with Mr. Phelan and me, Jake surprised us by arriving unexpectedly at the house. A Catholic priest named Father Boyle accompanied him. The young man turned red when he saw the three of us seated around the dining room table. Removing his dripping hat and holding it in front of his waist, he said, "Granddad, I need to speak to you. Privately."

"I can go to the kitchen," I said, removing my napkin from my lap and rising. "Dr. Wakefield, you would be welcome to join me there."

"No, no, missy, you and the doctor stay here," Mr. Phelan said and patted my hand. The grandson scowled at the gesture. "Jake and I can go."

Jake helped Mr. Phelan to his feet and handed him his cane, and together they walked through the door that led to the kitchen.

"Father Boyle, please have a seat," I said. "Let me pour you some tea."

"No, thank you," he replied in a reedy voice and remained standing near the fireplace with his hands behind his back. He was a thin man, dressed in plain black.

I glanced at John in bewilderment. He winked and picked up a popover. "You're missing out on quite a tasty repast," he observed to Father Boyle. The priest did not answer.

As I refilled John's teacup, we heard Mr. Phelan shout, "I will not have a young pup like you telling me what I can do in my own house. There is not a thing wrong with that girl."

"Granddad, wait! Please read this letter I received from Rhode Island."

My cheeks flamed as I realized I was the "girl" they were arguing about. My heart pounded and my stomach grew queasy as I stared at the crumbs on my plate and tried to imagine what news could have come from home to provoke such a disagreement. My reputation there had been undeservedly maligned, but the friend who recommended me for this position knew all the gossip and still offered me this chance. The letter, whatever slander it carried, must have come from another source.

The shouting ceased, and after a minute, the kitchen door opened. Mr. Phelan made his way slowly back into the dining room, the tapping of his cane on the wooden floor punctuating his footsteps. Jake tried to take his arm, but the old man shook him off. After walking to within three paces of the table, he placed both hands on the head of his cane and leaned heavily upon it. "All right, missy, you tell me the truth. I like you, and I'll give you a fair shake. What in God's name did you do that was so terrible to make your own mother besmirch your name?"

I bunched up the tablecloth beneath my hands. "My mother wrote to Jake?"

"No, she wrote to me," Father Boyle said, "because she did not know

33

how to reach the boys. She was concerned about you living alone here with Mr. Phelan."

"That's absurd! His behavior toward me has been entirely proper."

Father Boyle cleared his throat. "That was not her concern. She feared that you would take advantage of the old gentleman."

Mr. Phelan shot the priest a look of venom. "I am not in my dotage, sir, and I'll thank you not to interfere in my affairs under the guise of protecting me." He faced me again and gentled his voice. "It's all right, missy. You can tell me whatever it is."

Even before he finished his sentence, I shook my head. "No! There are some things no woman should have to talk about. I will leave this house tonight rather than expose my private sorrows." I squeezed my eyes shut to keep from humiliating myself by crying. After a moment in which the only sound was the ticking of the mantel clock, I regained sufficient command of myself to say, "Mr. Phelan, I don't mean to spurn your offer of understanding. But please do not ask me to lay my soul bare before your grandson and this so-called man of God."

Father Boyle crossed his arms before his chest. "Then you will not defend yourself? Your mother's charges are serious. She describes you as a young woman of faulty character who cannot be trusted to live in the same house with an older man unless there is a vigilant chaperone."

Damn her, I thought. *Will she hound me to the end of her days?* Galling memories flooded my mind: the feel of my stepfather's hand upon my breast and his tongue thrusting into my mouth as I fought him, the crash of my bedroom door slamming open and my mother's shrill cries of outrage, the scorching shame of realizing that she would rather blame me than admit to her husband's betrayal.

I spoke to Father Boyle, "I will not explain myself to you, sir. You are not my spiritual guide, and your evident eagerness to judge me does not induce me to accept you as such."

"So we are at an impasse."

"We are not, sir!" Mr. Phelan cried. "This is still my house, and I will make my own decisions about whom I employ."

"But you pay her with my money, Granddad," Jake objected. "Mine and my brothers. And we three have decided to heed Father Boyle's council."

"So you defy the head of your family and turn me into a dependent against my will." Mr. Phelan drew himself up with difficulty and pointed his cane at the priest. "And you, sir, do you no longer preach the need to honor one's elders?"

His grandson flushed, but Father Boyle remained unmoved. "Jake honors you by protecting you from harm."

I stood and tossed my napkin on the table. Crossing to Mr. Phelan, I held his arm. "Forgive me. I do not want to leave you, but I cannot do as they ask."

He slumped and leaned on his cane again. "Forgive me, too, missy."

With a great effort of will, I walked from the room at a normal pace. Once I reached my small, second-floor chamber, tears began to stream down my face as I threw my clothes and scant possessions into my trunk. I also packed a carpetbag with a nightgown, some underthings, and my toiletries. To make sure that I left nothing in this house, I opened every drawer three times and looked under my bed twice. Several times, I had to stop working because tears blinded me. *What am I going to do? Now I have no job, and I can't go back to Rhode Island.*

As I descended the stairs, I saw through the rain-streaked window that dusk had fallen. In the dining room, the four men were exactly where I had left them except that old Mr. Phelan was sitting. Father Boyle and Jake stood stiffly by the fireplace, while John sat at the table, puffing a cigar and pointedly blowing smoke in the direction of the priest. His presence surprised me and filled me with gratitude. I had been certain that he would leave while I was packing and count himself fortunate to be shed of me.

I laid a hand on the old man's arm and bent down so he could hear me better. "Mr. Phelan, I left my trunk upstairs in my bedroom. I'll send for it tomorrow."

John stood. "No need. I can carry it for you."

"You?"

"I will not allow you to be cast out into the night unchaperoned. I intend to see you safely lodged in the boarding house or, failing that, the hotel." Without waiting for me to say which chamber was mine, John started upstairs.

A few minutes later, I heard him deposit my trunk in the hallway. Then he walked into the dining room. "It is still raining. Do you have an umbrella?"

"No, but I have a bonnet and cape. I will be all right."

I moved toward the doorway, but John said, "Wait." Turning to Jake, he said, "Aren't you forgetting something? You owe this lady wages through today."

The young man flushed angrily. "How much do you owe her, Granddad?"

"For two months." I opened my mouth to argue, but Mr. Phelan shook his head once in warning.

Looking as though he would rather strike me than pay me, Jake handed me several coins. John and I went into the hallway, where I put on my outer things. I picked up my carpetbag, he hoisted my trunk onto his back, and we walked out into the night.

The rain was steady, and the road was muddy. The Phelan house stood about a quarter mile from the center of town, and no wooden sidewalks extended this far out. We had gone only halfway when John panted, "I need to stop." He lowered my trunk and balanced it atop a nearby horse trough to keep it out of the muck.

We had halted in front of the livery stable, so I stepped under the overhang at the side where a large wagon was stored. John followed me. As I stood listening to the rain, I murmured, "What must you think of me?"

He stepped close behind me and said, "I told you before, I think you're a fine woman, Sarah Brown. And after today, a brave one."

"No, I'm not. I'm the most fearful woman I know."

John patted my back as though I were a child. "It takes spunk to stand up to such a hard-hearted pharisee."

Nervously, I felt for my coins through the fabric of my purse and checked to make sure that the drawstrings were pulled tight. "But surely, you must wonder why a mother would write such disparaging things about her own daughter?"

"I expect it had something to do with a man," he answered matter-of-factly. When I didn't answer, he asked quietly, "Was it your step-father? You never want to talk about him."

My cheeks burning with shame, I hesitated a long moment and then nodded. John huffed in disapproval and then said, "I'll wager a month's cigars that you took no pleasure at all in whatever attentions he forced on you."

I whirled to face him. "How can you possibly know? No one else has ever believed I might be innocent. And you didn't even ask for an explanation."

John sighed. "You forget, I'm a doctor, and as such, I've witnessed more than my share of human depravity. I've seen far too many young women violated and then blamed by their stepfathers, their uncles, and even their own fathers."

"He didn't—" I blushed fiercely at the thought of confiding my darkest secret to this man, but he *was* a doctor and seemingly the only person on my side. In a way, it gave sweet relief to finally talk about it to someone who believed me. "He tried, but I fought him. My mother walked in on us before.... He told her I tempted him shamelessly, and she—" Tears flooded my eyes, and my throat tightened so I couldn't speak. I bowed my head. John reached into his pocket and gave me a handkerchief. After wiping my eyes, I sat on an upended crate near the wall of the stable. "She kicked me out of the house. I had to go live with my uncle, who worked me like a servant. As if that were not enough, my mother reported my 'sin' to the ministers in town, and after that, I was no longer welcome in their churches."

I sniffed and tried to swallow back my tears. A flash filled the sky, and a crack of thunder followed. The rain outside our lean-to began to fall harder. "That's what I don't understand," I said miserably. "Why would she believe him instead of me? Does she love him so much more than her own child?"

John pulled his cigar from his mouth and peered at it. "Damn rain," he muttered and tossed it aside. "How long was your mother a widow?"

"My father died when I was six, and we lived with my paternal grandmother until her death. Then my mother took a job as a housekeeper at a boarding house for mill workers, but she didn't work there long before she married Pitt. My half sister was born when I was thirteen, so I guess Mother was a widow for about six years."

"I suspect that's your answer," John said, moving closer to me. Thunder boomed. "She was willing to do anything to make sure she wouldn't have to support herself and her children again."

"So she sacrificed me instead."

"Apparently." He rubbed the back of his neck and moved his head from side to side. "You know, I doubt she saw it that way. She probably thought she had to do whatever was necessary to keep the family together. I've seen plenty of women put up with worse just to keep bread on their children's plates."

"But I'm one of her children too!" I exclaimed. Then I fell silent as the truth stared me in the face. "But I wasn't. Not by then. I was in my twenties when it happened, so maybe...maybe she thought I could take care of myself."

"Really?" John asked, and for the first time I heard surprise in his voice. "Your stepfather didn't start bothering you right away after their marriage?"

"No. My mother had a late pregnancy and miscarried. She was sick for a long time, and that's when Pitt started to be nice to me. We hadn't gotten along very well before then, and God help me, I was happy when he began to buy me ribbons and taffy. It was like having a father again. When I found out what he really wanted, I felt a fool."

"You couldn't have known. I doubt you had any more experience of such things than a child." I shook my head. "What he did was abominable," John added in a rough voice.

I took off my bonnet and examined its bedraggled feather. "The worst of it is that I thought I could make a new start in Minnesota, but my mother seems determined to blacken my name even here. Now where can I go? No one in Shakopee will hire me after word of this spreads."

John took the bonnet from me and laid it on the wagon seat a couple of feet away. Then he held both my hands. "Sarah Brown, have you already forgotten what I told you the night we met? You should be a wife, not a shopkeeper and certainly not a servant."

I hesitated, afraid to assume too much. A flash of lightning illuminated his face long enough for me to see that, for once, he was sincere. The uncharacteristic expression made him look younger. A second later, thunder cracked, and I jumped. John laughed. He pulled me to my feet. "Sarah, I am asking you to marry me."

38

"Are you sure?" I asked and immediately felt foolish. What kind of response was that to a proposal?

"I'm sure." John placed his hand under my chin and bent his face toward mine. "May I?"

"Yes," I whispered, and he kissed me. His lips were soft, and the kiss was gentle, not demanding. The aroma of cigar smoke and damp wool that clung to him drove away the memory of my stepfather's reek of sweat and beer.

"What is your answer, Sarah Brown?" John asked softly.

"Yes." I put my arms around him and returned his kiss more ardently.

CHAPTER

5

OUR WAGON PASSES TWO SIOUX WOMEN STANDING ON BUFFALO ROBES at the edge of a field dotted with sheaves. The women are winnowing wheat by tossing it into the air from ridged boards and catching the heavier grain as wind blows the chaff away. Whatever they miss falls onto the robes so they can gather it later.

As that sight makes clear, the government road that leads to Redwood has changed a great deal since I last rode along it. The landscape has lost its untamed look and has begun to resemble the tidy Pennsylvania and Ohio farmlands I crossed years ago as I took the train to Minnesota. Agent Galbraith has kept the farmer Indians busy this spring and summer cutting timber and splitting rails. Bridges now span most of the creeks and sloughs, and many more fences line the road. The swiftness of the transformation shocks me—and if the loss of wildland distresses me, how must the Sioux feel? I want to protest when I see yet another fenced-in field, but I remain silent for fear that my companions might rebuke me. Most whites believe that uncultivated land is wasted, yet I cannot help but think that something precious is being destroyed in our haste to farm the prairie.

The loaded wagons of our convoy travel so slowly that it takes all day to cover the thirty miles between the two agencies. Fortunately, the early August sun doesn't set until about 7:30, so even though we stop to eat lunch, we should reach our destination before dark falls.

Late in the afternoon as we draw near the agency, we pass through several Mdewakanton Sioux villages—including those of Big Eagle and Little Crow. In each, tepees and bark lodges cluster around a common central area, and in Little Crow's village, a still-unpainted, two-story frame house stands. The sharp scent of freshly cut lumber hangs in the air. Bob, the teamster who drives my wagon, says that the government recently built the dwelling for the chief.

I have seen Little Crow only once, but I remember him as a handsome man in his fifties with an intelligent expression in his hooded eyes. John has told me a great deal about him, having learned bits of the story from Galbraith. Taoyateduta or "His Red Nation," as Little Crow was originally called, was a wastrel as a youth. He traveled out west where he hunted buffalo, traded furs and whiskey, became a proficient poker player, and married and divorced a couple of wives. The Sioux say he matured only after his father died, leaving the chieftainship to a younger half brother. Taoyateduta returned to his father's village to challenge that decision, and two of his half brothers shot him through both forearms, mangling his wrists and crippling his hands. His bravery on that occasion won him the band's loyalty, and he became chief, adding his father's name of Little Crow to his own.

As a leader, Little Crow is said to be educated, charismatic, pragmatic, and full of contradictions. He urges his people to farm but will not plow his own land. He dresses in white men's clothing but still wears a Sioux medicine bag. He attends Dr. Hinman's Episcopal mission but refuses to convert. Little Crow's paradoxes fascinate me, as I too struggle to find middle ground, striving to balance the strangling propriety of my New England upbringing with the freedom—and dangers—of my current life.

Our wagons pass an imposing stone warehouse and drive into the square at the heart of the agency. Redwood is far more developed than our agency at Yellow Medicine. More than a dozen structures surround the square—a barn, a blacksmith's shop, two warehouses, a dormitory, a boarding house, and several homes for missionaries and agency employees. Even before our wagons come to a halt, residents pour out of the buildings to greet us. A messenger on horseback had traveled ahead of us to report on yesterday's riot and warn them of our impending arrival.

Bob climbs down and helps me to alight, encumbered as I am by a wide hoop skirt and a sleeping child in my arms. Jimmy insists on jumping down unaided and cries out with delight when he lands on his feet.

My left arm, which bears most of Nellie's weight, prickles with needles, so I hoist her up to my shoulder and flex my hand to restore the circulation. As I watch Bob take down our trunk, I wonder what we are to do now that we are here. Then someone calls my name.

I turn to see Mrs. Humphrey walking toward me, holding out her hands. She is a lovely woman, with gleaming dark brown hair, a perfect oval face, and gentle, doe eyes. Her husband is the doctor at this agency. "Sarah, you and your children are to stay with us."

"Thank you, Susan." If I could have chosen a family to board with, I would have picked the Humphreys. Like us, they are New England transplants, and they have three children—an older boy, a son Jimmy's age, and a girl a few months younger than Nellie. "What a relief. I wasn't quite sure where I was to go next."

"Where else would you stay but in the home of John's colleague? As soon as we heard the news, Philander insisted that you lodge with us." She glances into the wagon and sees my satchel sitting on the floor by the backseat. "Is that yours?"

I nod and she pulls it down with a wince of pain.

"Are you well?" I ask as we walk around the wagon toward her house.

Lowering her voice so that no one but me can hear, she confides, "I am five months gone with child, and this pregnancy has been much harder than the others."

Her news surprises me. Then I see that her hoops are riding a little high. "I hope our visit won't put undue strain on you."

"Nonsense. It will be a rare treat to have another woman to talk to." She opens the door to her two-story frame house and ushers me inside. Jimmy follows, dragging his feet reluctantly, but as soon as we enter the hall, he sees four-year-old Jay standing at the turn of the stairs and runs up to join him.

"Make yourself at home," Susan says. "I'm going to go check on supper. I decided to make stew since we weren't sure when you would get here."

In the parlor, I gently lay Nellie on a sofa and look at my surroundings. The Humphreys' home has substantial furniture but far fewer cushions, knickknacks, and pictures than ours. I wonder at the difference. The two doctors each make the same generous salary of a thousand dollars a year, so I assume the Humphreys could afford a few more comforts. Philander Humphrey, however, strikes me as having a more austere nature than John.

Curiosity satisfied, I cross to a mirror and see that dust from the journey streaks my face. After I wipe it clean with a handkerchief, I turn away in disgust from the reflection—my drooping eyelids give me a look of perpetual disappointment, and my doughy cheeks and double chin make me look five years older than my hostess even though we are exactly the same age.

Dr. Humphrey walks through the door that leads from the surgery attached to the side of the house. He is a man with erect posture, and he wears whiskers along his jawline and a thick beard on his chin but no mustache. Seeing me in the parlor, he pauses in the doorway to inquire after John. I briefly describe the work that he's been doing, and then Susan calls us to supper.

Eight of us sit down in the dining room. I take the middle seat on one side of the table with my children flanking me. Jimmy sits atop a one-volume collection of Shakespeare, while Nellie is perched atop two thick medical books and tied by a sash to the spindled chair back. Across the table, the Humphrey children sit in a similar arrangement with Johnny, the twelve-year-old boy, between Jay and sixteen-month-old Gertrude. At the head of the table, Dr. Humphrey says grace, giving long-winded thanks for the food and our safe journey. My children are not used to such lengthy prayer, and I hold my breath, hoping that they remain quiet. They do, and after the "Amen," I pour them each a glass of milk. As Susan ladles up stew, Humphrey asks me about yesterday's attack on the warehouse.

"We saw the whole thing!" Jimmy scrambles up to kneel upon his book.

Dr. Humphrey points a fork at him. "Young man, in this house children are seen and not heard. Now be quiet, or I shall send you to bed without any supper."

My son sits back down, and his lower lip trembles. I long to defend him by explaining that John does not require such strict behavior on the part of his children, but I sense that such a protest would antagonize Dr. Humphrey and make our stay here more uncomfortable. Instead, I say, "Since our house is the building nearest to the warehouse, we did witness everything. In fact, several warriors forced their way into our home and demanded axes from me."

Susan gasps and covers her mouth. Her husband asks, "Were you hurt?"

"No, they merely wanted tools and did not accost me in any way. But as you can imagine, the experience was terrifying." I go on to describe the confrontation at the warehouse and how the soldiers brought the situation under control.

Dr. Humphrey nods and makes no comment about the young lieutenant's bravery or Galbraith's cowardice. "I heard that a messenger arrived here in the afternoon to tell Little Crow of the riot, and he responded by riding upriver as quickly as he could. He did not show up at the warehouse yesterday?"

"Not that I know of. He may have gone directly to the Indian encampments."

Dr. Humphrey reaches for another slice of bread and launches into a denunciation of the unfair practices of traders at Redwood, particularly the way they inflate the Indians' debts they record in their books. "It is an iniquitous system and a major source of the Sioux's discontent."

He progresses from that topic to a condemnation of slavery, ending with bitter complaints that most Christian denominations refuse to endorse abolition. "I have long since ceased to attend any formal church because I cannot tolerate their shilly-shallying on this, the essential question of our time."

I can tell from the way Susan smiles at him across the table that her husband neither requires nor expects a verbal response to his tirade, so I feed my children in silence and merely nod whenever Dr. Humphrey pauses for breath.

Tired as I am, I lie awake for a long time thinking of my husband. After only a single evening with Philander Humphrey, I see John in a new, more flattering light. He has his faults, as I well know, but he is a far more loving father than the disciplinarian who rules this household. John is tolerant of our offsprings' childish ways, and he enjoys listening to their prattle at mealtimes.

There was a time, long ago, when he was similarly patient with me. Right after our marriage, he was extraordinarily gentle because he feared that my stepfather's improper behavior might have made me skittish about men. On our wedding night, John promised that he would never force me to do more than I was willing, and little by little, he taught me what I needed to know about conjugal relations. Those first weeks with him were the happiest of my life.

Relations outside the bedroom did not go as smoothly. At first, John found it sweet that I feared myself not good enough for him, but soon, he grew tired of my desire for reassurance. I think he even began to wonder whether a farmer's daughter was a fitting match for a doctor. So I learned to stifle my doubts, worked hard to make a home that reflected his station in life, and diligently read Shakespeare and other works of literature to make up for my lack of education. John never saw those efforts as accomplishments worthy of notice. If anything, the accouterments of gentility I worked so hard to acquire for the house only made him feel penned in by cushions and gewgaws.

My self-doubt is not the only quality that grates on him. After six years of marriage, he has grown tired of my occasional unconventionalities. One of the most glaring contradictions in my husband's character is that he resents having to conform to orthodox behavior, but he demands it of his wife. Whenever I come home from the Sioux camp, he complains if he smells the pipe on me. He disapproves of my smoking with Sioux women, even though I have explained that to refuse would be a dire insult. As a result, I carry a small perfume bottle filled with vinegar so I can rinse the telltale odor from my breath on the way home.

Sighing, I shift to find a comfortable position on the cornhusk mattress, which rustles so loudly that I fear it will wake Nellie, who sleeps with me. Fortunately, she doesn't stir. It surprises me that the Humphreys did not transport cotton-stuffed mattresses out to the agency along with their other furniture. Cornhusks are cheap but so lumpy that few people use them if they can afford anything better.

In contrast to Dr. Humphrey, John does not begrudge his family the comforts of life. Despite the tension and sometimes outright unhappiness between us, I could have done far worse than to marry John Wakefield.

The question that plagues me is whether I can do anything after all these years to win back his affection. If I were to become more self-sacrificing and submissive like Susan Humphrey, would John love me again—or would such behavior only annoy him?

I wish to God I knew.

Tuesday morning after breakfast, Dr. Humphrey leaves for his surgery. When Johnny goes outside to chop firewood, Jimmy and Jay tag after him. "Stay away from that axe," I call after my son.

Carrying our babies, Susan and I enter the parlor. We set the girls on the floor with a couple of rag dolls and John's old tin cups, which are currently Nellie's favorite playthings. As Susan and I sit at the worktable, I notice that her face is pale with dark smudges beneath her eyes. The Humphreys do not employ a servant, so Susan's workload is much heavier than mine. The cuffs and collar of her blue gingham dress are threadbare, further confirming her difficulty in keeping up with her chores, not that she is the type of woman to complain.

She brings up her workbasket from under the table and takes out the pieces of a flannel shirt she is sewing for her oldest boy. After matching the left front piece to the back, she begins to pin the side seams, making sure to match the lines in the plaid. Because we left home in such a hurry, I did not bring any work with me, so I ask, "May I help with your sewing?"

Susan looks up in hope but then shakes her head. She removes the pins she holds between her lips and answers, "I couldn't ask a guest to do that!"

"But I would enjoy it. I hate to be idle, and surely, with three young children, you must have more than enough to do."

"Well, all right." She wipes her hands on her apron and crosses to

46

a trunk that stands beneath the front window. "I keep all my fabrics and patterns over here."

Together we bend over the trunk and sort through the well-used patterns for boys' shirts and baby gowns and the various lengths of fabric folded into neat bundles. Near the bottom, I spot a large piece of calico with a coral background and a green trellis pattern surrounding cream rosebuds. Some of it has already been cut into sleeves for a woman's dress. "What beautiful fabric! Is this for you?"

"Yes." She straightens up to rub her lower back, and her face creases with pain. "It's a dress I began for myself at the beginning of the summer. Then Johnny went through a sudden growth spurt, and I had to stop to make him trousers. When I found out I was expecting, I decided I might as well wait until after the baby comes."

I stroke the cotton fabric and think how much I would enjoy working with such pretty colors. "Would you mind if I sewed this dress for you? I used to do a bit of work as a ladies' seamstress in Shakopee." A queer look crosses Susan's face, and I fear that I have overstepped my place. "I would not dream of taking over the project if you really want to make it yourself."

"No, it isn't that." Still rubbing her back, she returns to the worktable and sits down. "I feel guilty sewing for myself when the children need so many things."

"Let me do it for you. It will be my way of thanking you for your hospitality, and you'll have a new dress to wear after the baby comes."

"All right." Susan blushes prettily.

I run a practiced eye over her figure. Although she isn't a thin woman, I estimate she weighs at least forty pounds less than I do. "What happened with your last pregnancy? Did you keep the weight?"

She shakes her head. "Only for a few weeks afterward. But this time feels so different, I don't know what to expect. My back aches terribly today, and that has never happened before."

"I can do the cooking while I'm here, so you don't have to be on your feet so much. As for the dress, I will make it a little bigger than your usual size. If it turns out to be too loose, it will be easy enough to take in the seams."

Susan reaches out and clasps my hand. "Oh, Sarah, your coming here just now may turn out to be a godsend."

We spend the rest of the day sewing and chatting amiably about our children, and in the late afternoon, I cook supper while Susan sews in a corner of the kitchen. Doing so makes her feel lazy and ashamed, but her backache continues and I insist that she remain seated for the sake of her unborn babe. I also make her promise to tell her husband about her discomfort as soon as they are alone for the night.

Wednesday morning, Susan says she is better, so she refuses to allow me to do all the cooking. Other than that, we follow much the same routine as the day before, and I make substantial progress on the dress. I convince Susan to let me have a bit of cream lace I found in the trunk to trim the collar, even though she had been planning to put it on a gown for Gertrude. "Look how well it matches the roses. You must let me use it on this bodice."

She presses her lips tightly together, and I can almost hear her arguing with herself, struggling to reconcile her desire for a bit of adornment with her deeply ingrained belief that she should sacrifice for her family. Finally, she gives in by saying, "All right, if you would enjoy doing so."

Late in the afternoon as we prepare supper, Susan reaches around to rub her lower back. Then she clenches her jaw to keep from crying out as she lifts a heavy pot. "Please, go sit down," I tell her. "I can do this on my own."

"That wouldn't be fair to you," she says breathlessly.

I put my hands on my hips and stare at her in exasperation. "You said you thought my visit was a godsend. Are you refusing the help the Lord has sent you?"

Susan blinks, and tears fill her eyes. "No, of course not." She sits in the corner chair she occupied yesterday. "You're a blunt-speaking woman, Sarah Wakefield."

"A trait that has gotten me in trouble on more than one occasion," I admit. "I think my husband might prefer it if I were sweet-tempered like you."

She laughs, and the momentary tension between us dissolves like frost on a sunny morning. "I like you the way you are."

In the middle of the night, I wake to hear a woman's moaning. Nellie and I are in the Humphreys' extra room, across from the master bedroom. Jimmy is in the small front bedroom with the two other boys.

Throwing a shawl over my nightdress, I step into the hall. Through the closed door of the Humphreys' bedroom, I hear Susan cry, "No!" and then weep.

Dr. Humphrey exits their bedroom and looks startled when he sees me there. "How can I help?" I ask him.

He grasps my arm so tightly that it hurts. "Go gather up all the sheets and towels you can. I'm not sure where Susan keeps them. She's losing the baby." As soon as he says that, he returns to the bedroom.

The miscarriage takes hours. Susan bleeds and bleeds but does not expel the last tissue from her womb until morning. By the time it is all over and she has fallen into exhausted sleep, a pile of blood-soaked sheets lies on the bedroom floor. Only then does Dr. Humphrey go out into the hallway, lean against the wall, and cry.

I leave him to his grief and carry the soiled linens downstairs. After placing them outside the back door, I light the kitchen stove, put the kettle on to boil, and grind coffee beans. As the first streaks of light paint the sky, I go to fetch water from the spring. I will have to do a great deal of laundry today.

By the time I return, Humphrey is sitting at the kitchen table with his head in his hands. "Why would God do this?" he murmurs. "Susan is the most godly woman I have ever known."

"Dr. Humphrey, God does not cause evil. He comforts us in our tribulations."

"Yes, yes, you're right." He rubs his face and looks at me ruefully. "I truly thought that I was going to lose her."

"But you didn't. God spared her. It may take time, but she will get well again."

He nods, but his posture remains slumped.

"When she wakes, what do you want me to feed her? I was thinking of making beef broth because she lost so much blood, but I will do whatever you say."

"Broth would be good. And strong, sweet tea. She will fret over the children, but I do not want her to get out of bed."

"You can rely on me," I say as I take out the iron skillet to cook him some breakfast. "I will look after the children and the house. She won't have to do a thing."

"Thank you," he says quietly, sounding like a far different man from the one who lectured his way through mealtime the last three nights.

The days pass more quickly than I would have thought possible. Susan is very weak from loss of blood, so she remains in bed, and I take charge of the household. Caring for five children is much more work than looking after two. Thank heaven, twelve-year-old Johnny is accustomed to bearing much of the responsibility for his siblings, so I let him monitor Jimmy and Jay while I focus on doing the housework and tending the two baby girls.

With all the household chores, I barely have an hour or two a day to spend sewing in Susan's bedroom so she can have a bit of company. Her spirits are so melancholy that I fret over her. All I can think to do is to continue working on her dress so she will have something pretty to wear when she is finally up and about.

On Sunday, Susan insists that I should attend services if I wish. So Jimmy and I go to Samuel Hinman's Episcopal church, the mission of St. John the Evangelist. The Reverend Mr. Hinman has been here only two years, but even in such a short time, his congregation has grown so much that they need a larger church. To one side of the existing building is a partially built stone structure that looks as though it belongs in New England. The thick walls are built of irregularly shaped stones mortared together. The front of the building features a small gabled entryway protruding from a larger gabled end that has a round opening for what I suspect will be a rose window. After gazing at it for a moment, I decide that it is going to be lovely despite its incongruence in this landscape. Then I take my son by the hand and walk into the wooden church where the service will be held.

It is the first time I have been in close proximity with the Sioux since the attack on the warehouse six days before, and I confess to being nervous as we find seats in an empty pew. My fear soon subsides as I see many familiar faces that I recognize from our time in Shakopee. Almost all the men have cut their hair and donned the collared shirt and trousers of white men.

The service is of great interest because I have little familiarity with the Episcopal form of worship. Most of the other missionaries on the reservation are Presbyterian. The Episcopal service is more formal, more Catholic, based as it is on an official prayer book. However, Dr. Hinman has adapted the service to suit his needs by translating many prayers into Dakota and also preaching in that language.

The Indian congregants display reverence for the ceremony. As I gaze at their solemn faces, I find it hard to reconcile their behavior with the rage I saw last week. The contrast between these quiet worshippers and the warriors who attacked the warehouse demonstrates what a civilizing influence Christianity is upon the red man, I think. The men who lifted their hands in anger last week are savages compared to these Christians.

Then unexpectedly, I remember the Bible verse that proclaims, "Thou hypocrite, first cast out the beam out of thine own eye; and then shalt thou see clearly to cast out the mote out of thy brother's eye." Who am I to judge any of the Sioux? If I were forced to hear my two babies crying day after day from hunger, might I not turn to violence? Humbled by that reflection, I fervently pray that the annuity payment arrives in Minnesota soon and that life on the reservation will return to normal.

CHAPTER
6

IN THE AFTERNOON, PHILANDER HUMPHREY CARRIES SUSAN DOWN-stairs so she can eat Sunday dinner with us. She is alarmingly pale, but he says she is recovering.

As soon as everyone is seated, Humphrey says his usual long-winded grace, but instead of concluding it, he falls abruptly silent. Susan adds, "And we thank you, Lord, for sending Sarah Wakefield to us in our hour of need."

Only then does Humphrey say, "Amen."

To celebrate her improved health, I have made a special meal of chicken and dumplings. As I dish up the food, Humphrey says to me, "This morning while you were at church, I spoke to a man who rode down from Yellow Medicine yesterday."

I freeze with a soup plate in hand and look at him apprehensively. Surely, he would not tell me bad news about John in such an offhand manner. Even so, I am breathless as I ask, "Is everything well? Has there been more trouble?"

He shakes his head. "Everything is fine, although it was touch and go for a while. After your wagons left, the Dakota began to strike their tepees, and people feared they were preparing for war. Galbraith told Sheehan to arrest the men who conducted the warehouse raid, but Sheehan didn't think he had sufficient strength, so he sent to Fort

Ridgely for reinforcements. In the meantime, Little Crow arrived and demanded that more goods be handed out.

"When Captain Marsh reached the agency, he ordered that blankets and provisions be distributed from the stores, and when the traders balked, he threatened to arrest them. He insisted that everyone attend a council. After two days of palaver, Galbraith finally agreed to open the storehouses and give the Sioux all the supplies they would normally receive with their annuity. Then the Indians broke camp and left."

I exhale deeply and hand Susan her plate. "So the trouble is over."

"The gold payment still has not arrived, so I don't think we're completely out of the woods, but things have calmed down considerably."

"Galbraith is a wicked man!" I exclaim as I dish up the children's food. "If he had distributed supplies weeks ago, all this trouble could have been averted."

"I don't think he is wicked so much as incompetent," Humphrey replies.

"Well, the end result is the same!" I sit down. As my gaze falls upon my full plate, I realize that irritation has ruined my appetite.

After we finish our dinner, Susan returns upstairs to rest and I settle the two girls down for a nap in my bedroom. Humphrey goes outside to smoke a cigar on the small front porch, and I begin the gargantuan task of washing dishes and cleaning the kitchen. The afternoon has turned blazing hot, so I decide to set out a cold supper of bread, cheese, and stewed fruit tonight.

As I work, I wonder how John fared during the tense events of this last week. Was he at any of the meetings? Did he dose his nerves with whiskey, or did he relish living on the edge of danger without the responsibilities of a married man? The more I think over Dr. Humphrey's news, the more hurt I feel that John did not send a message with the man who rode down here yesterday.

The cleaning finished, I walk through the house drying my hands on an apron. I pause at the foot of the stairs and, hearing only silence from above, step out onto the porch. "On days like this, I crave lemonade."

Humphrey laughs. "We'll know civilization has truly come to Minnesota when we can get lemons west of St. Paul."

Leaning against one of the pillars, I gaze across the dusty square where long shadows stretch across the grass. "Redwood looks like an established village. It isn't as lonesome here as out where we live."

"Are you sorry John moved you to Yellow Medicine?"

"No. At least, I wasn't until all this trouble. I've never seen such pretty country, and...." I hesitate, wondering if he will understand what I'm about to say. In the pause, I hear the dull clopping of horse's hoofs and the rumble of an approaching wagon. "I felt like I had gone a fair way toward making friends among the Sioux."

He grunted. "I wouldn't take that too far. From what I understand, if you form too much of a tie with them, they consider themselves entitled to share all you own."

"Do you think so?" I ask, but I'm not really listening for an answer. The horse that walks into view looks exactly like our Lady, followed by our medium-sized, two-seat farm wagon with my husband in the front seat.

"John!" I wave to him. He tips his hat to me and steers Lady in our direction.

Humphrey steps down from the porch and grabs the mare's bridle. "I can take the wagon to the stable. I imagine you would like to talk to your wife."

John climbs down, but instead of coming to me, he takes off his hat and slaps it against his leg to knock the dust from the brim. He brushes off his unbleached linen frock coat before stepping onto the porch. "Hello, Sarah Brown," he says in a low voice that caresses my name as it used to when we were courting.

Instinct warns me against responding with too much emotion. I remain leaning against the pillar and say, "A week apart seems to have damaged your memory, sir. My name is Wakefield."

"So it is." John takes my hand, pulls me into the house, shuts the front door, and kisses me. "I missed you."

"I missed you too," I say. He kisses me again with mounting hunger, and I wonder sourly if he missed *me* or simply the ability to satisfy his carnal appetites. Then I berate myself for the unkind thought.

A moment later, John recollects that we are standing in another man's house and pulls away. The interior has grown dim as the sun outside sinks closer to the horizon. After glancing into the parlor and down the hall, he frowns and turns to me. "Where is everyone? Why are you and Philander here alone?"

My heart thrills at the idea that he might be jealous. "The boys are outside playing, and the two girls are taking a nap. And Susan—" I stop, appalled that I could have forgotten about Susan.

"Oh, John." My voice breaks. "She miscarried on Wednesday, and she is still convalescing upstairs. I've never seen so much blood."

"I'm sorry, chicken." he says, reverting to an endearment that he hasn't used in years. He embraces me again. "So you've been running the household?"

I nod and burrow my face into the coarse linen of his summer coat. He sighs, and his ribcage falls with the expulsion of air. "I want you and the children to come home. Do you think you can leave her?"

His voice wavers. As I stand in the shadowy hallway, a blinding flash of insight illuminates me. For six years, I have defined myself as a vulnerable, maligned woman who needs the shield of her husband's strength to protect her from the world. How could I have failed to see that beneath his mordant wit, John has frailties too? In his own, un-acknowledged way, he needs me.

"I think they might be ready to manage on their own," I answer, "but we ought to ask to be sure."

He nods. "I have so much to tell you."

"A messenger came down from Yellow Medicine this morning," I say as we walk into the parlor, "so we heard most of the agency news. I know that Galbraith finally opened the storehouses and the Sioux have left."

"Yes, that's right." John sinks onto the horsehair sofa. "I hope I never again live through another week like this one."

Looking at him in concern, I say, "I was planning a cold supper to-night, but if you prefer, I can cook something hot."

"No, that's all right." He grins up at me. "But I surely do wish you had baked one of your pies this afternoon."

I laugh. "When we get home, I'll make as many pies as your heart desires."

Over supper, Humphrey says that he will not hear of my offering to stay longer. "Your place is with John. I'll see if some of the other agency wives can stop in for an hour or so each day."

"How is Susan doing?" John asks.

"She isn't regaining her strength as much as I would like, but I think she will recover in time."

I bite my lip to keep from rebuking him for allowing her stamina to be depleted by years of overwork.

That night, at John's insistence, we pull a drawer out of the dresser, line it with a shawl, and tuck Nellie into it so he and I can sleep alone together. As soon as we get into bed, John unbuttons my nightgown and caresses my breasts. My body responds swiftly. When I feel slipperiness between my thighs, I pull up my gown. He positions himself between my legs. The cornhusks beneath us rustle. As John enters me and moves in rhythm, the mattress emits telltale crackling and popping noises that cause him to freeze. "Dammit," he exclaims in a low voice. He starts to move inside me again, but it is no use. The mattress is loud, the Humphreys lie across the hall, and our amorous mood evaporates.

John rolls over onto his back, muttering imprecations. I want to giggle at the absurdity of the situation, but I know that would offend him. Moving slowly to create as little noise as possible, I straddle him, take his member in my hand, and pleasure him manually. After he obtains release, he throws his head back and murmurs, "Oh God, Sarah. Thank you."

I stand, kiss his forehead, and go to clean myself.

In the morning we eat an early breakfast and prepare to leave. By clinging to the banister and descending one step at a time, Susan makes her way downstairs to see us off. She is wearing the new coral calico dress, and I smile to see how well it looks on her. The bright fabric brings color to her wan complexion.

When we go outside, Jimmy complains about leaving Jay, so I promise that we will try to visit soon. I too am sorry to leave the Humphreys. If we lived nearer to each other, Susan and I might develop a warm friendship, something I haven't had with any woman since my mother and stepfather ruined my name.

We climb into our conveyance, an open wagon with two seats and a narrow area for cargo in back. John sits in the driver's seat, and I sit on the backseat with the children. Once we have passed the Sioux villages and are driving in the open countryside, I lean forward to tell John about my visit to the mission church. "I saw many Indians that we knew in Shakopee, and they were as well-behaved as the white congregants. Dr. Hinman is doing good work among them."

John reaches into his inside coat pocket for a cigar and temporarily holds the reins between his knees so he can trim and light it. "I wish he'd tell them to stop their thieving. Mary said three of your chickens disappeared last week. Although, who knows? She might have taken them herself."

"Mary wouldn't rob me," I say firmly. "I'm surprised the Sioux haven't stolen my hens before this, hungry as they are."

Jimmy stands up and tugs his father's sleeve. "We could get a dog to guard the chicken coop!" he says, all excitement.

"Whatever gave you that idea, cricket?" John asks, laughing. I enjoy seeing how much more easygoing he is with children than Philander Humphrey is.

"Johnny took us all 'round the Lower Agency, and I saw lots of guard dogs. We could get one and keep him tied in the backyard except when I want to go fishing, and he could bark if someone tries to take Mama's chickens."

"Fishing!" I exclaim. "When have you ever gone fishing?"

"I went with Johnny a couple of times when he was done with all his chores. It was fun. He showed me how to make a fishing pole from a sapling. I could teach you, Father, and we could go fishing on Sunday sometimes."

John shoots an amused glance over his shoulder. "I suppose we could at that."

Surprised to learn of this unsuspected activity, I say, "But if you boys went fishing, what happened to the fish? You didn't bring them home to be cleaned and cooked, at least not that I recall."

"Oh, we didn't catch anything," he answers. "Johnny said that's 'cause me and Jay wriggled around and talked too much. But I bet I could sit still enough to catch a fish as soon as I turn five."

I laugh, but as we bounce along in the wagon, uneasiness settles in my stomach. The thought of my son playing by the river upsets me. It never occurred to me that the boys would go down there without asking; Dr. Humphrey assured me that he has forbidden his children to go swimming. Perhaps it is time to take the boy more strictly in hand.

Scooting forward and leaning close to John, I say, "I've been thinking. There's no school where we're living, and your appointment is likely to last until the next president is elected. Do you think I should start teaching Jimmy his letters this fall?"

John puffs his cigar and, shifting it to the side of his mouth, says, "I suppose it is time. Once we're sure the trouble with the Indians has died down."

"And the weather cools," I say, moving back in my seat and taking off my bonnet so I can fan myself with it. A minute later, I put it back on for protection from the August sun.

We drive along until we reach the large Indian burial mound about halfway between the two agencies. There we stop and sit beneath the shade of a black maple to eat a picnic of hard-boiled eggs and bread.

After lunch, I lean against the tree and allow Nellie to nurse. John removes his coat and drapes it over the wagon seat. When he does so, I notice that he is traveling with his pistol tucked into the waistband of his trousers. He lies on the grass with his hat over his eyes, and Jimmy curls up next to him.

As they nap, I use the time to think about changes I could make to improve our marriage. Now that I know he missed me, I feel on firmer ground than I have for years, but that doesn't mean I am happy with our relationship. One of the best times for us was when I assisted John in Shakopee as he treated wounded Sioux. I felt like more of a real helpmeet then. However, after a few minutes of trying to think of a way to assist him in his work now, I realize that goal will be difficult to accomplish once I start teaching our children. No, I tell myself, a better course of action would be the one I decided on during my stay with the Humphreys: to be more cheerful and less emotionally demanding. I need to earn John's respect as well as his love. The idea comes to me, yeasty and unformed like a lump of dough, that if I were a stronger person, my husband might resent me less and be less cruel. If I were more self-sufficient, I could encourage him to go off on occasional excursions or hunting trips to satisfy his craving for adventure. Might that not ease his discontent?

While these thoughts still churn in my mind, John rises and brushes debris off the back of his clothes. Within minutes, we are on the road again. After we travel about an hour, I see small puffs of dust rising above the spot where the road dips below the horizon. I scoot forward and clutch John's shoulder. "Do you see that up ahead?"

"Yes, I noticed it a couple of minutes ago."

Placing my mouth behind his ear, I lower my voice so the children cannot hear me over the jingling and creaking of the wagon. "Do you think it's a war party?"

"Too soon to tell," he answers, but he transfers the reins to his left hand and pulls out his pistol with his right.

"Do you want me to come up front and drive so both your hands are free?"

John glances at me sideways and shakes his head. "No, I would rather you watch over the children."

By then, it's obvious that whatever is kicking up dust is moving toward us—but slowly, so it probably isn't caused by a troop of riders. Sure enough, after about ten minutes more, we can make out the dark blue uniforms of marching Union infantry, and I expel a sigh of relief. Wordlessly, John puts his pistol away.

We meet the infantry in a low dip in the road. The column, which has four soldiers abreast, stretches back more ranks than I can count. One of the officers calls, "Halt!" about the same time that John pulls Lady to a stop. Jimmy instantly climbs up and stands on the backseat so he can see what's going on.

An officer who is riding a large black horse at the rear of the column swings out and moves up to talk to us. He is wearing a captain's uniform. "Dr. Wakefield." He touches his hat and nods at me. "Ma'am."

"Captain Marsh," John says. "Where are your boys heading?"

"Back to the fort, sir."

"I am astonished, Captain!" I exclaim. "Did you leave any soldiers at the agency to protect us from further trouble?"

"No need, ma'am. All of the Indians have departed, satisfied now that they have received their much-needed supplies."

"But Captain—"

"That's enough, Sarah," John says gruffly over his shoulder. "I'm sure these men know their duty."

Chastised—and ashamed of myself for violating my resolution to control my nerves—I subside in my seat.

"Double file, men. March!" Captain Marsh orders, and the column of men splits into two lines that pass on either side of our wagon. Jimmy, still standing on top of the seat, salutes them, but the soldiers keep their eyes to the front and do not return the gesture. As soon as they bypass us, they spread back out into their four-file column. Captain Marsh salutes Jimmy smartly as he rides past, and my son sits down with a huge grin on his face.

I expect that John will start the wagon on its way again, but he sits there for several minutes, scratching his side whiskers. Then he turns halfway in his seat. "I need to talk to you. Would you come sit up here for a while?"

Glancing at the children, I bite my lip. "I don't think Nellie is able to hold herself on a backless seat."

He sighs in exasperation. "Set her on the floor. This is important."

"All right." As John sets the brake and jumps down from the front seat, I move Nellie to the floor of the wagon and reach into my drawstring purse for some crackers I brought along in case I need to soothe the children. I give several to each child. "Jimmy, keep a close eye on your sister. Do not let her crawl around."

Then I hike up my hoop skirt, climb over the wall of the wagon, and stand on the side step. John gives me a supporting hand as I climb into the front.

Before we get underway again, John takes out a cigar and goes through the routine of lighting it. He gently slaps the reins across Lady's back. "Walk on."

He waits until Lady has pulled our wagon up the incline and we can see the road stretching out ahead of us for a couple of miles before he says, "I'm sorry, Sarah. I wasn't counting on the soldiers leaving our agency before the gold payment got here. I never would have come to get you and the children if I'd known."

"It's not your fault," I say softly, surprised by his apology.

"We have no way of knowing if that money will ever arrive, and I have little faith that the supplies Galbraith distributed will keep the Sioux satisfied for long. Now that they've had a taste of forcing us to do what they want through threats of violence, they're likely to use those tactics again."

Chills sweep over me despite the intense heat, and I grip the edge of the seat. Glancing back at the children, I say, "So you think there will be more problems."

"I'm not sure," he says. "At the very least, I expect us to have trouble with begging and thieving all summer. I should have left you where you were."

"We can't stay with the Humphreys forever. They have their own troubles."

"I know." He chews on the end of his cigar. Then he snatches it out of his mouth and growls when he sees how soggy it has become. "I have another plan. I want you and the children to go east for a while. That way I'll know you're safe."

A wave of nausea adds itself to my chills. "What do you mean by 'go east'?"

"You should take the children to visit your mother."

I turn sideways to confront him. "John, you know I haven't spoken to her in years. I'm not even sure where she's living any more."

"Where else would she be but in the house where you left her?"

"You know what she did. I can't go back there and ask her to take me in."

"Not even to protect your children?" he asks, his tone cutting.

I refuse to rise to the bait. "I am perfectly willing to take them to safety, but why do we have to visit her?"

"Because she's your mother, Sarah, and she has a right to meet her grandchildren. Your stepfather died years ago, so it's time to heal the breach."

"I would rather be robbed by the Sioux," I say, rubbing my hands together.

"Don't be ridiculous. I am trying to do what is best for the children."

"Why can't we visit your sister Lucy?"

He stares at me. "My sister is persnickety. I don't think it's a good idea for you to go there without me. You have to visit your mother."

"Have to?"

"Yes, Sarah, have to. Or if not your mother, then your brothers or uncles. I want Jimmy and Nellie to know both sides of their family."

To my distress, tears fill my eyes. "John, please don't ask me to do this."

John slows the horse slightly and reaches over to place his hand atop mine. "You faced down six angry warriors at the door to our home a week ago. Surely you can stand up to one old woman." He squeezes my clasped hands.

I laugh sharply. "Only if you let me borrow your pistol."

John chuckles and leans over to kiss my cheek. "You're a formidable woman, darlin'. You don't need anything but your own strength."

Really? I think. *So why do I feel so defenseless?* The thought of seeing my mother again frightens me more than the Sioux.

CHAPTER

7

BY THE TIME WE REACH HOME, IT IS NEARLY SIX O'CLOCK IN THE EVENING. Mary meets us in the hall, and I ask her to take the children upstairs and wash their grimy faces. Then I enter the parlor, remove my bonnet, and gaze around at the familiar things that make this room so homey: a pair of porcelain vases, more than a dozen family photographs, a framed lithograph of the well-known painting "Shakespeare and His Friends," and an assortment of bright pillows, one of them embroidered with a lighthouse and seagull to remind us of New England. My sense of joy at being back in my own house is marred by the knowledge that John wants to send me away again.

When he carries our trunk in the front door, I call, "It's too late in the day to cook a full dinner. I thought I might make pancakes and fried ham. Is that all right?"

"Fine," he says in a strained voice as he carries the trunk upstairs.

All four of us are tired and sore from the long, bumpy wagon ride. During supper, the children whine about not wanting to drink their milk or eat their ham. As soon as we finish eating, I put Jimmy and Nellie to bed. When I come downstairs, John is at his desk making a list on a sheet of paper. He glances up when I enter the room. "The stage from Fort Abercrombie will come through sometime tomorrow. You should be ready to go early to make sure you don't miss it."

"Tomorrow?" I move close to him. "John, we can't leave tomorrow.

I have to wash all our clothes and take our cold-weather things out of storage. If we're going all the way to Rhode Island, we probably won't return until late autumn."

He sets down his pencil. "But the stage runs only once a week. If you don't go tomorrow, it will be seven days before you have another chance."

"That can't be helped." I stretch to ease my sore back, sit in a near-by armchair, and unbutton my high-top shoes. "We'll be on the road a week or more. We cannot start such a trip with a trunk full of dirty clothes."

"Why didn't you wash them at the Humphreys'?"

"I intended to do so today. I had no idea when you were coming to get us."

He frowns but cannot refute my logic. "Well, come look at this itinerary."

Sighing, I push my aching body out of the chair. When we moved here a year ago, we journeyed by steamboat from St. Paul to Redwood, but the boat was a charter that does not run regularly. John points at the first item on his list. "As I said, the stagecoach from Fort Abercrombie comes through every Tuesday. You'll spend the first night at New Ulm and reach St. Paul on the second day. Then you can catch the stagecoach for Galena, which will take three days. In Galena, you can board a train to Chicago, where you can transfer to a train heading east."

After adding up estimated travel times for each leg of the journey, I say, "So we'll be in transit ten days."

"Something like that."

"John, do you have enough cash on hand for a trip like this?"

He doesn't meet my eyes as he answers, "I have enough for the fares and your meals. I'll have to mail you the money for the return journey."

An emotion as prickly as skin rash sweeps over me. John isn't very good at saving money, and I have a sudden fear of being stranded in Rhode Island while he tries to acquire the necessary funds. Squaring my shoulders, I rebuke myself for the thought. Whatever other faults he has, John loves his children, and he will do whatever he must to bring us back as soon as the troubles are over.

Putting an arm around his shoulder, I say, "I know you think this is the right thing to do, but I hate the idea of being separated for such a long time."

He reaches up to pat my hand. "If it were the two of us, Sarah, I would let you make your own choice. But we have to protect the children."

His words fill me with dismay because they reveal a deeper worry than he has admitted. John would not talk of protecting the children if he feared only theft.

"I know," I say, but in my heart, I exult that I have bought a seven days' reprieve before I have to leave for the East. If the gold payment comes before then, I may not have to go at all.

After breakfast on Tuesday, Jimmy reports that men are gathering outside the agency building. Fearing another riot, I rush out our front door, only to see that the crowd is composed about equally of mixed bloods and young men from the surrounding farms. Most of them have knapsacks or burlap bags tied with string, and a few carry guns.

"Mama, what are they doing?" Jimmy whispers.

"I don't know. Maybe they are forming a militia to protect us. You know that the soldiers went back to the fort yesterday."

"Are they going to start drilling?" he asks. "Can I watch them?"

After hesitating a moment, I say, "Do you promise to stay inside our fence?"

"Yes, Mama."

Leaning down, I say sternly, "I mean it, Jimmy. If you disobey me and go bother those men, your father will punish you."

Jimmy frowns and digs his big toe in the dirt. "I promise."

I sigh. Although I'm not sure I can trust him, I have so much to do today that things will be easier if he isn't underfoot. Patting him on the head, I say, "Good boy," and go inside.

The first thing I do before the day grows any hotter is to bake John the pie he wanted. Early this morning, I sent Mary to the wooded area along the river, and she came back with a pail of wild raspberries and blackberries. As I roll out the crust and Mary hulls the blackberries, she tells me about her mother, who is ill with fever. "I'll make some broth you can take to her," I say as I ease the crust onto my pie pan.

While the pie is in the oven, we go upstairs to look through the children's winter clothes. Jimmy has outgrown the pants I sewed him last year, but I planned ahead by making them loose and taking up substantial hems, so I think they will fit if I lengthen them. I decide to pack his brown broadcloth suit for autumn, along with two summer suits. One pair of shoes and his Congress gaiters should be enough; I'm hoping we won't be gone long enough for him to need winter boots.

As I set aside the trousers, I hear stomping feet outside, so I go to the window. The crowd of about thirty men has formed itself into a straggly double-file column and begun to march down the road toward Redwood, with Galbraith at the head. "That's strange," I murmur and head downstairs to do laundry.

When John enters the kitchen two hours later, I'm standing at the stove frying chicken. Because he won't get much home cooking while I'm away, I've decided to fix his favorite meals all week. I turn a chicken leg in the hot lard and glance at John to see if he's pleased. Instead, his mouth is set in a grim line, and he holds a glass of whiskey.

"Send her away," he says quietly, nodding toward Mary, who stands at the table chopping cabbage.

"Mary, fetch more water for the next load of laundry. I'll make the coleslaw."

"Yes, ma'am." Mary hurries outside.

I turn two more pieces of chicken to make sure they won't scorch and then say, "What's wrong, John? You have a face like thunder."

He takes a slug of whiskey. "That fool Galbraith. He recruited thirty men from around here and marched them off to fight against the South—and he plans to pull more from Redwood. I know the president is desperate for troops, but this is the wrong time to take able-bodied men off the reservation. Doesn't Galbraith realize that the Sioux are still mad as wet hens?"

As I take in his words, fear strangles me in its vise. I lay my fork on the stove. "How many people remain at the agency?"

"Givens and a few other employees. Galbraith's family. The store clerks. Oh, and the missionaries, of course."

So the agency is not quite deserted. Slowly, I let out my breath and go back to turning pieces of chicken. "What do you think will happen?"

"I don't know. I wish to God you had caught that stage today."

"John, we talked about this. It's not my fault."

"I know." He places a hand on my back. "I never thought coming out here would turn out like this."

He sounds as lost as a little boy, and I swallow my terror and say in the brisk tone I would use to reassure Jimmy, "Maybe it will be all right. Nothing has really happened yet." As I move to the table to make dressing for the coleslaw, a hopeful thought occurs to me. "Do you think maybe Galbraith heard that the annuity is finally on its way and that's why he decided to leave?"

John shakes his head. "No, I asked him that. He hasn't heard anything, but he says he is confident that the worst of the unrest is behind us. If you ask me, the man is a coward and looking for a reason to get away from here."

"But surely he wouldn't leave his wife and children behind if he was afraid of trouble." I put bacon grease, vinegar, sugar, salt, pepper, and dry mustard into a pan and carry it to the stove to make a hot dressing. "Besides, enlisting in the Union Army isn't going to keep him out of danger."

John barks with laughter. "By God, you're right." He picks up his empty glass and goes to the parlor for a refill.

Although I try hard not to show my anxiety, the news that so many men have left the reservation unnerves me. I have never been one of those people who wanted to live on the undefended frontier; we came out to Yellow Medicine because we thought the Sioux had been pacified and were far along in the process of adopting white culture. Like so many missionaries and Indian agents before us, we underestimated how strongly the Sioux love their traditional ways.

Now, the stories I've heard about Indian attacks haunt my days and disrupt my nights. As a little girl in Rhode Island, one of my heroines was Anne Hutchinson, who spoke out against the narrow teachings of the Massachusetts Puritans. She emphasized faith in the mercy of God rather than rigid adherence to a legalistic code—a doctrine that comforted me when I suffered the condemnation of clergymen but which got Hutchinson herself in trouble in Boston. Excommunicated, she moved to what became Rhode Island and established one of the first settlements there. Four years later, after her husband died, she moved to Long Island Sound. There, hostile Indians killed her and all of her children except for one daughter, whom they took captive. The possibility that my children and I now face a similar danger sobers me, and I redouble my preparations to travel east.

By Sunday, I have washed, mended, and altered the clothes I plan to take, and I spend the afternoon packing. Instead of making me feel better, the accomplishment increases my sense of dread. All day, I go to our windows, expecting at any moment to see a war party descend upon the agency. Each time, I see only the empty stretch of grass between the buildings. The settlement is quiet. The calm should reassure me, but somehow it doesn't. Instead, I feel as though we are surrounded by a hostile force that is noiseless only because it awaits the right moment to strike.

When John comes home for midday dinner on Monday, his face is white. He pulls me into the parlor away from Mary and the children. "I've changed my mind about you catching the stage tomorrow. I want you to leave today."

"Today? How?"

He moves to his desk, unlocks the tin box he keeps there, and counts out coins. "You know George Gleason, don't you?"

"Yes, of course." Gleason, a pleasant young man who likes to sing and tell jokes, works as a clerk at the Lower Agency.

"He rode up here on Saturday to visit some of the other bachelors, but now he's about to go back to Redwood. He's offered to drive you and the children to Fort Ridgely if I let him use our horse and wagon. With his horse and Lady hitched as a team, you'll make better time."

John keeps his back to me as he puts the coins into a small leather pouch. After a moment, I say, "But why go to all that trouble? Then you'll be stuck here without a horse to pull your buggy. How will you make medical calls if you need to?"

He shrugs. "Oh, I expect I can always borrow a horse." He turns toward me, but his gaze slides away from my face.

"But it's only one more day until the stage comes."

"Sarah, don't argue," he says sharply. "I've made up my mind. As soon as we eat dinner, you and the children are setting out for Fort Ridgely. You can catch the stage there late tomorrow."

Pushing past me, he leaves the parlor and I have little choice but to follow.

By two o'clock, George Gleason has loaded our trunk and satchel. John lifts Jimmy into the wagon. A terrible presentiment of disaster—like the heaviness that comes just before a storm—oppresses me, and I cannot shake off the premonition that I will never see my home again. Impulsively, I say, "Give me a minute," and rush back into the house.

I go upstairs and walk slowly through the two rooms of our sleeping area. A host of memories flit through my mind: nursing Nellie in the rocking chair, cutting out clothing patterns on the worktable, making love with John in our big, black walnut bed. Will I ever again do those things in this place? My gaze settles upon the bottle of perfume on my dresser; John sent away to Chicago for it last Christmas. I snatch it up, tuck it into my purse, and walk downstairs.

Entering the dining room, I approach my birdcages and whistle at my canaries. One of them warbles in reply, and tears spring to my eyes. Then the front door crashes open. "Sarah, what are you doing?"

I walk back into the front hall and see John standing there with his hands on his hips. "I thought you were ready to go."

"I am, but I forgot something, so I ran upstairs to get it." If I tell him that I am saying farewell to our house, he will ridicule me.

When I walk out the front door, Gleason is already sitting in the front seat. He is a round-faced man with curly black hair and blue eyes, dressed in checked trousers, a green-striped shirt, a brown waistcoat, and a straw hat. A small brown-and-white terrier sits to his left.

I hike up my skirt, and John helps me onto the side step and then into the wagon. As I settle onto the backseat, I realize I forgot to kiss him good-bye. Now it is too late. He places Nellie on my lap and turns to talk to Gleason. "Drive fast so as to get to the fort early. Don't spare the horses."

Facing me again, John reaches for my hand and squeezes it. "When you change coaches in St. Paul, send me a letter, so I'll know you made it there safely."

"All right."

John steps closer to the side of the wagon. "Come here, son. Let me hug you."

I glance toward Gleason, who is watching us with an uncharacteristically somber expression. I sense that the two men are keeping something from me. "Do you have a pistol with you, Mr. Gleason?"

"Yes, Mrs. Wakefield, don't you worry about that." He grins broadly. John releases Jimmy and steps back, and Gleason slaps the reins, saying, "Get up, now."

I turn to watch John as the wagon moves away and see him wipe his eye. I have never known him to cry, and my sense of foreboding grows suffocating. "What did my husband tell you that he didn't tell me, Mr. Gleason?"

"What a question to ask, Mrs. Wakefield!" Gleason cries with forced gaiety. "Here's your husband sending you on a nice holiday, and all you can do is fret."

"But—"

Gleason cuts me off and starts singing a Stephen Foster song:

I dream of Jeanie with the light brown hair,
Borne, like a vapor, on the summer air;
I see her tripping where the bright streams play,
Happy as the daisies that dance on her way.

I sigh and turn to my son who is still standing, grasping the side of the wagon. "Sit next to me, Jimmy. We have a long drive ahead of us."

Gleason continues to sing as we descend the hill on which the agency stands. Down in the valley of the Yellow Medicine River where the traders live, Mr. Garvie runs out of his store and waves for us to stop.

As soon as we halt, he approaches. Gleason's dog barks at him, so he remains a couple of steps away. "I have terrible news. Yesterday, Indians killed some people in the Big Woods, up Acton way."

Gleason appears unsurprised. I ask Garvie, "Sioux Indians or Chippewa?"

"Sioux. Some of Little Crow's band. And the Indians down at the Lower Agency are holding a council right now to decide whether they should kill all the whites or leave Minnesota and go to the Red River."

"Thank you for warning us." As Garvie returns to his store, I tell Gleason, "Take me back home. We'll be safer there than on the road."

"No, ma'am." He tilts his hat back. "Your husband heard these reports this morning, and that's why he asked me to take you down to the fort. And I'm in a hurry to get on home to Redwood. Once I'm there, I'm going to round up four or five hundred Indians and send them here to defend the whites."

"But Mr. Garvie said they're having a war council in Little Crow's village, and you know perfectly well that we'll have to drive right past it." Gleason sets his jaw stubbornly and gathers up the reins, but I grab his arm. "Listen to me. We've gone only a quarter mile, so it won't take you any time at all to drive us home. Then you can drive the wagon to Redwood."

"Lord, how you go on. Doc Wakefield made me promise on my soul's honor to take you and the children down to Fort Ridgely, and that's what I'm bound to do. You women just don't understand these things."

With that, he urges the horses into a trot. Gleason commences to belt out song after song, his baritone voice booming over the silent countryside. We drive for two hours without stopping, and my fears increase with each passing minute. Usually, we meet lots of teams on the road, but today, we are the only travelers. Finally, I tug Gleason's arm. When he stops singing, I say, "Don't you see that something must be wrong downriver? We haven't met another person all afternoon."

Gleason hoots. "Some women are never happy. If the road was crowded, you'd be complaining about the dust."

"That's not true, and you know it. I tell you there's something dreadfully wrong. I've felt a premonition of danger growing all day."

"Stop being so nervous. I swear you must drive your husband to distraction with all your hysterics."

"I am not having hysterics. I'm being sensible. You're the one trying to make a joke out of everything even after we've been warned about hostile Indians."

He snorts in disdain. "I know those Lower Agency Indians better than Stewart Garvie does, and I tell you there is no danger at all. Now if you don't stop nagging me, I will never take you anywhere again."

"I didn't ask you to take me this time. That was my husband's doing."

"Well, pardon me!" he snaps and falls silent. As if to emphasize that he won't give way to my fears, he urges the team to go even faster.

Soon after we conclude this debate, we reach the Indian mound where John and I picnicked last week. We climb to the top of a hill, and Gleason halts the wagon to allow the horses to rest.

Ahead of us, thick columns of black smoke rise into the distant sky. "Look!" I point at the horizon. "Indians are burning the agency."

"Oh, no, they're not. Probably the sawmill caught on fire, or maybe it's a wildfire on the prairie. Yes, by gum, I'll bet that's what it is."

"No, you're wrong." Holding Nellie tight to my bosom, I stand. "My children and I are getting out of this wagon right now. You can go on without us."

Gleason turns around in his seat to face me. "By durn, you're a troublesome woman. I'm just doing what your husband told me, and it's mighty unpleasant to have you fuss at me hour after hour. I wish to high heaven I'd never agreed to take you to the fort, but I did agree, and I'm not going to fail to carry out my promise. Now you sit back down again and be quiet, or I'll tie you to your seat."

I stare at him in blazing fury. Then Jimmy tugs my skirt and asks plaintively, "Mama, if we get out here, where will we sleep?"

When I glance down at my son, I see that he is biting his lip in an effort not to cry. I look from him to the surrounding landscape and realize that there are no nearby cabins where we can seek shelter. As terrified as I am of going forward, I grudgingly admit that it makes more sense to stay in the wagon. At least, Gleason has a pistol. "Don't worry," I tell Jimmy. "We're not getting down."

I resume my seat and say tartly to Gleason, "All right then, have it your own way. Go on. They will not kill me. They will shoot you and take me prisoner."

"Why, who are you talking about? Those Lower Agency Indians are just like white men. You must not act so hysterical."

I'm so furious at the way he condescends to me that I do not bother to answer. Instead, I gaze at Nellie, who is napping in my arms. She has grown pink with sunburn, so I drape a shawl over my shoulder to protect her.

We drive on in silence that is thick with resentment. Gleason doesn't even hum. A short time later, Lady wheezes as the team pulls the wagon up another low hill, one that normally would cause her no strain. We have pushed the horses hard today, and the smoke-filled air must be causing them difficulties. "Shouldn't we get out to lighten the load for the horses when we go up slopes?"

Gleason gives me a sideways glance. "No, ma'am. I'd ruther you stayed in the wagon."

We reach the top of the hill, and Gleason points ahead. "Lookit there, Mrs. Wakefield. See how foolish you are? Joe Reynolds's cabin is standing."

Reynolds runs a way station for travelers in this place, and he also teaches agriculture to the Indians in Shakopee's village. I look down the slope, but it is difficult to see anything because a great haze of smoke hangs over the valley, especially in the low areas. The silhouette of the cabin is visible, but I cannot tell whether it is damaged. Gleason pulls out his pocket watch. "It is now a quarter past six. We'll stop to have supper at Old Joe's and by eight o'clock we'll be at the fort."

His calculation makes no sense. It's taken us more than four hours to come twenty-two miles. How he thinks we're going to travel fifteen miles in little more than an hour is beyond my comprehension, but I am too heartsick to argue. Despite the friendly cabin directly ahead of us, I feel certain we are driving toward our deaths.

As we start down the hill, I notice two Indians walking toward us on the right. To my relief, one is a man I recognize from the time we lived in Shakopee; in fact, I recently saw him at Dr. Hinman's church. He is a farmer Indian named Chaska, who usually wears the shirt and trousers of a white man. In the past, he cut off his long hair, but now it has grown out to just below his shoulders and is plaited into braids. Today, he wears the traditional breechcloth and leggings of his people. With him is an Indian I don't know, but I can tell that he clings to the old ways because his braids reach to his waist. Both men carry double-barreled shotguns.

"Mr. Gleason, take out your pistol," I say as the two warriors near us.

"Be quiet. These are just two boys out hunting." The dog stands on the seat and barks, and the Indian with the long braids scowls.

His fierce expression frightens me, so I urge Gleason, "Make the horses hurry. We need to get out of here."

Instead of doing as I ask, Gleason pulls on the reins, causing the team to halt. "Where are you boys going?"

The Sioux, who are walking beside the horses, clear the animals' rumps and come into the open. The moment Gleason asks his question, the long-haired Indian raises his shotgun and fires. The bullet hits Gleason's right shoulder, twisting his body and forcing it backward. He falls against me, crushing Nellie against my breast. His blood splatters my skirt. Jimmy screams and crawls under the seat.

Then the same Indian shoots Gleason a second time, this time in the bowels. The blast is so violent it propels him out of the wagon, and he lands on his side with his back to me. The terrier barks furiously and jumps down. Lady rears up in terror and tries to run into the fields, but the other Indian, Chaska, grabs the traces and forces the animals to halt. He speaks to the mare in a low voice, and I wonder that anyone could gentle an animal right after committing such savagery to a human being. Gleason moans in pain behind me.

Once the horse is calm again, Chaska approaches the side of the wagon. "Are you the doctor's wife?" he asks in English.

Stunned that he would speak to me so civilly, I nod. Chaska, who looks to be in his late thirties, has a Roman nose and smallish eyes placed close together. He gazes at me with a kindly expression if such a thing is possible in these horrible circumstances. "Yes, I am Mrs. Wakefield. I remember you from Shakopee."

"I remember you," he says and, to my astonishment, reaches out and shakes my hand. Lowering his voice, he says, "Do not talk much." He nods at the man who shot poor Gleason. "That man is a bad man. He has too much whiskey."

"Oh," I say and clutch my stomach; I feel nauseated.

Chaska goes back to the team and, grabbing the bridle of Gleason's horse, pulls the team in a wide arc to reverse the direction of the wagon. As we come around, I see Gleason writhing on the dirt road and hear him gibbering in agony. His dog stands guard nearby. The murderous Indian is reloading his shotgun. He raises it in my direction, and all my joints melt with terror. "Please!" I cry and press my daughter to my breast with my hands covering the back of her head. Without thinking, I cry out in English, "Don't shoot. Spare me for the sake of my children. I will do everything for you. I will cook, sew, wash, chop wood, anything you ask. But please don't kill me."

The Indian scowls and points his gun directly at me. Only then do I remember that Chaska told me to be quiet. I hold my breath.

Suddenly, Gleason cries, "Oh, my God, Mrs. Wakefield!" A look of distress crosses Chaska's face. The scowling Indian whirls around and shoots Mr. Gleason a third time, and he lies still.

The murderer turns. Stalking to the wagon, he raises his shotgun and points it at my temple. I close my eyes and send up a silent prayer.

An instant later I hear a scuffle and open my eyes to see that Chaska has knocked the weapon from the other Indian's hands. I gasp in relief and stretch out my hands in a placating manner. "Please, I beg you, spare me."

The murderer growls and slaps my hands so viciously that tears fill my eyes. Chaska takes his arm and leads him a few steps away, urging him in Dakota not to harm me. Because I have some knowledge of their language, I learn that the violent Indian is named Hapa. He rushes back, picks up his gun again, and takes aim, but Chaska interposes himself between us. They argue vehemently, speaking swiftly. In my distressed state, I fail to understand more than about half of what they say. For a second time, Chaska leads his companion away from the wagon. I try to catch my breath, at the same time straining to hear their words. A few minutes later, Hapa charges me again. A vision flashes into my mind of my children sitting on the prairie, crying helplessly over their dead mother. Then I imagine all three of our corpses on the open prairie, bleached bones and scraps of faded fabric scattered amid the tall grasses. But before Hapa can shoot, Chaska knocks away his shotgun once more.

As the two men argue, Hapa mentions the name *Galbraith* with rage. I realize that Hapa believes I am Henrietta Galbraith, wife of the Indian agent, and he wants to kill me—and do so savagely—because of his great hatred for the man. At that, I grow so faint I can barely remain upright. Chaska urgently tells him who I really am and reminds him of the time John and I treated the Sioux after battle. He takes Hapa by the arm and recounts several other stories about kindnesses I have done for their people. For the first time since I saw the smoke-filled sky, I allow myself to hope.

The argument goes on for what seems like an hour, and as time passes, my optimism fades. The rage in Hapa's voice convinces me that death will strike me at any instant. My bones ache from nervous tension. The dreadful, coppery smell of blood fills the air, and a long smear of it stains my left sleeve. At long last, the two men return to the wagon and Hapa leans over the side to get closer to me. "I know you. You are agent's wife," he declares in English.

"No, I am the wife of the doctor," I say, doing my best to keep my voice calm. "Chaska," I make sure to pronounce it *Chas-kay* as the Indians do, "has been to my house in Shakopee, and many of your people have visited me in Yellow Medicine. I do not like the Indian agent Mr. Galbraith. He is a bad man."

He glares at me through narrowed eyes, then turns to Chaska. "She can live."

Chaska climbs into the driver's seat, and to my horror, Hapa sits beside me, pointing his gun at my breast. Nellie starts to cry and I try frantically to shush her.

Hapa growls and says to Chaska in Dakota, "She can live, but I will kill these children. They will be much trouble."

"No!" Chaska says in a loud voice, speaking so emphatically that I can translate with ease. "I will keep them. I have no children. These will be mine. You must kill me before you touch them."

My heart quails at the thought that he means to take my babies, but then he glances over his shoulder and briefly shakes his head. I look back at the body of Mr. Gleason, and when I see the dog nudge him and whimper, I start to cry. Chaska says, "You must not look anymore. You will only make this man angry."

Turning halfway around to his left, he says to Hapa in Dakota, "Get out and shoot him again. Do not leave him with any life in him to suffer."

Hapa answers, "You have not shot today. Get out with me and you do it."

Chaska glances toward me, searching my face as though seeking confirmation that I understand his motives, but I am too frightened to respond. The two Indians jump off the wagon and walk back to Gleason's body. After pointing his gun at Gleason's head, Chaska pulls the trigger. The gun snaps but does not fire, and I wonder if it is even loaded. Grunting, Hapa raises his gun and shoots Gleason one last time. Chaska reaches for the dog, but it backs away, barking furiously, so he leaves it alone. The two men return to the wagon, and we drive away.

CHAPTER

8

As I travel down the road with my captors—one of whom points a gun at my breast—my imagination conjures terrible images. New Englanders grow up hearing bloodcurdling stories about King Philip's War two hundred years ago. Now, one tale from that conflict comes to mind, that of an English captive tortured mercilessly. First, the Indians amputated each of his fingers, slicing through the skin around the joint where it meets the hand and snapping off the finger the way I might pull the leg off a roasted chicken. Then they performed the same grisly operation on his toes and forced him to dance after each amputation. After that, they broke both legs and finished him off by clubbing him to death.

My stomach churns as I remember how we children used to gather around autumn bonfires and frighten ourselves with that story—safe in the knowledge that New England would never again experience such violence. No such assurance holds true for Minnesota, and I cannot help but wonder if Chaska has spared me from death only to lead me toward a more horrifying peril.

If I should die, what will happen to my children? Since Chaska has sworn to keep them, will he raise them as Sioux? Or will he find a way to return them to John—if, indeed, John still lives? The realization that I don't know whether my husband is alive makes me feel even more defenseless.

After a half hour's ride, we pull off the main road and arrive at an Indian encampment that has many cook fires but few tepees. At the sight of what looks to be 200 people milling about, I tremble. Will most of them be like Chaska, who has been to school and learned some of white society's ways? Or will they be like the murderous Hapa?

Chaska pulls on the reins. As soon as the wagon stops rolling, Hapa jumps down and strides away as though nothing had occurred between us. After setting the wagon brake, Chaska helps Jimmy get down and then me.

By this point, many Sioux are gathering around us. I bend down and whisper to my son that he must be quiet and well behaved. Then I face the crowd.

A cry goes up from the women. To my astonishment, I know many of them. This must be the village of Chief Little Six; his people used to camp near Shakopee, which means "six" in the Dakota language and was named after the current chief's father. During the time I lived there, hardly a day passed without one or two Indians coming to my door to beg, and I never turned a single one away without food.

Three older women rush toward me. The first woman takes my hands, the second pats my arm, and the third pulls Jimmy into an embrace. All three are crying. Their grief at seeing me taken prisoner causes my own tears to flow. My companions lead my children and me to a common area around which cook fires burn.

Several women spread rugs on the ground, and one of the older ones brings me a pillow and urges me to rest. For a moment, I hold the cushion to my chest, afraid to make myself vulnerable in their midst. The woman sees my fear and says, "Your husband saved our men. Now we will protect you and your children."

At that, I collapse on the rug and weep. Nellie starts to wail, and Jimmy crouches down next to me, patting my shoulder and saying, "Mama, what is wrong? What did that Indian do to you?"

For the sake of my children, I inhale deeply, pull a handkerchief from my pocket, and wipe my eyes and runny nose. Then I give Jimmy a wobbly smile. "I was thinking about poor Mr. Gleason."

Jimmy puts his hand in mine, and Nellie crawls on my lap. The air is filled with wood smoke and cooking smells, and the sky has turned the silvery purple of a plum. Crickets chirp a chorus beneath the sound of women chatting as they work.

After half an hour, the woman who promised to protect us brings my children and me a watery stew of wild turnips and squash. "Mama, I don't like this," Jimmy complains after his first spoonful.

"Hush," I rebuke him. Residents of the encampment continually walk past to stare at us, and I am afraid someone will take offense at Jimmy's words. Lowering my voice, I say, "These people do not have much food, and they are giving you the best they have. Thank the woman for your supper when she comes back."

Jimmy takes another spoonful of stew and grimaces as he chews it.

I have very little appetite, but I force myself to eat the meal to avoid insulting the women. Bless their hearts, they do everything they can to make me comfortable. One woman offers me a second cushion, while another brings us cups of cool water. When Nellie starts to cry and beat her tiny fist against my bosom, a Sioux woman brings me a shawl so I can nurse my daughter without exposing my breasts to the warriors who traipse by and make crude jests. Their taunts convince me that it is only a matter of time before some enraged member of the tribe kills us.

A feeling of utter hopelessness descends upon me. What do eating, drinking, and sleeping matter if I am about to die? The women continue to reassure me that my children and I are safe, but I interpret their guarantees as wishful thinking. The men of the tribe, not their wives, will decide the fate of any prisoners.

Shortly after I finish nursing Nellie and lay her sleeping form on the rug, a mixed-blood man I remember from Shakopee sits down cross-legged in front of me. He says in an oily tone, "I feel very sorry to see you here, Mrs. Wakefield. You will probably be spared a few days, but you will be killed in the end because the warriors' lodge has sworn to kill everyone who has white blood in their veins."

"Then I should be equally sorry for you," I retort. "You are a half-breed, are you not? That means they will not let you live either."

He rubs his chin and smiles. "You are clever and not so easily terrified as the other white women. You saw right through my little joke."

"It was not at all funny."

He laughs. "Indian humor and white humor are different." Then he leans closer to me and lowers his voice. "But now I will talk serious with you. I saw how you cried when you arrived in camp. You must not carry on so because it goes against our ways and will turn many Indians against you."

Before I can answer, Chaska approaches. When he sees the children sleeping, he beckons me, and we walk a few steps away. "You had better go with me to a house where there is another white woman. We are not going to put our tepees up tonight, and your children will take cold sleeping on the prairie."

For a second, I am too panicked to answer. Why does Chaska want to take me away from these kind women? Has Chaska been told he must bring me before the council for judgment—or that he must kill us himself? My mind recoils from the myriad of possible dangers, yet I am even more afraid of offending this man who saved my life. Placing a hand on my throat, I croak, "I will fetch the children."

I return to where they doze and bend down to wake Jimmy. At the same time, I whisper to the mixed-blood man, "Chaska says he will lead me to a house where we can sleep, but I don't know if I dare believe him. What should I do?"

"Chaska is a good man, and you must trust him. Listen to what I tell you. As long as you live with us, you must respect our ways. Try to be pleased with what people do for you. Act as though you have confidence in us, and the people will come to love you and treat you better. Doing this may save your life."

Someone approaches from behind, so I hurriedly whisper, "Thank you!" Then I shake Jimmy once more. When he complains, I say, "Get up now; we are going to a house." Picking up my girl, I turn to see Chaska standing there. I take Jimmy by the hand and announce, "We are ready. Can we bring my trunk with us?"

"No, we go a long way. We leave trunk in wagon. I will carry your bag."

His reply intensifies my suspicions, but I try to hide them. Chaska leads me out of camp and across a meadow toward some woods. My heart pounds so hard that I feel certain he must hear it, so I cover by saying, "Goodness, what a heavy dew has fallen. My skirts are becoming quite wet with it."

Chaska merely grunts. Up in the sky, a last quarter moon hovers above the treetops. It is faintly yellow in color. I once again seek to engage Chaska in conversation. "Isn't this a sticky evening?"

He gestures for me to be quiet and leads us into the trees. "Mother," Jimmy murmurs crankily, "where are we going?"

"Hush!" I say and increase my speed to keep up with Chaska. My wide skirts keep catching on weeds and branches in the dark. The trail is too narrow for both Jimmy and me to walk side by side, so I push him to go ahead. The poor child must do a half-run to maintain the pace our guide is setting.

Judging from the amount of time we walk, I conclude that we cover about a mile before we reach a cluster of dwellings. Chaska lifts the flap of a tepee and gestures for me to enter, an action that confuses me because he said we were going to a house. When I step inside, I see two warriors and another white woman. She sits to one side, crying, hugging herself, rocking back and forth, and muttering in German. A tiny baby, swaddled in a blanket, sleeps on the ground beside her.

The two men greet Chaska, who points at me and answers in Dakota. The men nod. One of them barks out a statement, in the midst of which I hear the phrase *big dress.* Chaska turns to me. "You take too much room in tepee. You must remove—" I panic at the thought of undressing, but then he makes a rolling gesture with his hand. "Circles."

"Oh. My hoops? Yes, I can take them off." All three men watch me expectantly. Blushing hotly, I ask, "May I be left alone?"

Chaska's eyes widen, and his lips twitch in the hint of a smile. He nods and translates for the other men. They look surprised but leave without protest. Before following them, Chaska says, "My people approve of women who are modest."

As soon as he leaves, I set Nellie on the floor by Jimmy. Then, I pull up my skirts and reach under my bodice to untie the tape around my waist. As I free myself from the bell-like contraption, the German woman frets, *"Ach, alle meine federbetten. Meine fünf wundervollen federbetten. Sie haben meine federbetten genommen."*

I step out of my hoops, which have dropped to the ground, and cross to the weeping woman. Putting an arm around her shoulder, I ask gently, "Are you all right? Have the Sioux wounded you?"

"Nein!" She wipes her eyes. "All I own have I lost. The Indians came to my cabin. They killed all my family. My man," she says and then lapses back into German. *"Und mein Vater, mein Bruder, meine Schwester."*

"Your father and brother," I guess from the sound of the words, and she nods her head emphatically.

"Ja, ja. And my sister. Only my babe and I survive. The Indians made to stab me and I cried, 'Don't! I will give to you my house, everything I have, and I have much money.' All I own was into a wagon loaded. Me and my babe too. They drove right away down the road to the river and in great haste crossed. The Indians remembered then that my hidden money they had left, so they sent me back alone while they held my babe. After I returned, they brought me to this camp."

"And they have not...," I glance at my children and whisper, "abused you?"

"Nein. But—" She weeps. "Two weeks only have passed since this child was born. I am weak, and the Indians did not leave even one feather bed for my comfort." Her voice rises to a wail. "All my five feather beds gone. I picked the feathers myself in Old Germany, and now they will not give me even one to sleep on."

I stare in horror as she resumes rocking back and forth. *All this fuss for a feather bed? Doesn't she care that she saw her family killed before her eyes?*

The tiny baby starts to mewl, but the woman does not seem to hear. Her lack of reaction makes me understand that she is in shock.

"Frau," I say and tug on her sleeve, but she jerks away from me and huddles more tightly into herself. The infant's crying grows louder. My own breasts leak in response, and I pick up the child to feed him myself.

That action rouses the German; she lunges to take the baby from my arms. *"Mein Säugling!"* she exclaims and, unbuttoning her bodice, holds the child to her breast. I retreat to the other side of the tepee to rejoin my children.

The two strange Indians return through the flap, carrying George Gleason's clothes. The green-striped shirt and checked trousers are too distinctive to mistake. Then Chaska enters, leading Gleason's dog tied to the end of a rope. As soon as Jimmy sees it, he rushes forward, and the animal leaps up in excitement. Chaska smiles and drops the rope so that the dog can run to my son and lick his face.

The other two Indians go through Gleason's things. They pull out his pocket watch and, chuckling, hold it up to show that the crystal is broken. The men turn out all Gleason's pockets, demonstrating that they are empty. One pocket has a small hole in the seam, and the Indians poke their fingers through it and laugh. Watching them, I realize with indignation that Gleason lied. He never had a pistol; he was merely humoring me when he said he did. Oh, what a foolish, reckless man.

Chaska turns to me. "Come. I will take you to a house now."

We leave, with Chaska in the lead, Jimmy and the dog following, and Nellie and me bringing up the rear. As we pass through the settlement, Chaska points out a tepee with a jagged, red-ocher border around the bottom. "Remember this tepee."

"All right." I look around me. Most of the others are either more elaborately decorated with paintings of bison or horses or not decorated at all. "Why?"

"It is the tepee of my mother. If you need protection, come to her."

I nod.

Just beyond the tepees stands a rectangular house made of thin poles lashed together and covered with bark. The structure has a sharply pitched, A-shaped roof. A drying platform constructed of poles forms a sort of portico at the entrance.

When I enter it, I have to blink until my eyes adjust to the unexpected brightness. The interior is almost as well lit as the home of a white person. Several candles are placed around the room and a fire burns in the center, its smoke rising through a vent hole in the roof. The house is occupied by two Sioux women and three boys, two of them several years older than Jimmy. My son ducks behind my skirts. Sitting against the wall opposite me is another captive woman. She is about my age and has ash-blonde hair worn in a braid coiled around her head. When she sees me, she speaks frantically in German. I lift my hands, shake my head, and ask haltingly, *"Sprechen sie...*English?"

"Nein," she says mournfully.

I turn toward the Sioux then because Chaska is speaking to the old women. One of them stands and makes a bed for my children and me by spreading out buffalo robes and laying a blanket across them. Chaska says to me, "Sleep. Tomorrow morning, we will leave for Red River. When you rise, go to my mother's tepee and ask her to dress you like an Indian. You will be more safe."

He leaves before I can question him. I want to ask why we are going to the Red River, which forms the boundary between Minnesota and the Dakota Territory. Does that mean we are fleeing the state? The thought terrifies me.

The woman who made my bed gestures for me to lie down. She blows out the candles, and we retire to our respective pallets. I place Jimmy and Nellie next to the wall, so I can lie between them and the others. The dog curls up at Jimmy's feet.

As I lie there, my thoughts fly to John. What has been happening at the Upper Agency? Have the Indians there killed the whites and burned the buildings? Is my husband alive or dead?

Outside, people constantly walk past our house. Shots are fired and warriors let out whoops of triumph and rage. Farther away, women wail and what I take to be a medicine man chants, conjuring his spells over some ailing person.

A terrible scream rends the night, and my children stir in their sleep. The horrible sound unleashes my anger. What in God's sweet name was John thinking to send us into the very heart of danger with as useless a protector as George Gleason? Swift on the heels of that thought comes shame. How dare I think unkind thoughts about the poor man who lost his life trying to drive me toward safety? But I cannot deny the truth. If only he had listened to me, he might still be alive and I might not be a prisoner.

Another volley of gunshots goes off close to our house. Rolling onto my back, I stare up at the ceiling, dimly lit by the embers of the dying fire. *John,* I think, *why did you send us away? It would have been better if we could have faced this together.*

My mind conjures a vision of my husband, standing in the dim hallway of our home, loading his pistol as he hears Indians attacking the agency. I imagine his last conscious thought being, *At least I made sure that Sarah and the children are safe.*

The whoops outside the house merge with the war cries in my mind, and I feel certain that John is dead. Pressing my hand tightly over my mouth, I force myself to remain silent even as I weep.

CHAPTER

9

ALL NIGHT, I FRET ABOUT WHAT WILL HAPPEN TO US—IN PARTICULAR, Jimmy and Nellie. Chaska's words *I will keep these children* ring in my ears, and I grow fearful that the Sioux plan to kill me and raise my babies as their own. Like any mother, I want my children to live long, healthy lives, but I want them to be raised among their own people. I want my boy to go to college as John did and my girl to marry an upright man who will provide for her and her children. The thought of them growing up superstitious and wild, of Jimmy being taught to scalp and torture, of Nellie being traded to a man for the price of a horse, makes me want to pull out my hair and screech. I would rather see them dead.

At last, I fall asleep, but soon after sunrise, noises in camp awaken me. The German woman sleeps on her pallet across the room, but the Indians who slept here last night are gone. I tiptoe to the door and peer outside to see whether the Sioux are beginning to depart for the Red River. However, only men appear to be leaving. Each of them is bedecked with war paint and carries a weapon.

Gleason's dog trots over to me and whines. He still has a rope tied to his collar, so I grab it and step outside so he can relieve himself. Already, most of the men seem to have left. Even so, I duck back into the house and pull the dog with me. The last thing Chaska told me was to go to his mother's tepee to get Indian clothing, but I'm afraid to walk through the camp as long as any of the warriors are here.

My children remain asleep, so I sit, leaning against a woven backrest at the end of the pallet, and absentmindedly stare before me. Today was the day we were supposed to catch the stage. I wonder if it will run or if someone will warn the driver not to come onto the reservation. For an instant, I imagine eluding my captors, managing to reach the road just as the stage comes along, and flagging it down so I can ride to civilization. Quickly, however, I dismiss that idea. Angry Sioux roam the countryside. I would be risking my children's lives if we attempted such an escape.

Soon one of the Sioux women returns carrying a basket. She comes in with her gaze fixed upon the ground, but when she notices that I am sitting up, she glances at me and exclaims in Dakota, "White woman, what are you doing?"

She then stands where she blocks my view of the other captive. Lowering her voice, she says, "It is not good to stare at a person who sleeps. If you do this to our people, you will offend them."

Self-justification rises to my lips, but I quickly comprehend that this woman is trying to protect me with a warning about how to behave. "Thank you," I say.

The woman beckons me to the center of the room and tilts her basket to display several small rounds of fried bread. Speaking slowly in Dakota, she says, "I have no flour. I went to ask other women for bread to give you and the German."

Tears sting my eyes. "Will you share these with us?"

"Thank you for your good manners. I do not need this bread."

My experience of Sioux culture makes me suspect that I should not fuss over her hospitality, so I change the subject. I speak haltingly as I translate my thoughts into Dakota, "Chaska said we would go to the Red River this morning."

"Not today. Little Crow sent his warriors to attack soldier fort."

"So that is where the men went."

She nods. I turn away, ostensibly to wake up my children, but really to keep her from seeing my consternation. Fort Ridgely is not much of a fort; it has no stockade. Instead, it is a cluster of buildings on the wide-open prairie. If the Sioux attack in force, they may over-run the facility without difficulty—and then who knows how long my children and I will be held captive, assuming we are allowed to live. Yet, as much as I hope for a decisive white victory to end the war, I am terrified that Chaska might be killed. If he dies, who among the Sioux will protect us?

After we eat, I look outside and see that the camp is quiet. Tak-ing my children and Gleason's dog, I walk to the tepee of Chaska's mother. The flap is open, so I call a greeting in Dakota and am invited to enter. I set Nellie down and bend low to get through the opening. Even a short woman must duck to enter a tepee.

Once I am inside, I recognize Chaska's mother from Shakopee. She is a short woman, who looks to be in her late fifties; her dark braids are streaked with silver. Her broad face, lined with age, is composed. Halt-ingly, I explain that her son sent me here to change into Indian attire.

How humiliating it is to give up my fashionable, Zouave travel cos-tume with its skirt and short jacket, both smartly decorated with black braid. True, the clothes are stained with blood, but I might be able to soak that out if I were at home.

In place of the suit, I wrap a piece of navy broadcloth lengthwise around myself, tie a sash around my waist, and fold the upper part of the fabric over the sash to make a narrow skirt that has two layers. Over this, I put on a blouse of cheap, printed cotton. On most Sioux women, the blouses reach past their hips, but because I am tall, mine does not, and when I button it, it strains across my bosom. Chaska's mother insists that I remove my shoes and stockings and put on moc-casins. They are not new and their contours feel strange. Then the old woman makes me sit down so she can take out my hairpins and plait my hair into two braids.

When she has finished, Jimmy, Nellie, and I go back outside. Women and children wander through the camp, all of them eager for news of the battle. I hear laughter and turn to see the cause. A split rail fence runs along the road that passes by the camp, and against one of the upright posts, someone has propped a full-length mirror plundered from a settler's cabin. The Sioux women and children are having a wonderful time parading before the glass.

One woman sees me and giggles. She comes over and, taking my arms, marches me to the mirror. My reflection dismays me. Although my hair is brown rather than black and I lack the prominent cheekbones of the Sioux, at first glance I resemble an Indian. Even on close inspection, I might pass for a mixed blood. I made this change to blend in for safety, yet the sad-eyed woman who stares back at me is a stranger, and for an unsettling instant, I wonder if Sarah Brown Wakefield even exists any more. Has my soul drifted away from my body the way smoke rises from a tepee?

By mid-morning, the day grows blindingly hot, and I get a headache from the sun beating down upon my unprotected head. I lost my bonnet sometime yesterday, and my other clothes are still in the trunk at the first camp. Here the tepees stand on open prairie, so I cannot even sit beneath a tree. I find a place beside a large shrub growing next to the road and sit there to wait for news of the battle. Many Sioux women do the same, and an uneasy silence settles over us.

After about an hour, someone gives a sharp cry of alarm. A woman rushes into the clearing and speaks to the other Sioux women. Soon all of them scurry about, calling their children and gathering bundles. Those that have erected tepees immediately start to unfasten the canvas coverings and take them down.

Grabbing my children's hands, I hurry to the tepee of Chaska's mother. She stands outside talking to a neighbor, who hastens away as I approach. Chaska's mother does not bother with her tepee but instead picks up a skin bag that sits by her feet. "We must leave this place. Some bad Indians come to kill captives."

My chest squeezes in upon itself in terror. I pick up Nellie and my satchel, and tell Jimmy to grab the dog's rope. Chaska's mother leads us away. In a few minutes, we enter some woods. My heart is pounding as much from fright as exertion, and my side aches. Twigs and prickly leaves scratch my unprotected calves as we hasten down the trail. All the time we walk, I strain my ears to discern whether anyone is following us, but I hear nothing except my own heavy breathing, the tramp of our feet, and the noise of breaking branches and rustling leaves as we pass.

After about twenty minutes, we arrive at the first camp I visited last night. Several women question us, and as Chaska's mother answers, one of the younger women folds her arms across her chest and glares at me. She is a pretty woman. Her face tapers to her chin, and she has large eyes beneath beautifully curved eyebrows. Right now, however, hatred mars her beauty.

At last, Chaska's mother tells me, "These women have heard of no trouble. We can rest here."

She leads us to a grassy area beneath a spreading elm. As I sit down and lean back gratefully against the tree, I spot my husband's wagon standing empty on the far side of the camp. *"To'kiya cayo'hnaka mitawa?"* I say, hoping I have used the correct form to ask, "Where is my trunk?"

"I do not know anything about it," Chaska's mother murmurs, but she will not meet my eyes. She sets down her bag and goes to fetch water.

After she leaves, the beautiful woman strides up to me. "We do not have food for captives. I wish my husband shot you."

"Your husband? Are you Chaska's wife?"

For some reason, that question enrages her more. "No. The other."

"Hapa," I whisper.

She leans close to me. "He will kill you. He will dash your children's heads against a rock."

"Winona!" The cry forestalls whatever Hapa's wife was going to say next. She steps back and whirls around to see Chaska's mother, who stands there, disapproval on her face. "You do not honor your hakata by speaking so."

Winona jerks up her chin. "As you say, Ina," she mutters and walks away.

The old woman hands each of my children a cup of water. "Forgive my daughter. Her heart has grown angry as she sees her sons go without food."

"Your daughter?" I ask. "She is Chaska's sister?"

The old woman sits on the ground, bending both knees and folding her legs to the right side of her body. "Chaska's father had two wives, my sister and me. I bore Chaska, and six winters later, my sister bore Winona."

"So she is your...sister's daughter?" I don't know the Dakota word for niece.

Chaska's mother shakes her head. "I am her mother. My sister's children are my children and my children are hers. We are both their mothers. My son has told me it is not this way among the whites."

"No. We have only one mother and one father, unless one of them dies and the other remarries." My throat tightens with bitterness as I think of my stepfather.

"I am sorry for you."

I stare at her in shock, fearing that she has read my mind. Then I understand that she simply means she prefers her kinship customs to ours.

Chaska's mother opens her leather bag and pulls out a cloth-wrapped object. She pulls back the fabric to reveal a small but precious lump of maple sugar. Wrapping it again, she lays the bundle on the ground and pounds it once with a rock. Then she hands it to me. "Give this to your children."

"Thank you." Humbled by her generosity, I feed my children the pieces of sugar. After they finish, I let myself lick a few of the powerfully sweet crumbs. The taste reminds me of childhood days when my family gathered clear maple sap in the early New England spring. That was our custom in the years before my father died and my mother had to leave the farm so his brother could work it.

Chaska's mother pulls needlework from her bag. I watch with interest as she sews dyed porcupine quills onto a piece of leather about twelve inches long and two inches wide, with a curved point at one end. From its shape, I suspect it will be one side of a knife sheath. The quills are colored cream, red, yellow, and black, and the design is made up of multicolored squares that form a stepped diamond.

Jimmy, who has been letting Gleason's dog lick sugar granules from his chin, stands and searches the ground. After a moment, he finds a stick about as thick as my thumb. He tosses it and calls, "Fetch, Buster. Fetch." We don't know what Gleason called his dog, so the name surprises me. Chaska's mother laughs as she watches my son and the animal play.

Nellie sucks on the first two fingers of her right hand. "Bustah," she mutters around the obstruction in her mouth. I run my fingers through her baby hair.

A young woman hurries up to us and speaks to Chaska's mother. I pick up the word *Sisseton* and wonder what has happened. The people of Chaska's village are Mdewakanton Sioux, the same band as Little Crow's people. The Sisseton and Wahpeton peoples live on the western half of the reservation near the Upper Sioux Agency.

The young woman rushes off, and Chaska's mother turns to me. "The Upper Indians are coming to cause trouble. We must move again." She pauses to stare at me. "Wait. I can make you look more Indian."

After returning her needlework to her bag, she scrapes soil from the ground and, grabbing my left hand, rubs earth onto it. "See?" She places her hand next to mine, and I see that my dirty skin is closer to hers in color. "You will be more safe."

I know she is right, but I have always prided myself on my cleanliness, so coating myself with grime feels degrading. After darkening my face, hands, and calves, I call Jimmy and repeat the process with him. I take off his shoes and socks and his little jacket, leaving him with only a shirt and trousers. I can do nothing about his bright hair, which marks him indelibly as a white child.

Nellie is easier to disguise with her naturally dark skin and hair. All I need do is remove her dress, stockings, and shoes, leaving her in nothing but a diaper and a little shift. She looks enough like an Indian child after that to pass all but the most severe inspection.

After I have done what I can to perfect our appearance, we trudge back through the woods to the place where we slept last night. My whole body is tight with fear, and my daughter feels ten pounds heavier than she did this morning. When we near the encampment, Chaska's mother tells us to remain in the trees while she goes ahead to make sure her tepee is safe. She disappears from sight. I set Nellie on her feet to ease my aching back and whisper to my children to stay silent.

A rustling in the leaves causes fear to rise like vomit in my throat. A chipmunk, tail high, scurries across the trail and into the underbrush. Buster barks and strains at his rope, but Jimmy holds it tight. The dog emits one last indignant woof and falls silent. I go limp with relief. Then I realize that Buster's strident alarm must have carried a far distance, revealing where we are. I bite my lip and listen for signs that someone is approaching. Have the warriors returned from battle? Perhaps we should move deeper into the trees.

Then, Chaska's mother comes toward us. Her lined face breaks into a smile and she beckons for me to come forward. I sigh and, picking up Nellie once again, slog toward her. Already, I have come to trust this woman as my guardian angel. I wish I knew what to call her besides "Chaska's mother," but the Sioux are reluctant to share their personal names with people outside their family.

By the time we reach her tepee, I teeter on the edge of collapse. If I were at home, I would recline on the sofa in the parlor and ask Mary to make me a cup of tea and some buttered toast. Instead, I am a homeless captive on the open prairie. Some twenty miles away, a battle rages that may decide whether I will be executed. The rumors and false alarms have left me so ragged that I hardly care whether I live or die so long as I don't have to suffer torment. I imagine John dead, lying in the smoldering ruins of our house, and despair weighs upon my heart like lead. My only reason for living is that I will not leave my children alone to be raised as savages.

Gazing at the road beyond the split rail fence, I decide not to go inside the tepee. If news comes from the fort, I want to hear it as soon as possible.

Chaska's mother ducks into the tent and comes out with an iron pot, cornmeal, and a handful of dried berries. She tells me she plans to cook a little gruel. "Should I fetch water?" I ask, embarrassed at how much she has waited upon me.

She shakes her head, picks up a pail, and heads toward the creek.

After she leaves, a wizened old woman sits beside me. Her long braids are pure white at the top, but toward the tips, they are faded brown—a record of long life as revealing as the rings of a tree. She says her name is Lightfoot. "You have handsome children." She reaches out to touch Jimmy's white-blond hair.

"Thank you."

She strokes my son's head. "When the men return, they will kill you. We will keep these children. When they are big, we will sell them

94

back to our Great White Father. He will pay us much gold, and the traders will not get it."

My mouth drops open. Seeing the horror on my face, the toothless crone smiles. Her glee causes something inside me to snap. I grow breathless with dismay as my mind latches upon the necessity to save my children from being raised by malicious creatures like this witch.

My gaze darts around the camp, searching for Chaska's mother. I see the woman who led me to the mirror this morning. Her laughter then was a friendly thing, and the memory of it gives me hope that she might help. I stand, lift Nellie into my arms, and rush to her. "Do you have a knife? May I use it?"

She reaches into a leather pouch at her side, pulls out a knife, and hands it to me without question. In my frantic state, I take that as confirmation I am doing the right thing. Glancing around swiftly, I spot a flat outcropping of granite a few yards away. It reminds me sharply of an etching I once saw of Abraham sacrificing Isaac, and my resolve stiffens. I stride toward it, calling for Jimmy to follow me. When we reach the projection of rock, I lay my baby girl upon it, positioning her so her head hangs over the edge. She whimpers. "Son, hide your face in my skirt."

His lip trembles as he gazes up at me. Then he obeys. "Forgive me," I whisper. I seize Nellie's hair, pull her head lower to make her neck go taut, and raise the knife. What I am about to do is so horrible that I stand there frozen, trying to work up the resolve to end our captivity in the only way that is left to me.

Shouting erupts behind me. Before I can strike my daughter, some women grab me from behind. I strain against their grip but cannot force my arm down. My whole body trembles with the effort. Another woman rushes up and removes Nellie from the makeshift altar. My baby screams. At the sound, I drop the knife, which clangs upon the granite. Then I droop, and the women who restrain me allow me to sink to the ground. Someone pulls my little boy away, and he shouts, "Mama!"

Chaska's mother kneels beside me. "White woman, why did you do that?"

I stare at her in despair. "Lightfoot said the Sioux plan to kill me.

They will hold my children for money. I will not let that happen."

Chaska's mother shakes her head. "Lightfoot is old. Her talk is foolish. I am sorry she troubled you."

I rest my forehead upon her knees and cry. The old woman smooths my hair and makes shushing noises.

"*Ina, Ina!*" I cry, using the Dakota word for mother. Then, horrified that I let myself slip into such familiarity, I jerk upright and wait to be rebuked.

To my relief, she smiles. "Do not fear. My son has sworn to protect you."

"Thank you." I wipe my tears away with my sleeve. When I try to rise, my muscles are so weak and quivery that I stumble and press one hand against the rock to steady myself. My glance falls upon the knife, glinting in the sun, and I go cold with horror at the madness that seized me. "My baby!" Sweeping my gaze over the assembled women, I find the one who holds my daughter. "Give her to me."

The woman hands me my baby girl, and I clutch her to my bosom. Chaska's mother says, "Come to my tepee. You can sleep there."

Sleep, I think. *Maybe that's what is wrong with me. I need sleep.*

CHAPTER

10

Someone is shouting, but the words are garbled as though traveling through water. As my brain struggles to decipher the sounds, I make out a repeated phrase: *"Wašicuŋ wiŋyaŋ! Wašicuŋ wiŋyaŋ!"*

When I open my eyes, I am lying in a tepee with my children. The canvas on one side of the structure glows golden with late afternoon sun—except where a dark silhouette is cast upon it. The strange words emanate from that spot. I rub my gritty eyes and recognize the voice of Chaska's mother calling in Dakota, "White woman! White woman!"

"Haŋ!" I reply, raising my voice so she can hear me.

"May I enter?" she asks in Dakota.

"Haŋ."

The old woman pulls back the flap and ducks through the opening. As soon as she is inside the tepee, she speaks rapidly and gestures with animation. I have to ask her to speak more slowly. "A man comes to kill you," she says, picking up Nellie from the pallet. Chaska's mother puts my baby girl into a cloth sling that she positions on her back. "Take a blanket. Hold your boy's hand. We must go."

I shake Jimmy roughly and pull him to his feet. "Leave me alone!" he cries.

"We have to go now!" I say in English as I pick up a blanket and then my satchel. "A bad man is coming to hurt us."

Chaska's mother leaves the tepee before me, pausing first to look out the flap to make sure we can exit safely. Once Jimmy and I are outside, she hurries to the right. Jimmy wants to bring the dog, which is tied to a sapling, but I tell him no. Buster barks sharply as we hurry away from him.

Within moments, we reach the bark house where we slept last night. By the front entrance sits an old man, who is carving a wooden bowl and watching over a little child who plays in the dirt.

In a low voice, Chaska's mother tells him our story. He nods at key points and, after she finishes, says, "You must flee to the woods."

Chaska's mother turns and says, "Come, white woman." She leads me onward past the bark house, out of the encampment, and toward a band of trees.

We enter the woods, following a narrow trail that meanders around outcroppings of rock. I put Jimmy ahead of me and keep my hands on his shoulders. The trees and underbrush are thick, and the sounds of the encampment fade away. As we head deeper into the forest, the distinctive three-part song of a wood thrush sounds overhead. Its melody, the most beautiful of all birdcalls, cuts through my terror and reminds me how much I love this country. I find myself wishing for a peaceful day at home, reveling in the simple joys of gathering eggs and seeing a red-tailed hawk circle against the pale blue sky. Then my gaze falls on the crown of Nellie's head, bobbing as she rides on the old woman's back. My heart lurches with the desire to protect her, and once again, I land back in the threat-filled present.

Chaska's mother leads us to a deep ravine, whose walls form a V-shaped valley. She starts to climb down. Trees grow up to the bank's edge, and I grab a gnarled root to steady myself as I scramble down the steep slope after my son, who descends as nimbly as a squirrel. When we reach the bottom, we stand on a margin of land between the ravine walls and the flowing creek.

We walk along the stream to a place where the bank is nearly vertical and shrubbery overhangs the edge, providing concealment from anyone who searches from above. The land bordering the stream here is extremely narrow, and three boulders block our way—the nearest one stands close to the ravine wall, while the other two line the creek's edge. Chaska's mother points to them. I remove my moccasins to keep them dry and place them and my satchel on the boulder farthest from the creek. Then I place my folded blanket as a cushion on the middle and largest boulder and sit on it with my feet in the stream. The water reaches to my ankles. Jimmy sits on the smaller rock to my right. A thicket of shrubbery blockades the path beyond the boulders, and large clumps of scouring rush and cattail grow to my left.

"You sit here," Chaska's mother says. "Keep children quiet. I will come for you in the morning." She removes Nellie from the sling and sets my baby on my lap. Then after handing me a bag of crackers and a tin cup, Chaska's mother leaves.

Her departure makes me feel bereft, recalling the abandonment I felt as a six-year-old child when I finally understood that death had stolen my father from me forever. Have my poor darlings suffered a similar loss? I hug Nellie more tightly.

The air is hot and muggy, so I enjoy having my feet in the creek. Then black flies land on us and bite. I wave my left arm in the air to ward them off.

Jimmy leans against me. "Mama, why do the Indians want to kill us?"

"Shhh," I say. Every instinct warns me not to speak, but somehow I must make my boy understand. "It's a long story. The government owes them money, so they cannot buy food. They are hungry and that makes them angry."

"But we didn't take the money," Jimmy protests. I lay my finger across his lips and he lowers his voice. "Why do they want to hurt *us?*"

I run my fingers through his hair as I think of a way to explain. "Do you remember when we lived in Shakopee, and the neighbor's cat scratched you?"

"Yeah. Stupid cat."

"And do you remember going over to Mrs. Tompkins's house a couple of weeks later? What did you do when you saw the cat in her parlor?"

"I dunno," he said, but I can tell from his grudging tone that he does remember but doesn't want to admit it.

I rub his scalp in a gesture of comfort. "You hid your face in my lap because you were so scared that cat was going to scratch you like the other one did. Mrs. Tompkins told you Boots was a sweet kitty, but you weren't having any of it because you were so sure that all cats were mean."

"So what?"

"Well, some Indians feel that way about us. Some white people have hurt them, so they don't like any whites. Just like you didn't like any cats for a while."

Jimmy is silent for a long minute and then says, "But I do like nice cats now."

"I know you do, honey, and I'm proud of you for learning that every cat is different. That's why we must be careful how we behave in the Indian camp. We have to be kind and helpful, and we mustn't complain even when we're hungry."

"Hungry!" Nellie interjects and tugs at the front of my blouse.

Reaching into the bag Chaska's mother gave me, I pull out a couple of crackers and give one to each of my children. Then I continue, "We have to show the Indians that not all white people are their enemies. Do you understand?"

Jimmy eats his cracker and says, "I think so, Mama."

We fall silent. I focus on the sensation of cool water rushing over my tired feet. After a few minutes my shoulder aches from fanning away flies, so I rest my arm in my lap. Only seconds pass before a fly bites Nellie's cheek. She starts to cry, so I quickly unbutton my blouse and give her my breast to quiet her.

An instant later, a mourning dove calls loudly in the woods above, followed by the warbling cry of a screech owl. This is the wrong time of day for an owl, so I suspect that the birdcalls were made by warriors on the hunt for escaping captives. Placing my hand beneath Jimmy's chin, I tilt it to make him look at me. I lay my finger on my lips. Then I point to the shrubbery overhead, use my fingers to imitate a walking figure, and finally make a slashing gesture across my throat. My son's eyes grow big and he hides his face in my side. I lay my hand on the back of Nellie's head and pray that she remains content to nurse until the danger passes.

Before long, someone moves in the bushes above us. I hold my breath and shut my eyes tightly as though that could make me less visible. Fear clutches my throat like an icy hand. In our hurry to get away, we probably left a trail that will be easy to follow. My only consolation is that no rain has fallen for more than a week, so the dirt path is hard—and both Jimmy and I are wearing moccasins. Perhaps our hunters will assume that Indians made the tracks.

I am afraid to breathe, but my lungs are growing tight, so I cover my mouth with my hand and exhale. The rustling above grows fainter, but that change brings no relief as the tracker seems to be moving toward the place where we clambered down the bank. My entire body tenses, and I glance about. The walls of the ravine are too steep; I will never be able to climb up them unassisted, not though a dozen devils were behind me. Dear God, I wish I had John's pistol.

A scream splits the air. The stealthy noises overhead change to crashing as the searcher runs away from the ravine deeper into the woods. Shouts and a desperate sobbing reach me from a distance, and my eyes fill with tears as I imagine some unknown captive being tracked down like a deer. Nellie releases my nipple and stares upward in fright. My poor, sweet child has finally discerned that we are in danger. That knowledge breaks my heart.

I hear thrashing and a muffled cry, but no shots. Perhaps the captive has been dragged back to camp, although I shudder to think what awaits her there. I try to force such morbid speculations from my mind, but the effort is useless. Whatever is happening to that captive now came perilously close to being my fate.

My children and I are so petrified that none of us moves for a long time even after the sounds of pursuit and struggle fade away. The sun sinks so low in the sky that the entire ravine is in shadow, and I thank God because I hope the approaching darkness makes us safer. Miraculously, the flies stop biting.

As my fear ebbs, I grow more aware of my physical discomfort. My tailbone throbs from the unyielding seat, and my feet in the stream are icy cold. I know I should walk back and forth to keep my circulation going, but I am afraid to move. My bladder has been full for over an hour, but I am too terrified to attend to it.

After placing Nellie on her brother's lap, I bend down to get some water—being careful to dip the tin cup into the flowing stream above my feet. Then I give each child a handful of crackers and take a half dozen for myself. It is a meager supper, barely enough to keep our stomachs from growling, but our supply is small, and I do not know how long we will have to make it last.

The food makes me feel a little better, so before taking my daughter back, I wade downstream a few paces, careful not to slip on any of the algae-covered rocks in the streambed. After struggling to pull up the narrow and now-sodden skirt, I squat and relieve myself. The blessed release of pressure makes me feel not only more comfortable but also in a strange way safer.

After wading back to the boulders, I take Nellie on my hip and use my right hand to steady Jimmy as he wades down the stream to do his necessaries. My girl is still in diapers, which are wet through, but I don't have any dry cloths with me.

As we pick our way back to our seats, I make out distant shouting, followed by gunshots. The commotion draws nearer. I freeze midstream, but then realize how foolish it is to stand where we can be seen. I gesture for Jimmy to return to his boulder, and I carry Nellie back to ours, moving slowly to minimize splashing.

For a long time, raucous yells and laughter resound through the woods, and I wonder if the warriors are returning from battle. I suspect from the noise that at least some of the men have been drinking. *Dear God,* I pray, *do not let them find us.*

Eventually, the woods grow quiet again except for the occasional rustling of animals and windblown branches. The sky turns grey, and the gloom in the ravine grows deeper. As I begin to hope that danger has passed, I hear a soft chittering and then a gnawing. My heart leaps in fear. In the water near the cattails, a small pointed head with slicked-back fur and beady eyes emerges from the water. It is a muskrat with a tuber in its mouth. Another muskrat swims up to it and then dives under the water.

As I hear the animals' soft plashing, I realize the wind has dropped—leaving us more vulnerable to discovery. My children and I sit quietly as twilight deepens. Suddenly, a cool breeze rushes downward and along the length of the stream. Thunder booms, and raindrops as big as pennies pelt us. Within seconds, the rain is falling so thickly that I can no longer see past the cattails a couple of yards away.

The parched ground is too hard to soak up the rain, so sheets of muddy water pour over the edge of the bank and drench us. Despite our discomfort, I am grateful for the storm because it surely makes it harder for any searchers to see. To my astonishment, angry warriors shout above us even as the storm rages.

Terror roots me to my boulder. My children and I have nowhere safer to go than this miserable spot, so we remain beneath the waterfall.

Unexpectedly, the words of a Charles Wesley hymn come to me. Pulling my children even closer, I duck my head and sing softly so only they can hear:

Jesus, lover of my soul,
Let me to Thy bosom fly,
While the nearer waters roll,
While the tempest still is high.
Hide me, O my Savior, hide,
Till the storm of life is past;
Safe into the haven guide,
O receive my soul at last!

The first verse is all I know, but it is enough to turn my petrified heart to my Maker, and I pray as I have never prayed before: I thank God for keeping us safe thus far and fervently petition for continued protection. Imagining my husband lying dead, I beseech God to have mercy on John's soul and to remember his good deeds rather than his weaknesses. "And if John still lives," I whisper, "keep him alive and enable me to protect our children so we may all be together again."

The very moment I utter that hope, lightning strikes a tree up on the bank, perhaps fifty yards downstream. I yelp in alarm and then cover my mouth. My mind utters the silent plea, *Lord, if it is not your will for us to live, let the next bolt of lightning hit this spot so that we do not have to suffer a vicious death.*

Seconds later, lightning strikes farther away from us, and my poor fluttering heart believes that God has given His answer. For some reason, whether my husband still lives or no, God wants me to go on.

After a few more minutes, the rain eases to a gentle, steady shower. Still, a sheet of water falls on us. The temperature has dropped perhaps fifteen degrees since the storm began, and I feel chilled in my wet clothes. Nellie, who is practically naked, shivers. Rising halfway from my seat, I take the blanket I've been sitting on and unfold it. Parts of it are soaked, but it has dry patches too where my body shielded it from rain. I drape the blanket around all three of us. It is made from wool, so even if it gets wet, it will help keep us warm.

Despite my efforts, Nellie's teeth chatter. I press her to my bosom and frantically wonder how to keep her from taking a fever during this long night. Then, as though God himself planted the thought in my mind, I remember that I have a flask of medicinal brandy in my satchel. What a miracle it seems that neither Hapa nor any of the other Indians has found it since our capture.

I move Nellie to Jimmy's lap and tell him to hold the blanket tightly so it doesn't fall in the water. Then, moving cautiously because of the near-total darkness, I step into the stream and bend down to fill our cup. I set the cup upon my boulder and reach carefully for the satchel. My hand brushes against my moccasins first, and I smile grimly at the memory that I placed them there to keep dry. Then I retrieve the satchel and, after opening it, dig around until I find the precious flask. "Thank you, Lord," I breathe as I close the satchel and place it back on its perch.

Hardly a glimmer of light shines in this place. I cannot even see to measure out the brandy. For an adult, I would give a couple of teaspoons of pure spirits, but I dare not use such a potent dose on my children. After a few minutes' thought, I decide to drink about a third of the water from the cup and then, using my fingertip to gauge the level, add brandy until it is nearly full. Once I have done this, I tuck the flask into my bosom to keep it safe. Then I give the cup to each of my children, making sure that neither one drinks too much. Afterward, I wrap us all up in the blanket again.

The brandy does the trick, and soon both Jimmy and Nellie slumber, leaning their weary bodies against me. The storm continues, but I have grown resigned to the feeling of water running down my face and into my blouse. I do not think I have ever been so sopping wet in all my life.

Now that the rain is falling more lightly, the sounds of shouting, screaming, and shooting in the forest increase, and I grow even more certain that the warriors have been partaking of whiskey or some other form of "firewater." A pounding noise convinces me someone is rushing upon us, but then the tightness in my chest reveals it to be the accelerated beating of my own heart.

A moment later, a silvery snout rises from the water near my feet. I shudder at the thought that a wolf has entered the ravine to hunt us down in our helpless condition. My muscles tense with the expectation of fangs sinking into my calves. Then I see that it is only one of the muskrats, and I go limp with relief.

Now that my children sleep, I have no motherly duties to distract me. Once again, my imagination conjures up a horrible vision of John, his chest caved in from the blow of an axe, his scalp torn away, a pool of blood beneath his head. I shut my eyes, as though doing so could blot out the picture, but it only grows more vivid.

For an instant, I consider drinking the brandy to find oblivion, but I tell myself sternly to keep the spirits in case my children need them. Besides, brandy would likely put me to sleep, and I must stay alert.

A particularly ferocious howl rends the night, and Jimmy stirs awake. "Mama, take me home, and put me in my own little bed," he murmurs, rubbing his eyes. "What do you sit here for? My father will not like his boy to sit out of doors all night."

"Why, Jimmy, you know that we must hide here in the ravine from the Sioux."

He sighs. "I forgot about the Indians. I will be still."

I give Jimmy another dose of brandy and water, and gradually he drifts back to sleep. "Dear Heavenly Father," I whisper, "I know that you are all powerful and can save us if you will. Keep us through this terrible night."

This time, no lightning bolt comes in answer to my prayer, but I tell myself it doesn't matter. "Faith is the substance of things hoped for," the Bible says, "the evidence of things not seen."

I muster what little determination I have left and say, "Lord, I believe. Help my unbelief."

Then I make up my mind to think of ways to endear myself to the Indians who hold me captive. Though my emotions recoil in horror, I must do whatever I deem necessary to survive both the tempest tonight and the larger storm.

CHAPTER

11

In the early hours, long before I can detect any light in this narrow ravine, the songbirds of the forest above start singing the dawn chorus: the piercing *cheerup* of the robin, the complex whistle and warble of the song sparrow, and the harsh *oh-ka-reeee* of the redwing blackbird. About half an hour after the serenade begins, the curtain of inky black slowly lifts from the sky, giving way to a backdrop of grey-blue that will soon lighten to gold-hemmed azure.

Poets often use sunrise to symbolize the dawn of hope, but after our long night of fear, this first hint of a brightening sky serves only to deepen my dread. As soon as it is full light, the Indians who have been searching the woods will easily find my children and me and drag us back to camp. Or perhaps they will kill me here and leave my bones to be picked over by foxes, rodents, and crows.

As soon the sunlight grows strong enough to poke its fingers into our hiding place, I discover that my children and I are slime-covered from sitting beneath the muddy torrent. I remove the blanket from our shoulders and fold it up, encrusted as it is with mire. Our clothes and faces are as filthy as the coverlet. I use the underside of my sleeve, the cleanest piece of cloth I have, to wipe off my cheeks and chin.

The day quickly warms, and a whining noise proclaims that mosquitoes have awakened. Within seconds, a hot sting inflames my right cheek. Nellie burrows her face into my bosom, and I open my blouse so she can suckle—even though I am not at all certain I have any milk to offer after having eaten so sparsely.

Fortunately, my body does not fail me. Nellie latches onto my nipple, closes her eyes, and settles into a contented rhythm. While she nurses, a mosquito lands on her temple close to her eye, and I shoo it away. Another immediately alights on her plump cheek. As I wave at it, I glance at Jimmy and see three red welts rising on his face. Even so, he makes no complaint. The night of terror has taught my darlings that they must hold their silence no matter what discomfort they feel.

Remarkably, as the light grows stronger, the sound of searchers in the woods fades. A few faint cries sound, and then human noises cease. After several minutes pass, broken only by the natural sounds of the forest, I slump in relief.

The leaves of the branches hanging over the ravine glow green-gold in the morning light. A mourning dove calls in plaintive counterpoint to the merry rushing of the brook. Our situation, however, is far from idyllic. The mosquitoes attack without mercy until my children's faces run with blood, yet neither one cries out. They continue to stare upward, searching for signs that our enemies approach. I hate to see them so troubled, so I pull out a few crackers and divide them among the three of us. Then, on second thought, I put mine back in the bag. We have already eaten more than half the supply, and I fear running out.

The air is humid after all the rain that fell last night. I lift Nellie, rise slightly from my seat, and do my best to rearrange my weight more comfortably. My tailbone aches as though it has cracked from sitting on granite.

To pass the time, I whisper the story of Hagar and Ishmael to my children. The wife of the biblical patriarch Abraham drove his concubine and eldest son into the wilderness, where they ran out of food and water. When Hagar began to weep because she did not want to see her son die, God sent an angel to show her a well and to promise that Ishmael would live and father a great nation.

"I wish God would send an angel to us," Jimmy murmurs. "I wish he would bring us bread and eggs."

Laughing softly, I play with his hair. "God doesn't send angels to Earth anymore, honey. That happened only during Bible times."

He heaves an adult-sounding sigh. "How long do we have to sit here, Mama?"

"Until Chaska's mother comes to get us."

"I wish she would hurry," he mutters and leans heavily against me.

I am so weary from the long hours of terror that I doze. Suddenly, my head jerks up from my chest and my eyes fly open in alarm. Glancing around, I wonder if I was asleep for ten minutes or an hour. I cannot tell.

Time crawls more slowly than a slug over sand. Craning my neck to look overhead, I see from the angle of the sun that it is not yet mid-morning. Even so, I am surprised that Chaska's mother still hasn't come. As I contemplate the silence in the forest, anxiety assails me. Has the village departed for the Red River without us? For an instant, my heart rejoices that we may have escaped our captivity with so little effort; then I plunge into despair. I cannot possibly climb the steep walls of this ravine by myself, let alone carrying my children. Is this narrow canyon destined to become the grave where we three will starve to death?

As though reading my mind, Jimmy complains of hunger. Reluctantly, I give my children more of the precious crackers. Again, I take none for myself. If Chaska's mother does not return by nightfall, we will run out of provisions. As I search my mind for possibilities, I remember the muskrats I saw last night. Could we eat cattail roots as they do? Or could I, perhaps, find a way to trap the rodents? I have heard that their meat is greasy and unpleasant, yet I know that Indians eat them in late winter when other sources of food are exhausted.

Something rustles in the shrubbery above us, and I freeze. Then comes the low voice of a woman: *"Waŝicuŋ wiŋyaŋ! Waŝicuŋ wiŋyaŋ!"*

Hoping it is Chaska's mother, I reply, *"Haŋ!"* Tightening my hold on my children, I wait in trepidation as someone scrambles down the bank. For several moments, I cannot breathe. Then I see the short figure and lined, bronze face of my guardian angel coming toward us.

Instantly, I weep tears of relief. Leaning Nellie against my shoulder, I try to stand, but my lower limbs have no more sensation in them than slabs of meat, and I collapse back onto my seat. My circulation has grown sluggish from the hours without motion and the exposure to the chill waters of the stream.

Chaska's mother rushes to me, crying in Dakota, "Are you hurt?"

"No, but my legs are..." I fall silent, searching for a way to describe my condition in her language. "My legs are cold and asleep."

Chaska's mother puts Nellie in a sling upon her back. Then the old woman lifts my right leg and rubs the calf and foot to knead life into the half-paralyzed limb. My skin tingles uncomfortably under the friction. "The men who want to kill you are gone. They have gone to attack more settlers."

"Did they take the fort?"

She shakes her head and rubs my left calf. "They did not go to fort. Yesterday, they attacked the German town."

New Ulm, I think, but before I can ask for confirmation, she says, "You must get up now and walk. The people have moved across the Redwood River."

So that's why the forest is so quiet this morning. Bracing my hands upon the boulder, I push myself to a standing position. A thousand needles pierce my feet and my legs cramp, but they do not give way. I wade ashore and put on my soggy moccasins. If the band has moved to the other bank of the Redwood River, we will have a much longer walk than we did last night.

"When we reach my tepee," the old woman says, "I will give you dry clothes and coffee."

I nod and beckon to my son, who scampers over the boulders and hops down behind me. He is barefoot, and I wish I hadn't been so quick to remove his shoes.

We walk to the place where we descended into the ravine. Chaska's mother scales the incline with Nellie on her back and then gazes down at us. I push Jimmy ahead. He climbs, but within seconds, he loses his footing and slides back down until he comes to rest against my legs. As a result, thick mud coats the lower half of his body and my shins.

Jimmy pushes himself up from the ground and shakes the muck from his fingers. "Try again, son," I say. This time, I place my hands on his bottom and shove him upward, while Chaska's mother reaches down to pull him to the top of the bank. As I push, my weakened legs collapse and I fall to my knees.

The scene before me blurs, then my vision goes partially black. I put both hands to my temples and breathe deeply until the dizziness passes. Chaska's mother says, "White woman, hurry. We must go."

Gloomily, I shake my head. "I cannot climb the bank. I have no strength."

"You must try." The old woman looks behind her and then disappears from view. After a minute, she returns dragging a large branch; it must have snapped off in the storm last night because it still bears green leaves. Chaska's mother extends the limb toward me. "Hold this. I will pull."

"But I am too heavy for you." I rake my fingers across my scalp. "Take my children to safety. And pray, do not let them forget me."

"White woman, do not give up. Take hold."

Even though I think it is useless, I obey her peremptory command and grab the branch. Chaska's mother sets her feet apart to brace herself and pulls the branch upward about a foot. Rather than let go, I take two cautious steps up the slimy slope. The old woman says something to Jimmy, who grabs one of the side branches that stick out from the main bough. When she is satisfied that he is holding on tight, she removes her right hand from the thick central stem of the branch and repositions it about eighteen inches lower down. Then she pulls again. I take two more steps. Mud squishes beneath my feet, which slide precariously, but my grip on the branch keeps me upright. For the first time, I hope I might escape this accursed ravine.

We repeat the operation twice more, but the second time, my feet abruptly slide out from under me. The entire length of my body pitches forward until I am lying prone on the incline, still clutching the branch. The fall knocks the wind from my lungs. When the shock wears off, I dig my toes into the sodden bank and push myself upward like a worm.

After a few more minutes of upward struggle, I manage to grab one of the tree roots extending from the eroded bank above my head. Once I have done so, Chaska's mother is able to drop the branch and sit down. She pants heavily, and I feel wretched for causing the poor woman so much fatigue.

I take a minute or two to catch my breath and then climb by burrowing the toes of my moccasins into the nearly vertical wall. Within
a few minutes, I have ascended high enough to wrap my arms around
a tree trunk and scrabble my legs to the top of the bank. Once I suc-
ceed in exiting the ravine, I lie upon the ground gasping for air and
crying from sheer amazement at my escape.

Chaska's mother allows me only a few minutes of rest. "We must go."

Even though I am unsteady, I follow her down the trail through the
woods. Spotting a fallen branch about four feet long by the side of the
trail, I pick it up to use as a walking stick. Sensation has returned to
my legs, which ache in protest at bearing my weight. I am light-headed
and hunger pains plague my stomach, but no relief is possible until
we reach camp.

It is not yet midday, but the temperature is blazing. Even so, by
the time we have traveled fifteen minutes, I begin to shiver as though
we were hiking in winter. I say nothing but concentrate on placing
one foot in front of the other and maintaining the pace that Chaska's
mother sets.

After what seems like an hour—but could not be so long—we arrive
at the house where the children and I slept two nights ago. Gratefully,
I sink upon the rough wooden bench outside the front entrance, the
very seat where we saw the old man carving. Chaska's mother disappears into the building. Content to wait while she does whatever she
wants, I lean back against the wall and doze.

Some time later, Chaska's mother stands before me, saying, "White
woman, wake up. Drink this."

I shake my head and wipe my eyes. Then I focus on the tin cup she
holds in her hands. It holds a blood-red liquid. "What is that?"

"Tea made from white willow bark. It will help your pain."

Because I have heard of this folk remedy from John, I do not hesitate to drink the concoction—although it is one of the most astrin-
gent brews I have ever forced down my throat. Once I empty the cup,
Chaska's mother takes it back into the house and returns with coffee.
This beverage is more to my liking, and I drink it gladly. Soon, the
pain in my limbs eases and my shivering subsides. I rise. "I am ready."

At first, the energy I gained from the coffee enables me to keep up with the hardy older woman. We scarcely go half a mile, however, before I start shivering again. At the next settlement, Chaska's mother goes from tepee to tepee to beg another cup of coffee for me.

Once I have downed that restorative beverage, we resume our journey. Chaska's mother refuses to travel by roads or existing trails, saying they are too unsafe. Instead, we plunge into unbroken woods that are thick with berry bushes intertwined with wild grapevines and ivy.

Chaska's mother does not bother to look for breaks in the undergrowth but pushes straight through the thicket as though deadly killers pursue us, and I wonder if she misled me when she said the dangerous men were gone. I do my best to follow without complaint, but maintaining a stoic silence is difficult as brambles slash my arms and legs. Some of the gashes are deep and will certainly leave scars.

Jimmy too does his best to be a brave little man as thorns tear his bare feet until they are covered with blood. Only once does he cry out, "Oh, oh!" My heart aches for him, but I say only, "You must keep quiet so angry Indians do not hear us." I tell him this in Dakota, so that Chaska's mother will know that we are trying to behave in a way she would consider proper.

Fighting through the forest exhausts my pitiful store of strength, and before long I am shivering and staggering again. When we come to a place where we see a stand of tepees through the trees, Chaska's mother goes ahead to make sure that the Indians there are not hostile to whites. Then she brings me into the village and procures another cup of coffee for me.

After I have rested about fifteen minutes, we set out again. Because of the delays and the difficulty of grappling with unbroken terrain, a journey that should take an hour stretches to more than two.

In early afternoon, we wade through a marshy area and arrive on the bank of the Redwood River. The water is flowing swiftly, no doubt because of last night's heavy rains. Chaska's mother removes Nellie from the sling and holds her high in front of her body before wading into the river. After tossing aside my now-useless walking stick and grasping Jimmy's hand, I follow.

At first I feel no alarm. Then, when we have gone about ten feet from the shore, the bottom of the riverbed slopes downward, and the water reaches my thighs. The current is so strong and alive that it feels like a large dog butting against my body. I halt and do my best to gain a firm foothold. Then I pick up my son and brace him against my hip. How I find the strength to do so, I will never know. Needs must when the devil drives, as the saying goes.

Ahead of me, Chaska's mother lifts Nellie above her head as they reach the center of the river. The water touches the bottom of the old woman's chin. Telling Jimmy to put his arms around my neck, I hoist him higher. When I reach the same spot a few seconds later, the water is up to my armpits. The onward rush of the river is so fierce that remaining on my feet is a struggle. After a few tense seconds, we reach a shallower part of the river, and I exhale in relief.

As we emerge onto the bank, I set my son upon the ground and look down ruefully. My clothes, which had begun to dry, are sodden, and I fear that the chills will soon afflict me again. At least, the top layer of mud has been washed away, so that my blouse and skirt are merely dirty rather than caked with mire.

Then I peer at our surroundings. Here, thank heaven, is a trail we can follow. Knowing that we are so close to our destination strengthens my resolve, and we set off. This time, a short journey brings us to the clearing where Chaska's band is setting up camp.

No tepees have been erected. Instead, each family is gathered next to its wagon, and the women work at making dinner. I can smell wood smoke and coffee. The latter holds little appeal to me after all I have drunk this day.

We're safe, I think as Chaska's mother leads us in a circuitous path around several wagons to get to her campsite. But when we reach it, my heart sinks. Winona is there, stirring some sort of stew in an iron kettle. Her two young sons, who look to be about three and seven, play nearby. She looks up and scowls at me, but when she sees her aunt beside me, says nothing.

In a low voice, Chaska's mother tells me, "It is our custom for families to place their tepees side by side. You must get along with Winona and her husband. My son will see that they do not harm you."

"I will try," I whisper. Glancing in Winona's direction, I notice that she stands by *our* wagon. My trunk is visible, and I want to ask for a change of clothing, but I decide to wait until Chaska returns so he can make the request for me.

Chaska's mother spreads a robe on the ground to make a place for me to sit, and she hands me a clean cloth to diaper Nellie. Then she goes to fetch water so my children and I can wash. As soon as she leaves, Winona comes to stand over me. She folds her arms across her chest and glares at me. Then a shrewd gleam enters her eyes. "Are you a friend to my people?"

"Yes, I have always tried to treat them kindly."

"Then give me your earrings."

My hand flies up to my earlobe. I am wearing a pair of earbobs John gave me for my last birthday; each one has an arrangement of three gold leaves, from which hang a cluster of amethyst beads that look like grapes. They are my favorites, but that matters little if I can use them to placate the hatred of this vixen. I remove them without hesitation— but not without regret—and hand them to her. She removes her cheap tin hoops and puts them in my ears. "We trade," she says and laughs.

I nod but say nothing. My throat is so tight from unshed tears that I cannot speak. *A small price to pay for your life,* I tell myself.

CHAPTER

12

AFTER I WASH, CHASKA'S MOTHER GIVES ME A LOOSE SACQUE TO WEAR instead of my wet things, but in that whole camp, there is no private place where I can change, so I offer to help the old woman put up her tepee. First we erect a tripod made of three pine poles lashed near the top with a rawhide strip whose long end is left hanging. One by one, I lay other lodge poles in the tripod's crotch. Chaska's mother follows behind me, making sure each pole is placed evenly around a circle. I ask, "Have you heard from Chaska?"

"No. Not since he rode away yesterday."

"Wasn't he one of the warriors who came back to camp last night?"

"No."

I glance back at her. Although she maintains a stoic expression, I sense her worry about her son. I too am troubled by his continued absence.

When she is satisfied the poles are placed correctly, she has Jimmy take the rawhide lash and walk around the tepee three times to secure all the poles tightly.

The old woman ties the cover—now that her people can no longer hunt bison on the plains, they use canvas—to another pole and lifts it into place. Walking in opposite directions, Jimmy and I stretch the cover around the frame.

The old woman pulls the edges together above the door and reaches up to secure the overlap with wooden lacing pins. Placing a hand on her shoulder, I say, "I will do it. I am tall."

After I finish, Chaska's mother teaches me how to tie round stones into the hem of the cloth and run rope from those makeshift anchors to pegs in the ground.

Once the tepee is up and I have changed my clothes, I go back outside. One of the friendly women in camp brings beef stew for my children and me. I suspect that we are dining upon a cow rustled from a nearby farm, but I hardly care. My depleted body desperately needs the sustenance.

After we eat, Chaska's mother and one of her neighbors place a couple of robes in the shade beneath my husband's wagon and encourage me to rest. Gratefully, I lie down with my two children, who doze off quickly. Tired as I am, my mind conjures up the specter of every conceivable evil. Restlessly, I stretch, search for a more comfortable position, and try to quiet my mind by reciting Psalm 23. I do not sleep.

After a while, stealthy footsteps capture my attention. I open my eyes to see the legs of four women gathered near the wagon. I recognize the moccasins of Chaska's mother. "You must wake her," a woman says softly. "Warn her of danger."

"I am awake." I ease myself from beneath the wagon without disturbing my children. As I stand, my legs ache painfully.

The three visitors all speak at once: "Someone threatens you." "An evil man." "He wants to kill you."

"Hapa?" I ask.

"No. Another."

Chaska's mother tugs my sleeve. "You must go to the woods again."

At the thought of enduring another such night, my knees buckle and I grab the side of the wagon. "I cannot walk so far. I am too exhausted. My enemy would surely catch me and kill me on the way."

I hear a commotion to the north. Even though fear has settled in my stomach like a lead sinker, I step away from the wagon and look to see what's happening.

Beyond the cluster of tepees stands a hut made of green boughs. A middle-aged Sioux, wearing a white band across his forehead, moves into the clearing before the structure. He leads a woman whose wrists

are tied before her. She has coppery hair and wears a brown gingham dress.

They disappear into the hut. Although I want to run away, horror
tethers me to the spot. Time distorts, so I cannot tell how many minutes pass before a heartrending shriek emanates from the doorway. The
man with the white band comes out brandishing the woman's dress
triumphantly over his head. He spreads it on a shrub and leaves the
area—to fetch another captive, I fear. Two men exit the hut carrying
a white body, which they toss into a wagon, and drive away.

I whirl around. The women, including Chaska's mother, have vanished. Quivering with terror, I crawl under the wagon. I feel safer there,
even though I know it makes a poor hiding place. As if to demonstrate
my folly, a white man—the only one I have seen since poor Gleason
died—rushes up and squats to speak to me. In a heavy German accent,
he says, "We will shortly all be killed. The squaws are very excited.
'Go to the woods,' they tell me, but 'It is useless,' I answer."

"Please go," I whisper. "You will wake my children."

"Bah!" he exclaims and hurries away. I gaze at the cherubic faces of
my babies, wondering if they truly will be angels before nightfall. My
eyes fill with tears as I ponder whether I should find a heavy rock and
dispatch them before the murderer comes. Surely, it would be more
merciful for them to die in their sleep than to suffer the horror of seeing their mother dragged away to be executed.

I extricate myself from beneath the wagon and search the area. Before I find a stone large enough to do the deed, Chaska's mother approaches. "I will hide you in my tepee. You must not talk." She picks
up Nellie and puts her in a sling on her back.

I wake up Jimmy and we follow the old woman into her tepee. When
I realize that she expects me to lie on the ground covered by a buffalo
robe, I protest, "I am too large. Anyone who comes inside the tent will
see me hiding there."

"Quiet," she says and goes back outside. Bringing in the buffalo robes
we were using beneath the wagon, she folds each one lengthwise and
piles them on top of each other to make a sort of embankment.

I understand then what she intends, and Jimmy and I lie flat in the
space between the folded robes and the canvas tepee wall. Chaska's

mother lays two more robes on top of us. "Does the pile look flat?" I ask her.

"Yes. Do not talk."

Despite her assurance, I feel certain I am too large to escape detection. Crouched beneath the hides, I imagine that I look like a kneeling buffalo calf. Surely, I will be discovered and killed.

To my surprise, that conclusion does not distress me the way it would have a week ago. Resigning myself to the worst, I whisper, "Jimmy, can you hear me?"

"Yes, Mama."

"If anything happens to me, stay with your sister and take care of her."

"O.K." His glib answer shows he does not grasp the gravity of our situation.

"You must remember your name."

"I know my name." Jimmy's voice rises in indignation, and I place my fingers over his lips.

"I mean your full name—James Orin Wakefield—and that of your sister. Remember that her name is Lucy Ellen. Nellie is a nickname."

"All right, Mama. But why?"

I squeeze my eyes tight in a spasm of pain over my inability to shield my darlings from the world's cruelty. "Son, a bad man may come to kill me. If that happens, remember who you are. That way, if your father or uncle should still be alive, they might be able to find you after the war is over."

His little hand creeps up to rest on my neck. "Mama, will they kill me too?"

"I hope not. They may adopt you and raise you as an Indian. But you must always keep in mind that you are white. You must remember your name."

"Yes, Mama," he whispers, this time as solemnly as I could wish.

We fall silent. The robes atop us are heavy and uncomfortably warm. The smell of tanned leather fills my nostrils. The ground beneath us is unyielding, and my already sore back grows so stiff that I can hardly keep from groaning.

After a time, I inch closer to the tepee wall and lift the edge of the robes. On the canvas, the shadow of Chaska's mother marches back and forth like a soldier on guard duty. "Any news?" I call in a low voice.

"No. Be quiet."

Using a small rock, I prop the tepee cloth a couple inches off the ground. By turning my face to the side and poking my nose past the edge of the robes, I can get fresher air. Closing my eyes, I lie there and pray silently that God will save me from death so I can raise my children.

The heat beneath the robes grows so oppressive that I drift into a stupor. After an indeterminate amount of time, a sharp keening jolts me awake. Lifting the edge of the tepee cloth again, I peer outside and see the old woman kneeling, sobbing, and covering her face with her hands. "Ina, what is wrong?" I cry, calling her "mother" because I don't know another name to use.

"Chaska,...dead." She grovels on the ground and rubs dirt upon her face. Her voice rises in a harsh, wordless lament.

I let the tepee cloth fall to the ground and inch more deeply under the robes. My heart contracts with terror as I contemplate what lies ahead. Not just the tortures I will no doubt undergo but the dread possibility of eternal damnation. The churchmen I have known here and in New England do not deem me a true Christian because of the stain upon my past. "Heavenly father," I pray, "forgive me my trespasses and receive me into glory. I have always loved you, and I believe in the saving work of your son, Jesus Christ."

A voice deep within me replies, *Then trust Him,* and a miraculous calm descends upon my spirit. In a soft, quavering voice barely above a whisper, I sing,

Just as I am, without one plea
But that Thy blood was shed for me,
And that Thou bidd'st me come to Thee,
O Lamb of God, I come! I come!

Jimmy puts his little fingers upon my lips and says, "Shhh, Mama."

I fall silent but do so happily. That single stanza of the well-loved hymn has restored my hope in God's grace. Feeling at peace, I turn my thoughts to my husband and pray for the repose of his soul. Perhaps, if my children are murdered with me, all three of us will find John in the world to come.

"Jimmy," I whisper, "you may die and go to heaven soon."

"O, Mama! I am glad, ain't you? Heaven is supposed to be a nice place."

I pull my boy close to me there in that suffocating space beneath the robes and hold him tight to my bosom. Poor little lad, he has no idea of what will have to transpire before we reach the pearly gates.

After several minutes pass, I lift the tent cloth again. Chaska's mother is still kneeling in the dirt keening, and Winona squats beside her with an arm around her shoulder. "What has happened?" I ask. "What news have you heard?"

Chaska's mother answers, "Chaska dead. You will die soon. That man is a very bad man."

"How am I to be killed?" I ask, thinking it would be better to know what is coming than to live in this torment of uncertainty.

Winona shoots me a look of pure malice. "Stabbed!" She points to her heart.

Withdrawing into the shadows again, I leave a gap between the tent cloth and the ground so I will know when my killer approaches. I have a sick horror of slow, agonizing deaths, and the thought of being knifed terrifies me more than any other way of dying except to be burned alive.

"Grant me courage," I pray. My innards feel as though they have turned to liquid, and I fight the urge to relieve myself. I do not want my killer to drag me from my hiding place stinking of urine.

As I take several deep breaths to calm myself, an unexpected sound catches my attention: a soft neighing that sounds like my mare, Lady. Chaska rode away on her when he left yesterday morning. Can the news of his death be wrong?

Pushing my face close to the opening, I hear an answering neigh from Gleason's horse, staked near the wagon. Then a whinny that I am certain is Lady's. Excitedly, I raise the tent cloth further, just in time to see Chaska ride into view.

I drop the tepee cloth and throw off the suffocating buffalo robes that cover us. "What is it, Mama?" Jimmy asks.

"Chaska has returned." I head for the tepee opening and then halt and bite my lower lip in trepidation. What if we are still in danger?

As I stand there, hesitating, Winona throws open the flap and says, "Come out. Chaska has come. It is safe now."

When I emerge blinking into the sunshine, I see Chaska and his mother standing face to face without touching. The old woman's tears have ceased. As she gazes up at her son, she uses one hand to hide her exuberant smile. Chaska speaks so quietly that I cannot make out his words. The dignity and deep unspoken emotion of the scene before me moves me almost to tears.

After a couple of minutes, he turns and, seeing me standing there, comes toward me. *"To 'ked yauŋ he?"* he asks: "How are you?"

"Taŋyaŋ wauŋ ye," I say because it will make a better impression to say that I am fine than to complain about my troubles.

Chaska nods but peers intently at me for several seconds. He is a couple of inches shorter than I am, so he tilts his head back slightly to gaze at me from beneath half-lowered eyelids. The scrutiny brings a blush to my cheeks.

Standing so near to him, I notice that he smells of horses and sweat. He has crow's feet at the corners of his eyes and a few strands of silver in his hair.

After several seconds, he reaches out to shake my hand. His palm is rough and callused, but his steady grip is reassuring. "Do not be afraid. He will not dare to hurt you while I am near; if he comes near, I will shoot him."

"Pidamaya ye," I answer: "Thank you."

Chaska goes away to tend the horses, and I take my daughter back from the old woman. When I ask Ina if I can help her, she tells me to take my ease. For the rest of the afternoon, I sit quietly in the sun. Everything is so tranquil that I can hardly credit the scenes of violence I witnessed a few hours ago. Soon Jimmy and the dog Buster are playing together happily. Nellie sits on the grass, reluctant to stray from my side, so I make a clover chain to amuse her. "Fwowers!" she says and giggles.

Occasionally, I catch sight of Chaska going about the camp, and his presence calms me. A memory from early childhood comes to me: once when my parents and I were driving back from my grandmother's farm, I fell asleep in the back of the wagon. When we arrived home, I woke as my father's strong arms carried me into the house; I felt so secure that I went back to sleep even before he tucked me into bed. The knowledge that Chaska will protect me makes me feel almost as safe.

Toward the supper hour, the old woman sits near me to make bread and smoke a pipe. For the first time, we have a chance to chat about ordinary things, and I learn that Chaska is a widower. His wife and only son died of smallpox during the previous, harsh winter. I experience a rush of sympathy for him as I imagine how I would feel if I lost my Jimmy.

At bedtime, Ina explains that in a Sioux tepee, everyone has a traditional sleeping place. As the tepee's owner, the mother is responsible for tending the fire and stores of food and water. Her place is close to the entrance on the right side as one goes in because that is where supplies are kept. The husband's place is usually the center back. Any sons sleep along the left side of the circle with the oldest near the back and the youngest near the entrance. The daughters sleep in corresponding positions along the right. "You will sleep in a daughter's place," Ina tells me, "with your baby. Your boy will sleep on the man's side of the tepee next to Chaska."

Mindful of the warning the woman in the bark house gave me, I lie on my side and stare at the tepee cloth rather than the pallets belonging to Chaska or Ina. Nellie curls between me and the wall, and we both fall asleep almost immediately.

The next day dawns grey and cloudy. Chaska's mother accepts my offer to fetch water, so I pick up a pail and walk down to the Minnesota River. To my surprise, no one objects to my leaving the camp unaccompanied.

Our camp is near a fairly low place in the river. As I gaze at the flowing water, I imagine fording the stream and secreting myself somewhere on the north bank. Surely I could make my way cross-country to safety, that is, if I did not have my children. Jimmy is too young to walk so far, and Nellie is too heavy for me to carry more than a short way. For an instant, I contemplate making my escape and coming back with soldiers to rescue my babies, but then I dismiss the idea. The whole country is aflame with war, and the army has too much to do to go after two specific children. With a heavy heart, I draw water and head back to the camp.

In the space between our tepee and Winona's, the younger of Winona's sons sits on the ground dragging something through the dirt. Stepping closer, I see that his plaything is my best collar; it is made from fine European lace, and I prize it highly. *"De mitawa,"* I tell the boy: "That is mine."

He holds it out to me. Winona rushes out of her tepee. Snatching the collar from the boy, she pulls a knife from the sheath at her waist, makes one cut in the edge of the collar, and grasping it in both hands, rips the lovely thing in two. Digging her fingers into the lace itself, she tears at it until it looks like a tattered spider web. She throws the collar on the ground, pivots on her heel, and reenters her tent.

I turn to see Chaska's mother watching me with an impassive expression. Knowing it would be difficult for her to take my side, even if she thinks her daughter is wrong, I hand her the filled pail and say in Dakota, "Here is the water."

She nods.

Not long after that, rain starts to fall. Chaska remains in camp, but most of the time, he is in another tepee meeting with the men. My children and I stay with Ina, and I help her with sewing and food preparation. At no time do we speak of Winona and her hatred.

At noon, Chaska tells us that we must move again—closer to Little Crow's village, which has become the headquarters of the hostile Sioux. Despite the steady rain, we take down the tepee, stow our things in the wagon, and travel east with the band. The showers stop before we reach our destination, but the sky remains overcast. The air retains a damp heaviness, and my spirits remain low as I help Ina erect her tepee.

Sometime during that night, crashing thunder wakes me, and I sit up with a jolt, thinking I am back in the ravine. Then I see that I am indoors, but a gale as violent as a hurricane lashes the tepee cover violently. Enough rain blows through the smoke vent that the fire at the center of the tepee sputters.

Powerful gusts of wind snake beneath the bottom of the tent cloth. As I watch, the straining canvas pulls a lodge pole off the ground and deposits it an inch or two away. Many of the poles on my side of the tepee are "walking" in this way, and the dwelling is losing its conical shape. Suddenly, a large portion of the cloth on my side becomes unmoored, and the fierce wind tips the entire structure over onto its side. One of the lodge poles grazes the side of my head as it falls; thank God it misses Nellie. The next thing I know, we are all sitting outside in a whipping rain.

Chaska's mother grabs my arm. "Come, white woman." She hurries under the wagon, and I snatch up Nellie and follow. Chaska and Jimmy join us moments later.

Gazing out at the curtain of water, I wonder if heaven is weeping for all the innocent lives lost this week. Will we continue to experience nightly inundations until the conflict ceases? If so, am I doomed to die of drowning or pneumonia rather than a scalping? The thought arouses a grim humor in me, and to the surprise of my companions, I begin to laugh.

CHAPTER

13

AFTER SEVERAL HOURS, THE RAIN STOPS; WE WAIT ABOUT FIFTEEN MIN-
utes to make sure the storm has truly passed and then crawl out from
under the wagon. The clouds have thinned, and a waning crescent
moon emits just enough light to see the chaos spread out before us.
The tempest overturned not only our own tepee but also most of the
others in camp. Dark figures move to and fro, trying to set things to
rights. Chaska goes off to see what he can learn.

In every direction, small campfires are being lit by old women, who
croon over the flames as they coax them to life. The sight reminds
me of the witches in *Macbeth*. As I watch the old women moan and
fan their fires, a peculiar, dizzy sensation passes over me—causing me
to wonder if the old ones are casting a spell to strengthen the tribe's
hold over its captives during this period of disarray.

Sick and weary, I lean against the side of the wagon. Chaska's
mother asks, *"To'ked yaun he?"*

"Miye wamatuka ye," I answer: "I am tired."

She reaches up to check my forehead. The instant her skin makes
contact with mine, my fearful fancy about witches falls away, replaced
by shame that I let myself be prey to diseased imagination. The women
of this camp are worried mothers just as I am and, except for Winona
and Lightfoot, they have been kind.

"Tayca'ykatapi duhe ŝyi," Chaska's mother says: "You have no fever."

I nod in agreement.

She turns away. "I must put up my tepee."

"I will help." Straightening, I lift my children into the wagon and tell them to stay put. Then I begin to disentangle the lodge poles from the tent cloth.

Winona emerges from her tepee, one of the few that remain standing. Her mother asks for dry wood from her stores, so we can start a new fire. Winona agrees, but she stands there for several minutes with her arms folded across her chest. I sense rather than see her watching me.

Ina and I lay out all the poles parallel to each other, and then we lift the tent cloth section by section and whisk mud off it. As we work, Chaska returns. "Do not put up the tepee."

"Why not?"

He glances at his sister's dwelling. Even though Winona has gone back inside, he motions for us to step a few more feet away from her tepee. "The warriors attack the fort today. I must go with them."

His expression is guarded, but I fancy a plea for understanding lurks in his eyes. *If he is reluctant,* I wonder, *why must he go? Does he think he must take part to protect his family?*

I have not considered that there might be dissension and coercion among the Sioux, but as soon as the idea occurs to me, it makes sense. The women are clearly divided about the war; it only makes sense for the men to be split over the issue too.

As these thoughts race through my mind, Chaska lowers his voice. "I am afraid to leave you and your children here. Hapa might return and kill you."

I interrupt him, "Do not ask me to go to the woods."

"No." He lays a reassuring hand on my arm. "You had better come with me to my grandfather. He lives in a brick house a short way from here. We will pass it on our way to the fort. You can travel in the wagon."

"Thank you."

"We will leave soon. Wait here. My sister will help you to get ready."

I open my mouth to object, but Chaska says, "Do not fear. Hapa is not here."

He strides to the open space before Winona's tepee and declares in a loud voice. "It is good that Tanka-Winohiŋca wears the dress of an

Indian, but I wish that someone would paint her face like one of us."

Without a backward glance, he walks away. Almost immediately, Winona pokes her head through her doorway and beckons for me to enter.

Although I find their indirect method of communication curious, it is clear what I am expected to do. Taking a deep breath, I gather my children and tell them not to say anything while we are in the tepee. Then I bend down to enter. The first thing I see inside the dwelling is Winona's two boys sleeping on the men's side. Winona points to a place just inside the door, and I sit there with my children. She crosses to a pile of household objects and sorts through them. While she does so, I notice that my trunk sits near the back of her tepee.

Winona returns to me carrying several colorful ribbons; a small, quilled buckskin bag; and a bison-horn bowl containing a dab of animal grease. Silently, she unfastens my braids and runs a carved-antler comb through my hair. Then she rebraids it and wraps ribbons around the plaits in crisscross fashion. After tipping a small amount of ground red ocher from the bag into the bowl, she mixes the grease and powder into a paste and uses it to paint the part of my hair and red circles on my cheeks. As she kneels before me, my gold earbobs, hanging from Winona's ears, glint in the firelight.

Standing and backing up a few paces, Winona regards me critically. She rummages around in a stack of folded clothing for a moment before tossing me a new pair of moccasins, colorful leggings, and a blanket to wrap around my shoulders. "Wear those. Then you will look like Indian woman."

Quickly, she paints my children's faces and tells me I am ready to go.

"Pidamaya ye," I say, thanking her even though I know perfectly well she acted only to comply with her brother's wishes.

When I go back outside, birds are singing and the sky has started to lighten. Chaska has harnessed Lady to the wagon; if his mother and Winona need to strike camp, they will use Gleason's horse to pull a travois.

Unsure if I will see Chaska's mother again, I thank her for all her kindness.

"Waŝicuŋ wiŋyaŋ, taŋyaŋ uŋ wo," she answers: "White woman, be well."

"Taŋyaŋ uŋ wo," I echo her.

With Chaska's help, I climb into the front seat of the wagon. He lifts my daughter into my arms. After watching Jimmy clamber onto the rear seat, Chaska takes the driver's seat next to me and clucks at the mare.

We leave the camp in the twilight that precedes dawn. As we pull out onto the broad prairie, I am surprised to see several dozen warriors traveling in the same direction. Now I understand why Chaska wanted me to look more like a Sioux woman, and I pull my blanket over my head to hide my brown hair. Fortunately, the morning is cool enough that the action does not look suspicious.

Chaska wears a shirt and leggings, but most of the other men wear only breechcloths. Their naked bodies are ornamented in a variety of ways: bison-horn headdresses; eagle feathers; beaded chokers; bear-claw necklaces; and red, white, black, and yellow war paint. I have never seen such a fearsome looking group of men.

The warriors ride horses decorated with ribbons, feathers, and bells, which jingle as we cross the prairie. The men boast about what they will do in the coming battle. They laugh harshly and make fierce gestures that freeze my blood.

Soon, they chant a war song. At the sound, my heart floods with pity for the people at Ridgely, who have no idea what a frightful force is about to fall upon them.

I confess, I pity myself too. Little did I imagine as John drove us home from Redwood that I would soon be crossing the prairie as part of a Sioux war party. How has it come to pass that I must ride with men whose intent it is to wipe out my people? To any casual observer, it must look as though I support their deadly mission. I feel deeply mortified to be riding in this train, but I have little choice.

As the sun rises, Chaska halts the wagon before a small brick house surrounded by tepees. He hurries my children and me inside. An old man with bent posture and silver hair rises to greet us. Chaska introduces him as Eagle Head, his grandfather, and tells me that the old man does not speak English. Eagle Head's skin is deeply lined, and the lower half of his face has the sunken look that comes from losing one's teeth. A tiny old woman—a more shriveled version of Ina—stands behind him, but no one introduces her.

The main room of the house has an iron stove in one corner; a fire is burning within and a covered kettle sits on top. The warmth emanating from the stove feels comforting after the chill outside. The old woman gestures wordlessly toward the table, and my children and I sit. Then she serves us small portions of corn mush.

Chaska remains standing and refuses the offer of breakfast. "I must go," he tells me. "I will stop tonight to take you back to my mother's tepee."

Bereft, I follow him out the door and watch him drive away. Before going back inside, I take in my surroundings. Several women walk about the camp, fetching water and gossiping with neighbors, and after a few seconds, I realize that I know many of them. Some of them are acquaintances from Shakopee.

An old woman exits a tepee about forty feet away, and I am pleased to recognize her as the kindly Sioux woman whites called Mother Friend. When I cry out to her, she turns in my direction, walks closer, and peers at me without recognition. I remove the blanket from my head. "It's me. Mrs. Wakefield."

Her mouth drops open. She rushes up and clasps my hands. "My daughter, why are you here?"

"My children and I are captives." Mother Friend wails at the news, and I have to wait for her to calm down before I can explain, "Chaska is our protector. He brought us here to stay with his grandfather during the attack on the fort."

"Where are your children?"

I nod at the dwelling behind me. "In this house."

"Bring them to my tepee. I will care for you today. I go fetch water. Come when the sun has climbed one finger higher in the sky." She holds out her hand at arm's length to show me that the sun is now four finger widths above the horizon.

"I understand."

Mother Friend hurries away and I go back inside to inform Eagle Head of my plans. After about fifteen minutes, I walk outside to check the position of the sun and see that it is time for us to go.

When we enter Mother Friend's tepee, she tells me to sit in the place of honor at the back. She clucks in dismay at the crusted-over bites on my children's faces and the cuts on my boy's feet. "I will take good care of you," she says.

First she has me remove my sacque, which is filthy from crouching in the mud last night, and gives me a blanket to wrap myself in. "I will wash this."

About fifteen minutes later, Mother Friend returns and tells me that my dress is drying on a bush in the sun. She heats water and gently washes all the scrapes and scratches on my children and me. As she does so, I recount everything that happened during the last few days. When I finish, she shakes her head. "Not all my people want this fight."

She gazes at me wistfully. "When I was a girl, all this land was ours. It is a good land, and we were happy. Then whites came like waves of locusts, too many to chase away. We tried to live peacefully, but the traders do not deal fairly with my people. Now our young men want to drive all whites from the land. They are foolish children. We cannot win. This war will cause great suffering for both our peoples."

"This war has already caused me great suffering," I retort, but instantly regret the words. I lay my hand on her arm. "Mother Friend, I know that not all Sioux are hostile. Just as you know that not all whites are cruel."

We gaze sadly at each other, two women caught in a man's conflict brought about by greed and dishonesty on one side and anger and desperation on the other. She sighs. "Your boy must not go about with bare feet. I will make him moccasins."

Since I do not know how to sew leather, I cannot offer to help. I am always interested in learning new skills, though, so I watch as she cuts out the soles of thick rawhide and tops of soft leather.

The process also fascinates my son, who asks, "Can I have beaded tops?"

"Jimmy, it is rude to ask for something extra," I scold him in English. "Be grateful for what she offers."

Even though Mother Friend speaks little English, she understands my tone of rebuke. Laughing, she strokes my son's hair. *"Siceca owasin haŋpikce'ya owaŋyag waŝte ciŋ'pi,"* she says indulgently: "All children want handsome moccasins."

She explains to Jimmy that she has no time to bead these because she must finish before Chaska returns tonight. Then she adds brightly, "When your sister is old enough to bead moccasins, the first pair she makes will be for you. And when you are old enough to hunt, you must give your first kill to be cooked in her honor."

Jimmy turns to me with a puzzled expression.

"Listen to Mother Friend," I tell him, although her implication that my children will grow up as Indians troubles me. "You know that I always tell you to watch out for your sister."

"Yes, Mama," he drawls, bored by talk of responsibility. "Can I play outside?"

"All right, but leave the tent flap open and stay where I can see you."

After he leaves, I ask, "Why did you tell my son those things?"

I want her to explain why she assumes my children will be raised as Sioux, but Mother Friend interprets my question a different way: "Is it not this way among whites? Among my people, brothers and sisters have a respect relationship. We call it the hakata relationship." *Hakata.* Ina used that term when speaking to Winona, but I didn't know her well enough then to ask what it meant. Mother Friend goes on, "They must never be too familiar or make demands. Instead, each one must always think of ways to please or honor the other."

"That explains it," I murmur in English, and she looks at me quizzically, so I explain the indirect way that Chaska asked his sister to help me this morning.

Mother Friend nods. "Yes, that is the hakata way. Chaska has publicly taken you under his protection. He must not demand that his sister help you, but if she honors him, she will."

"But she acts with malice toward me when he is not near."

Mother Friend frowns and stops stitching. "What do you mean?"

I summarize the hateful way that Winona has treated me.

"She should not do so." Mother Friend frowns pensively. "Did you not tell me that Chaska calls his sister's husband a bad man? Usually, that is not done. A hakata should honor his sister's choice even if he thinks it a poor one. As children, we are taught to settle our differences and live with our kin in peace, yet this family has discord. I fear you will continue to have trouble from Winona and her husband."

"What can I do?"

She begins sewing again. "Be respectful. Stay away from Winona and her husband. Let her keep your things. Perhaps that will appease her anger."

I sigh. Isn't it enough that I am caught in a war between whites and Indians? Why did I land in the midst of a family squabble too?

Shortly before midday Chaska's grandmother comes to fetch my children and me for dinner. Mother Friend protests, "No, many times, she has given me cooked food in her tepee in Shakopee. Now she must stay and eat bread with me."

After Chaska's grandmother leaves, I go outside to check whether my dress is dry. Finding that it is, I take it back into the tepee and put it on.

Mother Friend's two daughters join us a few minutes later, bringing fried bread and *wasna*—dried buffalo meat mixed with suet and crushed cherries. As we eat, the daughters try to cheer me by complimenting my son and daughter and telling amusing stories about their own children. I smile to show my appreciation, but I fear my expression betrays my anxiety. The elder daughter says, "When our father returns, we will ask him to paddle you in a canoe down the river to Mankato."

"Would he do that for me?" I exclaim, hardly daring to believe the offer.

"We will ask."

The idea that I might be free by the end of the day fills me with restless energy. After we finish eating, I offer to wash the bowls, but the daughters will not hear of it. They clear away the remains of the meal and leave us alone to gossip. Mother Friend takes out her *ca'ŋnuŋpa* and asks me to smoke with her before she goes back to work on Jimmy's moccasins. As she stuffs her pipe with tobacco, I hear a distant crack that could come only from a rifle. Several other shots follow the first.

Even though I know it is safer to stay inside, I cannot bear to remain ignorant, so I order Jimmy to stay in the tepee with his sister, drape the blanket over my head, and go outside. Mother Friend and I follow other women heading east.

Our encampment is on high ground. All the land around here is scored with ravines, some of them long and deep. From where I stand, I see warriors sneaking through a gorge that runs toward Fort Ridgely. The men have grasses and prairie flowers sticking up from their headbands to further disguise their approach. When they reach the far end, they climb the embankment and rush forward. The sound of firing guns grows constant.

I hold a hand over my mouth as I listen to the battle a few short miles away. My emotions war within me like a dog and a wolf fighting for mastery. If John is still alive—and despite my fears that he must be dead, I have not completely lost hope—he is more likely to be at Ridgely than anywhere else. Because of that, I know I should pray for the whites to defeat the Sioux, but I cannot. Chaska is one of the attackers, and my heart quails for him as much as it does for John, not only because my safety depends on Chaska but also because he is a good man.

While I stand with the other women—yet separated from them by my divided loyalties—I notice them casting sideways glances at me. Several times I catch the muttered phrase *Pa baska,* meaning, "Cut off your head." I blink and maintain a stoical expression so they will not know they have upset me.

As I debate whether to return to the tepee, a loud boom announces that the soldiers have begun firing artillery. The other women scream in panic. Mother Friend grabs my arm and stares at the sky. "It does not rain. Why does it thunder?"

"That noise is not thunder. It is the great guns of the white soldiers. These guns fire large balls." I indicate their size with my hands. "The balls fly apart into many sharp pieces and kill many men."

Mother Friend stares at me open-mouthed. Around us, the women murmur as they pass my explanation one to the other. The sound of shelling grows steadier, and the gaps between explosions are filled with the low roar that comes from a hoard of men shouting. A thick column of smoke rises into the sky.

After a particularly hellish explosion, coming I suspect from two pieces firing simultaneously, the rumor that the Sioux are being slaughtered spreads down the line. Panic sets in, and the women rush back to camp. I follow Mother Friend even though I am not convinced retreat is necessary. The smoke I saw must mean the Indians are burning some of the buildings, and if the Sioux are setting fires, they must still be engaged in the fight and not wiped out as the women fear.

Mother Friend and I collect my children and follow the other women a quarter mile west to a deep, wooded ravine. To my surprise, I see two other white women in the crowd ahead, too far away for me to speak to them. Each is in the custody of a Sioux family, and each wears American clothes.

Nearly all the women and children from camp, as well as a few old people, flee to the ravine; once there, everyone tries to hide by crouching behind a shrub or climbing into a tree. We all remain as motionless and silent as possible, and time slows to a crawl. The layers of heavy foliage prevent us from hearing the sounds of battle except for the muffled booms of artillery. The tension of not knowing what is happening scrapes my nerves raw.

Finally, a young lad of about ten jumps down from the leafy branch where he had secreted himself and runs from the ravine. About an hour passes before he returns, but when he does, he no longer moves stealthily. Instead, he shouts: "The battle goes on. Our men still fight. Few have died."

Chattering breaks out instantly, and the Sioux emerge from their hiding places and head back to camp. A woman with two daughters walks ahead of us on the trail; when she hears Nellie speak English, she turns to smile at us. "Do your children like candy and nuts?" she asks me in Dakota. I nod and she gestures that they should cup their hands. When they do, she gives each of them as much shelled walnuts, hard candy, and maple sugar as they can hold.

"*Wopida unkenic'eyapi,*" I tell her: "We thank you." When she turns away from us again, I shake my head and wonder if I will ever understand these people. One minute they are threatening to kill me and the next they are spoiling my children. The longer I am with them, the more I understand that their attitudes toward whites are neither uniform nor predictable.

Nellie allows me to share her treats, so I suck upon a peppermint as we walk. As we near camp, the women call out to each other cheerfully, as seemingly certain of a positive outcome now as they were of a disaster two hours ago. I can scarcely keep from exclaiming in disgust at their foolishness. If someone had thought to check out the earlier rumor before spreading the alarm, we would have all been spared needless anxiety.

Mother Friend and I return to her tepee, where she works on Jimmy's moccasins. The events of the afternoon have left me so agitated that I pace back and forth as much as I am able in that confined space. After a few moments, Mother Friend says, "My daughter, do not walk wildly inside the tepee. Nobody does so."

Her words stop me short. *Nobody does so.* Sioux elders use that expression to teach children how to behave. Does Mother Friend think I am acting childishly? My cheeks burn with embarrassment as I take my place beside her. After taking a moment to swallow my anger, I say, "Mother, please show me how to sew the moccasin so I may be more useful."

CHAPTER
14

NIGHT FALLS. EVEN THOUGH THE SOUNDS OF THE BATTLE DECREASE AND finally fade away, Chaska does not come for us. My children, worn out from the long day and satiated with treats, fall asleep without eating supper.

As Mother Friend and I prepare a simple meal, Eagle Head comes to the tepee carrying a rifle. The old man lays down his gun and sits cross-legged inside the doorway. "A messenger has come," he says in Dakota. "He says the warriors will stay by fort tonight. A chief will come to our camp to kill you and other white women."

"What can I do?"

Eagle Head stands. "Flee to woods. I will go with you."

Dread settles upon me like a dark shadow. Will these threats against my life never cease? No matter how I change my behavior to please the Sioux, someone always wants to murder me. I feel so hopeless that I am about to tell Eagle Head to leave me here to die when Mother Friend hands me a baby carrier. "You and your girl must go, my daughter. Leave your boy here. I will watch over him."

I grasp Mother Friend's arm. "Will he be safe? Will the chief not kill him?"

"No," Eagle Head answers. "He comes to kill white women only."

With tears in my eyes, I gaze at the white-blond hair of my sleeping boy. We have never spent a night apart from each other since the day that he was born, and my arms ache at the thought of being separated from him.

"We must hurry," Eagle Head says in his old man's voice, which lisps because of missing teeth. He picks up his rifle and holds it diagonally across his chest.

"All right." I gently lift my sleeping daughter and hand her to Mother Friend, who makes a sling of a blanket and puts Nellie upon my back. She shows me how to wrap it around my arms to keep it in place. "Are you sure my boy will be all right?"

Mother Friend comes around to face me and holds up her right hand, palm out. "I will die rather than let him be hurt. The Great Spirit hears me."

I hug her and follow Eagle Head into the night.

Making a sign for me to remain silent, the old man leads me through the village and across a clearing toward the woods. We plunge into the trees and pause as he considers which direction to take. A sense of panic seizes me, and I glance back the way we came, expecting to see armed warriors on our trail. "We must go," I hiss.

Eagle Head points toward the right, and I take off through the trees. Terror drives me like a whip across the back of my legs. Now that we have decided on this course, I want to get as much space between me and the camp as possible.

The band of woods, located on the bluff that rises on the north side of the river, is long but narrow. I try to stay near the center, as far as possible from either border. Trails are difficult to find at night, but I don't let that stop me. I plunge through the undergrowth, ignoring the brambles that tear at my clothes and skin.

After about an hour, Eagle Head calls, "Stop!"

I halt and look back. My eyes have adjusted to the dark, and I see him bend over and press his hands to his thighs. "I am old. I am tired."

Biting my lip to stifle a complaint, I move into the shadowy area among three trees and wait for him to catch his breath. My stomach growls, and I realize that in my haste to get away, I forgot to ask Mother Friend to pack some food.

After a couple of minutes, shouts erupt somewhere behind us. "We must go," I whisper, and Eagle Head nods. He still breathes heavily, but I am too frightened to linger, so I set off, directing my footsteps toward the gloomiest part of the woods.

We have gone only a short way farther when my daughter stirs upon my back and murmurs, "Noo noo."

For a moment, I am tempted to ignore her, but I know she will cry loudly in frustration if I don't attend to her needs. "Yes, darling. Let me find a place to sit."

Not far ahead of us is a fallen log. When we reach it, I feel along the length of the trunk, carefully sit down, and lower Nellie from the sling. I place her on my lap and open my bodice so she can suck.

Eagle Head remains a respectful distance away from us; even so, the bellows-like puffing of his lungs is audible. I hold my own breath and strain to detect other sounds in the forest beyond his wheezing. For a long time, I hear nothing. Then the distant report of a rifle punctuates the night.

Somehow, I manage to disengage Nellie without precipitating a protest and move the carrier with her in it onto my back. Once again, Eagle Head and I plunge into the darkness, heading ever farther from camp. I have no idea where we are or how far we've come, and I suspect that Eagle Head doesn't either.

After nearly an hour, Eagle Head calls to me again. His voice is strained and hoarse. "We must stop. I am an old man. I will die."

In frustration, I halt next to a tree and lean my forehead against its trunk. My breath too comes in labored gasps. My limbs tremble with fatigue. Yet, despite my exhaustion, a steady drumbeat sounds in my mind: *run, run, run.*

Lifting my head, I search the darkness for shelter. What I long to see is a stand of fir trees with wide, needle-filled branches that can screen us from view, but conifers are rare in this part of Minnesota. The faint moonlight glimmers off a colony of straight, white tree trunks, and I deduce that we are in a grove of aspens. They are tall and narrow, and even their lowest branches are way above our heads. Exasperated, I pound my fist against the nearest bole.

Then I notice that ferns fill many of the gaps among the trees, and some of the plants reach three feet high. Their plumy fronds would not be a sufficient hiding place in daylight, but in the dark, they might suffice—if I can lie down among them without flattening the plants.

When I explain my idea to Eagle Head, he says, "You can rest a short time."

Carefully, I wade into a large bed of ferns, trying to step between plants instead of upon them. When I find a place where the land dips into a hollow, I remove Nellie from my back and lie down with her in my arms. As I hoped, the surrounding fronds extend higher than my prostrate body.

To my surprise, Eagle Head doesn't follow us into the bank of ferns. I call to him in a hoarse whisper, "Will you not rest?"

"I sit against a tree and watch. You sleep."

"Thank you," I say, but I doubt I will slumber. My mind chitters away about danger, as wary as a squirrel that spies a human approaching its winter stash.

Nellie curls up facing me with her tiny fist holding the cloth of my bodice. I kiss the top of her head and say a prayer for Jimmy's safety, followed by my usual prayers for John and Chaska.

Then I close my eyes. Forest noises surround me: creaking branches, rustling leaves, the hooting of an owl, and the skittering of a small animal. Just as I begin to relax, the stealthy sound of someone or something picking its way across the forest floor captures my attention. Whatever it is comes toward me from the opposite direction to where Eagle Head sits guard.

My eyes fly open, and my whole body tenses. Straining my ears, I detect a very slight creaking. The conflicting demands of concealment and curiosity pull at me. After a few seconds, the desire to know my peril wins out and I cautiously push myself up on my elbow to peer through the feathery tops of ferns. A dark silhouette stands among the trees about five feet away. The moonlight is faint, but my eyes have adjusted to the dark. With great relief, I discern the outline of a white-tailed doe. As I watch, the animal stomps its left hoof twice and cocks its head—as fearful of predators as I am. The doe makes a loud blowing noise and leaps away.

Expelling a great sigh, I sink back down. My heart is racing so hard I can scarcely breathe; I force myself to inhale and exhale slowly three times. Then I gaze at the dark canopy created by overarching branches above my head. Despite the benign nature of my encounter with the deer, this ferny hollow no longer feels safe.

Moving as silently as I can, I wake Nellie and nurse her again. After putting her back in the sling, I go to Eagle Head. "We have been here too long."

"Yes."

The old man and I wander the forest for several more hours, sometimes backtracking, but most often going in our original direction. Sometime during the night, Eagle Head begins to limp. Several times we stop to allow him to rest.

Finally, the eastern sky lightens through the trees, and Eagle Head turns south toward the Minnesota River. After a few minutes, we emerge from the trees and head down a steep trail toward the bottomlands.

"I must go to camp to see if it is safe. You stay here," he says.

"On these flatlands? Why did you not leave me in the forest?"

"I have to see river to know where we are," he answers and scans the area around us. We are standing at the edge of an open meadow dotted with haystacks. Not a building or shrub is in sight.

"Come," he tells me and crosses to the nearest haystack. Stopping, he turns to me. "I will pull out hay. You hide in center. Then I cover you."

Horrified, I step back. "I need air!"

"I will make hole." Eagle Head bends to scoop hay out from the middle of the stack. Nervously, I glance around, hoping that no one is watching from the trees we left behind.

Within a few minutes, the old man creates a large enough hole for me. I take Nellie off my back and hand her to him, and then I position myself, kneeling on the ground in the space and sitting back on my heels. Eagle Head places my child in my lap and begins to loosely restack an outer wall of hay, trying to leave a hollow center. When the stack reaches to the top of my chest, he holds up one finger in an enigmatic gesture and hurries away.

A couple of minutes later, he comes back with three sticks, each about two feet long. By positioning them horizontally and shoving their ends into the edges of the remaining opening, Eagle Head creates a grill to preserve a pocket of air between my face and the outer wall.

Despite this, I feel panicky at the thought of being enclosed. When Eagle Head starts to place a layer of hay stems over the sticks, I recall Edgar Allan Poe's story "The Cask of Amontillado," which I read in *Godey's Lady's Book* when I was a girl. As all but a tiny hole of daylight disappears, I feel a nearly overpowering urge to cry out, "For the love of God, Montresor!"

Before departing, Eagle Head says he will come back for us as soon as he sees that the village is safe. Left alone with my baby, I settle in, thinking that our stay there will be two or three hours. The sweet smell of hay surrounds us, but the temperature within the stack is very warm—at least ninety degrees—and the air does not move. Perspiration pours down my face.

Before many minutes pass, I realize I made a serious error in the way I've positioned myself. Already my knees ache, and my feet and lower limbs prickle from the weight upon them. Lifting Nellie partway off my lap, I shift my legs. When I do so, some of the hay falls off the grill, leaving a narrow gap in the coverage. Frightened, I settle back down. The pain in my knees grows more excruciating. Eventually, I discover that if I am very careful, I can rise to an upright kneeling position to take the weight off my lower limbs. To do this, I have to hold my daughter in my arms, and her weight soon forces me to sit back on my heels.

Nellie fusses, so I allow her to nurse even though I am weak from lack of nourishment. The light through the tiny opening in front of me grows brighter. I close my eyes and attempt to sleep, but I am in too much discomfort. My lower limbs are numb and my knees feel like they have ground glass inside the joints.

After perhaps an hour, I hear men's voices, close enough to my hiding place that I can identify the language as Dakota even though I cannot discern their words. Nellie, who has been amusing herself unbuttoning and rebuttoning my bodice, squeaks in alarm. I press my hand tightly over her mouth. She squirms and tugs at my fingers, and a muffled cry escapes. In an agony of desperation, I put both hands around her throat and choke her into silence. Her face turns dark purple and, after a few seconds, she goes limp.

I release her and cover my mouth with both hands to keep from screaming. *My baby, my darling girl.* The blood rushes in my ears as I stare at my daughter's motionless body. Surely she can't be dead! Yet, she seems utterly lifeless. The voices speak again, moving farther away. Horror and shame overwhelm me, and I imagine bursting out of the haystack and begging the men to kill me.

Suddenly, Nellie's hand twitches. I put my fingers to the side of her neck and feel a pulse. Overwhelmed with joy, I hug her to my chest and rock back and forth a few inches as I offer thanks to God that I haven't killed her.

She groans softly. Pulling her away from my body, I gaze into her face. Her eyes flutter open. As soon as she sees me, her face puckers up into an expression of injured outrage. I cover her mouth gently and say in my softest whisper, "Don't cry. There are bad men outside."

Nellie frowns but does not make a sound. Instead, she reaches up to touch her throat, which is already turning purple. "I'm sorry!" I whisper, pulling her into my embrace. "I had to keep you quiet. It saved our lives from the bad man."

She says nothing, and I rock her back and forth. Then I push her slightly away from me, so I can gaze directly into her eyes. "Do you promise Mama to stay quiet?"

She pushes out her lower lip, which quivers, and tears pool in her eyes. Then she hides her face against my bosom.

As the morning wears on, the outside temperature climbs, and the interior of the stack grows even more airless. The aroma of hay, which I considered sweet at first, grows cloying. Because I am perspiring so heavily, I am losing liquid at an alarming rate. The inside of my mouth is as dry as flannel.

While I sit there, I imagine the faint sound of trickling water. The next time I lift my weight off my heels, I place my ear close to the grill, and the sound grows more distinct. Surely, there is a brook close by.

For an instant, my heart leaps with joy, until I realize I don't dare leave my shelter to look for it. Buried as I am, I have no way of knowing if enemies are nearby. Exposing myself in the open field would be foolhardy. And even if I succeeded in fetching water, how would I rebuild the haystack?

"Doggone it," I mutter, "this is just like Tantalus." Now that I know water flows nearby, all I can think of is my cottony mouth. Resolutely, I tell myself that Eagle Head will return soon, but that reassurance does not ease my parched throat.

Digging my fingers into the surrounding wall, I find a spot where the hay is moist. I pull out a handful and draw each stem through my lips one after the other to suck out what little water I can.

So the day passes, but Eagle Head does not return. Hour after hour, I nurse my daughter despite my growing weakness, muffle her with my hand when I hear noise outside, dismantle the haystack from within to find small bits of moisture, and bob up and down like a jack-in-the-box to redistribute the pain in my body. By late afternoon, I no longer have the energy to lift myself.

My heart sinks when the golden light that seeps through the thin outer layer of hay starts to fade. We have been here since sunrise, a period of about fourteen hours. The thought of remaining inside this haystack all night fills me with panic. As soon as darkness falls, I will have to dig my way out and search for water.

Once I make that decision, my thoughts turn to my boy. Is Jimmy still with Mother Friend? Once night falls, he will be afraid for me—and if he should cry in distress, one of the hostile Indians might kill him. Leaving him was a mistake, but what could I do? I thought we would be back by morning and it was better to let him sleep. If Eagle Head does not come back for me, I will try to make my way back to the village to look for my son.

As I slump in place, waiting for full darkness, I hear a voice and the sound of scratching outside. Seconds later, a hand pulls away the hay and the three horizontal sticks making up the grill. Eagle Head's white-haired head pokes through the opening. "Come out."

Nellie lifts her head from my bosom, but when she sees him, she whimpers in alarm.

"No, darling!" I exclaim. "The bad man is gone. This is our friend."

By then Eagle Head has cleared enough hay to free us. I set Nellie on her feet and tell her to walk into the field. Pushing against the ground, I attempt to rise, but I cannot. My knees are locked, and my lower limbs have no feeling in them. If Chaska were here, I would ask him to raise me to my feet, but Eagle Head is too feeble to lift a heavy woman like me, so I crawl out into the meadow. The sun has not yet set, but it is so low on the horizon that only the upper half of the disk is visible.

"Why were you gone so long?"

"Be quiet," he hisses. "The warriors did not take the fort. Some of the Indians are ugly. If you talk loud, they will kill you."

With difficulty, I maneuver myself into a sitting position and massage my knees. "I have no strength. I need food and water."

"I have nothing. Wait until we reach tepee."

"But I heard water. There must be a stream here."

"No. Now hurry and stand. We must go."

I press a hand to my forehead. Could I have imagined that sound? It was so real, yet I no longer hear it. The thought that it was a hallucination terrifies me.

Eagle Head makes an impatient sound, so I force myself back to a kneeling position and bring one knee forward to place my foot flat on the ground. My calves throb with the renewed sensation of blood pulsing through them. I press my palms against the forward knee to push myself up, dragging the other leg with me. As soon as I am erect, a wave of dizziness passes over me, and I sway back and forth. Eagle Head puts an arm around my back to hold me upright.

When the faintness passes, I ask, "How far to camp?"

Eagle Head frowns and makes a chopping motion with his forearm in the direction that the river flows. "Far. It will be night before we get there." I remember then that the Indians do not measure distances in miles—or time in hours.

"How is my boy? Is he with Mother Friend?"

"I do not know."

He does not look at me as he says that, and I grow convinced that Jimmy has been killed. The camp is not large; Eagle Head must know what happened to my son. He doesn't want to tell me the news because he is afraid I will make a fuss and draw the attention of hostile Indians. My eyes fill with tears, and an icy pain settles in my heart. What do I have to live for if both husband and son are dead?

My gaze falls upon Nellie, standing a couple of feet before me, sucking her thumb. I hold out my hand to her and tell her to walk by my side. For the first part of our trek at least, I will not be able to carry her.

The three of us inch our way across the field. My feet are still numb, so I keep stumbling because I cannot feel the ground beneath them.

Twilight deepens. At the edge of the meadow, just before we reach the trail to the top of the bluff, I find a rut that holds a few cups of water. I bend down and scoop it up, drinking several handfuls and offering some to my daughter. The water tastes of mud and decaying plants, but to me it is better than the finest wine.

By then, the sky is dark. Afraid of losing my baby, I lift Nellie and put her into the carrier on my back. For more than two hours, I walk in a daze, following Eagle Head. Never in my life have I been so tired and hungry, and as I stagger along, I silently plead, *Help me, help me, help me.* Either God hears my prayer or my body has reserves of strength I've never suspected because somehow I make a four-mile trek.

As we approach a cluster of tepees, I recognize that this isn't the place where I left my son. Instead, Eagle Head has brought me to a large encampment and leads me to the tepee of Chaska's mother. "Why are we here?" I demand. "I want my boy."

"Chaska said bring you here," Eagle Head answers gruffly. "Wait in tepee."

With my heart in my throat, I throw back the flap and duck through the entrance, only to find an empty tent. I rush back outside and run up to a woman who cooks dinner nearby. "Have you seen my son? A little boy with white hair."

The woman, a stranger to me, shakes her head wordlessly. Whirling around, I look for someone else to ask and spy Winona walking toward me.

The sight of her chills me, and I straighten to my full height. I will not let this bitter enemy see either my fatigue or my fear.

"You have returned," she says when she reaches me.

"Where is my boy? Do you know?"

"He is with Ina nearby. After breakfast, I went to my grandfather's house and carried the boy back here. He has been with us all day."

I blink. The nearest campfire is ten feet away, so the light isn't strong enough for me to read her expression. Yet I notice that her voice lacks its usual bitterness.

"And Chaska?" I ask. "Is he well?"

"Yes."

Then the voice that is dearer to me than all others cries out, "Mama!" I turn to see a small form with shining hair race across the camp and fling himself at me. Grasping me around the legs, my son sobs as though his heart would break.

My own chest feels as though it will explode with joy. Somehow, I drag him into the tepee—a difficult task since he refuses to let me go. Once inside the tent, I shrug my way out of the carrier, set Nellie on the ground, and kneel down to take Jimmy into my arms.

He cries and cries, but gradually, as I rub his back, his shuddering sobs abate. Between sniffles, he says, "Oh, Mama, I thought you was dead and I was left alone with the Indians." Tears well up in his eyes again, and he trembles.

"Shhh, it's all right. I'm here now," I murmur.

"I cried until I was sick. Oh, Mama, are you back for good? Put your arms around me and kiss me." When I comply, he embraces my neck and whispers into my ear. "I thought you and Nellie had gone up to heaven to be with Father and left your boy all alone."

Nellie, who has been watching us in silence, cries and tugs my sleeve. With a start of shame, I realize the poor thing is still wearing the soiled diaper she has had on the whole time we were hiding. Quickly, I kneel and change her, using a Sioux ointment made from bison grease and clay to soothe her chafed bottom.

Then, because my knees ache from their all-day ordeal, I arrange myself so I'm sitting on the ground with my legs out straight before me, both my children on my lap, and my arms encircling them. "You'll never guess where we spent our day," I say to Jimmy.

Ina enters the tepee, carrying a kettle, so I pause to greet her. "You are well?" she asks me.

"Now that I have my son with me, I am well."

Jimmy hugs my neck again.

"Your boy cried for you all day," Ina says, her back to me. "We could not quiet him. A half-breed named Roy took him to see an ox killed, but it did not help."

Jimmy exclaims, "I could not help it, Mama! They would not tell

147

me where you were. I thought you might be shot like the ox, and it made me cry harder."

Stroking his hair, I murmur, "Never mind. It's all right now." To Ina, I say in Dakota, "The boy and I have never been apart. I am sorry he caused trouble."

Ina turns to me in surprise. "He was no trouble. I felt sorry for him." She uncovers the kettle, ladles up bowls of thin stew, and hands them to me.

"Thank you. You are very kind to my children and me."

"Do not speak of it."

As soon as we have eaten, my children and I go to bed. Jimmy refuses to lie on the men's side of the tepee but rather sleeps on my pallet. Because of my sore legs, I have trouble getting comfortable, but whenever I stir, he whimpers and trembles in his sleep. Finally, I lie on my back with a child on each side, my arms wrapped around them. I remain awake a long time, staring at the stars through the smoke vent at the top of the tepee. *Are you in heaven, John?* I wonder. *Can you see your poor, miserable wife and children? Oh, how I miss you and wish we were all together again.*

CHAPTER

15

EARLY THE NEXT DAY, INA GATHERS THE HOUSEHOLD GOODS INTO A BUN-dle. *"De aŋpetu Peźutazi ekta uŋyapi,"* she tells me: "Today, we are going to Yellow Medicine."

My heart skips. If we go there, I might finally hear what happened to John. At the very least, I will see if my house still stands, and if it does, I might find clothes or other supplies to ease our captivity. Feeling both excitement and dread, I offer to help Ina prepare for the move. She tells me to fetch water and make coffee.

When I return to the tepee with a filled pail, I find Chaska talking to his mother. He wears a breechcloth and fringed leggings but no shirt. Although he is middle-aged, his lean form is strongly muscled, much more so than my husband's. John and I did not lead so active a life as the Indians do, nor did we ever lack for food. Already, living among the Sioux has changed me. After only five days, I have lost enough weight to make my clothes fit more loosely.

Chaska breaks off his conversation and says to me in English, "We change plans. We stay here three more days. Then we go to Yellow Medicine."

"O.K." Stung by disappointment, I turn away and fill the coffeepot.

As I measure out coffee grounds and Ina prepares porridge from the flour of dried prairie turnips, a man calls for Chaska to come outside. Fear flares within me, and I stare after him as he goes out the tepee door.

Once I place the pot on the fire, I wake my children. Jimmy starts when I shake him. He throws his arms around my neck. "Mama, I am so glad to see you this morning! I was afraid you and Nellie would be gone again."

"We're both here. Now get up and wash your face and hands."

I pour water into a basin, hand him the piece of soap Ina gave me, and turn to rouse Nellie. After changing her diaper, I wash her face and untangle her hair with my wooden comb. As I return it to my satchel, the flap to the tepee door flings back violently. Chaska enters scowling and exclaims in English, "I wish I could kill all the Indians!"

"Why? What do you mean?" I exclaim.

He ignores me and, stepping next to where Ina stirs the porridge, speaks to her quietly. She nods, removes the kettle and coffeepot from the fire, and leaves.

"Chaska, what is wrong?" I demand.

Rubbing the side of his jaw, he gazes at me and presses his lips into a thin line. "A man in a nearby tepee is drunk. He waves his gun and says he will shoot all white women. I spoke calmly to him, but he grew more angry. He said I had become white and he would shoot me too."

I reach out to touch his forearm. The gesture is inappropriate, but I cannot resist the tide of emotion flooding me. "We bring trouble to you. I am sorry."

He brushes my hand away. "I will not let him kill you." Then he walks to his side of the tepee and picks up his rifle, which is rolled in cloth and tied with rawhide to keep it out of the hands of my children.

As he unwraps the weapon, we hear the report of a gun and a woman's shriek outside. Chaska calls to his mother, and Ina pokes her head through the opening. *"Akicita wašicuŋ wiŋyaŋ o,"* she reports: "A warrior has shot a white woman."

Chaska barks a command and nods toward the outdoors. The old woman withdraws and closes the flap. Presumably, he has told her to keep watch.

As soon as she is gone, I ask, "Should we run away?"

He shakes his head. "We cannot go outside. He looks for white women."

Tossing away the rifle covering, he gestures toward a spot between the door and the fire. "Sit here with your children behind you. I will sit in front with my gun. If the bad man comes, he will have to shoot through me to hurt you."

I settle my children and take my place. Chaska sits cross-legged before me with his rifle held so he can aim it quickly. The words he uttered when he entered the tepee come back to me, and I lean forward to ask, "Why did you say you want to kill all the Indians? You are an Indian."

Chaska does not take his eyes off the door but turns his head slightly so I can see his profile. "I walk in both worlds. I went to English school, and I listen to your holy men. They say the Great Spirit made all men and we are brothers."

"I believe this."

"I know it. But many whites do not. And some of my people. Too many of our young men want this war. They want to drive you back toward the rising sun."

He pauses, and his shoulder muscles tense beneath his bronze skin. Turning his head to stare straight ahead, he says, "Your medicine is better than ours, and you are skilled at growing food. I want us to live in peace. I want my people to learn your ways, so our children do not go hungry or sicken and die."

Like his son, I think sadly. I want to convey that I do not look down on Chaska as other whites do, so I ask, "And what would you like whites to learn from your people?"

"Do not take more than you need," he answers instantly. "Keep your word."

We agree on this, I think and murmur a well-known verse from the Bible: "As ye would that men should do to you, do ye also to them likewise."

Chaska grunts, which I interpret as a sarcastic commentary on the failure of whites to live by their own religion. Chastened, I sit back and wonder why people are so greedy and cruel. Should not their faith make them better? As I know all too well, too often the most religious people are also arrogant and judgmental.

After a few minutes, Jimmy says, "Mama, I am hungry. When can we eat?"

"Feed your children," Chaska says.

I find two bison-horn bowls and scoop up some of the now-cool porridge. After handing a dish and a spoon to Jimmy, I return to my place, set Nellie on my lap, and feed her. If I let her do it herself, she will end up with porridge in her hair.

Chaska glances over his shoulder. "You do not eat?"

"No. I am not hungry." No need to tell him that fear has stolen my appetite.

He grunts again.

Nellie dislikes the porridge and clenches her teeth so I cannot put the spoon in her mouth. Sighing, I set the bowl aside and open my blouse to nurse her. From the corner of my eye, I see Jimmy grab her portion. The hunger we have suffered this last week has taught him not to pass up any chance to eat.

When Nellie finishes feeding, she falls asleep on my lap. About an hour passes before Ina reenters the tepee smiling. She speaks to Chaska quietly, and he lays aside his gun. "My mother says Indians brought many mules from the fort. The bad man forgot his anger. He put down his gun and went to claim one of the animals."

"Do you know what happened to the woman he shot?"

He questions his mother and then tells me, "The man shot her through the legs. She lives."

The relief that washes over me leaves me dazed and weak. Pushing myself up from the ground, I add a few sticks to the cook fire and set the kettle and coffeepot back on it to heat our long-delayed breakfast.

After we eat, Chaska goes out to learn more about the events of the morning. Before leaving, he tells me, "Stay in tepee. Do not go out unless you have to."

Staring directly into his eyes, I nod my assent.

Chaska picks up his rifle and exits but leaves the tepee flap open. That action reassures me. Surely, he would close it if he were worried about a renewed attack. When Jimmy asks if he can go outside to play, I grant him permission as long as he stays where I can see him through the opening.

Ina sits down beside me and takes out the knife sheaf she was quilling a few days earlier. "Can I help you?" I ask in Dakota. "What chores can I do?"

She considers for a moment before saying, "I have cloth. Do you want to make your daughter a dress?"

"Yes, thank you."

Setting down her project, she goes to look in her stores and comes back with a small piece of yellow calico with tiny red flowers, large enough to make a knee-length shift for Nellie. Laying out the fabric on the floor, I try to think of the best way to sew without a pattern. After a moment, I find the dress Nellie was wearing when we were captured to serve as a guide. I fold the calico fabric in half with the printed side facing inward so I can cut two identical pieces simultaneously. Then I pull a scorched twig from the fire and use the burnt end to trace the outline of a simple shift on the wrong side of the material.

My anxieties ease, and I find myself humming as I use Ina's scissors to cut out the pieces. Jimmy stands just outside the doorway where he throws sticks to Buster. Nellie sits on the floor of the tepee playing silently with a cornhusk doll Ina made her. Holding the cloth next to my child, I squint to imagine her garbed in it. With her dark hair and dusky skin, she will look pretty in this bright outfit.

Ina works alongside me. Often when I glance up from my stitching, I catch her watching me with a hint of a smile. After some time, the old woman strokes Nellie's cheek and rises. Ina goes over to the place where she got the fabric and returns with a length of red ribbon and five cowrie shells drilled with fine holes that I can use to ornament the little dress.

A lump fills my throat. "Thank you for your generosity."

She shrugs and resumes her quillwork. "Do not speak of it. These are old things I have no use for."

After deciding to sew the shells to the dress in a curve that parallels the neckline, I baste them in place to see how they will look. As I knot the thread securing the last one, something blocks the light coming through the open doorway. I tense with fear that one of my enemies has found me. Instead, two white women duck down to peer through the *tiyopa,* or tepee opening. "There she is," one says, and they enter without asking permission.

One of them is in her twenties, slender with light brown hair and an arm in a filthy sling. She would be pretty under normal conditions, but today her eyes are red-rimmed. The other woman is in her forties and stouter, although not as large as me. Each of them wears a cotton dress that is torn and stained with dirt and blood.

The two stand hunched over because of the tepee's slanting walls and stare at me with matching expressions of incredulity. "We heard there was a white woman at this end of the camp," the older woman says.

Ina sets aside her handiwork and welcomes them in Dakota. Seeing the blank looks on the visitors' faces, I translate.

When the younger woman realizes I understand the Indians' language, she glances at the older woman with raised eyebrows. After a moment's hesitation, they sit down near the *tiyopa.*

"You certainly have made yourself at home here," the young woman says. "When Martha told me she'd heard one of the doctor's wives was here, I said no, I'd seen only squaws in this part of the camp. My goodness, I doubt your own husband would recognize you."

A hot blush rises upon my cheeks. "My protectors told me I would be safer if I dressed this way."

"Your protectors!" Martha exclaims. "Your captors, don't you mean?"

"No, I do not. Chaska saved me from certain death at the hands of a drunken man. He and his mother have hidden me from danger several times."

The two women exchange glances, and Martha says, "No doubt, they are keeping you alive for nefarious purposes of their own."

Their stony faces make it obvious that they have little interest in anything I have to say about my situation, so I refrain from commenting. The younger woman says, "We came to ask you to accompany us as we walk through the camp looking for other white captives. There's safety in numbers."

I shake my head, wondering that they feel safe enough to wander about. Don't they know what's been happening? "I can't. Chaska told me to stay inside."

"My, my," Martha murmurs. She glances from sleeping pallet to sleeping pallet as though counting them. "You seem very eager to do this Chaska's bidding."

Her implication infuriates me, but I refuse to acknowledge it. Instead, I say, "Surely, you know what happened earlier! Chaska is trying to protect me from the hostile Indians in camp. It is safer in the tepee. I have my children to look after."

The young woman picks up the little dress I'm sewing and fingers the cowrie shells. "I see that you are dressing your daughter like a savage too. Is that your idea of looking after her?"

"My one and only idea is to keep her alive," I answer hotly. "I will do whatever I must to accomplish that. Any mother would do the same."

The young woman turns pale, stumbles to her feet, and rushes from the tepee. Martha glares at me. "The day she was taken prisoner, Jane saw the Indians bash her baby's head against a tree. If you had sought out your fellow prisoners to see how they fared instead of consorting with savages, you would have known that."

A wave of nausea passes over me. "That's dreadful. Please tell her how sorry I am for her loss."

My words of condolence do not soften Martha's flinty expression. "You seem to have cajoled these heathens into treating you well."

"This family does, but I have also been in great peril. I have had to hide in haystacks and ravines to escape drunken brutes who threatened my life."

"What a dramatic tale! You are not the only one in danger, you know," Martha retorts, gathering her skirts in her hand so she can get to her feet.

"I never said I am," I reply, but she is already out the door.

As soon as we are alone, Ina asks, "What is wrong?"

"They are angry," I answer, too demoralized to hide the truth. "They say I am too friendly to Indians."

Ina grunts. "They sound like those who talk about Chaska. Some of our people are angry that he took you into our tepee."

I nod but do not look at her. Instead I gaze down at my hands. Are my two visitors correct? Am I betraying my race, and somehow betraying John, by trying to get along with the Sioux? Surely, if my husband is alive, all he cares about is our survival. John will know that I haven't become a *squaw* just by adopting Indian dress; in my heart, I am as white as Martha or Jane.

Raising my chin, I gaze at my surroundings. Although the Sioux way of life is more primitive than the one I am used to, living this way should not corrupt me as long as I maintain my womanly honor. Surely, it cannot be wrong for our two races to befriend each other. If more people did so, this war might never have started.

Yet as logical as my opinions appear to me, few other whites share them. Once again, I am an outsider. Why am I so out of step with everyone I know?

As I return to my sewing, I remember attending First Day meetings with my Quaker grandmother long, long ago. The way the Friends sat quietly to listen for God's guidance seemed strange and mysterious to me. My grandmother tried to explain about the inward light, that part of God within everyone, but I was too young to locate the evidence of such a divine spark within myself. Now, I wonder if I have finally found it, because no matter what the other captives think, I know that I can do only as my conscience directs.

The rest of the day passes quietly. Chaska returns in the late afternoon, but he is in a pensive mood and sits outside the tepee. We do not speak again except for the polite phrases necessitated by eating together.

I feel so depressed when I lie down on my pallet that night that I cry tears of self-pity until I sink into sleep.

Hours later, the loud shout of *"Waŝicuŋ wiŋyaŋ! Wiŋyaŋ waciŋ!"* awakens me.

Now what? I think as I push myself to a sitting position. The tepee is lit only by the glowing embers left from the day's fire, but I see a hulking figure inside the *tiyopa*. As my eyes adjust, I recognize Hapa. He reeks of whiskey, and he sways as he bellows, *"Wiŋyaŋ waciŋ!"*

My blood runs cold as I translate his words: "I want a woman!" Hapa steps toward me and draws a knife. In English, he says, "You must be my wife or die."

Terrified, I shriek, "Chaska! Help!"

Ina sits up and puts a hand on my arm. "Be quiet," she says in a low voice. "Do not provoke him. My son will not let him hurt you."

As she speaks, Chaska rises to his feet. "*Taĥaŋ,* do not do this. You have a wife. Go back to my sister's tepee."

"No. I want this woman."

Chaska grabs his brother-in-law's arm. "You are a bad man. Your wife, my sister, lies in the next tepee. I have no wife, and I don't talk bad to the white woman."

Growling, Hapa breaks free of Chaska. He steps closer and waves his large knife in front of my face. The fear that holds me captive gives way to sudden rage, and I shout, "Kill me then! I will not lie with you. I would rather die."

"Stop talking!" Chaska yells at me. He grabs Hapa's arms from behind and pulls him back. When he has his brother-in-law at a safe distance from me, Chaska moves around to face him. Pointing at the men's side of the tepee, he says, "You lie down. I have no wife. I will take the white woman."

Hapa pulls his gaze away from me and stares at Chaska in befuddlement. After an instant, he nods and says, "That is right. You take her, and I will not kill her."

Laying a hand on his brother-in-law's arm, Chaska steers him toward the pallet. "Yes, as soon as I know her husband is dead, I will marry her."

"No!" roars Hapa, waving his knife again. "Take her now, or I will kill her."

Frantic, I grasp Ina's hand. "What should I do?"

"Do not be afraid," she whispers. "My son is a good man. He will not hurt you."

At the same time, Chaska says, "Yes. Lie down. I go to her now."

Hapa rubs his face with his left hand and drops heavily onto the ground next to Chaska's pallet. My heart clutches when I see how near he is to my son. Then Chaska starts toward me.

As soon as he reaches our side of the fire, he says quietly, "You must let me lie down beside you, or he will kill you. He is drunk. I cannot talk to him."

Scooting back a little way, I murmur, "No."

Chaska squats before me. "My wife is in the spirit world and can see what I do. I will not harm you."

I glance at Ina, who nods, so even though I am trembling with fear, I move to the edge of my pallet. Chaska lies down between his mother and me. Curling on my side, I face away from him. Nellie murmurs, "Mama," and snuggles closer to me. *Dear God,* I pray, *do not let her realize what is happening.*

After several minutes, loud snores rise from the opposite side of the tepee. I feel Chaska shift closer behind me, and I freeze with dread. He murmurs, his mouth next to my ear. "Do not fear. I have sworn an oath to return you to your husband the same way you were when I took you. I had a wife. I know how a husband feels."

He is so near I can smell his sweat and the grease in his hair. The sensation of having a masculine body next to mine evokes disturbing images, and I force myself to remember John to keep from having improper thoughts.

Then I recall the two women who visited this afternoon and wonder what they would say if they could see me now. Would they pity me because of the danger I just escaped, or would they blame me for allowing this pretense of a marriage? But I know the answer to that. They would say the only honorable thing I could have done was to let Hapa kill me.

Tears ooze from my eyes, and I whisper to Chaska. "Every day, someone threatens me. Why do your people hate me so much?"

Chaska replies, "Little Crow speaks against you. You are his only prisoner from Yellow Medicine. He wants you to suffer for the things Galbraith has done."

"But I do not like Galbraith either."

"Do not fear. Little Crow may be angry, but you have friends here. We will keep you safe as long as we can."

"And how long will that be? When will the war end?"

"I do not know. The fighting does not go well. But Indians have killed too many whites to stop."

"How many?" I ask, expecting him to say twenty, maybe fifty.

He hesitates before saying, "Hundreds."

I gasp. The land must be swept clean of white settlers, I think, and wonder how long I will remain a prisoner.

Hapa's snoring grows even louder. "He is asleep," Chaska says after a few more minutes. "I will go back to my pallet."

"Wait!" I roll onto my other side to face him. "Thank you. You are a good man."

For a moment, we remain motionless, our bodies turned toward each other, our faces just a few inches apart. I can hear his breathing, as I know he hears mine. *This was a mistake,* I think. *What if he assumes that I want him to kiss me?*

Then Chaska says, "Sleep now," and crawls away.

CHAPTER
16

LATER IN THE NIGHT, A STRONG GALE KICKS UP OUTSIDE. THE MOANING and sighing of the wind sounds like the wailing of tormented souls: murder victims wandering the earth, unable to find peace. *Is John among them?* I wonder and then chastise myself. Until I learn otherwise, I must cling to the hope that he lives.

I long for sleep, but my nerves are overwrought. My fevered brain replays the confrontation with Hapa, and the memory is more terrible than the actual event. My mind snags upon the most horrifying details—Hapa's threatening posture, the gleam of the knife, the rage in his voice—and cannot shake free of them.

Shuddering over my near escape, I try to banish the unpleasant images by reminding myself of the way Chaska saved me, but that line of thought also has pitfalls. Even without indulging in amorous congress, sharing one's bed with a man produces feelings of intimacy. My cheeks grow hot as I remember how conscious I was of Chaska's breathing and how, as we lay on the same pallet, I could not resist envisioning the muscular form I had noticed earlier in the day. Ashamed, I caution myself not to weaken the guard I must keep upon my honor.

Uneasily, I wonder where this "sham marriage" will lead. If I remain with the tribe very long, how can I avoid becoming Chaska's wife in truth—especially if my husband has been killed? And if John is dead, what reason do I have to return to the white society that scorned me before my marriage? I don't even know if any white settlements still exist. If Chaska is right about the death toll, the southern part of the state must be depopulated. I could do worse than to stay with these kind people. Chaska is a good man. Together he and I could work to build a bridge between whites and Indians to prevent future hostilities.

But as soon as I imagine us living together as man and wife, shame washes over me. *Stop it! You feel beholden because you owe Chaska your life. That's all. No matter what he does for you, he is an Indian, and you must not love him.*

Even to contemplate such a thing is to trespass on forbidden territory. Few white women marry outside their race, and those who do lose their status as respectable women. I have worked too hard to overcome my mother's slander to make such a misstep now. While I might admit in my innermost heart that Chaska could make an admirable husband, he isn't for me.

Biting my lip, I glance at my sleeping daughter and thank God that I have not betrayed my wicked thoughts to anyone. I roll on my back, gaze through the smoke vent at the stars, and silently recite the Lord's Prayer. Gradually, the twinkling orbs fade, and the sky fades from deepest indigo to slate grey.

As morning dawns, the winds grow fiercer. The canvas walls vibrate, and the tent poles begin to "walk." I sit up, fearing that the tepee is about to collapse. Sure enough, just as I decide to wake Ina, the dwelling lifts from its mooring. The bottom skims over our heads and then the structure collapses a short way away.

My son jerks up with a cry. "Mama, where are you?"

"Right here," I call. Then I see that the wind is billowing out the fallen tepee cloth and pushing it along the ground away from us, so I run to grab it.

Chaska comes to help by pulling out the lodge poles that are tangled in the canvas. As we work together to fold the tent cloth, I push down the unwelcome thought, *You make good partners.*

Hapa sits up and groans. He grabs his head with both hands and staggers away down the path—in search of whiskey to ease his headache, I suspect.

Trying to erect the tepee in this storm would be futile, so we store our household goods in the wagon and sit under it wrapped in blankets. Nellie sleeps on the ground to one side of me, while Jimmy sits on the other side between Ina and me. Buster lies at my feet. Chaska stands by the wagon as though on watch. Winona and Hapa's tepee still stands, but no one suggests seeking shelter there.

When it is fully light, Ina departs for the woods to cook breakfast within the windbreak of the trees. I offer to help, but she tells me to stay with my children.

Once she leaves, I blush at the thought that we must look like a man guarding his wife and children. Chaska clears his throat as if he too is self-conscious. He says, "I must check my sister's tepee to make sure it does not fall."

Leaving the wagon, he finds a rock and uses it to pound the stakes of the tepee more securely into the ground. After a minute, Winona exits the *tiyopa* to see what he is doing. "Ina's tepee fell again?" she asks.

"Yes."

"The white woman does not know how to put it up properly."

Still squatting by the tepee stakes, Chaska shoots her a look of reproof. "Teach her to do it better."

Winona folds her arms across her chest in the gesture of resentment I have come to know well. "I will not help her. I do not want her here."

"Whether she stays or goes is not your decision, my sister."

She tosses her head. "That woman causes trouble in my tepee."

Her words sting like a slap across the face. Even though I do not blame myself for Hapa's behavior, I now understand why Winona hates me so much. I would be angry too if I saw John lusting openly after another woman.

Chaska stands. "Your husband drinks too much and has bad thoughts. The white woman does not make him do such things. A man should control himself."

"And a man should look after his own people before helping the enemy," she retorts before ducking back into her tepee.

Scowling, Chaska comes over to the wagon and reaches into it for his rifle and the deerskin bag that holds his powder and bullets. "When my mother returns, tell her I go hunting," he says and then walks through the encampment in the direction of the forest.

When we are alone, Jimmy crawls onto my lap and leans against my bosom—an old comfort-seeking behavior that he stopped doing months ago. "Mama, when are we going to go home?"

"I don't know. Not until the war is over, I guess."

He plays with the end of the ribbon tied around my braids. "Do you think Father is at our house?"

"I don't know. I don't know if he is there or at the fort or—" I halt. Even though I confided my fear that John is dead to Jimmy days ago, he doesn't seem to comprehend what that means. I remember when my father died, I kept hoping he would walk in the front door as though returning from a journey. It was months before my childish mind could accept that death is irreversible, and I was two years older then than Jimmy is now. Why should I force my boy to that unhappy conclusion when we still don't know for certain that John is gone? "Or if he is searching for us," I conclude instead.

"Maybe we could leave clues for him to find." Excitement fills Jimmy's voice. "You could write notes to say where we are, and I could run around leaving them where Father might find them."

"We can't do that," I answer, regretting that I must squelch his enthusiasm. "If the Indians found out, they would be angry. They might hurt me."

Jimmy throws his arms around my neck. "Oh, Mama, why can't we go home? I know we could find our way."

"You know the Indians won't let us." I take hold of his shoulders and move him back so I can stare into his face. "Listen to me. I don't want you to think of ways to escape. Your job is to be a good boy and help me look after your sister."

"But, Mama—"

"No, I want you to promise me that you will not make any plans for how to escape or go back home. Promise?"

His sigh of disgust sounds so much like his father that my heart aches. "All right, Mama. I promise."

When Ina returns with a kettle of gruel, she tells me that she saw Chaska on his way to the woods. Another warrior accompanied him.

We eat under the shelter of the wagon. The windstorm lasts for hours, and time passes slowly as we wait for the weather to change. I tell my children stories until the gale finally ceases.

As Ina and I put up our tepee, a gaggle of little boys come ask Jimmy to play. I expect my son to shy away from them, but he asks, "Can I, Mama? Please?"

Pressing my lips together, I glance at Ina. She murmurs something about it being good for boys to be together, so I swallow my fears and agree. "Don't go far," I warn him. "Come back in time for supper."

My gaze lingers after him as he runs off with his new friends, and I am relieved to see that they intend to play in the open space within the circle of tepees. I go back to tying anchor stones into the hem of the tent cloth. Mindful of Winona's criticism this morning, I vow to be more careful pounding in the stakes.

The afternoon has turned pleasant after the ferocity of the windstorm. Even after the tepee is standing, Ina and I remain out of doors. Sitting down next to her, I say in my most formal Dakota, "I wish to ask for your help."

"Yes, my daughter, what is it?" she responds, and my spirits lift at hearing her grant me the familial title.

"I want to learn how to sew a pair of moccasins. I want to give them to your son to thank him for protecting us."

Ina puts down her quilling and gives me such a penetrating stare that I wonder if my suggestion violates some taboo. Or worse yet, have I signaled that I have inappropriate feelings for Chaska? I press my lips together and wish I had not spoken.

Finally, she nods. "I will teach you." She disappears into the tepee and comes back with rawhide. Together we cut out the pieces and then she asks, "Do you want to sew beads on the tops?"

I look up in surprise. Because Ina is using quills on the sheath, I assumed those are the only decorative items she has, and I was resigned to making plain moccasins because I don't know how to quill. But if she has beads...

"May I?" I ask.

Ina nods again and pulls several folded paper packets from the buckskin bag that holds her sewing supplies. She lays them in a row on the ground, and when we open them, I find seed beads in a variety of hues. The glimmer of sunlight on the tiny glass ornaments gives me a rush of pleasure. I finger them, considering the colors.

"What picture will you make?" Ina asks.

Frilly designs like flowers seem inappropriate for as serious a person as Chaska. As I roll a sky blue bead between my fingers, a simple geometric design forms in my imagination. "A stripe," I say in English, frustrated that I do not know the Dakota word. I use a stick to draw an outline of a moccasin in the dirt, sketch a band down the center of the vamp, and divide it into horizontal stripes. Ina nods. "I will use black and green and blue and white," I explain, pointing at each stripe as I name its color. "For land and water and sky."

Ina gives me a look of surprise mingled with respect. "It is good."

Happily, I thread my needle and settle in to stitch the beading. Before long, I find myself wishing for my thimble. The rawhide is much tougher than fabric, and the skin of my index finger grows rough from pushing the needle through it. Even so, I enjoy myself. Some people find beading monotonous, but this type of repetitive work always calms my spirit.

As I reach the end of the first row, I notice movement next door and see Winona emerging from her tepee. Draped across her arms are two of the best dresses from my trunk. She calls to a neighbor, who comes over to join her.

Dropping one of my dresses in the dirt, Winona holds up the other one and the two women laugh at how large it is. Winona does not look my way, but she speaks loudly enough for me to hear. "I am going to cut this and make coats for my sons. There is enough cloth here for a tepee. I can give some to you."

Tearing my gaze away from the humiliating scene, I see Ina watching me. She gives a tiny shake of her head, and I smile to let her know I am not going to respond.

Winona and her friend continue to laugh for some time, but I remind myself that her rudeness is an expression of jealousy, not a response to anything I've done. If I were married to Hapa, I would be bitterly unhappy too. Turning to Ina, I ask about life when she was a girl, and for the next hour, she tells stories as I bead.

I sit facing the forest, and toward the end of the afternoon, a man emerges from the trees, carrying a bundle wrapped in what looks like a deerskin. "Chaska returns," I say and gather up my work to put it away so he won't know about the moccasins until they are finished.

By the time I emerge from the tepee, Chaska has arrived and unwrapped his bundle to display a large quantity of venison, already butchered into roasts, ribs, shanks, and loins. Listening to him talk to Ina, I learn that he and his companion divided the deer and Chaska was allowed to keep the hide because he made the kill. As he speaks, he sets aside a sizable chunk of meat and nods brusquely toward his sister's tepee. Ina puts the piece into a cook pot and carries it next door.

Chaska takes another roast, wraps it in rawhide, and puts it in the tepee. "Tomorrow I will take this to Eagle Head. The old ones do not get much meat."

I gaze at the remainder of the venison spread out before us. "There is still so much left."

Ina returns in time to hear my words. "Tonight we will cook a feast and share with anyone who passes by. But we will not cook all the meat. Tomorrow we will dry some of it into jerky. Then I will teach you how to make *wasna.*"

She hands me a knife and tells me to cut the fat from the venison and set it aside. While I comply, she builds up her cook fire and constructs two frames on either side of it. When everything is ready, we push sharpened green stakes through several pieces of meat and set them over the fire to roast.

Before long, the smell of sizzling venison fills the camp, as potent an invitation to a party as ever existed. People come by, ostensibly to congratulate Chaska on his luck in the hunt, but really to share in the bounty. The chunks of meat take varying amounts of time to cook, so for a couple of hours, Ina and I are kept busy turning spits, removing roasts as they are done, and cutting meat into small servings. Some women bring bread, while others bring vegetable stew or a kind of pudding that contains dried berries. As darkness falls, laughter and conversation fill the camp. For the first time in a week, I do not feel afraid.

When I wake early Sunday morning, the tepee is empty. After eating a piece of bread, I go outside to find my children playing with the dog, which is tied to a tree to keep him away from the meat. After greeting me, Ina says that Chaska has ridden away to take food to the old ones. On the rawhide before her lies the remaining venison. She picks up one chunk at a time and uses a sharp knife to shave each one into extremely thin slices.

Ina has already removed the roasting frames we used last night. "Start a fire," she tells me. "We need embers to dry the meat."

I pile tinder in the center of the fire pit and lay kindling over it in a square, log-cabin structure. Once the fire is going strong, I add larger logs so it will burn a long time. Then I join Ina in cutting slices of venison.

By the time all the meat is sliced, we have a thick bed of coals. We lay a triangle of three sturdy poles across the flat stones that outline our fire pit. Ina and I drape the slices of meat on sticks and set them horizontally across the triangle of poles so the meat hangs down over the embers. Once we have finished, I ask, "When will the meat be dry?"

Ina shrugs. "Maybe when the sun is halfway to the horizon."

Because we have to maintain the fire, we bring our needlework outside. Two of Ina's friends stop by our camp, and she sets her quilling aside to smoke a pipe with them. They offer it to me, and after taking a puff, I thank them and pick up my beading again. As I finish the black stripe and move on to the green, I remember that this is Sunday and start humming hymns.

Intent on my work, I pay little attention to the sound of approaching footsteps until a familiar voice says, "I see what you mean. I would not have recognized her either."

I look up to see Martha, the woman I met a few days ago, and Jannette De Camp, one of my former neighbors from Shakopee. Mrs. De Camp is a plain-faced, sturdy woman with a discontented personality. Her husband, Joseph, was awarded the job of running the mill at Redwood about the same time John became the Upper Agency physician. They have three children and, from the looks of Jannette's figure, a fourth is on its way. "Mrs. De Camp, I am sorry to see you in this place. Are your children with you?"

"Yes, Mrs. Wakefield." She looks around pointedly, and I rise to fetch a rug from the tepee for my visitors to sit upon. When I come back outside, I find Mrs. De Camp examining the piece of rawhide I've been beading.

With a curl of her lip, she drops it to the ground. As the two women sit on the rug, Jannette says, "Are you making moccasins for your husband?"

My face flushes. I try to hide that reaction by bending down to pick up the beaded rawhide and dusting it off. "No. I think John must be dead."

Martha demands, "Is that why you have taken an Indian husband? We heard that you married this Chaska you are living with." She says the name *Chas-kuh* instead of the Dakota pronunciation *Chas-kay*.

I glance toward Ina and her friends, who have fallen silent, causing me to suspect that some of the women understand English and want to hear how I answer. If I deny that Chaska and I are married, word will get back to Hapa and he will be enraged at our deceit. Yet, how can I allow these white women to believe that I have done such a thing?

Martha and Jannette stare at me accusingly as my silence lengthens. Finally, I say, "I am trying to make myself useful so the Sioux will stop threatening my life. That's why I do things like cook and fetch water."

"They allow you to go to the river by yourself?" Martha demands, her voice rising.

"Yes," I reply, surprised at her apparent anger. "I have freedom to move about the camp as long as Chaska senses no special danger."

"Then for God's sake, why don't you wade across and escape?"

"Without my children? How could I do such a thing?"

Martha sputters as though about to argue, but Jannette interrupts. "You have plenty of food." She jerks her chin at the drying venison. "I thought these people were supposed to be starving. They keep telling me they have nothing to eat."

I sigh in exasperation at their determination to find fault with everything and at their foolishness in criticizing the Indians within earshot. "Chaska went hunting yesterday. Now, Ina and I are drying the leftover venison so we can make *wasna.*"

Both women give me a blank look, so I say, "Oh, you must know what I mean. Some people call it pemmican. It's made of dried meat powder and rendered fat."

To my astonishment, Martha scowls and struggles to her feet. Glaring at me, she says in a voice quivering with rage, "Of course, I know what pemmican is. The savages carry it with them when they go on the warpath. How can you assist them in their bloody deeds? Is that your idea of being *useful?*"

"I'm not preparing the men for battle. Ina and I are simply preserving food so it doesn't go to waste. It's no different than you or I," I gesture between us, "putting up garden produce for the winter."

"Yes, it is," Martha retorts. "When I put up a jar of pickles, those are for my family, not the bloodthirsty devils who massacred my neighbors."

She reaches out to help Jannette rise.

"For the love of God, come to your senses, Sarah," Jannette says quietly. "Remember that you are a white woman, not a heathen like these people. Stop debasing yourself."

Before I can think of a suitable reply, the two women hurry off as though they fear my company will contaminate them.

CHAPTER

17

NOT LONG AFTER MARTHA AND JANNETTE STALK AWAY, INA DECIDES THE jerky is dry. Earlier in the afternoon, she tried to snap off a small piece, but the meat bent rather than tore, and sinews were visible in the fold. *"Sica!"* she had exclaimed, meaning "bad." Now, when she performs the same test, the meat breaks apart easily.

I spend the evening using a stone to pound the jerky into a fine powder and then grind the last of Ina's dried berries. While I work, Ina renders out the fat I set aside yesterday, strains it, allows it to cool, and renders it again. Shortly before bedtime, we combine the three ingredients until the powder is moist enough to hold together. We form the *wasna* into balls and store them in a hide bag.

By the time I go to bed, my upper back and arms ache from the hours of grinding. My "mattress" is little more than two strips of carpeting, and usually I take a while to fall asleep on the hard surface, but within moments, I feel myself slipping into exhausted slumber. Before I completely drop off, however, Chaska enters the tepee with two men I have never seen before. Both wear traditional Sioux dress, but one has short hair, a sign that he is probably a Christianized Indian. I sit up.

Chaska says, "You must take your children and come with me."

"Why? What is happening?"

"Sometime I will tell you. Now we must go."

My stomach twists with fear. *It must be bad,* I think and reach for my leggings and moccasins.

Moving to the men's side of the tepee, Chaska squats down and tells my son to climb on his back.

"Mama?" Jimmy asks, his voice high with fear.

"Do as he says." Even though Chaska will not say what the trouble is, I trust him. To ease my boy's anxiety, I ask, "Won't it be fun to ride piggyback?"

As soon as I've put on my legwear, I stoop to pick up my daughter, my satchel, and a blanket. Then I nod to indicate my readiness. The two strangers duck through the *tiyopa,* and Chaska and I follow them out into a drizzling rain. The night is very black with no moon.

I put the blanket over my head as a shawl. When we set off toward the forest, the two strangers move to flank Chaska and me as if guarding us from danger. Or perhaps they are under orders to deliver me to the chiefs as a prisoner.

Don't even think that, I tell myself as we set off. *If you cannot trust Chaska after all that he has done, who in the wide world can you trust?*

On we walk, leaving the encampment far behind. In the dark, I stumble over roots and humps in the ground. I cannot tell whether I have passed this way before. Images of the white woman I saw being led to her death haunt me, making me suspicious of our silent escort. Even though I believe Chaska is truthful and honorable, how do I know he is not being forced to surrender me against his will?

Stepping closer to Chaska, I whisper, "Where are we going?"

"Keep still!" he answers.

His refusal to explain unnerves me. The farther we walk, the more convinced I become that our taciturn guards are leading me—and perhaps Chaska too—toward death. Once more I question him, but again he replies, "Keep still."

After that rebuff, I give up and try to prepare myself for whatever may come. Tears run down my face as I silently recite Psalm 23.

Finally, after we walk for more than an hour, I see the glowing embers of fires, and a few minutes later, we enter a small encampment. Our two guards fall behind us as Chaska leads me to a tepee. He halts at the *tiyopa* and calls, *Tuŋwiŋ,* which means aunt. Only after a female voice invites us in, does he move to enter the tent, beckoning for me to follow.

The tepee has only one occupant, an old woman. Her hair is faded to dull pewter rather than being visibly streaked with grey. She has the same small eyes as Chaska, a broad nose, and an unusually wide mouth. The skin of her face is deeply crinkled. Chaska sets Jimmy upon the ground, waves in my direction, and tells the woman in Dakota that I am the wife of the doctor at Yellow Medicine.

The old woman nods and gestures for me to sit.

Glancing back at me, Chaska explains in English, "This is my father's sister. I am going to leave you here. But first, I must explain to her."

He squats before the old woman and whispers to her in Dakota so softly that I cannot make out what he says. She keeps looking from his face to mine, and the more she hears, the sadder her expression becomes. I grow uneasy.

Abruptly, Chaska hands the woman a small hide bag and stands. "I will come for you in the morning," he says to me and leaves without any other explanation. I don't even know if the old woman speaks English.

As Chaska's aunt gathers robes and blankets to make us a bed, I thank her in Dakota for giving us shelter. She halts next to me and smiles at Nellie, who still rides in the sling on my back. The old woman says hesitantly, "You are welcome."

"You speak English!"

Chaska's aunt shrugs. "A little."

When she has finished making the pallet, she says, "You sleep now." She turns away so I can retire in privacy.

The bag Chaska left with his aunt contains *wasna,* so that is what we eat in the morning. Judging from the sparse furnishings of the tepee, I'm not sure Tuŋwiŋ has any other provisions. Nellie doesn't like the *wasna,* but I convince her to eat a few bites. Then, as I nurse my daughter, I ask Tuŋwiŋ if her husband is away with the warriors. She shakes her head. "My husband died many winters ago."

After our meal, I go outside to sew. I have been storing the makings of Chaska's moccasins in my satchel, so at least I can work on them while I wait for him to return for us. As I settle to my beadwork, Tuŋwiŋ joins me with sewing of her own. Throughout the morning, many women stop by the tepee to ask who I am and why I am here. When Tuŋwiŋ mentions my husband, most of them nod in recognition.

About midday, as I sit in the sunshine with my children playing nearby, I hear the commotion of riders returning to camp. "Scouts," Tuŋwiŋ tells me in Dakota. "They rode to Yellow Medicine to see if it is safe for the people to move there."

Soon one of the women I met this morning races up to Tuŋwiŋ. I discern the Dakota words for *husband, doctor,* and *head,* but I cannot translate the rest of her rapid-fire speech. Tuŋwiŋ turns to me with a grave expression.

"Red Bird says the riders brought news of Yellow Medicine. All the whites have been killed."

I drop my beading in my lap. "John? My husband?"

Red Bird says something more to Tuŋwiŋ, who tells me, "The doctor was shot. Warriors cut off his head."

For a moment, her words make no sense. Then, as the gruesome image invades my mind, nausea sweeps over me, followed by chills. My hand flies up to cover my mouth as a terrible cry is wrenched out of me: "Johhhnnn!" I bend low over my lap and dig the heels of my palms into my eyes to keep from envisioning the events Red Bird described. John is dead, not only dead but also dismembered. Why would the Sioux do that to a man who had saved their lives?

My mind conjures up such vivid memories of my husband that, for an instant, I sense him here beside me. I smell his pungent cigars and the whiskey fumes that so often cloud his breath. I recall his hands upon my skin, coaxing me until I think I will burst with desire. I hear his baritone voice with its New England accent, so like my own. Then the sensations evaporate, and I am alone again in the midst of an Indian camp. Alone and at the mercy of my captors.

Jerking upright, I look wildly at the surrounding tepees. At least one warrior must be here somewhere. I must find him, throw myself at his feet, and beg him to kill me. I cannot bear another day of threats and privations. Why should I go on suffering like this when I have nothing left to live for? John was all I had.

Still crying, I rise to go searching for someone who will agree to execute me quickly. But before I can act, Jimmy runs up and throws his arms around my legs. Nellie follows after him, crying and sucking her thumb. Instantly, remorse strikes me. How could I have forgotten my darlings?

Forcing back my tears, I hold out my hand and say, "Come to Mama, Nellie." She approaches me warily. Her reluctance makes me wretched; she never displayed any fear of me until I choked her in the haystack.

Freeing myself from Jimmy's grasp, I kneel on the ground and pull my baby into my arms, wishing that my intense love for her could pass through my skin and be absorbed by her own. Then I enfold my son into our embrace. "A lady told me that your father is dead," I say gently. "He has gone to heaven to be with Jesus." My tears flow again, raining down upon their contrasting brown and blond heads.

After several minutes, my grief drains away, leaving me with fatigue and despair. Again, I feel an overwhelming longing to die and rejoin my husband. Despite all our problems, I loved John and felt grateful to him for saving me from ruin. What will happen to us without him?

I sit back on my heels and gaze at my children. Jimmy places one palm against my cheek and leans his face in close to mine. His blue eyes reflect worry. "Mama, will we have to be Indians now?"

"I don't know," I say, but his question, so astute for a young child, takes up residence in my heart like a prophecy. Perhaps that is what we must do. If the war goes on much longer, the surviving whites will surely flee Minnesota. I may have to convince the tribe to adopt us. As a family, we will spend our days struggling against starvation and counting ourselves blessed if we gather enough food for mere subsistence. My life as a Dakota woman will certainly be far shorter than my life as a white woman would be, which I may come to view as a mercy.

Standing, I brush off my clothes and bend to pick up the beaded moccasin top from the dirt. It reminds me of Chaska, whose compassion is the only reason my children and I still live. If we become permanent members of the tribe, will he continue to look after us or will he weary of the burden? Perhaps the best way to ensure our survival would be to really marry him. That is, if he would do so. Chaska has not shown the slightest desire for me. Can I win him over so he would want me as his wife? The very thought brings a hot flush to my face. He is a kind man, and I know he would never hurt me. But to accept someone of another race into my bed... The idea causes my heart to pound, whether from fear or something more unseemly, I cannot tell.

Nellie plops down on the ground and inserts three fingers into her mouth. Looking up at me, she plaintively asks, "Noo noo?" The moment is mundane, an exchange that passes between us every day, yet it clarifies my dilemma. These last few days, I have been excavating through years of accumulated sediment in my mind—layer upon layer of Christian teachings and social attitudes—and now, the spade of my conscience strikes the bedrock of my own truth. With my husband dead, I have only one duty left. I will do anything within my power to save my children. I will lie, steal, kill, or if necessary, take an Indian lover. Most white women would rather die than submit to such dishonor, but I don't believe a mother has the right to hold her virtue more precious than her children's lives.

Anyway, hasn't Chaska shown himself to have as much integrity as any white man? He certainly has more honor than my mother's second husband, for all that my stepfather prided himself on being a hardworking, honest Welshman. Pitt Vaughn was certainly not alone in his hypocrisy. I've known many a white man, even those who professed to be "Christian," who take unfair advantage of women.

Oh, but to give myself to an Indian! Everything within me revolts at the idea. Even if Chaska were the noblest Sioux alive, he still isn't white. If I were to take such a step, I would cut myself off from my own people forever. No one in white society would ever believe I did it for my children; the gossips always assume the worst of those who defy convention. They would say I must have an unnatural interest in carnal relations to live with a man of another race.

My head throbs, and a wave of sadness washes over me. *Oh, John,* I think. *Why didn't we pack up and drive to Mankato as soon as we knew the Sioux were restless? Why did you value your professional reputation above your family's safety?*

I realize that my husband faced a decision very similar to the one I'm grappling with now—whether to heed society's expectations or to do what he thought was best. John buckled under the pressure to remain at his post, and now he has paid for it. As sharply as I regret his death, it has freed me from the need to act as he would wish. I alone am responsible for these children, and I must do what I think is necessary to keep them alive.

Chaska returns in the evening. I want to ask him why we fled during the night, but he barely glances at me. Instead, he goes into the tepee with Tuŋwiŋ and stays there a long while. His behavior makes me wonder if I have angered him. I blush at the memory of my internal debate about whether to marry him. If I didn't know better, I would think he had read my mind and been offended by the idea.

About an hour later, Ina arrives at our encampment. "You and your children must come back to my tepee."

"Is everything safe now?" I ask.

She gives me a strange look and does not answer directly. "We all leave for Yellow Medicine in the morning on our way to Big Stone Lake."

The lake lies on the border between Minnesota and the Dakota Territory. The thought of going west with my captors deepens my fear that I might never get back to white society. My already depressed spirits plummet. Two days ago, I was looking forward to seeing my home again, but now that I know it is the site of John's murder, I don't see how I shall bear it.

Disconsolately, I call my children and gather up my few belongings. Ina helps me put Nellie on my back, and we trek back toward her tepee.

A short way beyond the encampment, we see an Indian riding a horse. He pulls up and exclaims in surprise, "You are the doctor's wife!"

I smile at him, but Ina scowls and whispers to me, "Hurry on. He is Sisseton and will kill you."

"But Ina," I say. The old woman hisses at me and gestures for me to be quiet. I nod to the warrior as we pass but say no more, perplexed by Ina's fear. The Sioux of Minnesota are divided into four bands; the Mdewakanton, which is Chaska's group, and the Wahpekute are the lower bands who live near the Redwood agency. The Sisseton and the Wahpeton are the upper bands who live at Yellow Medicine. I do not believe the Sisseton are my enemies; in fact, I think they would protect me from Little Crow if they learned of his hatred. But if the Mdewakanton and the Sisseton distrust each other, there is little I can do to change Ina's mind.

After we have walked about half an hour, I notice Jimmy cross his arms over his abdomen and hunch over. He halts, and I ask if he needs to find a place to relieve himself. At that moment, he has an attack of diarrhea, which stains the seat of his pants and flows down his legs.

He weeps from shame. "It's O.K., honey. It's not your fault that you can't hold it when you're sick. It even happens to grown-ups."

Ina leads us to a nearby stream, and we get Jimmy out of his pants. While Ina washes his legs, I swish the pants around in the stream, but they don't come clean. I will have to wash them again with soap when we get to Ina's tepee. Contrary to the common belief that Indians are dirty, Chaska's relatives always wash their hands and comb their hair before eating. I have a wash dish and bit of soap in my part of the tepee, and I will have to see if lather will scrub out the stain. This pair of pants is the only one he has because Winona took all his other clothes for her boys. In the meantime, I tear a piece of fabric off one edge of my skirt and make a little loincloth for Jimmy to wear under his shirt.

Once we reach Ina's tepee, I beg her to ask Winona for a change of clothing for Jimmy, but the old woman merely shakes her head and turns away. I know she does not want to get involved in the dispute between us. So I go to the river to do my laundry as best I can. After I come back and spread the wet pants on a bush to dry, I sit down to rest. Ina immediately tells me to get up. If we are going to leave in the morning, we have much to do. Sighing, I remind myself that I have determined to fit into tribal life as best I can. Then I set to work.

CHAPTER
18

As we pack our belongings to leave for Yellow Medicine, a scout rides into camp with the report that white soldiers are on their way to attack us. The news races from tepee to tepee like a prairie fire. Women call out to each other in alarm, and the pace of preparations grows frantic. The warriors—who consider domestic affairs beneath them—adorn themselves with paint, prepare their weapons, and harness their horses.

Ina and I work all night and get everything stowed away in the early hours of the morning. Ina plans to carry a massive pack, which feels as if it weighs eighty pounds. I wish I could assist her with the burden, but I must carry Nellie and keep my eye on Jimmy, who is still sick with bowel complaint.

Shortly before dawn, Winona comes bearing the lantern that she took from my wagon. By its light, she plaits and beribbons my hair, and paints my cheeks and my part red. "We are going into Sisseton country," Ina says as she watches us. "We must make you look like Indian woman."

When Winona finishes, I ask for footwear.

"We travel barefoot so we don't put holes in our moccasins."

"But I always wear shoes. My feet are not like an Indian woman's feet. They are too soft to walk barefoot across the prairie."

Winona folds her arms across her chest and smiles maliciously. "You must learn to do so. If you cannot keep pace with us, we will leave you behind, and other Indians will kill you."

Ina clucks in disapproval. Tossing her head, Winona gathers her things and returns to where her children lie sleeping, wrapped in a blanket. I gaze pleadingly at the old woman and say softly, "Could you not give me moccasins?"

She shakes her head and walks away. The noise of camp increases as the sky brightens. When coral and gold streaks of light rim the horizon, Ina places Nellie in a sling upon my back.

Ahead of us, an Indian travois is placed upon a milk cow, and the unfamiliar poles lying across the beast's back terrify her so that she twists her neck to look back at them, mooing pitifully. Not far from that an Indian pony that has never felt a harness is being forced to pull a buggy. The animal suddenly bucks and rears and roars in protest, but cannot escape the traces. In its desperation, the pony knocks down a woman carrying a pack as large as Ina's. Her baby falls to the ground and squalls, and her pack breaks open, spilling flour, beans, blouses, moccasins, and two young kittens.

At last, the sun rises above the horizon. Daybreak is the signal everyone has been waiting for, and the entire camp departs, heading west. The women do most of the hauling, either by carrying packs on their backs or leading horses attached to travois or driving wagons. Most of the warriors ride. They race their horses up and down along the outside of the moving train, rear their animals for show, and let out war whoops.

I follow Ina and Winona, working hard to keep the sling holding my baby high upon my back. The tall prairie grasses make it difficult to see what's ahead. Within minutes, I step upon a thistle growing low in the midst of the grasses and get prickles embedded in my sole. Knowing that my companions will not stop, I press my lips together and try to ignore the irritation in my foot as I hurry along.

The women walk at a much brisker pace than we have used before. Struggling to keep up, I call out, "Why are we running?" The exertion causes me to pant out the words.

Ina does not stop but calls back, "Sisseton are coming. They will kill you."

Again I wonder at her fear. During my time at the Upper Agency,

I came to know the Sisseton well, and they are no more hostile than Chaska's people. Although the Sisseton started the troubles by raiding the warehouse at Yellow Medicine, they are not the ones who began the killing; from what Chaska told me, four Mdewakanton warriors did that.

I cannot demand further explanation because I am too winded. As we trot along the prairie, Nellie slips partway down my back. Adjusting the sling as I walk is nearly impossible. I had prided myself on learning to use a sling as well as an Indian woman, but that was when I was walking at a moderate pace, not running through four-foot-high bluestem prairie grass.

Jimmy, who is somewhere behind me, calls in a panicky voice, "Mama, Mama, don't leave me. I cannot walk so fast as you!"

When I look back over my shoulder to find him, my grip on the sling loosens and Nellie slides down below my hips and bounces uncomfortably against the back of my legs. She cries, and I am forced to stop. "Ina, wait! Please help me!"

Ina sees our predicament and comes back to us. *"Sica!"* she exclaims: "This is bad." Reaching us, she addresses me in a torrent of Dakota: "Why can you not carry your child? We cannot stop. We must travel quickly." With impatient movements, she readjusts Nellie's position. Then she turns to Jimmy and sees his tear-stained face. "What is wrong?"

He gulps and says, "I am a little boy. I cannot walk so fast."

Usually, Ina is indulgent with my children, so I expect his difficulties to soften her heart. Instead, she scowls. "You have to run. Enemies are coming. Your mother can carry only one child."

"Hau, Uŋci," Jimmy answers, respectfully saying, "Yes, Grandmother." When we start moving again, he tells me, "I will be good, Mama. I won't complain."

Although I feel indignant on his behalf, Ina's words remind me that the scout warned of danger. I swivel my head from left to right. More than just our band is fleeing. In every direction, hundreds of Indians move across the open prairie, all making for the crossing on the Redwood River. As if spurred on by the sight of so many heading toward their destination, Ina and Winona canter more quickly.

Near the river the land grows marshier, and the bluestem grasses give way to prairie cordgrass. This species is coarser with serrated edges, and it slices my skin as it whips against my feet and calves. Within fifteen minutes, my legs are flayed from a hundred tiny sword cuts. As we hurry along in the heat, sweat trickles into the wounds, making them burn. I worry for Jimmy, who still wears only a loincloth with nothing to protect his bare legs. Glancing back at him, I see his face scrunched up in pain, but he maintains a stoic silence.

The Redwood is a narrower river than the Minnesota. Upon our approach, I notice that its level appears to be lower than it was a week ago when Ina and I crossed it; the flats along the edge are wider than they were then.

The swarms of people trying to cross halt our progress toward the riverbank. I refrain from pointing out how useless it was for us to run ourselves ragged only to stand here and wait. Ina sets her pack down, removes the waterskin fastened to her belt, and allows each person in our party a single swallow. We must be sparing because the river is too churned up with mud to refill the skin here.

The chaotic scene before me would be humorous if we did not fear for our lives. For a hundred yards on either side of me, teams are trying to cross the Redwood. Many wagons stick fast in the muddy riverbed, so their drivers must climb down to push them free. Often when the wheels begin to roll, the person doing the pushing falls headlong into the river and jumps back up again sputtering.

In their impatience to cross, the warriors gallop up and down the bank, shouting and firing guns into the air. The noise upsets the animals; some freeze stock still where they stand while others plunge forward recklessly. The older boys do their best to imitate the antics of the men. The women scold them, but it does no good. Many young children wail in fright.

The day has grown warm and oppressive. The air is dense with humidity and the sun beats down upon our unprotected heads—the Sioux do not wear hats except in the coldest weeks of winter.

While we wait to cross, I use a bandana dampened with river water to clean Jimmy's legs, which are bloody from innumerable cuts and scratches. His skin must sting unbearably, and yet, he presses his lips tightly together and refrains from crying to show our captors that he is as brave as they are. How quickly he has learned that the

Sioux admire courage. I am grateful my boy is proving so adaptable because that trait will help keep us alive, yet it troubles me as well. Do I really want him to act so much like an Indian?

Finally, the crowd ahead of us clears. Before wading into the river, I find a way to tie the sling holding my baby more securely so she won't slip down my back and drown in the water before I can rescue her. Then I follow Ina into the stream.

Even though the river is lower than last week, the water is still up to most people's upper arms and the current is strong enough to be dangerous. Before we go very far, the water threatens to submerge my son and I must pick him up. With my twenty-pound baby upon my back, my forty-pound boy upon my hip, and the dangerous undertow swirling around my legs, I struggle to remain upright. Remembering the burdens that others carry, I admonish myself to persevere.

At the deepest part of the river, Ina pauses to see if I need help. Offended that she thinks so poorly of my capabilities, I shake my head and push through the water on my own. Within another couple of minutes, the level drops, and I expel a sigh of relief.

Moments later, a middle-aged Indian who rides one mule and pulls another halts in the stream in front of me. "Where are you going?" he asks me in Dakota.

"Yellow Medicine," I answer, squinting up at him because of the sun.

Ina tugs my sleeve and says in a low voice, "Be quiet. He is Sisseton."

The warrior smiles at me. "You are the doctor's wife."

"No, I am Indian woman," I say because of Ina's warning.

At that, he throws back his head and laughs. He exclaims in English, "I know you! You must not tell lies. You are no Indian woman; your eyes are too light."

Still laughing, he clucks at his mule and heads for the bank.

Uneasily, I walk beside Ina the rest of the way. The old woman mutters, "*Sica!*"

We reach the edge of the river and struggle up the bank to dry ground, where I set Jimmy down on his feet. Once I straighten, I see the ruins of Joe Reynolds's cabin: a blackened fieldstone chimney and a few charred beams. It reminds me of my ill-fated ride with George Gleason and how he believed we could stop at this house for dinner on our way to the fort. Then the man I met in the river approaches me again, leading his two mules. He says, "Mrs. Wakefield, don't you recognize me?"

I peer at him. He has a benevolent expression, collar-length hair, broad cheekbones, and a mole upon his chin. That distinguishing mark looks familiar, but I am too frightened to think clearly. After gazing at me expectantly for a moment, he leans closer and whispers, "I am Paul, don't you know me? You must come with me to my tepee."

"Paul!" I exclaim. *Little Paul,* we called him at Yellow Medicine. He is a half-Sisseton–half-Wahpeton man who was educated at the Lac Qui Parle Mission and converted to Christianity. He is also President of the Hazelwood Republic, a group of self-governing farmer Indians who live a few miles west of the Upper Agency. Paul is fond of saying that he has changed himself into a white man, and I have never seen him in Indian dress before.

"I am happy to see you," I say, ignoring Ina's hiss of disapproval behind me.

"Come with me to my tepee," he says again. "I will protect you."

"Thank you, but Chaska and his family are taking care of us." I gesture toward Ina, so he will realize that my children and I are not unaccompanied.

"Which Chaska?" he asks the old woman in Dakota. It is a common name, given to all first-born sons just as Winona is given to all first-born daughters.

After scowling at me, she answers, "My son is Wicaŋhpi Wastedaŋpi."

Paul nods and turns to me. "He is a good man, but I can help you more. We have thirty miles to go to Yellow Medicine. I will let you ride one of my mules."

For a moment, the offer tempts me. I glance at his medium-sized beasts. Mules are stronger than horses, so either one of them should be able to carry my weight, but although I am experienced at riding bareback on a horse, I am leery of doing so on a mule. Their gait is different from that of a horse and their backs are narrower, so bareback riders tend to slip from side to side.

"I don't think I can ride a mule without a saddle."

"It is a long way to walk," Paul answers in a wheedling tone that unsettles me.

Jimmy tugs at my skirt. "Mama, please say yes. I cannot walk so far."

His appeal reminds me that, not only will I have to keep my own balance upon the mule, but I will also have to carry my children. I truly do not think I can do it. Paul watches me with a peculiar glint in his eyes, and my discomfort grows. "No, Jimmy, I'm sorry, but I don't know how to ride a mule bareback."

Paul scratches his chin above the mole. "I can take the boy with me." I think he means that if I go on one mule, he will take my son on the other, but that is not how Jimmy interprets his remark.

"Oh, yes, Mama, please let me go with Paul. I will be safe with him."

Jimmy's face is alight with that pleading expression any mother knows all too well. How soon he has forgotten his terror at being separated from me five nights ago. Placing my hands on my hips, I say to him, "You will cry for me when night comes because I shall walk and not get to Yellow Medicine for two days."

"No, Mama, I will not cry if I can ride. It will kill me to walk so far. Do let me go with Paul."

Uncertain what to do, I look to Ina, but she has turned away from what she sees as a foolhardy conversation. Chaska is driving the wagon up the bank, so I wave to him. He approaches, brakes the wagon, and jumps down. Beckoning him to come closer, I tell him about Paul's offer and whisper, "Do you think I should go?"

A look of annoyance flits across his face, very like the irritation John used to display whenever he thought I was dithering instead of making a quick decision. I fully expect a rebuke, but Chaska walks over to Paul and speaks to him for several minutes. Then Chaska returns to me. With a nod of his head, he indicates that he wants to move a couple of yards farther away.

His face remains expressionless as he says, "You can go with Paul if you wish. But know that he wants you to be his wife. He says that since he is as good as a white man, he should have a white wife. He has been trying to get one for many days."

I shoot an indignant glance toward Paul, who has squatted down to talk to my son. "He did not say that to me! He offered me a ride, nothing more."

Chaska shrugs. "The choice is yours."

"But I do not want to marry him. I do not want to marry anyone."

Chaska lifts his eyebrows in what appears to be amusement. "I have other news that will make you happy. Paul says your husband is alive."

"Alive! But the scout in your aunt's village said that he was dead."

Shaking his head, Chaska asks, "Do you know John Other Day?"

"Yes, I know him," I answer impatiently. Other Day, another farmer Indian who lives at Hazelwood, is notorious among settlers for having married an English woman he met when he traveled to Washington for treaty negotiations. Rumor has it he met her in a brothel. "What does he have to do with my husband?"

"Paul said that Other Day led a group of sixty people from Yellow Medicine across the river and through woods to safety. Your husband was with them."

I press both hands to my cheeks and stare at Chaska. My lungs feel as though someone had punched the air out of them. "Do you think I can believe him?"

After glancing over his shoulder, Chaska nods. "I do not think he lies. Paul and Other Day rescued the white girl stolen by Inkpaduta."

Abbie Gardner. In March 1857, about the time I began to suspect I was carrying my son, a group of renegade Wahpekute led by Inkpaduta attacked several frontier settlements near Spirit Lake in Iowa. The raiders killed about forty people and captured four young women, only one of whom came back alive—thirteen-year-old Abbie Gardner. If Little Paul and John Other Day were part of the group that rescued her, then they have previously acted against their own people to help whites in distress. That makes Paul more trustworthy in my eyes.

"So John is alive!" A large grin breaks across my face, as if of its own volition. "My husband lives, and I must stay alive so I can return to him."

"Yes," Chaska says, but he narrows his eyes as though perplexed. Perhaps his mother never told him about the time I tried to kill my children.

Ecstatic, I twirl like a little girl at her first party and rush to my son. Lifting him, I laugh. "I just heard the most wonderful news. Your father is alive. He's safe!" Mere words are not enough to express my exuberance, and I dance with Jimmy in my arms until I am dizzy. Still laughing, I set him back on the ground.

When I smile at Paul in gratitude for the news he brought, he misinterprets and asks, "So you will come with me?"

"No, I will walk with Chaska's mother."

"But you will let me ride, won't you, Mama?" Jimmy asks.

I see his badly cut legs and think, *Why not? I can trust Little Paul.* I place my hand on Jimmy's shoulder and ask, "Are you sure you won't miss me too much? Remember how you cried for me the other night."

He scowls, not liking to be reminded of babyish behavior. "That was because you didn't tell me good-bye, and I didn't know where you went."

I am so happy about our news that I cannot bring myself to deny my son's desire. But first I must check whether Paul really wants to burden himself with a child. "Are you sure it won't be too much trouble?" I ask.

Paul grins and taps himself on the chest. "No, I will take good care of him."

"O.K. Thank you." I focus my attention on my son. "Do everything Paul tells you and don't misbehave. Do you promise me?"

"Oh, yes, Mama. Thank you." He hugs me around the legs, turns away to go with Paul, and looks back to me one last time. His lip trembles slightly. "You will walk as fast as you can, won't you?"

His display of anxiety moves me. "Yes, Jimmy, I will hurry to find you."

He gives a solemn nod, much as his father would, and sets off with Paul.

I turn to rejoin Chaska and Ina. As I do, I see a white girl, about fourteen years old, staring at me with a scornful expression. She has a stocky body; a round face with pretty, upturned eyes; and thick, dark braids coiled around her head. When I walk past her, she mutters, *"Hure!"* and spits on the ground. I do not need to speak German to know that I have been called a whore.

Keep walking, I tell myself. *She's only a child.*

As we come out of the band of trees that runs along the river and start across the open prairie, I see the full extent of the exodus. The procession spreads out a full mile in width, and it extends a mile or more ahead of us and several miles behind. Yet, the teams and walkers are not dispersed with gaps between. Rather, everyone crowds together as close as they can.

I have never in my life seen such a collection of vehicles: oxcarts, chaises, buggies, farm wagons, fine coaches, peddler's wagons, baker's carts, and even a Conestoga wagon with its distinctive flared shape. Most of the vehicles are decorated with green boughs, American flags, or bunches of colored ribbons.

The Sioux have also decked themselves out for the occasion with finery plundered from settlers' homes. To my eyes, their taste in fashion leaves much to be desired. Many warriors ride about wearing women's bonnets trimmed with ribbons, plumes, and lace, and I swear a few young bucks wear ladies' drawers over their leggings. One chief proudly sports a white eyelet dress with puffed sleeves; the bodice is unbuttoned to the waist to show off a prized bear-claw necklace.

The women wear silk and satin dresses—some just the bodice and others just the skirt—over their everyday clothes. On their bosoms they display necklaces and brooches, and their ears twinkle with pearls, gold hoops, and rich gems. My heart aches for the original owners of the jewelry; farming is a grueling life without much luxury, and these bits of finery were perhaps the only things of beauty those women owned. The treasures may even have been family heirlooms, passed down from generation to generation, now taken as spoils of war on the American frontier.

Even so, I cannot keep from laughing. Some Indians attempt to play stolen musical instruments as we travel, so our march is accompanied by the screeching of fiddles, the tuneless hooting of flutes, and the incessant banging of Indian drums. Accompanying this are Dakota chants and the repeated shouts, "Hi! Hi!" Between the ludicrous outfits of my companions and the noise our procession makes, I feel as though I have joined a circus.

Laughing at the wild parade provides me with a much-needed distraction from my poor, torn feet. The tall, sharp-edged grasses continue to slice my skin, and thistles and other stinging weeds disgorge thorns into my flesh. My lower limbs and feet bleed so much that I cannot see how bad the damage is for all the gore.

When we stop for lunch, Chaska takes one look at the pulpy mess and calls for his mother. I sit on the ground as Ina kneels before me, washing my legs and feet, and then wrapping them in cloth that holds medicinal herbs. After she finishes, we eat a light lunch of crackers, maple sugar, and water. Because of all the walking we did that morning, I am still hungry, but I swallow my complaints.

As the procession starts to move again, I rise and gasp at the burning in my feet. I hobble to where Nellie naps in the shade of the wagon and begin to put the sling back on. Chaska comes to me and says, "You drive wagon."

My mouth drops open in surprise, but I quickly close it again. "Thank you," I tell him. I want to say more but don't wish to embarrass him in front of his people. It is not the Sioux way for men to pamper their womenfolk.

Not long after we set out, the pedestrians and vehicles ahead of me begin parting as if to circumvent a large boulder. When we reach that place, I realize with shock that they are avoiding the naked corpse of George Gleason, still lying upon the open prairie nine days after we were ambushed. I would never know who it was if I did not recognize the place where I sat while Chaska and Hapa debated my fate.

Horror draws my gaze to his mortal remains, and I am glad not to have much in my stomach. Mr. Gleason's body is swollen; the skin is darkly discolored with bloody blisters across its surface. Insects swarm in a cloud above him, animals have fed upon his limbs, and something has pecked out his eyes. The smell is unspeakable. I put the hem of my blouse over my nose, but that doesn't help much. The only thing that keeps me from vomiting is the terror of what the Indians might do if I show such weakness.

As soon as we pass the spot, I breathe deeply to fill my lungs with fresh air. The sun still shines, but my day has turned gloomy with despair. No longer do I rejoice in knowing that John lives. Instead, I find myself dreading what I might find when we reach the spot that used to be my home.

CHAPTER
19

ABOUT AN HOUR AFTER WE PASS GLEASON'S BODY, A SCOUT GALLOPS UP and shouts that white soldiers are closing in behind us. Instantly, everyone takes off for the only cover within sight, a small thicket about a hundred yards ahead.

As women and children scurry through the woods, the warriors prepare themselves for battle. Each one finds a spot behind a tree or fallen log where he can cover the prairie we just crossed. Many shoot their guns to test that the weapons are in working order and then reload.

When Ina halts next to an ash tree near the far edge of the woods, I set the wagon brake, rise from my seat, and gaze in a full circle around me, wondering where my son is in all this confusion. The close-growing trees and milling Sioux make it difficult to see very far, and I cannot spot the small tow-headed figure my heart longs for. Has Paul traveled on ahead, or is he somewhere in this band preparing to fight? If he is here, why doesn't he send Jimmy to me for safety?

I bite my lower lip as my mind envisions dire possibilities. Perhaps the child succumbed to heat stroke from riding in the hot sun without any hat. Or perhaps he had another bout of diarrhea that left him so weak Paul abandoned him along the way. Why, oh why, did I ever entrust my precious boy to someone I barely know?

As I frantically scan the scene, Ina sheds her pack and approaches the side of the wagon. "Come, white woman," she says in Dakota. "Help me set up camp."

"Where will we put the tepee?" I ask as I climb down.

"No tepee. If soldiers come, we must run."

Taking off my sling, I set my baby girl on the ground and prop her against a wagon wheel. "Do you want me to fetch water?"

Ina shakes her head. "The river is far away."

Upon learning that we must make a dry camp, I instantly grow aware of my parched throat. My mouth tastes like the dust I inhaled as I rode in the middle of that caravan, and all I can think of is rinsing it with cool, clear water. I turn away to hide my dismay and look for blankets amongst the household goods.

Nearly an hour passes, yet the expected battle sounds do not commence. Once again, the Indians seem to have panicked because of a false report. The position of the sun tells me that it is late afternoon, so even if we learn that the report of imminent attack was false, I doubt we will travel farther tonight.

My throat grows increasingly scratchy, and my tongue sticks to the roof of my mouth as I create makeshift beds for us under the wagon. After I finish, I sit in the shade of the wagon with Nellie upon my lap. The child murmurs, "Noo noo," and pulls at the front of my blouse, but I dare not nurse her when I am so dry.

As I jiggle her on my knee to distract her, my thoughts turn back to Jimmy. Is he somewhere in this group, or has Paul carried him to Hazelwood? I cannot shake off the premonition that he is lost to me forever.

And where is my husband? Chaska said that Other Day led the refugees away from Yellow Medicine, so most likely John is at Fort Ridgely or in St. Paul. Does he suspect that we are still alive, or has he given up hope? Either way, the closer I come to my former home, the farther it seems I journey from my husband.

I cannot help but wonder why the Indians are so intent on traveling to Yellow Medicine. Perhaps they are leading me to my home only to kill me there.

The thought is so horrible that I shake my head to chase it off. Gazing at Ina's creased face as she smokes her pipe, I tell myself that neither she nor Chaska would willingly take part in such a cruel scheme. Haven't they endured the criticism of their tribe for sheltering me, and hasn't Chaska made every effort to provide for us? But what if the tribe turns completely against them? In such a circumstance, could I expect them to defend me to the death? I would feel horribly guilty if one of them were to die for me.

As I fret, Chaska strides up carrying a large cloth bag, which he sets at his mother's feet. Ina glances into it and exclaims, *"Kuŋta!"* She pulls out a plum and bites into it. Juice runs down her chin.

Chaska bends down, removes three plums from the bag, and drops them in my lap.

They are small, purple, egg-shaped plums with the characteristic dusty white bloom upon the peel. When I bite into one, I discover that they are the sharp-flavored variety whites use for canning rather than eating, but I don't care. In my desperate state, the tart juice is more refreshing than a sweeter fruit would be.

I tear off some of the greenish-yellow flesh and put it between Nellie's lips. She narrows her eyes, puckers up her mouth, and begins to cry. Chaska laughs at her as he takes a plum from the bag and bites into it. Bending down to gaze at her, he says, "Good!" and rubs his belly. The sudden proximity of his face startles Nellie so much that her eyes widen and she stops crying.

"Try another bite," I say, giving her a second morsel of the flesh. She takes it without complaining, but I can tell by the exaggerated slowness with which she chews that she doesn't enjoy it any more than the first one.

Chuckling at her look of consternation, I finish my first plum and say, "All right, darling. Noo noo." I unbutton my blouse, place my daughter at my breast, and take another plum for myself.

Every time I close my eyes, I see Gleason's decaying corpse, and sleep flees like a frightened rabbit. As the camp noises around me subside, the incessant chirping of crickets takes their place, and my disturbed mind interprets the sound as my boy crying in the dark.

Before dawn, Nellie wakes up wailing, and I discover that she's caught the bowel complaint that afflicted Jimmy. Perhaps it is a good thing she didn't eat much fruit last night, I think, as I lift up her legs and pull away the reeking, laden diaper. Because we have very little water, I use leaves to wipe her clean before swaddling her in a new cloth. I scratch a hole in the ground with a knife and bury the soiled diaper so I don't have to carry it with me in the morning.

Dawn breaks, Ina rises, and we consume a meager breakfast of crackers and a mouthful of water each. Then we set out on the last leg to Yellow Medicine. Again, Chaska lets me drive the wagon. I place Nellie in a makeshift bed under the seat where she will be protected from the sun. The poor mite is so depleted from her illness that she quickly drops off to sleep.

As we travel, I scan the jostling crowd for my son. I ask passersby where Paul has gone, but no one knows a Sioux man with that appellation, and I cannot recall his Indian name. Worried, I pray for my boy's safety.

Nellie awakens and whimpers. She calls for me, and I answer, "I'm driving the wagon, sweetheart. I cannot stop." Her fretfulness changes to sobbing, and I fear that it will annoy the Indians traveling alongside us. "Nellie, baby, you're not alone. Mama is right here. Don't you see my skirt right next to you?"

The next thing I know, a tiny hand grazes my left ankle. I feel a tug as my daughter's fist closes upon my skirt. "That's my good girl," I croon.

The air is full of moisture, and haze hangs on the horizon, although the sky above is clear. About two miles out from camp, we come upon a stream where Ina fills her waterskins. After carefully disengaging my clothing from my daughter's grip, I disembark from the wagon. I pull a tin cup from my satchel, dip it into the flowing water, drink deeply, and then wake up Nellie to give her some. The child's forehead burns with fever, so I place a damp cloth across it before climbing back into my seat. Ina smiles wearily at me as she hoists her pack and resumes walking.

Before long, we pass the home of Joseph R. Brown, the previous Indian agent on the reservation. Brown, whose wife is part Sisseton, understands Sioux culture well and was far more successful in the post than Galbraith. When President Lincoln took office last year, however, Brown lost his appointment. He consoled himself by erecting a fine stone mansion for his large family. The house, finished early this summer, would have graced the finest neighborhood of any Eastern city. Three and a half stories tall, it was built of pinkish granite and featured a three-story veranda across the front façade, which boasted twelve shutter-flanked, glass windows.

Now Brown's pride and joy is nothing but a blackened shell. Brown's wife Susan is related to several chiefs, so if the Upper Agency Indians burned her home, I have little hope of finding anything left of mine. And what has happened to the Browns? Not a single clue to their fate can be seen among the charred ruins.

Now that we are a mere six miles from the agency, I sit forward in the wagon seat hoping to catch sight of our settlement, which is built on a bluff on the opposite side of the Yellow Medicine. A long time passes before I discern distant, dim shapes in the haze, which is thicker here near the river. Even though I strain my eyes to determine what has happened to my home, I cannot tell whether I am seeing buildings or the outlines of trees and shrubbery.

Soon we descend to the Yellow Medicine River, whose waters have carved their way through the surrounding bluffs for so many centuries that the streambed lies 600 feet below them. As we head downward, I lose sight of the silhouettes I'd been trying to read like tea leaves. Instead, as we reach the dale where the traders had their homes, I see with dismay that this area has also been put to the torch. My heart lies heavy in my chest as I cluck at the mare and drive to the crossing.

During the last day and a half, our procession has gradually spread out over the length of several miles. Because of that, the river isn't congested with crossers, and I traverse it in half the time it took to ford the Redwood. Once we reach the other side, Chaska rides up on Gleason's horse and tells me I must walk now. Lady must pull the wagon up a steep slope, so we need to lighten her load.

After checking on Nellie, who is fidgeting and sweating in her sleep, I climb down from my seat. Chaska leads the mare by the bridle up the steep trail, while I walk alongside the wagon bed holding its side for support. Our lack of food for the last two days takes a toll on me; I perspire and tremble as I trudge up the incline. The sun is at the highest point in the sky, and its strong rays beat upon my scalp until the resulting headache makes me want to scream.

When I turn to ask Ina if she still has some of that pain-relieving white willow bark, I can't locate her. I'm so astonished that she isn't there I let go of the wagon and crane my neck to search for her among the crowd streaming up the hill. Ina is nowhere in sight. I turn to alert Chaska and see that he's continued to forge ahead—so that now I am in danger of losing him too.

Driven by the terror of being separated from my daughter as well as my son, I hasten up the hill. At the same time, I fret about Ina. I didn't see her pass the wagon as I drove, so she must have lagged behind us. I hope she hasn't buckled under the weight of that heavy pack. For an instant, I consider calling to Chaska that we've lost his mother, but I doubt he would stop the wagon halfway up this precipitous slope.

As I half run, half walk up the hill, I pant so heavily that my mouth grows as dry as ashes. My throat feels scratchy and tight. Ina has our waterskins, so for the present, I can do nothing to quench my thirst.

Although I want desperately to catch up with the wagon, a painful stitch causes me to bend over and clutch my side. I slow my pace but force myself to keep plodding upward. Just when I think I cannot possibly put one weary foot ahead of the other, we reach the top of the hill. As soon as I reach level ground, I bend over with my hands upon my knees and gasp for breath. Blood pounds in my temples.

After a minute or so, I rise to a standing position. From here, I can gaze through an opening between stands of trees into the clearing where the agency was built. The large, two-story brick agency headquarters still stands—and beyond it, I glimpse the corner of my house. It looks to be intact.

For an instant, I gape at the unexpected sight, and then I remember my more pressing concern. I cross to where Chaska stands by Lady, stroking her nose and murmuring, *"Ŝuntaka waŝte"*—"good horse."

"I cannot find your mother. I have not seen her since we crossed the river."

Chaska stares over my shoulder. "The people still come."

"Do you think you should look for her? She is old. She might be hurt."

Chaska frowns. As he considers my question, Winona approaches with Maggie Brass, a Sioux woman who adopted an English name when she and her husband joined the Episcopal Church. Seeing the two together fills me with hope that this Christian woman might temper Winona's vindictiveness.

"Ina tuktetu he?" Chaska asks his sister. Winona shrugs, and in her rapid reply, I catch the words for "white woman"—no doubt, she is blaming me for allowing the old woman to become separated from us.

Chaska's face darkens, but he merely says that he will search for her.

After he leaves, Winona's two boys run up, followed by the German girl who was so rude to me yesterday. Ignoring me, Winona and Maggie create a shelter by making a small lean-to of tree boughs and draping a blanket over them. As I watch them, Maggie explains something patiently to the girl, causing me to wonder if Maggie has decided to adopt her.

I retrieve Nellie from her place under the wagon seat and gently wake her. "Mama," she says in a piteously weak voice. She rubs her eyes and tugs at my bodice.

Cradling my child in my arms, I move to sit under the shelter, but the two Indian women position themselves so there is no room for me. With a deep sigh, I sit on the grass next to the wagon and put Nellie to my breast. She latches on, but within a minute, she lets go and begins to cry. Because of my lack of nourishment, my body has nothing to give her.

When Maggie offers Winona's two boys water from her skin, I ask, "May I have a little water for my child? She is sick."

The two women exchange glances, and Maggie says, "No, white woman, get it yourself."

Her reply shocks me so much that my mouth drops open. Then I remember that Maggie's husband Good Thunder is a friend of Hapa's. That evil man's hatred continues to corrupt those around me, even those who should know better.

As I contemplate going down the steep hill to fetch water from the river and climbing the long way back up again, my heart quails. Suddenly, I remember that the settlement here at the Upper Agency has many wells. My sufferings for the last ten days have made me forget something I ought to have known right away.

I don't trust these women to look after my sick child, so I put Nellie in a sling on my back and rummage in the bed of the wagon until I find a pot. Then I set across the prairie to my home, which has a well right outside the door.

As I pass the agency headquarters, I see that in all directions, groups of Indians sit upon the green eating a midday meal and resting from the arduous river crossing. Several women stand around the well as I approach, and I am relieved to see them haul up the bucket. Thank heavens it hasn't been stolen. I wait my turn, draw water, drink deeply, and fill my pan.

I step away from the group, remove my daughter from the sling, and dribble water between her lips. She is awake but listless. I dampen the hem of my skirt and wipe her hot forehead, and then I check her diaper. She has not had another attack of diarrhea, perhaps because she hasn't eaten anything in nearly a day.

As I put Nellie back in the sling, I feel an overpowering urge to enter my home and see what remains in it. Turning toward the house, I see that the front door stands slightly ajar. The frame is splintered, and the door no longer latches shut.

Fear congeals within me as I cross to the stoop. With trepidation, I walk inside the building. In the parlor, the big pieces of furniture—the heavy tables, rosewood rocker, and green damask sofa—stand where we left them. But all of the vases, cushions, and decorative objects are missing. The floor is littered with pages torn wantonly from books. What hurts most is that our family photographs are gone.

As I stand there, taking inventory, the mewling of an infant comes from the floor above me. At first, I think my imagination must be conjuring a memory from the past, but the crying grows louder.

I set my pan on the nearest table and head for the stairs. When I reach the second story, I note that scavengers have been here too. Nothing remains in my children's sleeping area but Jimmy's bed. Even Nellie's cradle is gone.

The crying comes from the other room. Instinctively, I walk on tiptoe to the curtain that separates the two sleeping areas. As I draw near, I hear a woman murmuring to her babe. The cadence sounds like English.

"Hello?" I call. "Who's here?"

The woman goes silent and then says in a tremulous voice, "It's Elizabeth Brown. Angus Brown's wife. Who are you?"

"Mrs. Dr. Wakefield. May I come in?"

"Of course." She laughs nervously. "I fear that I've appropriated your bed."

When I push back the curtain, I find a pale, dark-haired woman, about eighteen or nineteen, with an infant lying next to her. We've seen each other at parties but have never spoken. She lets out an exclamation of alarm when she sees me in Indian dress, but I smile reassuringly. "Don't worry, child. I really am Mrs. Wakefield. And you're Major Brown's daughter-in-law. I worried about your family when I saw that the house had burned. Is everyone safe?"

"Yes, thus far. We were captured and taken to Little Crow's village, but my mother-in-law's stepfather, Chief Akepa, fetched us back to his own people." Elizabeth's arms tighten protectively around her baby, drawing my attention to the infant. "Ohhh," I exclaim. "He's so tiny. Did you just give birth?"

She nods shyly. "It's a boy," she says, pride in her voice.

"You are welcome to use this bed as long as you need it."

The girl bit her lip. "We've been hearing noises for the last two hours. Angus went out to investigate, but he hasn't returned. Can you tell me what's happening?"

"The Mdewakanton are crossing the Yellow Medicine River. I think we're going to Great Stone Lake, but I'm not sure. The plans keep changing."

"We?" she asks, suspicion flaring in her eyes.

"My children and I are captives. I must go with the Sioux, or they will kill me."

"I'm sorry," she murmurs, staring down at her baby. "I never understood before how terrible it is when your children are in danger."

"Don't fret. Your mother-in-law has powerful relatives to keep you safe."

A smile tugs at Elizabeth's lips. "Oh, Mrs. Wakefield, you should have seen her. When the Indians surrounded our wagons and threatened to kill us, she stood up and berated them in no uncertain terms.

She called out the name of every chief she's related to and announced that the rogues would answer to her kin if they harmed us."

"See there? You have nothing to fear."

Elizabeth bites her lip. "Little Crow didn't like it, having to release us to another chief. You said that you're traveling with the Mdewakanton? Is Little Crow with your party?"

Although I dread giving an answer that will increase her fear, I will not lie to this woman the way my husband and George Gleason lied to me. "Little Crow's band is not here yet, but they are following us. All the Mdewakanton are on the move."

The girl's face loses what little color it has. "Do not assume that things will turn out badly," I say hastily. "Put your trust in God."

Elizabeth nods, but a tear rolls down her cheek.

I pity the girl but also resent her. Even if she is taken captive again, she has her husband and his family to look out for her. I have no one but Chaska. "I must go," I say, "and you should rest."

Back downstairs, I hurry into the kitchen and check the pantry to see if any of our foodstuffs remain. As I expected, the shelves have been picked clean.

On my way back through the dining room, my gaze falls upon my birdcages, still hanging from their stands. I step close and see the desiccated bodies of my sweet songbirds. How cruel it was to leave them here to starve to death. The least the Indians could have done was to release them to fend for themselves.

Tears blur my eyes, and I lean against the dining room table. *I'm not going to get out of this alive,* I think. *I'm every bit as helpless as those canaries.*

I weep for several minutes and then press my lips tightly together and stand tall. "I will not give up!" I say aloud. Staring around the room, I think, *My husband is alive, and God has given me a protector. My children and I will survive.*

Holding my head high, I pick up my pan of water, leave the house, and stride across the green without a backward glance.

To my astonishment, as I draw near the wagon, I see that Ina has returned. Even more surprising, she and Winona are engaged in a loud argument.

Winona kneels on the ground, pulling items out of Ina's pack. "Where is it?" she screams. "Hapa wants it. What did you do with it?"

"I don't know," Ina answers. Her voice sounds spent, and she slumps with fatigue. When I gaze closely at her, I see a bruise on her forehead.

"Ina, what happened to you?" I cry, setting my pot of water on my trunk, which stands near the wagon, and rushing to her.

"Go away, white woman," Winona growls, but I ignore her and take Ina's hands, which have scrapes on both palms.

"I fell when I walked down the hill," the old woman says quietly.

I find a cloth in the wagon, dip it in water, and clean away the dirt embedded in the torn skin on her hands. "Did Chaska find you? He went to look for you."

Ina purses her mouth from the pain and shakes her head.

"There are so many people. You must have walked past each other."

Winona steps close to me and shouts in my ear, "Be quiet! You do not belong here." She shoves me backward and stands before her stepmother with her hands on her hips. "I put that bag of shot in your pack. Now it is not there. You stole it."

"Why would I do that?"

"To give to whites," Winona screeches. Her words are so irrational that I think she must have lost her mind. Obviously, the shot fell out of the pack when Ina tumbled downhill. Then I have a flash of recognition: *Winona is afraid. Of her husband.* Her sense of panic that she might be in trouble is all too familiar to me.

For an instant, empathy washes over me—until Winona screams at Ina once more. "You love the whites. That is why you give our family's food to this fat, lazy woman."

The angry words wake Nellie, who wails. I back away from them, wondering if my daughter and I could hide in my house until Chaska returns.

Ina draws back her shoulders, lifts her chin, and stares at Winona with hurt dignity. "Is this how you speak to your mother?"

"I speak the truth!" Pivoting on her heel, Winona stalks back toward the shelter where Maggie sits. After taking two steps, Winona halts and glares at me. "Tell your child to be quiet, or I kill her." She notices the pot of water on the trunk, snatches it up, and whirling around, hurls it at her stepmother. The metal container hits Ina in the head and splashes her with water.

The old woman wavers on her feet. I hurry over and put an arm around her shoulders to support her. "Are you hurt?"

"I am well," she says, but I'm not sure she's telling the truth.

"My house is near," I say. "Let me take you there."

She shakes her head. "No, I will go to my father. I saw him over there." Ina nods to the southwest.

I nod. "I will come with you."

"No." Ina pulls out of my one-armed embrace and grabs my hands. "Please stay here until my son returns."

My heart contracts with icy dread. "But Winona hates me."

"You must stay here to tell Chaska where I went. He will worry."

"But what if Hapa comes back? I will be in danger."

Ina shakes her head emphatically. "Hapa rides with the scouts. He will not come back until dark. Unless he starts to drink. Then he will not come back tonight."

Still, I hesitate. Ina squeezes my hands hard. "Please, white woman. I ask you for this favor."

I cannot refuse. She and Chaska have done so much for me, and this is the first thing she has asked in return. "All right." I smile weakly. "I will wait here and tell your son where you are. But how will we find you?"

"Ask the people to help you find Eagle Head."

I nod to show Ina that I understand. She takes a small pouch and sets off.

Dear God, I think as I watch her short figure disappear among the throng of Indians, *let Chaska come back soon.*

CHAPTER

20

I SIT ON THE FAR SIDE OF THE WAGON OUT OF WINONA'S SIGHT AND NURSE my child, who is so feverish that she takes little milk. After Nellie pulls away from my breast, I keep her on my lap to soothe her. Our brief idyll ends when she has a bout of diarrhea, soiling not only her diaper but also my skirt. I do my best to clean her. Then I bed her down beneath the wagon seat and head to the well for more water. As I pass the shelter, the German girl points out my stained garment to Winona and Maggie. Harsh laughter trails after me. Their abuse reminds me of the way schoolmates used to mock me for being fatherless and poor.

The fear that Chaska will leave me under the power of Winona and Hapa rises in my throat like choking phlegm. *You're all alone. Your husband is far away, your son is gone, your daughter is ill, and your protectors have left you alone with the two Indians who hate you most.*

To chase away my anxiety, I recite a verse from the Psalms: "Though an host should encamp against me, my heart shall not fear: though war should rise against me, in this will I be confident." But instead of lifting my spirits, the passage serves only to remind me that I live in the midst of enemies.

As if my loneliness isn't bad enough, my feet burn as though all the skin has been scraped off. I haven't looked under the bandages for more than a day, and I worry that the fiery pain means an infection has taken hold.

Only a few women are gathered at the well, and when they see—
and smell—the state I'm in, they allow me to draw water immediately.
I thank them in Dakota and explain that my little girl is sick. They
coo in sympathy.

I step away from the well and pour water on my skirt. As I scrub
at the stain by rubbing the fabric together, one of the women hurries
away. A minute later she returns and presents me with a sliver of soap.
Her simple act of kindness soothes my spirit like lotion on chapped
skin. I thank her and massage lather into the cloth.

After two washings, the stain fades, but its jagged outline remains.
At least I no longer smell like a latrine. With the last crumb of soap,
I wash my hands. Then I refill my pot with water and limp back to
our wagon.

As I draw near, I see that Winona and Maggie have dragged my
trunk to the shelter, where they sit pulling out my remaining dresses
and cutting them apart. Once again, the women laugh at the size of the
garments. The mockery hurts but not as much as before. After what I
have been through these last ten days, I don't long for beauty and elegance the way I used to. All I want now is to return to a simple life: to
sweep my house, tend my chickens, and bake pies for my family.

Back at the wagon, I pick up my daughter and gaze toward the slope
leading up from the river. The procession has thinned to a trickle, but
among the few people walking toward me, I discern a familiar form. I
wave. Chaska nods but keeps coming at the same steady pace.

When he arrives, I say, "Ina returned. She fell down the hill, but
she was not hurt badly."

He peers around. "Where is she?"

"She and Winona argued, and Winona threw a pot at her. Ina left
to go find her father."

Chaska's brow lowers and his jaw tightens. "Gather your things.
We will go to Eagle Head's piece of ground."

He fetches Lady, who is staked nearby, and hitches her to the wagon.
I climb onto the backseat with Nellie. Without bothering to remove
his sister's things from the wagon bed, Chaska climbs into the front.
He clucks at Lady and turns the wagon around. As we drive away, Winona runs after us shouting. Chaska ignores her.

Although I am glad to leave her behind, I grieve over the conflict between brother and sister. During my captivity, I have learned how strongly the Sioux believe that relatives must care for each other. While I don't blame myself for the discord in Chaska's family, I suspect that Ina and her stepdaughter would still be living together in peace if it were not for the strain of war and hunger. And I do blame whites for the fact that the Sioux are starving.

Chaska slows the wagon to ask bystanders if they know of his grand-father's whereabouts, and they direct us onward. When we find Ina and her parents sitting around a fire, Chaska jumps down from the seat. He goes immediately to his mother.

I climb down gingerly, not wanting to land too hard on my sore feet or to intrude on their reunion. After a couple of minutes, I pick up Nellie and walk toward the fire. By now the sun has set, and in the cooling air, the warmth of the flames is comforting.

Once again we make our beds under the wagon, and once again, I am wakeful all night, imagining that every noise signals the approach of enemies. Finally, just before dawn, I fall into a profoundly heavy sleep.

When my daughter's crying wakes me an hour later, my head feels stuffed with sawdust. I pull Nellie close and allow her to suckle as I regain alertness. Gradually, I become aware of bustling sounds and the aroma of wood smoke.

My stomach grumbles. When Nellie falls asleep once more, I button up my blouse, crawl out from under the wagon, and walk to the fire where the family is gathered. My feet are raw and swollen.

Ina sees me limping. Once I'm seated, she kneels before me and removes the cloth wrappings on my legs, hissing when she sees my feet. Several dollar-sized patches of bright pink, granulated flesh mar their surface.

She gives instructions to her mother, who fetches clean cloth, a bowl of water, and a packet of herbs. "You cannot walk," Ina tells me. She calls to Chaska, "Do you hear? White woman must not walk."

He comes over and stares down at me gravely. "I think the people will stay here a few days. She can rest."

"And if they decide to leave?" I ask.

Shrugging, Chaska says, "You will drive."

He turns away, but I call him back. "Do you know where my boy is? I asked many people yesterday, but no one has ever heard of a Sioux named Paul."

Chaska cocks one eyebrow. "I do not know where Mazakutemani took your son. If he does not bring the boy tonight, I will ride to Hazelwood to look for them."

I choke up with gratitude and nod in acknowledgment.

Once my feet are bandaged, Ina prepares breakfast, supplementing our meager stores with her parents' supplies. After about twenty minutes, she brings me a mug of coffee and a plate filled with dried venison and fried bread and potatoes. Even though I have scarcely eaten the last two days, I have little appetite. My hankering for my son takes up all the empty space in my body.

As I sit giving tiny pieces of bread to Nellie, who seems to be better, Jannette De Camp comes toward me. She cradles her baby boy in her arms, and her older two sons, aged four and nine, trail after her.

"Good morning, Mrs. Wakefield." She gingerly lowers herself to the ground and lays her baby in her lap. Her face is pale except for deep shadows beneath her eyes. Her lavender gingham dress is filthy and frayed at the hem. Her boys, dressed in tattered clothing, squat behind her. Their demeanor is subdued.

Jannette rubs her neck. "We had to huddle outside the tepee last night. The brave who holds us captive was shot at New Ulm, and his wound is festering. A medicine man worked over him all night, and we were not allowed to stay."

"Did you have a blanket?" I ask. The nights have been growing cool.

"No. These savages will not give me anything, not even my own clothes. I have begged them for something else to wear, but they just laugh." Jannette's eyes fix upon my plate. "They barely feed us. You seem well provisioned."

"This is the first real meal I have had in two days."

"I can't recall my last full meal. They give us scraps I wouldn't offer pigs."

I know full well that she is trying to wheedle me out of my breakfast, and I resent her assumption that I have been immune from hardship. Then I look at her two sons. The older boy, Willie, stares down, but tears glint on his lower lashes. The younger one, Joe, licks his lips openly as he stares at my food. I think of Jimmy and wonder if Paul is feeding him.

"Share this with your boys," I say, passing Jannette the tin plate.

She snatches it as though afraid I might change my mind and meticulously divides the food among her two children and herself. When the meat and potatoes are gone, she uses the bread to wipe up the grease, divides it into three pieces, and passes it out.

After swallowing the last bite, Jannette gazes at my coffee, which I quickly finish. She glances toward the fire to see if more food is available. With amusement, I note that Ina has cleared away all signs of cooking and is now sewing. Jannette turns back to me. "Thank you for giving us your breakfast."

"You're welcome. Will you be able to sleep in the tepee tonight? Is the warrior getting better?"

She shrugs. "I don't know. I hope he dies."

"You should not say such things. It will make the Indians angry, and they will treat you badly."

Jannette waves away my concern. "Oh, they don't speak English."

I happen to know that many Sioux are concealing how much English they understand, so they can better spy upon their captives, so I tell her, "Do not assume that. They may know more than you think they do."

"You overestimate their intelligence," she replies loftily. "They're children."

Ina calls to me sharply in Dakota and tells me that she has much work for me. Her peremptory tone surprises me because earlier today she told me to rest my feet. "I'm sorry," I say to Jannette. "I have to do chores."

"All right. Thank you again." She rises and leads her boys away.

I hobble over to Ina and ask in Dakota, "What do you want me to do?"

The old woman smiles roguishly. "Nothing. I wanted that white woman to leave. All she does is complain. I do not want my people to think you are like her."

I laugh for the first time in days. "Do not worry. We are not friends."

"Why did you give her food?"

"I felt sorry for her little boys. They looked hungry."

Ina shakes her head and murmurs the Dakota name I was given last summer, Taŋka-Winohiŋca Wašte—"large, good woman." She sets down her work, walks over to the wagon, and takes a fabric-wrapped bundle from under the seat. When she hands it to me, I unwrap it and find a piece of bread.

"Thank you," I say, and this time I eat it.

In the afternoon, Chaska sets off on Gleason's horse to look for Jimmy. I stare after him a long time, paralyzed by the yearning to see my boy again. Realizing that time will pass more quickly if I am occupied, I sit down to finish beading the moccasins. Ina sits by me with her own needlework. Her face is lined with weariness and her forehead is bruised, but she seems in good spirits.

As we work, a woman approaches us calling, "Winohiŋca Wašte?"

I glance up to see Opa, a woman I sometimes visit in the village near Yellow Medicine. Her husband has a farm near the agency. Opa's hair has a dull, washed-out color as though faded by the sun. Her cheeks are sunken because she is missing many teeth, so she rarely smiles, but her dark eyes light up when she sees me.

Rising, I say, "I am happy to see you. Are you well?"

She clasps my hands. "I am well. How are you? Where are your children?"

"My girl sleeps in the tepee. My boy visits Little Paul—Mazakute-mani."

She nods so vigorously her entire body sways. Turning to Ina, she offers a traditional greeting. From their words, I gather that they are related.

Opa sits, bending both knees and folding her legs to the right. She says to me, "I heard that you were taken prisoner. I did not know until today that you live with the cousin of my husband." She uses the term *tahaŋ'ši* for male cousin.

"Is your tepee in this camp?"

"No. We are with the Yellow Medicine Indians. Our camp is halfway to Dr. Williamson's house."

About a mile, I think, translating the distance into American terms.

Opa adds, "I was afraid I would not find you safe. As I walked to this place, I heard that many Indians are drunk."

"They must have found some farmer's stash of whiskey." On days when the warriors aren't fighting, they sit in camp drinking stolen liquor until they pass out. I will be glad when they have drunk their way through all the potables in the region.

"How is your husband?" I ask. At my urging, her husband Bit-Nose sought treatment from John last winter when he broke his wrist after slipping on ice.

"His hand is good."

"Does he fight in the war?" I ask.

"No!" Opa's reply is vehement. "Our village is friendly to whites. We want no part in this war."

Ina scowls. "We did not want war either. After the council voted to fight, what could my son do?"

The two women glare at each other, tension shooting off sparks between them. As the silence drags out, I decide to change the subject by asking about Opa's daughter—she and Bit Nose have a girl who is not quite old enough to marry. But then, we hear galloping hooves and a man's voice shouting.

Chaska rides up on Gleason's horse, which is so covered in sweat that it looks as though it has come in from a downpour. "A drunk Indian killed a white woman. You must hide."

"Where?" I jump to my feet. The moccasin pieces fall to the ground.

"Come with me!" Opa cries. "You will be safe in my village."

She ducks into the tepee and emerges moments later with Nellie on her back. I am down on all fours, scrambling to pick up the beads scattered in the dirt. "Leave those," Ina orders. "Go."

The urgency in her voice acts on me like a lash. Abandoning my sewing, I follow Opa as she runs to the fields north of the settlement. People stare at us as we pass tepees and cook fires, but no one interferes. Everything has happened so quickly that I barely comprehend how I come to be fleeing for my life.

We run into a cornfield and down a row, where I must duck to hide behind the five-foot-high plants. Rough leaves slap my face. I thought Opa would slow down once we reach cover, but she continues to sprint.

Nellie screams at me from her place on Opa's back, but I am too winded to call out reassurances.

Within minutes, I am stumbling and clutching my side, yet I hurry on. Even though I cannot hear anyone on our trail, I expect to be grabbed from behind at any second. The accumulated terror of the past days pursues me like a pack of rabid wolves, giving my legs unprecedented strength. Surprisingly, my feet do not hurt. My heart pounds. My vision is unnaturally sharp so that I retain vivid images of browning corn silk and the bright red dot of a ladybug even though I see them for the briefest of instants.

We reach the end of the cornfield and dash between mounded rows of potatoes, bent as low as we can make ourselves. When we reach the end of that field, we come out in the open—but are no longer within sight of the agency. I stop and rest my hands on my thighs.

Opa calls back, "Run!" Her command sends a new surge of panic through my veins. I race even though my lungs heave painfully. Finally, a cluster of tepees appears before us, and Opa slows to a walk.

When we reach her tent, she calls out to her husband and throws open the tepee flap. A pack of dogs rushes out, scaring me. A man issues a loud command from the interior, and the animals instantly sit at our feet. Nellie looks at them in open-mouthed astonishment and then issues a peal of delighted laughter.

Bit-Nose, a man with jagged scar tissue where the tip of his nose should be, comes out of the *tiyopa*. When Opa relates what happened, he says, "You are welcome here."

"Thank you," I say and ask if I may sit down. Now that we are no longer running, my feet pulse with a searing pain that keeps time to my heartbeat. Glancing down, I see that blood has seeped through the bandages.

Bit-Nose and Opa follow my gaze and ask what is wrong. After I explain, Opa sends her daughter, Grey Dove, to fetch water and bandages, while she prepares a paste of herbs. By the time they finish tending me, my pain has greatly diminished.

Opa tells me to rest. As she and Grey Dove prepare a meal, I amuse myself by watching the dogs wrestle over bones. Thirteen different animals make up the pack; most of them typical Indian dogs: medium-sized bodies, pointed snouts, erect ears, and coarse fur. Their colors range from blond to brindled tan to brown. They watch Opa closely as she cooks, but they are too well trained to steal food.

As word spreads of my arrival, women I know from the Upper Sioux agency come to visit me. One is Julia LaFramboise, a half-French–half-Sisseton woman who teaches at the school near the Lac Qui Parle Mission. She is a pretty girl with dark coloring, an oval face, and full lips. "Mrs. Wakefield," she calls as she approaches. "I saw your son James today."

I clap my hands. "How is he?"

"Well and happy. Paul and his wife are making a great pet of him."

"Oh! Thank you for telling me." Tears of relief flood my eyes, and I give Julia a watery smile. "And how are you? How are the Hugginses?" I ask, referring to the family she lives with at the mission.

Julia groans. "Amos Huggins is dead," she says, her voice hoarse. "Some men from Red Iron's village came to our house. They murdered Amos and told Josephine and me to take the children and run. We went to Chief Walking Spirit, and then my brother fetched me away from there in Indian disguise. I had to leave Josephine and the children behind."

I touch her arm. "I will pray that you receive happy news of your friends."

She nods. "Thank you, Mrs. Wakefield. Josephine's children are about the same age as your two little ones."

A wave of sadness flows over me. Whenever I think I find some good news in this bleak situation, something else bad happens. Will this terrible war never end?

I wake to the consciousness that, during the night, the big toe of my right foot has been rubbing an irritated spot on my left ankle. Gradually, I become aware of localized spots of inflammation on both legs and arms. Sitting up, I find tiny, hard pink bites—and red welts from scratching. As I examine them, a teeny, flat-bodied insect leaps from my clothing to my pallet.

Fleas, I think as I scratch my scalp. *Is there not one place among the whole Sioux nation where I can live in peace?*

Opa ducks through the *tiyopa* and bobs her head when she sees me awake. "Did you have good sleep?"

"Yes," I say, and it's not a lie. Although I'm miserably itchy at the moment, I slept soundly all night.

Bit-Nose and his dogs have left for the day. As Opa and I eat fried potatoes, I tell her about my troubles with Winona—feeling guilty for betraying Chaska's family problems but justifying it with the excuse, *She is their cousin, after all.*

"You stay with us," Opa says without hesitation. "We have room in our tepee. Bit-Nose likes children."

"Thank you," I say, despite having qualms. If I have this many flea bites after one night, how bad will it get if I live here all the time?

The mile-long dash to this village has worsened my poor feet so that every step feels as though I am walking on thorns. Opa tells me to rest. Without anything to keep my hands occupied, I am irritable, so I sit outside making a clover chain for Nellie. Although her diarrhea seems to have stopped, I continue to worry about her. Since our ordeal in the haystack, she has grown more babyish, and she speaks much less than she did before we were captured. Such a reversion to infancy is understandable, I suppose, but I wish I could ask John about it.

Mid-morning, a buggy approaches. Chaska is driving it and—my heart leaps—a small, tow-headed child rides with him.

Rising, I stagger toward them, crying, "My boy! My son!" I would not have recognized Jimmy if not for his hair. He is all done up in the dress clothes of an Indian boy: a buckskin tunic and leggings, decorated with fringe and feathers.

As soon as Chaska halts the buggy, a swarm of children converge on it. Jimmy stands up, delighted to be the center of attention, and shows off a new plaything, some type of slingshot made from rawhide. He grabs a green crabapple from a small pile on the seat and shoots it to the acclaim of his audience.

I reach the buggy, but he pays no attention to me. "James, aren't you glad to see your mother?"

He turns to face me. "Oh, yes. But I had such a nice time at Paul's. I want to go back again. Can we, Mother?"

"We'll see."

When I take hold of his arms to lift him down from the buggy, he scowls. "Do you think I am a baby? I can get out by myself."

I step back and watch him jump to the ground. Chaska laughs to see my boy's spunk, but my heart cracks a little. How did Jimmy get to be so independent in just two days? He *is* still a baby; he won't be five until October.

Chaska stays for supper and, agreeing that I am better off where I am, drives back to his mother alone.

My spirit is so buoyant that not even sore feet or itchy bites can keep me from celebrating having both my children back with me again. After supper, I take Jimmy and Nellie out to the prairie where they can run to their hearts' content through the licorice-smelling fields. As they cavort, I sing the songs we used to enjoy at parties—"Lorena," "Listen to the Mockingbird," and "My Old Kentucky Home"—and wander around gathering armfuls of asters, black-eyed Susans, and goldenrod.

When dusky lavender fills the sky, we head back to the tepee. On our way, I walk by two white captives who sit beside a fire. The women pointedly look away from me, but after we pass, one says loudly, "She acts glad to be a prisoner."

"What can you expect? That's the one who took an Indian husband."

I consider confronting them, but what would that accomplish? The plunge from civilized to primitive life torments me as much as anyone, but constantly bemoaning my state will only worsen matters. If those women do not see that for themselves, I pity them.

In the morning, as I sit outside helping Opa grind dried prairie turnips into flour, Jimmy shouts, "Paul!"

I absentmindedly scratch a flea bite on my arm as Paul rides up on a mule, tethers the animal, and comes to sit with us. Jimmy dances around behind him, but a sharp glance from me reminds him not to interrupt adults, so he squats behind our visitor.

As Opa goes to fetch coffee, Paul nods at the bowl and pestle I am using. "If you stay with me, you will not have to do that work."

"I like to be useful," I answer, not wishing to acknowledge the indecent proposal that underlies his words.

He rubs the mole on his chin. "But you are a white woman. You should not live in a tepee. If you come with me, you can stay in a house."

Opa hands him a mug of coffee and sits on the ground, grunting loudly. I'm not sure whether the sound expresses pain or disapproval. I smile at her and tell Paul, "Bit-Nose and Opa are my friends. It is an honor to stay in their tepee."

He frowns, clearly trying to think of a new argument. Jimmy takes advantage of the moment to jump up and tug the sleeve of Paul's calico shirt. "You promised to teach me how to make a spear."

Paul ruffles his hair, gives me an ingratiating smile, and leads my son toward the trees to choose a sapling.

Paul continues to pester me, arriving at our tepee at odd hours, bringing gifts of eggs or tomatoes, and asking me to come live with him. Each time, he offers some seemingly plausible reason—*I have chairs in my house, I have a Bible you can read, I have a fine garden and chickens*—yet everyone in camp believes that his primary purpose is to acquire a white wife. Each time, I deflect the question in such a way as to maintain the pretense that I don't know what he is really asking.

Toward evening of the second day, Chaska rides up, dressed in the fine, black wool frock coat he used to always wear to church.

"Ina sent your things," Chaska says, handing me my satchel. He dismounts from Lady and gives the horse a carrot that he extracts from a side pocket of the coat. I feel a pang of envy to see my mare nuzzle him affectionately.

As I ask after his mother, Paul rides up on his mule and hands me a letter from Mary Butler Renville, a white woman who married into the mixed-blood family that built the trading post at Lac Qui Parle. The letter says that some friendly Sioux from the Upper Agency have set up a camp apart from Little Crow's people. It promises that if I come with Paul, Mary and her husband John will protect me.

Refolding the letter, I bite my lip in consternation. The Renvilles are devout Christians, and I believe them to be sincere in their desire to protect white captives, but that does not mean Paul has been honest with them about his intentions.

The thought of Lac Qui Parle gives me an idea. Perhaps talking to someone who knows the people there better than I do will clarify matters, so I ask Paul if he will fetch Julia LaFramboise. "Why?" he asks testily.

"I want her advice."

Scowling, Paul walks off. As soon as he is gone, I turn to Chaska and tell him what the letter says. "What do you think? Should I go with Paul?"

He shrugs. "You may go if you want. I do not care. I swore to keep you so I can return you to your husband, but you may go away if you wish."

Annoyed by his indifference, I fold my arms across my chest and say no more until Paul and Julia LaFramboise arrive. I hand Julia the letter and stare straight into Paul's eyes. "Tell me the truth. In what way could I stay with you?"

His gaze slides first to Chaska, then to Julia, then back to me. "As my wife. But you need not do any work. My Dakota wife will do everything."

"Poor woman!" I exclaim. Now that Paul has spoken so boldly, I do not need Julia's advice, although I am glad to have witnesses to preserve my reputation. "How can you treat me so disrespectfully? You are a Christian. You know it is wrong to have two wives."

He opens his mouth to argue, but I refuse to let him speak. I gesture toward Chaska. "He is a better man than you. He treats me well and has never asked me to be his wife. Do not ask me this again."

Paul's face darkens with embarrassment and rage. Stalking over to where his mule is tethered, he unties it and rides away.

Opa, who had been listening to the exchange from inside her tepee, comes out to stand beside me. "That one will not give up," she says in a low voice. "I do not think you can stay here."

Stricken, I look at her. "Where will I go?"

She looks over my shoulder to Chaska, who says, "Get your children. I will take you to my aunt."

I nod and duck into the tepee to gather the few belongings we have left. Now that we've been told we have to move once again, I realize how minor a problem the fleas were. Staying with Opa and Bit-Nose felt like visiting good friends. How unfair it seems that, once again, I must search for safe harbor.

CHAPTER

21

WHEN CHASKA ESCORTS US TO HIS AUNT'S TEPEE, TUŊWIŊ GREETS US cordially, but her eyes hold anxiety. She lacks enough food to feed herself, let alone my family, yet at Chaska's request, she accepts us into her tepee without hesitation.

To alleviate the burden, Jimmy and I go foraging the next day in the abandoned gardens near the burned-out traders' houses, but all we find are a few ears of unripe corn and a handful of overgrown, fibrous green beans. Only our ravenous appetites made the resulting stew palatable.

As soon as I wake the next morning, I lie on my pallet counting the days since my capture. If I remember everything correctly, today is the last day of August, the fourteenth day I've been a prisoner. Autumn will arrive soon, and we will have to deal with cold as well as hunger. The thought worries me.

Sighing, I rise and change Nellie's diaper. She no longer has a fever, but her bowel movements remain soft, and I am at my wits' end to know how to cure her. I fear the green corn we ate last night will only make things worse.

My poor girl whimpers as I wipe her chafed bottom. To distract her, I sing a lullaby. As I fold a cloth into diaper shape, Jimmy walks up. "Mama, I'm hungry."

"I'm sorry. We don't have anything to eat."

"Can I go back to Paul's? He has food."

I fasten Nellie's diaper by knotting the corners and then face my son. "No, we cannot visit Paul. He was rude to me."

"But, Mama—"

"James Orin Wakefield, that's enough. I am in no mood for your fussing."

He runs back to his pallet and flings himself upon it. Instantly, I feel guilty for being so stern. Who can blame him for being cranky with an empty belly? Yet despite my regret, I can think of no way to make things up to him.

Soon afterward, Chaska drives up in our wagon, which is pulled by Gleason's horse. Beside Chaska sits his mother, and I walk out to greet her. On her lap, Ina carries a bolt of white canvas to make into a new tepee. She asks if Tuŋwiŋ and I will help her, and I say yes without hesitation. I can think of nothing I would not do for this old woman.

She hands me the cloth, and Chaska helps her climb down. I feel shy around him this morning—irritated that he was so unconcerned about the way Paul harassed me and embarrassed that I allowed myself to imagine I might mean anything to him. Inside Tuŋwiŋ's tepee are the beaded moccasins, finally finished, but now I cannot think what possessed me to make such a personal gift.

Ina takes back the bolt of canvas and carries it to where Tuŋwiŋ sits outside the tepee. I start to follow, but Chaska tells me to wait. He reaches into the back of the wagon, pulls out a small wooden crate, and hands it to me. It contains a five-pound sack of flour, a small bag of summer squash, and some potatoes and carrots. "For your children. So they do not go hungry."

"Where did you get this?" I ask in surprise.

"I bought it."

"You have no money. How could you buy food?"

"I sold something." His expression is evasive.

Instantly, I leap to the conclusion that Chaska has sold Lady and doesn't want to admit it. "My mare. You sold my mare without asking me."

His face takes on a mulish look. "I am no horse thief."

"Then what—"

"I sold my coat."

"Your good black coat?" He nods. Shame over my unjust accusation burns my cheeks. "That was your best garment."

He shrugs and stares at the ground. "Children must eat."

"Oh, my friend—" Emotion overwhelms me. I press my lips together and take a deep breath. "Wait here." I carry the box of provisions into the tepee. Unearthing the moccasins from under the robe where I hid them, I press them against my chest to hide the beading and take them outside.

"I...I have been working on a small thing...to thank you for your protection and...generosity." I stumble over my words because I fear he might take this gesture the wrong way. "You would honor me if you would accept this."

I hold out the moccasins on my outstretched palms. For a moment, Chaska is silent, and the gift sits there like a homely girl at a dance. Then he picks up one of the moccasins and runs a forefinger over the beading. "You made these?"

"Can't you tell? The sewing is poor. I have never worked with rawhide." I laugh at myself and suddenly feel better. Chaska's eyes meet mine, and I can see that my gesture moves him deeply.

"Thank you."

"It is a small thing after all that you have done."

"You have helped my people. Now I help you. It is the same."

"The same," I repeat softly, and I feel less alone.

Chaska nods. Taking the moccasins, he climbs into the wagon and drives off.

The glare of the sun reflecting off white canvas hurts my eyes. Ina, Tuŋwiŋ, and I each sit sewing a seam on a different section of the new tepee. Neither of the other two women seems to be bothered by the heat or intense sunlight. Earlier I suggested that we do our sewing in Tuŋwiŋ's tepee, but Ina wanted to work outside so we would have room to spread out the cloth.

I drink some water, wipe my face with a damp cloth, and go back to stitching. As I near the end of my seam, Mrs. De Camp approaches me. "Mrs. Wakefield! Your face is burned to the color of a raspberry!"

I shrug. "I cannot help it. I lost my bonnet the day I was taken captive."

"I have come to ask a favor," Janette De Camp says. "I wondered if, since you speak the Indian's language, you would ask them to give me a squaw dress like yours. The clothes I'm wearing are about to fall off me."

Shading my eyes, I look up at her. Her lavender gingham dress is even more threadbare than before. Some seams are splitting open—from wear and tear, not from the strain of her body. Like me, she has lost a noticeable amount of weight.

"My friends do not have extra clothing to give you," I say quietly, "and neither do I. All of my dresses have been cut up to make outfits for the Sioux."

Jannette wrings her hands pitiably. "You do not have to ask these women. Come with me to the tepee where I'm staying and ask the women there. They laugh at me, but they will listen to you."

I shake my head. "Why should they heed my request when they don't know me?" I set down my sewing and lead her a few steps away from Ina and Tuŋwiŋ. "Mrs. De Camp, listen to my advice. You have taken a wrong course with the Indians. Crying all the time, complaining about your treatment, and rejoicing when a Sioux dies will only make them hate you. They are all suffering and give you the best they can. If you would be patient and grateful, they would treat you better."

"Grateful?" she shrieks. Ina and Tuŋwiŋ look up and frown. "You think I should be grateful for being kidnapped and starved?"

Putting my hand on her arm, I adopt the soothing tone I use when one of my children has hysterics. "No, be grateful that they share their meager provisions with you and do not treat you the way the traders have treated them."

Mrs. De Camp puts her hands on her hips and glares at me. "Everyone says you have become an Indian lover. I defended you after you fed us the other day, but now I think the others are right. *Grateful!* Only a traitor would be grateful for the things that have happened to us." With that, she marches off.

"You did not take my meaning correctly!" I call after her, but she hurries away with greater speed.

I hug myself, discouraged over yet another squabble with a fellow prisoner.

And why do you care what Mrs. De Camp thinks? As if she stands before me, I hear my Grandmother Brown's voice: *Sarah Florence Wakefield, make up your mind once and for all. Are you going to spend the rest of your life seeking the approval of these starchy matrons? Or are you going to rely on your own God-given conscience and do what you believe to be right?*

The words of the New Englander philosopher Henry David Thoreau come to me: "If a man does not keep pace with his companions, perhaps it is because he hears a different drummer." That was easy enough for Thoreau to say. He was a cantankerous man, supported by influential friends and convinced of his own genius. I'm an ordinary, weak-spirited woman trying to keep my children alive. I have no interest in nonconformity for its own sake.

Yet, even as those thoughts flit through my mind, the flame of conviction flares up within me. I cannot knuckle under to the opinions of a foolish woman who lets her discontent overmaster her common sense.

For once in your life, forget about your reputation, I admonish myself. *Once this is all over, it won't matter what these women think. All that will matter is having survived the war and being reunited with John.*

In the afternoon, Chaska rides up on Lady. He wears leggings and a shirt, and he has a bag slung over one shoulder. He does not dismount. As Ina goes to speak to him, I steal a glance at his feet to see which moccasins he is wearing. His old ones, I note with a twinge of disappointment.

After a few moments, Chaska raises his voice so I can hear. "Scouts say lost cattle wander the Big Woods. I go with a group of men to drive them here."

I walk closer to them. "The Big Woods? Isn't that Chippewa country?"

He cocks his head as though my question puzzles him.

"Won't they attack you if you invade their territory to round up animals?"

Chaska scowls. "A warrior does not shirk danger when his people are hungry. Would you have me leave those cattle for our enemies to eat?"

I lower my gaze to hide my fear. "No. I understand that you must go."

"You should not stay here. If a bad man comes, my aunt cannot protect you. You must go back to Bit-Nose. My mother will take you there."

The thought of moving again reminds me of a game the Indians sometimes play, in which great crowds of men use giant sticks that end in spoon-shaped nets to carry a ball as they run down the field. At this moment, I feel exactly like one of those stuffed deer-hide balls being passed from player to player. I long to retort, *Then why didn't you leave me with Bit-Nose?* But I know the answer to that. The war has created so many shifting loyalties that Chaska must constantly reevaluate each situation. Three days ago, he moved me to get me away from Paul; now he has decided that the hostile Indians in this camp pose a greater threat.

"All right," I say. "I will pack up my things and go with Ina."

After spending one night with her cousins, Ina returns to Tuŋwiŋ's tepee. Although I am sorry to be separated from her, I am happy to be back with Opa and Bit-Nose—so much that I don't even care if fleas feast upon my ankles. Both of my children are safely with me, and although Nellie is not completely well, she has improved so much that she may be her old self soon. Maybe then I will hear her jabbering away as an almost two-year-old should.

Jimmy delights in running with the dogs and playing with other children in camp. Opa and I spend our days scouring abandoned homesteads for any food the raiders might have overlooked. In the pantry of one house set far back from the road, we find some flour and two crocks, one filled with lard and the other with molasses. That night we celebrate by making fried bread and serving it sweetened. The broad smiles on my children's molasses-streaked faces fill my heart with joy.

On my eighteenth day of captivity, Bit-Nose reports a battle. Three days earlier, four bands of Sioux—led by Grey Bird, Big Eagle, Red Legs, and Mankato—were on their way to attack New Ulm again when they spotted a column of U.S. soldiers in the distance near the creek whites call Birch Coulee. The Indians sent scouts who observed that the soldiers chose a poor camp site—too far from the creek to get water if they were under attack and too close to trees and high prairie grasses that could provide cover for encroaching Indians. The soldiers also failed to dig defensive entrenchments. At sunrise two days ago, the Sioux ambushed them.

Within an hour, the Indians had killed most of the army horses and inflicted heavy casualties on the soldiers. Those troopers who survived that assault hastily dug trenches and dragged animal carcasses into place to serve as barriers.

That evening, more than 200 American troops marched from Fort Ridgely to relieve the besieged soldiers, but Mankato and his warriors created so much noise that the jittery commander ordered his men to retreat. The next day, shortly before midday, Colonel Henry Sibley arrived with a much larger force. Rather than attack superior numbers, the Sioux melted into the prairie like the morning dew. Only two Indians died during the conflict, Bit-Nose tells us.

The news oppresses me. If U.S. soldiers are that poorly prepared to fight the Indians, then I do not see how the army will ever bring this war to an end. My heart sinks as I envision a life of endless captivity.

To my surprise, Bit-Nose draws the opposite conclusion. "Many thousands of soldiers will come now to avenge their fallen brothers," he says. "Our warriors made them look like children. They will have to defeat us to prove their skill as fighters."

While I do not care for his assumption that the deaths of soldiers are a sharper spur to action than slaughtered women and children, I take comfort in the thought that the army's response might be just beginning. Perhaps we may yet be rescued before winter sets in.

"Little Crow and his band arrived at Yellow Medicine this afternoon," Bit-Nose goes on. "He convinced the other chiefs that we must all leave this place. Tomorrow, we will start for the Red River, and we will not stop until we get there."

Swallowing hard, I offer a feeble protest, "I do not want to go so far. My place is here where my husband will be able to find me."

Bit-Nose says, "Little Crow would never allow it. He has given orders that any captive who refuses to travel with the people must be killed."

I stare down at my lap and nod, but secretly wonder if I could find a place at the agency where my children and I could hide.

Preparing for the journey does not take long; everyone has been expecting the move, so we unpacked very few things. Soon after dark, the family goes to bed. I lie on my pallet, listening to the dogs' snoring. For once, I am grateful for the noise because I hope it will keep me awake until the others fall asleep. Within seconds, however, my eyelids close and I drop into a heavy slumber.

When I wake, I suspect that I have slept for hours. I need to relieve myself, so I rise and quietly leave the tepee. The eastern sky has lightened from the black of night to a bluish grey. I walk in that direction, taking care to give tepees as wide a berth as possible.

By the time the cluster of agency buildings looms ahead of me, the stars have faded from the sky. In the growing light, I feel exposed and at risk. I pause behind a clump of shrubs and crane my neck to peer ahead.

Almost all of the tepees that stood here have already been taken down, so I can see all the way to the warehouse, the stable, and my home. Three men exit from the agency headquarters. Even from this distance, I identify one of them as Little Crow. One of the chief's companions strides over to the smoldering embers of a fire, jabs an unlit torch into it, and pulls forth a flaming brand.

A second man does the same, and the two of them go from building to building setting them alight. My own little house, the only wooden structure at the agency, is the first one set ablaze. As the flames catch hold, a searing pain twists my gut. The only belongings I had left in this world stood in that building. Now I am homeless and utterly bereft of possessions. Bit-Nose was right. This place no longer holds any safety for me.

The breeze blows the acrid smell of burning paint and varnish my way, causing my eyes to sting. Turning on my heel, I head back toward Opa's tepee, keeping under cover as much as possible.

CHAPTER

22

ABOUT HALF AN HOUR AFTER SUNRISE, I ARRIVE BACK AT CAMP. OPA, WHO is building the cook fire, gives me one of her closed-mouthed smiles. I say nothing about where I have been.

While she makes gruel, I put coffee on the fire. A droplet of water rolls down the outside of the pot and hisses when it nears the bottom. A tongue of flame shoots up, reminding me of the conflagration that just devoured my house, and sadness blankets me like falling soot.

As I stare absently into the fire, Bit-Nose drives up in a small, two-wheeled cart. The vehicle, once painted green, is chipped, stained, and patched with odd pieces of wood. It doesn't have a seat, so Bit-Nose stands at the front holding the reins, maintaining his balance with difficulty. The Indian pony pulling the cart bucks against the shafts. It is a sturdy beast, about fourteen hands high, with palomino coloring. Bit-Nose jumps down, grabs the animal's harness, and calms it by stroking its withers. Then he stakes out the pony and tells us to pack because we must leave after breakfast.

As the gruel and coffee cook, Opa and I load household goods from the tepee into the cart, piling layer upon layer of buffalo robes, blankets, backrests, dishes, pots, and clothing. When I carry out a half-empty barrel of crackers, Bit-Nose insists that it go in the front. "Why?" I ask as I move other items to make room for it.

"You will sit on it."

I stare at him in disbelief. "Me?"

"You drive. Opa says your feet are bad."

I stare in consternation at the precarious mound of items, which rises higher than my head. If I'd had any idea that I was going to be driving this vehicle, I would have taken more care in the loading of it.

The people around us are already breaking camp. After a hurried breakfast, Bit-Nose declares it is time to leave. When I take my seat in the cart, the raised edge of the barrelhead digs into the back of my thighs. I pull a blanket off the mound and fold it into a cushion. Even so, I remain uncomfortable; my feet straddle a crock of lard—melted to oil in this heat—and a crock of molasses pushes my right leg forward in an awkward position that strains my lower back. Bit-Nose lifts Jimmy and Nellie into the cart, and they scramble around until they find places to sit on piles of clothing near the front. "Hold on tight," I tell them.

Opa pulls on her pack, and Bit-Nose unties the pony. I flick the reins and, speaking in Dakota, order it to walk, but the beast ignores me and crops the grass. Only after Bit-Nose pats it on the rump does it finally move.

As we drive away, I fret about Chaska. Is he still gathering cattle in the Big Woods? Did his party have a confrontation with the Chippewa? Even though I trust Bit-Nose to protect me, the protracted separation from Chaska makes me feel forsaken. If anything happens to him, I doubt I will survive this war.

The pony bucks again, and I tighten the reins. Having spent my childhood on a farm, I have driven many a horse, but none compares with this one. I swear there must be mule in his background—even though I know full well that mules cannot breed. Clearly, this animal has not been trained to pull a cart. Whenever I tug one side of the lines, he turns in the contrary direction, and when I pull on the reins to slow him, he grows more rambunctious.

As a result of the pony's haphazard motion, pots, dishes, and vegetables keep sliding off the back of the cart. Opa and her daughter, who walk on either side of us, continually grab falling items and hand them to my son, who tucks them in wherever he finds space. All things considered, we get along fairly well.

We wend our way down from the high bluff where we camped to low ground so we can cross the creek. When the pony smells water, he plunges forward. I pull on the reins to no avail. Within moments, he is mired to the top of his forelegs in mud.

The cart appears to be sitting on solid, grass-covered ground, so after telling my children to stay put, I jump down. To my chagrin, I land knee deep in a bog, too far away from the cart to grasp its side for support. When I try to yank my leg free, the powerful suction of the quagmire pulls me off balance. I topple and land on all fours with my face only an inch above fetid swamp water.

Jimmy's bell-like voice calls, "Mama, what are you doing down in the mud?"

Opa comes around the back of the cart, halts where the ground is still firm, and calls to her daughter. After a few minutes, Grey Dove appears carrying a board she has borrowed from someone in the caravan. She inches forward, careful to stop short of the marshy area, and extends it to me. Opa stands behind her, holding onto her waist. By grasping the board, I pull myself out. Grey Dove laughs at the sight of me, covered in muck from neck to feet. For an instant, my cheeks burn with embarrassment, but then I look down at myself and join in the laughter.

Walking around to firmer ground on the other side of the cart, I unfasten the pony. As soon as he is free, he extricates himself from the bog, rushes to the creek, and drinks his fill.

With great effort, Opa, Grey Dove, and I pull the cart away from the marshy area. Opa's daughter puts the pony back in the shafts, and then we cross the creek.

As we make our way up the opposite bank, Jimmy sighs deeply. "Mama, why don't you turn around and drive to Shakopee?"

"Why, Jimmy, you know that the Indians will not let us."

He shakes his white-blond head and frowns like an old man. "Oh, dear me! What do you suppose God made Indians for? I wish they were all dead, don't you?"

Nervously, I glance to see if Opa or Grey Dove heard him. What a relief to see that they have fallen behind the cart and are talking together! "Son, I wish we could go back to Shakopee too, but I don't wish all the Indians were dead," I say quietly. "You wouldn't want any-thing bad to happen to our friends, would you?"

"I guess not. But I am tired of traveling, and I want to see my father."

"I do too, my boy. I do too."

That night, we camp about three miles west of Hazelwood. Opa fries up some bread and serves it with molasses. My children and I eat sup-per, sitting upon a piece of carpet placed next to the cart. Jimmy de-vours his sweetened bread with gusto, but Nellie has a poor appetite. Her forehead is warm again.

As I coax her to drink water, a woman calls, "Mrs. Wakefield? Is that you?"

Turning, I see Ellen Brown, the twenty-year-old daughter of the former Indian agent, walking toward me. She has her father's square face and round eyes, with the dark coloring of her mixed-blood mother. Like me, she wears Indian dress.

"Miss Brown." I smile warmly. "It's good to see you."

She stares at me intently. "Mrs. Wakefield, I would not have rec-ognized you if I met you on the prairie. You have changed so much since I saw you."

The last time we met was at a party in June to show off her father's new mansion—not three months ago, although it seems like a lifetime. "Yes, I'm very sunburned, and my clothes are muddy from a mishap I had today."

"It's not that." She clasps a hand over her mouth as if to recall the words.

"What do you mean?"

"Have you not seen a mirror recently?"

I shake my head, wondering in dismay what is wrong.

Ellen Brown lays a gentle hand upon my arm and whispers, "Your hair has begun to turn. Up at the roots, it's growing in pure white."

My hand flies up to my head as though I could feel the change. Tears sting my eyes, and I try to blink them away. *I'm only 32 years old,* I think. *John won't want me back if I look like an old woman.*

To Ellen Brown, I say, "It must have happened the first day I was taken. The shock of seeing George Gleason's murder and hearing

Hapa declare he wanted to kill me too. I've never been so frightened in my life."

She nods. "That would terrify anyone."

I smile, but my lower lip trembles, and I change the subject. "Is your family well? I saw your sister-in-law and her newborn baby a few days ago."

"Both mother and son are fine. My family is managing to survive, largely because my mother's relatives are part of the peace party among the Indians."

"Peace party?"

"Yes." She squeezes my arm. "They are trying to work out a way to save the captives. Take heart, Mrs. Wakefield. Not all Indians are your enemies."

"I know that." The image of Chaska arises in my mind. "I thank Providence daily because he has given me a protector among the Sioux."

As we gaze at each other, taking comfort in that simple exchange of hope, Jimmy walks up and tugs my skirt. "Mama, excuse me. Nellie is sick again."

"Forgive me," I say to Ellen Brown, "but I have to attend to my girl. The poor child has suffered from bowel complaint for days."

"I'm so sorry to hear that. I wish I had something that could help her," the young woman says and takes her leave of us.

I awake in the morning, expecting to travel again right after breakfast, but no one in camp shows any sign of moving. When I ask Opa about it, she answers, "Men brought back cattle. We stay here to prepare meat for winter."

"Oh," I say and wonder if Chaska is one of those who returned. Will he visit us today and perhaps transport me back to his mother's tepee?

The day passes, however, without his arrival. *Maybe he's glad to be free of us,* I think sourly.

For the next few days, the Indian women and I keep busy while the other white captives wander through camp gossiping and bemoaning their lot. I cannot understand why they don't help. Certainly, they will benefit from the food supply as much as anyone. But not only do they refuse to offer assistance, they also shoot me venomous looks for working alongside the Indians.

Opa and I toil from dawn till sunset butchering cattle, slicing and drying meat, and preparing jerky and *wasna.* As evening approaches, we switch tasks and cook kettle upon kettle of beef stew.

Each night after dark falls, the men arrive, each one carrying a wooden trencher. They eat their fill and, after smoking a pipe together, take out greasy packs of cards and gamble, wagering whatever possessions they have for the thrill of trying to win something from their friends. Often the same shirt or pair of moccasins is wagered and lost, night after night, exchanged from hand to hand.

Some of the men refuse to stop playing until they have nothing left to bet but their breechcloths, at which time modesty compels them to leave the game. Others play only a few hands and then lie down near the fire, pounding their fists upon their chests in the manner of beating a drum and singing songs about the *Isan Taŋka,* or Big Knives—one of their terms for white men. After an hour or two of such entertainment, they rise and demand more stew, so that the women must cook through the night until shortly before dawn.

After three nights of this, I am so exhausted that I stagger as I go about my chores. My weariness makes everything seem worse, and I am hard-pressed to keep from weeping. Since talking with Ellen Brown, I have managed to look at my reflection in the creek and confirmed that my hair is indeed turning white. I've also lost more weight. John has never minded that my face is plain, but he always set great store on my being "a fine figure of a woman." How will he adjust to having a skinnier wife? Will he still care for me as a husband should? How terrible it would be to reunite with my husband only to find that he no longer loves me.

I come upon Opa and Bit-Nose sitting outside the tepee, deep in conversation. As I approach, they fall silent and Opa glances at me uneasily. Instantly, my chest constricts with fear. "What is wrong? Has something happened to Chaska?"

"No, my cousin is well," Bit-Nose says. "But we are in danger. Lower

Agency Indians plan to attack the people from Upper Agency. They are angry that we keep a separate camp and have not gone to war. Our leaders have formed a soldiers' lodge to protect us. Fighting may happen soon."

My knees give way, causing me to drop heavily to the ground. Several of the dogs come over to sniff me, and I push them away. "But Little Crow wants to punish me for what Galbraith and the traders have done."

Opa nods. "Yes, it will go bad if they attack us and find you."

"Maybe I should return to stay with Chaska."

The old woman glances at her husband and back at me. "You are safe from Hapa here."

"I know." Biting my lip, I stare at the trampled ground and remember the belligerent songs the young men sing every night. If Little Crow's people attack this camp, riotous confusion will engulf us. It will be easy for some warrior to drag me off and scalp me to curry favor with his chief.

"Chaska is one of Shakopee's people, and Shakopee is Little Crow's ally," I finally say. "Little Crow's people will not attack his band."

Opa rubs her mouth and nods. "I want you to stay with me like a daughter. But you will be safer with my husband's cousin."

Bit-Nose rises. "I will send for him." Calling his dogs, he walks away.

About suppertime, Chaska rides up on Lady. He dismounts and, ignoring me, walks straight up to Bit-Nose. "I have not heard that Little Crow wants to attack these Indians. He has not crossed the creek."

"A party of his warriors rode to our camp and threatened us. They said we must join them. Maybe Little Crow did not want you to know this."

As one, the two men turn in my direction, and I know what they are thinking. Because of me, Little Crow no longer trusts Chaska. After a moment, Chaska nods. "It may be so. But why do you think Taŋka-Winohiŋca Waŝte will be safer with me?"

Bit-Nose steps close to him and lowers his voice. "Many chiefs from Upper Agency have formed a peace party. They speak of regaining the favor of whites. They want to take the captives away from Little

Crow and carry them back to their people." My heart leaps at this; it is the same thing Ellen Brown said.

Bit-Nose continues, "Mazakutemani and others went to speak to Lower Agency chiefs. They demanded the release of captives. Then Strike-the-Pawnees stood and said that if Mdewakanton must suffer and die, so must the whites."

Chaska shakes his head. "That is why Taŋka-Winohiŋca Waŝte should be here. Then she can go home when your chiefs release captives."

"I will not live that long," I say, interrupting them. "You told me Little Crow wants me to die. If his warriors attack this camp, they will seek me out and kill me."

"This is foolish talk. Little Crow will not attack. The Sisseton and Wahpeton have prepared themselves. The Mdewakanton will not attack an armed camp."

"You do not know that," I retort, shocking myself with my boldness in contradicting him—and in front of others too.

"We leave for Red River soon," Chaska says. "If you stay with Bit-Nose, you can ride in his cart. If you go with me, you have to walk."

"Why? I drove the wagon last time."

"Hapa has the wagon now and the other horse. He and Winona do not live near us anymore. We go separate."

My opinion does not waver. "I wish to go with you, even if I must walk. I will not stay here and wait to be killed."

Chaska lowers his brows and glares at me. Finally he says, "I will come back for you. I must find someone with another horse to help me carry your children."

"I can carry Nellie, and Jimmy can ride with you."

Chaska's jaw tightens. "No. It is better this way. I come back tomorrow."

Panic rises within me. Chaska sees it in my eyes, and his expression softens. "I will watch to see if Little Crow's people prepare for battle. If that happens, I will come and take you away tonight."

Pressing my lips tightly together, I nod.

The next morning, Chaska returns on Lady. At his side rides another man who looks to be about thirty. He wears a white shirt, ball-and-cone silver earrings, and a woman's black-lace shawl wrapped around his head as a turban. His horse is a beautiful grey gelding. Chaska introduces the man as his cousin Dowonca.

The plan is for the children to ride and for me to walk beside the two horses, carrying my few possessions in the now-battered satchel. Since Nellie is skittish with strangers, I hand her up to sit before Chaska. "She has been sick," I warn him.

He waves my words away. "If the child is sick, she cannot help it."

Bit-Nose lifts Jimmy up to ride before Dowonca. The younger man reaches into a bag and hands my son a piece of peppermint stick, to Jimmy's great delight.

"Travel with care, my cousins," Bit-Nose says.

Chaska nods, while Dowonca stares solemnly ahead. His horse prances impatiently. Opa steps forward to say good-bye, and I thank both her and Bit-Nose for their kindness.

As we set off, Chaska tells me that his mother's tepee is near Yellow Medicine on the far side of the creek, which means we have several miles to go. I ask if Ina has recovered from her bruises, and he answers simply, "Yes." I remark that the cattle drive seemed successful, and he grunts. After that, I fall silent, concluding that Chaska is still displeased about my decision to go back with him.

I trudge beside the two riders, tired of being treated like a child. Resentment bubbles within me like pus from a suppurating sore. Why should I not select which of two dangers I am most willing to face? I am a grown woman, and this is my life, mine and my children's. I have the right to make my own choices. My judgment has proven to be sound so far. If George Gleason had listened to me, we would have returned to Yellow Medicine and escaped to safety with John Other Day, as my husband did.

About an hour after we set out, a thick column of smoke rises into the sky ahead of us. Within minutes two more dark pillars ascend next to it. "That's coming from the mission at Hazelwood," I say.

Chaska nods. I think about the prosperous community I visited so often there; it had a church, a school, and Reverend Riggs's home.

"Why is Little Crow burning so many buildings?"

Dowonca is the one who answers, "He does not want the white soldiers to use them during fighting."

"Oh," I say. *Of course.* Little Crow is thinking as a general. The army could station sharpshooters on the upper floors and kill any Indians that approach. "That is too bad. It will take years to rebuild everything destroyed in this war."

Stony silence meets my remark, and I realize too late that perhaps neither of my companions regards that as a bad thing.

At the end of the journey, Ina greets my children and me warmly. Her new tepee is so clean and fresh that I feel almost as though I have entered a civilized dwelling. Even better is the knowledge that I no longer have to contend with Winona's foul humors or Hapa's threats.

My relief is short-lived, however. The day after our return, Nellie's illness comes back more violently than before. Whatever she eats or drinks runs through her, and she cries piteously from the scalding pain of continual diarrhea.

I feed her a bland diet: weak beef broth, plain bread, and starchy gruel. Ina brews a medicinal tea from red dogwood bark, and for a few brief hours, I dare to hope it will turn the tide, but then Nellie has her worst case of the runs yet. By noon, she is feverish and irritable. Her skin looks pasty, her cheeks are sunken, and her voice is as raspy as if she coughed all night. I sit beside her, murmuring, "Please, God. Please, God. Please, God." I fear that I am about to watch my baby die.

Ina's view of Nellie's condition is more sanguine. The old woman continues to dose the child with dogwood tea, saying it takes a few days to work. *We don't have a few days,* I think. When I remember all the medicines John kept in his office, now either stolen by the Sioux or destroyed by fire, I want to throttle the men who started this war. If only I could get calomel or laudanum or Dover's powder.

After two days and a night of anxiety, we hear from one of Ina's friends that the Williamson house still stands. Dr. Williamson is a doctor as well as a missionary, and I latch onto the hope that his abandoned dwelling might contain medicaments.

The next morning, Chaska, Dowonca, Jimmy, and I walk the two miles to the mission. Dread weighs on me heavily as we head toward the place; in more peaceful times, Jimmy and I often attended the Williamsons' church and shared many a meal with the genial, elderly couple and Dr. Williamson's sister Jane. Now, despite what we've been told, I fear that we will find nothing but a blackened ruin.

About halfway there, I hear the wild tolling of the mission bell. I glance at Chaska in alarm, and he gestures for us to walk more quietly.

Twenty minutes later, he points at a clump of shrubbery, and Dowonca leads Jimmy and me behind it. Chaska moves on ahead, keeping to cover.

He returns within ten minutes. "No danger. Boys play at mission, and doctor's house still stands."

I release my breath in relief, and we continue on. When we arrive at the mission, Chaska and Dowonca decide to question the boys to see what they can learn. I send Jimmy to look for food in the back garden, while I enter the house.

The interior shocks me. An earthquake could not have done more damage. Every piece of furniture and all the household goods are broken and thrown on the floor. Not one item of the Williamsons' belongings remains intact. The stove, bedsteads, cushions, dishes, books, and doctor's instruments have all been shattered or ripped to pieces. I sink to my knees and sort through the debris, praying to find something salvageable. When I find the medical powders, crushed pills, and smashed vials of syrup on the floor, I shriek in rage.

How could the Sioux have done this? They revere their elders, so why would they turn these elderly missionaries out of their home during a war? The three Williamsons are among the kindliest people I know. Of all the clergy I have ever met, Dr. Williamson most exemplifies the heart of Christ as I understand it from the Bible. He is a man of deep compassion and gentle judgment, and the people here at the mission loved Dr. Williamson as much as any of their chiefs. Why, oh why, would the Sioux do this to him when all he has ever done for them is good?

I walk outside, physically and emotionally spent. The clanging of the mission bell and the shouts of boys beat upon my ears. Chaska and Dowonca are nowhere in sight. I sink down upon the front step of the Williamson home, rest my head upon my folded arms, and sob.

After a minute or two, a small form sits next to me and a slim arm rests across my back. "Mama, are you hurt?"

"No." I struggle for breath. "I'm just sad. The Williamsons' beautiful home is ruined, and there's no medicine. I don't know what will become of your sister."

"Don't cry, Mama. You know we will get away soon. Then Nellie will get well."

Lifting my head, I wipe my cheeks with the back of my hand and give my boy a wobbly smile. "Did you find anything in the garden?"

His face droops with disappointment. "Tomatoes. But they aren't very red."

"Maybe they'll ripen after they're picked." I rise and reach for his hand. "Let's go see."

CHAPTER

23

THE NEXT MORNING WHEN I RETURN FROM RELIEVING MYSELF, I FIND Nellie sitting up on our pallet. Her eyes have lost their feverish look, and she says, "Mama, hungry."

"Oh, darling!" I kneel and take her into my arms. Her forehead is cool.

She pulls out of my embrace and exclaims, "Hungry!" I laugh and give her some crackers. Even though the fever has broken, I must be careful what she eats for the next few days. No meat until I am certain the diarrhea is gone.

As I go about the tepee hunting for suitable food, Ina enters through the *tiyopa*. She smiles when she sees my daughter. "Dogwood tea made her well."

"Yes, it did," I admit. Ina said that it would take a few days to work, and she was right. "Thank you for helping us."

Ina shrugs and turns away, downplaying her acts of kindness as always. Smiling to myself, I gather the ingredients to make cornmeal mush.

After breakfast, Nellie goes back to sleep. One of my regular chores is to fetch water for the tepee, so I pick up Ina's tin pail and set forth.

Even though the river is near our camp, my task is difficult because the bank is almost perpendicular here. Usually, I lay prone along the edge and lower the pail into the river, but when I haul the full container back up again, the weight wrenches my shoulder and the thin metal handle digs painfully into my fingers.

Today, I decide to use a different method. I take off my moccasins. Choosing a spot with overhanging shrubbery, I make my way down the steep bank and wade into the river. I fill the pail up to the brim and return to shore.

At this point, I realize the flaw in my plan. How will I ascend that steep bank? "You should have learned your lesson when you were stuck in that ravine," I grumble aloud.

Transferring the pail to my left hand, I grab an overhanging branch and pull myself up, digging my toes into the bank. Then I reach for a higher branch.

This time I mistakenly latch onto a twig, which breaks and sends me sliding. Mud streaks my legs, and the pail flies out of my hand, spilling water all over me. The pail lands on its side in the river and immediately starts to fill. In frustration, I lunge at it before it sinks. I make the arduous ascent, this time being careful to grab only branches that can hold my weight.

Once I am atop the bank, the obvious solution to my problem hits me. I should have brought a rope to tie to the pail's handle so I could dip it more easily into the river from up here. *Why did it take me so long to figure this out?*

I start to put on my moccasins but stop with one foot in mid-air. My feet are much too dirty. Which means I will have to wash in the water I have drawn and then get more to take back to the tepee. What a wasted effort.

Sitting on a boulder, I dip my right foot into the pail and reach down to rub off the mud. As I repeat the process with the left foot, one of Ina's friends approaches the river with a wooden bucket in her hand. Hers is attached to a rope, so I wave to her, intending to ask if I can use it. But as soon as she sees me, a look of horror crosses her face, and she rushes back to camp.

I look around to see what upset her, but nothing seems amiss. Even so, her behavior unsettles me. Hurriedly, I rinse out the pail several times before refilling it.

When I return to camp, I find Ina talking to Chaska in great agitation. She sees me, throws up her hands, and ducks into the tepee.

Chaska wears an uncharacteristically severe expression. "Is it so? Did you put your feet in the pail?"

"They were dirty. I had to wash them."

He scowls so fiercely that I take a step back. "You should not put your feet in the pail. No one does so."

I set the water down and hasten to explain, "I washed it after I used it."

Chaska makes a chopping motion with his hand. "Now the pail is dirty."

"But I washed it. I can wash it again."

He says something in Dakota, but even though I have grown almost fluent in the language, he is using one key word that is strange to me. I lift my hands in incomprehension.

"Wait here," Chaska tells me. "Do not touch the pail."

He stalks off, leaving me bewildered and shaken. I glance at the pail; it is a cheap tin container, old and much dented. How could it be ruined by what I did?

After several minutes, Chaska returns with an elderly man, who regards me gravely. "Chaska has asked me to explain because I have better English."

"Thank you," I say, reassured by his educated diction.

Gesturing to the container, he says, "According to Dakota belief, you committed a great sin by putting your feet in the pail. All the vessels in the tepee are sacred. No women are allowed to put their feet in them or even to step over them."

"But why?"

He lowers his brows. "I cannot explain. Men do not speak of woman things."

I frown for a moment before comprehending. He means a woman's monthly courses. They are afraid that I have contaminated the pot with my menstrual blood. "But I'm not—" I say and then stop myself. If they are that squeamish about the subject, mentioning it will only make my offense worse.

Once again, I seek to make amends. "But I rinsed it. And I can wash it again. You can watch me do so. I will use soap and wash it until you say it is good enough."

The man shakes his head vehemently. "You cannot make it clean!"

"I don't understand."

"It will not do. The pail is—" He frowns and scratches his nose. Then his brows lift as he finds the word he wants. "Polluted. They will never use it again."

"But that's the only pail they have."

He shrugs. "They will use waterskins until they can get a new one. You cannot make this one clean. It is not done."

With that he walks away. Chaska nods emphatically at me. He pours out the water and sets the pail upside down on the grass. He goes into the tepee, presumably to tell his mother that I have been suitably chastised.

After walking a short distance from camp, I sit behind a clump of bushes and rest my forehead against my upraised knees. My eyes sting from unshed tears.

Once when I was very young, we went to my grandmother's house for my cousin Elizabeth's thirteenth birthday, a momentous occasion on which she was going to receive an heirloom brooch that our ancestors had brought from England. When I entered the dining room, the sight of a beautifully decorated cake drove every other thought from my mind. I ran straight to the table, scraped off one of the marzipan roses, and popped it into my mouth. My cousin burst into tears. As my mother whisked me out the room, I heard Elizabeth wail, "It's ruined!"

After receiving a stern talking to, I went back and said I was sorry, an apology that Elizabeth grudgingly accepted. But we both knew my thoughtless act had tainted the occasion and perhaps even our relationship.

Now I am flooded with the same stomach-churning shame at having committed an act that cannot be remedied—yet in this instance, my remorse is tinged with anger. How was I supposed to know about their foolish superstition?

Suddenly, I remember an earlier incident. When I first began to live with Chaska and his mother, I noticed that they do not perform their morning ablutions in a washbasin. They take a mouthful of water and spit it onto their hands. It was only when I declared that I absolutely cannot wash myself that way that they begged a basin for my use. If I had paid more attention, I would have realized that it goes against their customs to wash in any of the tepee's vessels.

Stupid, stupid, I tell myself, and my tears begin to flow. After trying so hard to fit in with their way of life, I have committed a worse offense than any other captive. I feel as clumsy and out of place as a bison calf masquerading as a family dog.

No matter where I go, no matter what people I live with, I never fit in. What is wrong with me?

For days afterward, I take care to observe all the customs the Sioux have taught me, do my chores with my eyes cast down, and work as hard as any Indian woman. Yet I cannot get over feeling like a troublemaker. Each morning, the first thing I see upon exiting the tepee is the now-useless pail sitting overturned on the prairie. To compensate for my blunder, I take many trips a day to fill our waterskins. Yet, I do not complain about the tedious errand to any Indians and share my frustration with only one captive, a woman named Harriet Adams.

Mrs. Adams is a pretty girl, about twenty years old with fair skin, red-gold hair, and blue eyes. She and her husband John lived near Hutchinson. When I first met her here in camp, she told me they had been fleeing toward town when three Indians on horseback came after them. The Adams' oxen-pulled wagon was too sluggish to outrun their pursuers. They could see another wagon of white men farther ahead on the road, so John Adams leapt down, grabbed their six-month-old baby, and ran in that direction. Carrying the child slowed him, so Harriet called, "Put the baby down and hurry for help." She jumped from the wagon.

Within seconds the warriors were upon her. One dismounted, snatched the baby from her arms, and dashed his head against the ground. The little boy's body jerked once and then lay as limp as a rag doll. The warrior shot him. By this time, John had reached the other wagon and convinced the driver to turn back, but it was too late. The killer lifted Harriet Adams into the arms of one of his companions and jumped upon his own mount. The three Sioux galloped away.

Initially, Mrs. Adams's ordeal elicited the sympathy of other captives, but her subsequent actions curdled their pity into contempt. One of her captors took her into his tepee, and soon Harriet Adams was wearing Indian dress.

After that, other white women accused her of taking her child's killer as her lover, but I don't believe the charge. My impression is that she is a dazed bird with a broken wing. Sudden noises cause her to start, and whenever she fears anyone is cross, she smiles or giggles ingratiatingly. Because of that, some spiteful cats claim she enjoys being a captive. They have said the same things about me.

I pass her one morning as I am lugging water back to camp and she is on her way to the river. Stopping to catch my breath, I greet her and she gives me a timid smile. "How are you today, Mrs. Wakefield?"

Lowering my voice, I tell her about the misunderstanding regarding the pail.

"Isn't that strange!" She drops her voice to a whisper. "Some of their customs are so odd. I live in constant fear I will do something wrong and be whipped for it."

"You told me that the warrior who keeps you has been kind."

"He is! But his wife gives me angry looks and mutters under her breath whenever her husband goes out of the tepee."

I pat the poor girl's arm. "I will pray for your safety."

"Thank you." She picks up her bucket and continues toward the river.

Nearly a week after the incident with the pail, Chaska tells me that we are going to move again.

"To the Dakota Territory?"

"Not today. We will stop near Red Iron's village."

Red Iron is a chief of the Sisseton, one of the Upper Agency tribes that Ina and the other women fear so much—irrationally, in my view. I wonder whether Chaska believes there is friction between the bands. "Is Red Iron—" I struggle to word my question tactfully. "Is he an ally of Little Crow?"

Chaska presses lips together. "They are not enemies," he says slowly. "But Red Iron has not fought in this war."

I nod to show my understanding. Red Iron must be a member of the peace party I have heard about, but it would not be politic for Chaska to say that aloud. Even so, it must be a good sign that the Mdewakanton are going to join Red Iron's people. Perhaps Little Crow is ready to negotiate peace.

Early the next morning, Chaska hitches Lady to a loaded travois. It is the first time my mare has felt the burden of poles laid across her back, so she prances in alarm, scattering the goods packed on the triangular frame. Patiently, Chaska calms her and lifts Jimmy onto her back. The familiar presence steadies her.

Once again Ina tells me that I must walk barefoot across the prairie as Indian women do. A week ago I would have protested and reminded her of the damage my feet have already suffered, but today I acquiesce.

I put Nellie in a sling on my back and position myself alongside the mare. Ina pulls on a heavy pack and moves forward to lead Lady by the reins. As we walk away, I look back and see the abandoned pail still sitting where Chaska placed it. Years from now someone will find its rusted-out remains and wonder why it was left there, never knowing how much trouble the seemingly innocuous item caused.

The road to Red Iron's village is packed with carriages, buggies, and wagons, forcing those of us who walk to cross the prairie itself. We have not had rain for nearly two weeks, so the grass is dry and coarse, and it slashes my feet and legs. Three weeks of living with the Sioux have not been sufficient to give me the leathery skin of an Indian woman, but I tell myself that even if I do not have a tough exterior, I must be calm within.

However, the self-imposed task of quieting my heart proves even more difficult than ignoring the misery of my feet. I feel very sorry for myself. Despite hearing reports of a peace party, we seem no closer to freedom than we did the afternoon Hapa shot George Gleason. I am sick to death of being scolded by the Sioux and sneered at by other whites.

Salty sweat rolls down my legs and trickles into the open cuts on my feet causing them to sting. As the hot prairie sun broils my unprotected head, the heat distills my bitterness into a concentrated brew. My irritation is all the more galling because I dare not express it. Because of my blunder with the pail, my position feels even more precarious than it did when I was taken prisoner.

After about two hours, Ina glances back and sees me compressing my lips to keep from crying. She looks at my feet and clucks in dismay. "I am sorry you must walk," she says, her first kind words in a week. "All horses and wagons are loaded."

"I do not ask to ride."

Ina nods approvingly at my stoicism. She would not be so pleased if she could discern the seething self-pity within.

The prairie is so parched that our cavalcade stirs up clouds of dust from the road and grassland alike, and a brisk breeze blows it back on those of us who trail at the rear of the procession. I swallow hard, trying to work up enough saliva to moisten my dry throat. "Can I have some water?"

The old woman shakes her head. "We do not stop. We will eat and drink at Red Iron's village."

"Is there danger?"

Ina shakes her head again and says only, "The people do not stop." Then, in contradiction of her words, she abruptly halts the horse, hands the reins to Jimmy, and comes back to me. "Your daughter sleeps."

"Good. She must sleep to get strong again."

"We can put her on travois. You will walk easier."

I halt and let Ina remove the sling from my back. Together we tie Nellie to the bundle that is fastened to the poles on Lady's back. Within two minutes, we are marching across the prairie once more.

Without the weight of my daughter on my back, I am able to stand up straighter and roll back my shoulders. That relieves some of my discomfort but does nothing to ease my thirst or my wretched feet.

We reach a rough patch of ground, and the bumping of the travois wakes up Nellie, who begins to cry. Ina looks back and orders, "Make her quiet. Now."

Her angry response makes me wonder anew if enemies are on our trail. I take Nellie's hand and say, "Shhh, baby, Mama is here."

"Noo noo," my daughter pleads.

Half running to keep up with the horse, I untie her from the travois and take her into my arms. I unbutton my blouse, put Nellie into position, and make a cradle out of my arms for support. She instantly stops crying and latches onto my nipple.

Within a few minutes, my arms ache from her weight, which creates a terrible pull across my shoulder blades as I walk along. Yet, because of the order to keep her quiet, I dare not put her down until she decides she is satisfied.

My muscles grow more and more strained, and I have to grab both my wrists to brace my arms. Ina sees my predicament and moves close to me in case I need assistance. Determined to demonstrate my grit, I clench my teeth and continue to trudge forward without asking for help.

Finally, after an interminable length of time, Nellie dozes. Once again Ina ties her on the travois as I rebutton my blouse and rub my aching shoulders. The old woman nods at me, takes up Lady's reins, and starts walking again.

As I plod along, I feel proud at having proven my hardiness—yet also dismayed that I went to such lengths to make this old woman approve of me. Whatever possessed me? I could have thrown out my back, and then the Indians would really view me as a burden. Not a week ago, I was congratulating myself on having sound judgment, but lately all my decisions go awry.

A couple of Sioux women pass me on the left and laugh. "White woman, you have a dirty face," one of them calls.

I rub my cheek, and my hand comes away with a brown film. Between the blowing prairie dust and my sweat, my face is coated with grime.

We do not reach our new camp until midafternoon as I judge it from the position of the sun. At least six hours of walking without a break for food or water. I limp for the last hour or two and leave a trail of blood across the prairie.

By the time we stop, my feet are torn to shreds. I sink upon the ground. When Chaska comes near, I tell him, "I think I will die if I have to walk farther."

He sets his mouth in a grim line and folds his arms across his chest. "I told you to stay with Bit-Nose and ride, but you would not."

"I know," I say, ashamed again. "I am sorry I complained."

Chaska's expression softens. "You should go back with Bit-Nose now."

"No! I do not feel safe there." Despite the pain, I struggle to my feet. "Little Crow is angry with the peaceful Indians. If I stay with them, I might get killed in a fight between the peace party and the hostiles."

He glances around to make sure we cannot be overheard and answers softly, "You can stay here. I think the war will end soon. Soldiers will rescue you. If they do not come before river starts to freeze, I will put you in a canoe and take you to white settlements. But if we go now, the angry young men will kill us."

I nod, grateful that we finally have a plan to end this ordeal.

CHAPTER
24

EVEN THOUGH CHASKA AND I HAVE SETTLED ON A PLAN FOR THE FUTURE, we still face an intractable problem in the present: How can I march all the way to the Dakota Territory, which if memory serves, is some seventy miles from here?

When I express my concern to Chaska, he shrugs. I know he thinks I should go back to Bit-Nose so I can ride in the cart, but he refrains from mentioning it again. Instead, he goes to ask if the chiefs plan to leave for Red River tomorrow, leaving his mother and me to do the women's work of setting up camp. Before we erect our tepee, however, Ina insists upon tending to my wounds.

As she spreads balm on my feet and wraps them in cloth, we hear the thundering of many horses. Just beyond the edge of camp, nearly a hundred horsemen ride past with a scowling Little Crow at their head. I scan the riders but do not see Chaska.

Jimmy runs up. "What's happening? Are the soldiers coming?"

I gaze at him and, for an instant, I'm thrown back to the day six weeks ago when a war party rode past our agency on their way to raid the Chippewa. Back then, I feared that the mere sight of Sioux wearing war paint might give me a heart attack; now that woman seems like an overprotected stranger. Ruffling Jimmy's hair, I answer, "I don't know, son."

As Ina ties off my bandages, I ask her, "Should we put up the tepee?" Ina shakes her head. "I do not know. Let us cook food first."

Chaska returns while we are building the fire, and I notice his worried frown. When he touches Ina on the shoulder and nods for her to walk away with him, I burst out, "Please, tell me the news. I am not a child."

He scowls but gestures for me to come closer. When I do, he says quietly, "A large party of Sisseton with weapons met our people south of Red Iron's village. Red Iron will not allow us to cross his land. He told Little Crow, 'You started this war. We do not want you here to excite our young men and get us in trouble.'"

Fear constricts my throat. "What will happen?"

"No one can say. We must wait and see."

"Should Ina and I put up the tepee?"

Chaska lifts his hands palms upward. "We cannot go forward. The Sisseton will not let us. We cannot go back. The soldiers are there. We need a place to sleep."

As soon as camp is pitched, people gather in the central area between the tepees. Women cook kettles of meat as if for a feast, and two warriors set a pole in the middle of the ring. Glancing up, I see a long hank of red hair hanging from the top of the shaft. My stomach roils, and I take deep breaths to keep from being sick. No skin is attached to the hair, so it's probably not a scalp. I tell myself it must be a beard and hope to God I'm right.

As dusk falls, two warriors ride around the assembly, rearing their horses showily and letting out war whoops. Then a man, naked except for breechcloth and war paint, jumps into the clearing and dances around the pole, singing one of the Indians' rhythmic chants. When he is finished, he stands directly before the hank of hair, beats himself upon the chest, and shouts, "I killed two traders and took many things from their store while they lay there."

Shouts of triumph rise from the crowd, and several Indians, both women and men, dance around the man. Drums and chants accompany them.

I step back from our cook fire into the deepening shadows and whisper to Ina, "Why are they doing this? They have no victory to celebrate."

"They prepare themselves to fight. Go to my tepee and take your children."

I scoop up Nellie, who sits on a rug near the fire, and turn to fetch Jimmy, who plays with some of his Indian friends about thirty yards away. As I walk toward the boys, another warrior moves into the center of the clearing. This one is a frightening-looking fellow with heavily lidded eyes and a puckered scar along one cheek. The story he proclaims is so gruesome that it roots me to the spot: "I destroyed a whole family, for which I deserve much honor. This is how it happened. I came upon a farm and went into the stable to steal horses. The white man was there, so I shot him and smashed his head with the butt of my gun. After he was dead, I rushed into the house. The woman was making bread, and she screamed. I grabbed her by the hair and threw her against the wall. Her baby was in a cradle on the floor. I lay it in the bread pan and put it in the oven. The woman cried out and tried to stop me, so I shot her. Then I set the house on fire."

Shouts of vindictive glee rise into the night, causing me to wonder if I know these people at all. Trembling with horror, I stagger toward my boy. When he sees me, he rushes to my side and hides his face in my skirt.

We make our way to the tepee, where I throw myself down on the bed and gather my children into my arms. Jimmy's pallet is on the other side, next to Chaska's, but I don't care. Tonight I will keep my darlings with me.

Jimmy wakes me in the night by burrowing close to my side. "What's wrong?" I whisper.

"I'm cold!" His voice is piercing.

"Shhh!" I put my arm around him and pull our blanket up to our chins. Lifting my head, I realize he is right. Chill air seeps through the smoke vent at the top of the tepee, and I wonder if the temperature outside has dropped enough to make an early frost. "Don't wake the others," I whisper.

"But, Mama, I'm cold. Can't you build the fire?"

"No!" I answer, afraid that doing so might somehow violate the Indians' customs. "Go back to sleep."

My son pulls his head under the blanket, and I close my eyes. After a moment, I hear movement on the other side of the tepee. I hold my breath, afraid that we're in for a scolding. Instead, Chaska rises from his place, and without a word, drapes his blanket over my children and me. Then he returns to his pallet and lies down again with his back to the fire so he cannot see us.

The stalemate between Little Crow and Red Iron continues for days, preventing the Mdewakanton from journeying to the Dakota Territory. Now two large camps—one of friendly Indians and one of hostiles—face each other along the southern bank of the Minnesota River. When skirmishes break out between the young bucks, the friendly camp removes itself a few miles upstream. Little Crow's people break camp and move about the same distance, so that once again the two opposing sides of the Sioux people block each other's way.

Although I do not say so to Ina or Chaska, I thank God that we have halted. The thought of leaving Minnesota terrifies me.

Rumors swirl through our camp like scraps of paper borne by the wind. The day after Chaska gave us his blanket, I go to the river to wash clothes and take my place in a line of women who squat upon the bank performing the same chore.

One of the women calls out to me. "Did you hear about your friend?"

"What friend?"

"The girl with hair like fire who dressed like an Indian woman."

"Oh, Mrs. Adams. No, I have not seen her in many days."

"The Indian wife threw a knife at her husband for looking too much at the white woman. Now the white woman has gone to the other camp."

"Oh," I say, sad that the girl didn't say good-bye. It was a comfort to know one other white woman who had adopted Sioux customs as a survival strategy.

The women continue to swap news of various friends and relations. After a few more minutes of camp gossip, the woman next to me asks the others, "Did the messengers return?"

"No," another woman answers. "My husband says Little Crow expects them to return tomorrow."

The exchange startles me so much that I blurt out, "What messengers?"

Silence falls upon the group. The woman next to me narrows her eyes at me and says, "Little Crow sent two mixed bloods to the leader of the white soldiers."

I thank her for telling me and go back to washing out my daughter's clothes, working quickly so I can rush back to camp.

When I return, I find the old woman in the tepee. "Ina!" I call as I come through the *tiyopa*. "Did you know that Little Crow has sent messages to the army?"

When she looks up from the shirt she is mending, her expression is guarded. "Yes, I know it."

I sit down hard. "Why didn't you tell me?"

Ina looks down at her sewing and makes another stitch. "My son did not want to excite you. It is better to wait until we know what the white chief says."

Chaska doesn't trust me. He thinks of me as a child who cannot control her emotions. My cheeks burn with indignation.

"I heard it from other women," I say. "Tell me what you know."

Setting her sewing aside, Ina meets my gaze. "After the last battle, a mixed blood called Wakanhinape found a note that the white war chief left in a box tied to a stake in the ground. Wakanhinape brought the note to Little Crow."

"But the Battle of Birch Coulee was—" I pause, stymied because I don't know if the Dakota language even has a word for *week*. "Many days ago," I finally say.

Ina nods. "Chaska was in the council when the man brought the note. Little Crow did not want to be fooled, so he asked four or five different mixed bloods what the writing said. The white chief told Little Crow that if he had any proposals to make, he should send them with two messengers who carry a flag of truce."

"Do they talk peace?" I ask eagerly.

She shrugs. "No one knows. We must wait until the men return."

Wait, I think. *Always, wait. We've been captive nearly four weeks, and I am tired of being patient.*

By afternoon, I am so tense that my skin feels as if it will split open. When Nellie falls asleep for her nap, I go outside to watch Jimmy play with Gleason's dog.

I am sitting in the shade of the tepee, sewing in a desultory way, when shouting erupts at the edge of the camp. Looking in that direction, I see a group of warriors pushing several white woman and children ahead of them. The women, whose hands are tied, are crying. When they reach the clearing at the center of the tepees, one of the men bellows, "Listen to me, my people. The Sisseton have betrayed the nation. We found them trying to help these whites escape. We surrounded them and forced them to release the captives back to us."

I blanch when I remember how Chaska said his people would kill us if he tried to canoe me down to the white settlements. Calling my son, I lead him into the tepee to keep him from witnessing whatever violence might occur. Ina takes one look at my face and asks what is wrong. When I tell her, she says, "I will go see what happens. Stay here."

Sitting upon my pallet next to my daughter, I bow my head, cover my eyes, and sway back and forth.

"What is wrong, Mama?" Jimmy asks.

"I am scared," I admit, giving him a wobbly smile. "Everything is so volatile." He frowns at the difficult word, so I explain, "Everyone is excited and angry. I am afraid someone will hurt us before the war comes to an end."

"Don't worry," he says solemnly, patting my cheek. "I will protect you."

I hug him tightly, and he squirms to get free. "Mama! Stop treating me like a baby. I am a big boy now."

"O.K." I release him but ruffle his hair. "Your father would be proud of you."

"I think he would be proud of you too," Jimmy says generously.

Ina returns about an hour later and tells me that all is calm. The captives are under guard but have not been harmed. The warriors who recaptured them have gone to report to Little Crow.

"This has made more bad feeling between my people and the Sisseton."

I wonder if maybe Chaska was right and I should have gone back to Bit-Nose.

The next morning, Chaska leaves right after breakfast. When he returns midmorning, carrying two wooden buckets that he traded a lantern for, he finds Ina and me working with other women to dry corn and potatoes. He calls the two of us into the tepee and tells us that the messengers—two mixed-blood men named Thomas Robertson and Thomas Robinson—have returned. This time, Colonel Sibley's message to Little Crow is blunt: "You have murdered many of our people without any sufficient cause. Return me the prisoners, under a flag of truce, and I will talk with you then like a man."

I catch my breath and wait for Chaska to say more, but he remains silent, staring into the ashes of last night's fire. After a full minute, I ask, "What did Little Crow say? Is he going to release us?"

When Chaska looks up, his face is drawn. "Chief Wabasha's son-in-law spoke against letting the prisoners go. He said, 'The matter has gone too far to be remedied. We have got to die. Let us kill as many of the whites as possible, and let the prisoners die with us.' His words stirred the warriors in council."

Pain stabs my head, like a stake being driven through my temples. I squeeze my eyes shut and exhale. Then I ask in a croak, "So is Little Crow going to kill us?"

"He did not say so. He is going to send another message to the white chief Sibley. This time he will tell him that he has 155 prisoners and the Sisseton and Wahpeton hold others. He will also say the captives are doing well."

I expel a deep breath, and my shoulders drop from their hunched position. "He would not say that if he means to kill us."

"I hope it is so," Chaska says and exits the tepee.

Ina and I go back outside and resume preserving food. As we work, a mule-drawn buggy passes. It has two passengers, a young man with wavy, light brown hair whom I recognize as Tom Robertson, son of the former superintendent of farms for the Indian agencies, and another, darker man, who must be Tom Robinson. The other women also stop working to watch them pass. I say a quick prayer for the success of their errand and go back to tying ears of corn to a rack to dry.

About twenty minutes later, a party of warriors on horseback sweeps down the road after the two Toms. A woman with a baby on her back rushes up to us. "Those warriors ride after the mixed bloods. They plan to murder them."

"Why would they kill Little Crow's messengers?" Ina demands.

"Our young men do not want to make peace with white soldiers. After they kill the two men, they will come back and kill all the captives and mixed bloods."

Her words hit me like a physical force. A sound like wind roars in my ears, the earth seems to heave, and my vision goes black. The next thing I know, I am lying on the ground, my teeth chattering as though I suffer from deadly cold. Ina kneels next to me, rubbing my hands and murmuring, *"Waŝicuŋ wiŋyaŋ, waŝicuŋ wiŋyaŋ."*

I wish she'd stop calling me white woman, I think as I sit up. Vertigo assails me. Putting a hand to my forehead, I look at the old woman. "What happened?"

"You fell. We heard about danger, and you fell."

"Oh, yes," I reply as the memory comes back.

A friend of Ina's walks up carrying a mug of coffee, which the old woman hands to me. I take a sip. Glancing at the women around me, I ask, "Do you believe what she said?"

Ina shrugs. "I do not know. Do you want to hide?"

After finishing the coffee, I return the mug to the woman who fetched it and thank her. "When Chaska returns for the midday meal, I will ask him what to do."

Ina helps me to my feet, and I take a couple of deep breaths to make sure I am steady. Then I stoop to pick up the ears of corn I dropped when I fainted.

We work in silence for a time. Although I do not have another dizzy spell, I continue to feel physically sluggish, even as my mind races with fear that the Indians might slaughter all the captives rather than release us to Sibley.

As I go fetch another basket of corn, I spot a man I know from Shakopee walking a short distance away. Boldly, I hurry after him and call, "Dark Cloud, wait! Have you heard that the young men want to kill all the captives?"

He halts. "Some people say so. The chiefs have not agreed."

His answer is hardly reassuring, and my heart thumps with terror. Rash young men started this war without the chiefs' approval; they could just as easily go on an impulsive rampage against the prisoners. I lift my hands in a beseeching gesture. A way to save myself leaps into my mind. "But I am Chaska's wife."

Dark Cloud frowns skeptically. "Is it so?"

"It is. He married me after I moved into his mother's tepee. The young men will not kill another warrior's wife, will they?"

He shakes his head. "No," he says slowly. "If Chaska says you are his wife, they will leave you alone."

"Thank you," I say. Once again, a wave of weakness washes over me, but this time it is from relief, not fear, and I do not faint.

As I walk back, I see that Chaska has returned. I explain to him and Ina what I told Dark Cloud.

Chaska's face flushes dark. "You did very wrong to say so! There is no truth in the story."

I cringe before his anger. "You told Hapa I was your wife."

"I did so to stop him from hurting you. But you know the story is not true."

"But the young men are going to kill me. I have to do something."

Chaska shakes his head vehemently and rises to his feet. "It is dangerous to tell such stories now!" He moves toward the exit. "I must tell Dark Cloud it is a lie."

"Dangerous? How?" I call, but he leaves without answering.

I turn to Ina, who glares at me with her arms folded before her chest.

Holding out my hands to her, I say, "When I first came here, Chaska said I could tell that story if I was in danger. Why is it wrong now?"

"White soldiers are coming," she says, as though that explains everything. When I shake my head in bewilderment, Ina shoots me a scornful look. "You are foolish. If a white man abuses Indian women, the agent does not care. But if an Indian man touches a white woman, your people demand his death."

"Oh!" My mouth drops open in dismay, and I clap my hand over it.

How could I have been so stupid? "I am sorry. I will not say it again."

Her expression remains stern. "My son has protected you. When your soldiers come, will you protect him or will you lie to win the soldiers' favor?"

Impetuously, I raise my right hand. "I will tell the truth. I promise."

Ina nods. Turning back to the fire, she says, "Help me with the cooking."

The story that the two Toms would be killed followed by a massacre of the captives turns out to be yet another unfounded rumor. I draw comfort from the fact that no immediate purge is planned, yet the constant panics frustrate me. The night after Tom Robertson returns safely to camp, I recount the fable of the boy who cried wolf. Ina and Chaska laugh at the story, apparently not realizing that I mean it as a criticism of the constant false alarms.

The Sisseton and Wahpeton continue to block the Mdewakanton from traveling west, and our camp settles into an imitation of ordinary life. Sometimes warriors go off on scouting parties, but most of the time, the men remain in camp, playing cards and shooting at migrating ducks. I remain busy, making myself useful sewing short gowns for the women and shirts for the men.

After a few days of respite, Nellie's illness returns. Her diarrhea grows progressively worse each day. The dogwood tea no longer helps, and apprehension for my daughter quickly overshadows my fears for my own safety. Because of her illness, I must go to the river several times every day to wash out her diapers.

One morning when I arrive at the river with my buckets, several other women are there ahead of me. As I await my turn, I wearily lean my head back against a tree. I do not know how I will muster the will to carry on if Nellie dies. Sometimes I imagine weighing myself down with stones and jumping into the river. When my mood grows so black, I tell myself that Jimmy might be better off without me. He enjoys Indian life, so even if we do not make it back to John, he will thrive.

As I muse on these dark thoughts, from the corner of my eye I notice a rider approaching. To my surprise, he calls out my English name: "Mrs. Wakefield!"

I turn to see Comoska, a Christian Indian I know quite well. His wife worked for me one winter.

Comoska dismounts and hurries to me, taking my buckets, setting them on the ground, and shaking my hand. Afterward, he turns my palms upward to gaze at the blisters and calluses there. Tears fill his eyes. "Oh, Mrs. Wakefield, this makes me feel very bad."

His sympathy is so unexpected that all my defenses crumble and a sob escapes me. I sit on the ground, and Comoska sits next to me, both of us crying without restraint. After several minutes, I raise my chin and pull myself back under control. "I must return to work."

"Please, stay, Mrs. Wakefield," Comoska says in English. "My heart is heavy, and I have something I must say."

I turn to him with a quizzical look.

"You must put your trust in God," he says solemnly. "Many have tried to make me forsake the white man's God, but I know the true religion and so do you. Never forget that God has the power to save you."

Tears roll down my cheeks again, and all I can do is nod.

"Remember His eye is upon you, His arms are around you, and all will be well."

"Thank you. You speak words of true comfort."

Comoska rises and catches his horse's reins. "I will do all I can for you. I often pray for you and your children." He presses his lips tightly together and adds, "I believe God has a purpose for you, Mrs. Wakefield, and his will shall be done."

I stand too, wondering at his words. "Thank you," I say again. "Please greet your wife for me and tell her I hope she is well."

As I watch Comoska ride away, some of the oppressive heaviness lifts from my spirit. Is it not evidence of God's divine love that Comoska came to encourage me when I was contemplating giving way to despair?

CHAPTER

25

SEVERAL DAYS AFTER THE TWO MESSENGERS RETURNED FROM THEIR last mission, a scout on a lathered horse gallops into camp, dismounts and tosses the reins to a boy, and hurries into Little Crow's tepee. The news of his arrival races through the band. Women, children, and men gather within sight of the chief's tent. Chaska tells me to wait in Ina's tepee with my children and joins the waiting crowd.

About an hour later he returns with the news that Henry Sibley has left Fort Ridgely with 1,600 soldiers, who are making their way up the Minnesota River. "Little Crow says we must leave. Tomorrow, we turn away from the river and travel until we are far south of Red Iron's village. Then we will head northwest."

Toward Dakota Territory. My spirit plummets. A premonition tells me that once I cross the border, I will never come back to white society. Instead, my children and I will live and die as adopted members of the Sioux nation. I stare at Chaska and note that worry lines score his face more deeply than they did a month ago. I whisper, "Is this not a good time to escape downriver?"

He shakes his head. "The young warriors will follow and kill us."

"I do not want to cross the Red River. I am afraid that I will never see my husband again."

Chaska's dark eyes gaze at me with regret, yet he tries to reassure me: "I have sworn to return you to him. I will keep my word."

I nod and turn away, but my heart no longer believes that Chaska's promise will ever be fulfilled. The hostile Indians are too set against us.

At night, the memories of captivity narratives I read as a girl haunt me. Mary Jemison, taken from her Pennsylvania home during the French and Indian War, married into the Seneca tribe and lived with them the rest of her life, refusing to return to white society when she had the chance.

Her decision troubles me because I do not understand it. If I knew I would never be rescued, I think I could be content among the Sioux. Ina has become like a mother to me—certainly, a better mother than the one I left in Rhode Island. And Chaska is one of the most honorable men I have ever known. But given the opportunity to go home again, I would not choose Indian life. I am white, and even though white society has not been kind to me, I belong there.

As disturbing as Mary Jemison's tale is, I find Mary Draper Ingles's story even worse. In contrast to Jemison, Draper was determined to return home but had to cross hundreds of miles of wilderness to get there, nearly starving to death on the way. For a brief and frenzied hour, I imagine emulating her—eluding my captors during the confusion of the move tomorrow and escaping with my children by following the Minnesota River until I find Sibley's troops or reach Fort Ridgely. Could we do it? Could we survive long enough to make our way back to civilization?

One thing in our favor is that, instead of having to travel more than five hundred miles, we would have to go seventy at most. Yet, despite the much shorter journey, I must contend with problems that Mary Ingles never faced. For one thing, she was nearly ten years younger than I am and probably stronger. Second, she didn't attempt to flee with her children; the Shawnee had already taken her sons away from her, so she made her escape without them, something I would never do. But how can I run with two small children in tow? Nellie remains ill, and if we should have to sleep outdoors more than a night or two, exposure might kill her.

No, I tell myself. *You must stay with Chaska and his mother.* As the canvas wall of the tepee begins to brighten with morning light, I resign myself to my fate. Unless the soldiers overtake us, we will flee with the Sioux to the Dakota Territory or perhaps even as far as Canada, and I will live with these people forever.

Shortly after dawn, we leave, moving as quietly as a large band of people can cross a dry prairie. Again, I must walk, but my feet have healed somewhat from the last ordeal, and this time Ina has allowed me to wrap them tightly with protective cloth. Ina, Jimmy, and I walk alongside Lady, who pulls a travois, while Chaska goes up near the front of the caravan with other men.

As we travel, Two Shawls, a willow-thin woman with a crooked nose, comes alongside me. She is someone I have often seen talking to Winona. In a malevolent voice, Two Shawls says, "You will never go back to your people, Taŋka-Winohiŋca. If our men lose this war, we will kill the captives rather than let them go. I hope to kill you myself. I will render your fat and use it to make candles."

The image paralyzes me. Then Jimmy pushes himself between the two of us and brandishes his slingshot at the woman. "I will not let you hurt my mama."

Two Shawls grins a gap-toothed smile. "You have courage, white-haired boy. We may let you live and become one of the people." Laughing loudly, she stalks off.

Maternal instinct yanks me out of my stupor. Grabbing my son's shoulders, I whirl him around to face me. "Do not ever threaten an Indian again. If that had been a man, he might have killed you."

Jimmy pushes out his lower lip mutinously. "She is mean. She scared you."

"Dear God in heaven!" Squatting before him, I cup his chin in my hand. "I know you want to protect me, darling, but you are still a little boy."

He scowls. "I am not a baby."

I let out my breath slowly. "No, you are not a baby. But you are no match for a grown Indian."

Jimmy forms a fist. "I will be!"

Not wanting to shame him, I pat his head and rise. Ina watches us. "You have a brave son," she says in Dakota.

"Brave but foolhardy," I mutter in English and resume my trek.

Soon afterward, panic spreads through the procession, carried as always from woman to woman. "White soldiers are coming! They bring big guns."

Like a herd of sheep harried by a dog, we wheel about and race back to our former camp near the river, where we can shelter among the trees if the militia arrives. Despite the fact that the run leaves me breathless and bent over with pain, relief floods my soul. Today at least, we will not cross into the Dakota Territory.

Perhaps the soldiers will come quickly enough to prevent us from leaving the state. With 1,600 men armed with modern weapons, they should be able to bring this war to a swift close—something I would welcome as long as Chaska escapes harm. Then my children and I can put this long ordeal behind us.

As so often happens, the rumor proves to be false, and we reach camp without a sign of pursuit. That night, as we sit outside near the fire eating a meager supper, the old crier makes his way among the tepees. "All white women must be killed tomorrow morning," he calls as he walks up and down.

Forgetting propriety, I grasp Chaska's arm. "Now, can we leave?"

"Stop talking!" he exclaims and peers into the surrounding darkness to see if anyone overheard me. Then he gestures for me to go inside the tepee. Ina remains outside with the children.

When we are alone, Chaska says in a low voice, "Do not fear. For many days, Little Crow has told the council to kill the captives. A few young men agree, but no one else wishes to do so." Dropping his voice further to a whisper, he adds, "The people all know we will lose this war. Be patient."

"But the old man said they will kill us tomorrow!"

"Little Crow gives this order to force the warriors to do it, but the men will not obey. I have heard this."

As he turns to go back outside, I demand, "What if you are wrong?"

Chaska lets out an exasperated huff and faces me. "Do you not trust me? If they come for you, I will stand before you with my gun. As I did before."

Tears prick my eyes, and I glance downward, ashamed to look into his face. "I am sorry. I am frightened."

"We are all frightened." I hear the slap of canvas hitting canvas as he pushes his way out of the *tiyopa*.

Morning dawns with the crisp tang of autumn, reminding me that I have now been with the Sioux more than a month. I emerge from the tepee and glance nervously around the camp, but I see no sign that warriors are rounding up captives for slaughter. Instead, the old camp crier comes through again, this time shouting, "Little Crow says this: When white soldiers come, send out captives in Indian dress. Then the whites will kill the ones they come to save."

The idea is so ludicrous that I laugh. Even if all the white captives dressed like Sioux women, we would be hard to mistake for Indians. Few of us have black hair, and we carry ourselves differently than Sioux women do. Not to mention that we could call out to the soldiers in English as soon as they came near.

Chaska is coming from the river. He has his rifle over his shoulder and carries a dead mallard by its neck.

I turn to Ina, who is roasting potatoes in the fire, and tell her he is coming. She grunts in acknowledgement. "Wake your children. The morning meal is ready."

As we eat, Chaska tells us, "Scouts say Sibley has reached Yellow Medicine. Little Crow wants us to attack. My cousins and I must go."

"Why? You do not want to fight the whites. You should stay here." Another thought occurs to me. Little by little, captives have been sneaking away. Jannette De Camp and her children disappeared a week or so ago, and they are not the only ones. "We could cross to the friendly camp after Little Crow's people leave."

Chaska raises his eyebrows. "Now you wish to be in the friendly camp? You said you were afraid and refused to go there."

"I would go there if you came with me."

He shakes his head. "Mdewakanton are my people. I cannot leave them."

"But you abandon me," I say, angrily scraping most of my food into my son's bowl. "You go fight men who are not your enemy. You leave me alone surrounded by people who threaten my life."

He rises abruptly. "I do what I must do." Grabbing his rifle and ammunition pouch, he stalks out of our tepee.

Ina shakes her head. "You complain too much, white woman. We do not know what will happen. My son tries to stay friendly with both camps."

Glancing at the open flap, I lower my voice. "He told me the whites will win this war."

Ina shrugs. "Who can say? Things change every day."

All day, women of both races cluster like flocks of hens pecking at the juiciest kernels of gossip. I pass a group of white captives gloating over the idea that Sibley might defeat the Sioux and punish them for their depredations. "I hope every last brave swings from the gallows," one woman exclaims loudly enough to draw Indian glares. Annoyed by her reckless talk, I hurry away.

Closer to Ina's tepee, several Sioux women stand together exchanging rumors: "Little Crow threatened the friendly camp. After he returns from killing the white soldiers, he will destroy the friendly Indians and take their captives."

Another woman disagrees. "I hear that Standing Buffalo"—a Sisseton chief—"is going to attack our camp. He will take our horses and kill the white women."

I point out that such a scenario is hardly likely since the Sisseton are trying to protect the captives, but the women shake their heads. "There is not enough food. The Sisseton will kill us and the whites too, so they have enough to eat this winter."

Frustrated by their constant predictions of doom, I go about my chores, yet I remain skittish all day. We hear nothing about the men who went off to Yellow Medicine, and my stomach churns with fear. At midday, I am too anxious to eat. Picking up my mood, my children quarrel about their food and balk at my insistence that they remain safely inside the tepee. I finally allow Jimmy out to play with his friends because his whining is keeping Nellie from her nap.

Once she settles down, I go to fetch more water. As I approach the tepee carrying two filled buckets, an attack of lightheadedness hits me. In an instant, the world turns liquid and swirls about me. I put down my buckets and place a hand to my head. Ina hurries up to me, saying, "White woman, are you ill?"

"No, I am—" What is the Dakota word for *dizzy?* I make a twirling motion with my hand, and the old woman frowns.

Grabbing my arm, she pulls me into the tepee and makes me sit on my pallet, next to my napping child. After rummaging through her food stores, Ina hands me a piece of dried beef. "Eat this now." She goes outside to retrieve the buckets.

Jimmy runs into the tepee, trailed by Buster the dog. "Mama, are you all right?"

"Yes. Just tired and hungry." I smile reassuringly and tear off a bite of jerky.

I am stronger after eating, so I take the man's shirt I am sewing and go sit outside with Ina. Now that we are moving into autumn, cooler temperatures have replaced the oppressive heat of the summer, and it feels good to work in the sunshine. As we sew companionably side by side, pausing now and then to lift our heads and listen for riders, two of Ina's friends scurry up to us.

The taller, younger woman says breathlessly, "Come. White soldiers are near. We must hide in the woods."

I break off my thread with my teeth and say, "How can that be? Little Crow's men went to fight the army. The soldiers could not come here so quickly."

"Scouts report. They are coming."

Dropping my sewing in my lap, I gesture to the open lands beyond our camp. "If the army was coming, we would see dust rise."

The older of the two friends, a short squat woman who looks like a barrel, pushes her way forward. "You say this because you want the soldiers to capture us. You are a white woman. You try to help your people."

"No!" Ina interposes quickly. "She has seen the truth. The people run about like rabbits beneath the hunting hawk. We act from fear, not wisdom."

The short woman whirls on Ina. "The hawk may fly behind the cloud. It is not wisdom to crouch on the open prairie when we do not know where the hunter is. I will go to the forest with my family. You stay here if you are so brave." She narrows her eyes. "Maybe you stay to greet the soldiers because you think that will save your life. You want to tell them that you and your son are lovers of the whites."

"Stop this!" I exclaim, unable to remain silent as Ina is maligned. The growing disunity among the Sioux reminds me of a mirror I dropped once, creating a cobweb of fissures that changed a smooth, shining whole into a landscape of disconnected fragments. "It is not right for friends to fight among themselves. No one does so."

Their faces register shock that I, a white woman, would deliver the rebuke used for misbehaving children. After taking a deep breath, I say more calmly, "I do not wish to cause trouble. Ina and I will go to the forest if that is the people's decision. That way no one can accuse us of helping the enemy."

The short woman's expression remains stony, but after several seconds, she nods. "You have spoken well. We will go to the woods."

The rumor proves to be false as I knew it would, and after three hours of hiding in ravines, we return to camp. The women chatter happily, as if they hadn't been silly with panic a short time before. As we trudge along with them, Ina gives me a wry smile. "Rabbits," she whispers, and I laugh.

The sun has already set by the time we reach our tepee, so we have to cook in fading light. As night deepens, I find myself gazing out across the dark prairie and wondering when Chaska will return. Did he and the others fight Sibley's men today? Only a fingernail sliver of moon rises, so it is impossible to tell if anyone is coming except by listening. I feel helpless, not knowing whether my protector is alive. Did the army really bring up cannon to use against the Sioux? I have heard nothing that sounds like big guns, and surely the concussive noises would carry this far.

We speak little as we work, and I am certain that Ina must be sick with fear for her only son. I prepare corn bread and coffee, and Ina makes a stew with the duck Chaska shot this morning. Worry has dulled my appetite, and not even the savory aroma emanating from the kettle tempts me. Even so, when Ina hands me a dish, I force myself to eat. I have lost so much weight from the combination of scarce provisions and miles of walking that I fear for my health. If we make a run for the Dakota Territory, I will need all my strength to keep up with the caravan.

One thing that cheers me is that Nellie is better. Her bowel movements are firmer, so I feed her bread and potatoes from my stew but none of the greasy duck.

We finish supper. Still no word comes from the men. Ina keeps the kettle hanging over the embers of the fire, so the stew will stay warm. I expect she will sit here all night, smoking her pipe and gazing into the velvety darkness, praying to whatever god she honors for Chaska's safety.

She remains there like a statue as I clean the dishes, tell my children bedtime stories from the Bible, settle them onto their pallets, and listen to their childish prayers. When at last they fall asleep, I go out to sit by the fire. Without a word, Ina passes me her pipe, and I take a puff.

"What kind of man was Chaska's father?" I ask to take her mind off her fear.

"A good man. He was a good hunter, and he was kind to his wives. He kept the old ways, but he told our son to learn to live with white men. He saw that your people would keep coming in great numbers."

"He raised a good son," I say quietly.

"That is so."

She passes me the pipe again. Just then, the sounds of clopping hooves and murmured voices travel through the night, and Ina rises to stare toward the road. We see the silhouettes of riders passing before the glow of other campfires. I stand and put my arm around Ina's shoulder.

Soon Chaska rides up to our campsite, dismounts, and stakes Lady to the ground. "We did not fight," he says curtly as he removes the blanket from the horse.

"You must be tired," I say. "I will take care of the mare."

He gazes at me. After a long moment, he says, "Thank you."

"You must eat. The food is hot." Ina ladles up some stew. I move toward the tepee to get the curry brush.

I halt outside the *tiyopa*. In the flickering firelight, I see Chaska press his lips tightly together as though he debates whether to tell us something. Finally, he says, "There was no army when we got to Yellow Medicine. Little Crow is a bad leader. I will not fight for him again. Not unless he forces me."

Breathing a deep sigh of relief, I enter the tepee.

CHAPTER
26

WHERE ARE SIBLEY AND HIS MEN? I WONDER AS INA, THE CHILDREN, AND I trudge back to camp from the woods. Another false alarm sent us running for cover for the fourth or fifth time in two days. The panics occur so often I no longer count them.

Instead, I grow progressively more irritated by the rumors. Sibley's forces have reportedly been on the move for four days, plenty of time to travel the seventy miles from Fort Ridgely. I myself have gone sixteen miles in a single day. If a stout woman carrying a child can walk that far, shouldn't a trained militia be able to cover twice the distance?

For that matter, why did they wait so long to set out? According to my best estimate, the soldiers left the fort sometime around September 18—a full month after the war broke out. What could have delayed the mustering of the troops? By waiting so long, they have needlessly endangered all our lives.

The fact is, we captives are at the mercy, not only of the Sioux, but also of Sibley's dilatory nature. *Henry Hastings Sibley,* I think with a snort. *There is nothing hasty about that man.* If ever we meet, I shall blister his ears, even if he is one of the most prominent men in our state.

Just thinking of him makes me flush with rage. I fan myself with my hand and attempt to banish Sibley from my mind. Turning to Ina, I ask, "What do we have to eat?"

She shrugs. "If my son brings something from the hunt, we will eat that. If he does not, we will eat gruel."

I nod. We have stores of dried beef and potatoes in the tepee, but we must save those for winter, and likewise, we must keep the *wasna* in reserve in case we flee to the Dakota Territory—although that prospect is looking far less likely. The Sisseton still refuse to let us pass and insist that the captives be released to the friendly camp, a demand Little Crow persists in ignoring. The hundreds of white hostages are his one remaining advantage in this martial chess match.

When we arrive back at the tepee, I pick up the buckets and go for water.

Other women have reached the river ahead of me, and as I approach, I hear them gossiping. "I do not think white soldiers will come," declares one as she lowers a pail into the water. "They move as slowly as children on a berry-picking walk."

A crone cackles derisively, "They must not value their women or children. They do not hurry to get them back!"

The women fall silent as I make my way to the riverbank. Then the old woman speaks up, "Do you not agree, Taŋka-Winohiŋca Wašte?"

Turning to face them, I say in a level tone, "I think Sibley worries about his own scalp more than he worries about us. A man like him would never become a war chief of the Mdewakanton."

The Sioux women murmur appreciatively. "I do not think you would say that to his face," the crone asserts.

I set down my buckets and place my hands on my hips. "I will say it to anyone who asks. I am not afraid to speak the truth."

The old woman moves so close she has to tilt her head to gaze up at me. "If that is so, stay with us. Do not return to the whites. They do not value truth."

I wave her words away. "Whites are like any other people. Some are good, some are bad."

She shakes her head. "The whites say they are God's children and we are not. If you tell them some Indians are as good as whites, they will hate you."

Her words, sounding for all the world like an evil prophecy, cause me to shudder. "I cannot help that. If I ever return to white society, I will speak the truth. Many Sioux have been good to me, and I will say so."

"That is easy to promise," the old woman insists. "It will be hard to do when you are with your people. Are you strong enough?"

I meet her gaze squarely. "I think so. But who can say what she will do until the hour of testing comes?"

She nods. "It is so. I hope your word is true, Taŋka-Winohiŋca Waŝte. The other captives want to see us slaughtered."

"Not all do," I say, thinking of Julia LaFramboise and Ellen Brown.

As if reading my mind, she says, "Not the mixed bloods. But the other white women hate us. They do not heed your holy book as well as you do."

"Love your enemies," I whisper.

She nods again. "If my people lose this war, things will go bad for us. But it will be hard for you too. You must make a bitter choice, white woman. Listen to your God or listen to your people. You will not be able to do both."

I blink. I don't want to believe that my troubles may continue after the war is over. Surely, this old woman is wrong.

Shrugging, I say, "I cannot worry about that now. It is time to cook supper." I turn to haul up water from the river.

In the morning, as we sit outside eating gruel, a messenger wearing heavy war paint and carrying a rifle walks through camp shouting: "Every man who can carry a gun must come immediately. I will shoot all who refuse."

Chaska rises and goes inside to get his rifle. I jump up and go after him, even though I am not supposed to cross into the men's side of the tepee. "Do not go!" I whisper, making my voice as insistent as I can while keeping it low.

"I must," he answers as he checks his ammunition pouch.

"You said you would never fight for Little Crow again."

Chaska shrugs. "I was angry. I spoke in haste."

"No, you spoke true. He is a bad man who will get his people killed. Let the warriors go without you. Then we can escape with your mother to the friendly camp. Bit-Nose and Opa will welcome us into their tepee."

"Little Crow will say you stopped me from fighting. He will destroy us both."

I touch his arm. "I fear for you. The white soldiers are too many."

Chaska brushes my hand away. "It is not our way to hide behind a woman."

Tears of frustration flood my eyes, and I turn away. Crossing to my side of the tepee, I find my satchel and remove the lace-trimmed handkerchief I have carried in the side pocket as a reminder of my other life. I walk to the place where Ina keeps her stores, dig out the *wasna,* and tie three balls of it in the handkerchief.

When I turn back to Chaska, I see that he has changed into the moccasins I made him. My throat tightens painfully. I hand him the linen-wrapped bundle and say, "Take this. You will need food if you must go."

The corner of his mouth twitches, and his eyes convey gratitude. "Listen to me." His voice carries urgency. "Stay with my mother. Do not go outside the tepee."

"But what if the women run for the woods?"

Chaska frowns at my interruption, and I fall silent. "Do whatever my mother tells you. Do not talk to any white women. Do not talk to any mixed bloods. And do not run to the friendly camp."

"Why?"

"I cannot explain now. I have to water the horse."

"But—" I follow him out the *tiyopa.* Ina, who stands outside the door where she must have been listening, steps between us.

As Chaska stalks off toward the makeshift corral, the old woman says, "Thank you for remembering to wrap food for my son."

"It is nothing," I say to emulate traditional Sioux modesty.

"Mama, what's happening?" Jimmy asks in English, looking up from his bowl.

I explain that Chaska is going with Little Crow to fight the white soldiers.

"Oh." He uses his carved horn spoon to scrape up the last bit of gruel, creating a rasping noise that makes me want to scream. "I wish the soldiers would go away."

I kneel next to Jimmy and ask softly, "Don't you want the war to be over? Aren't you eager to see your father?"

"Oh, yes." His blue eyes regard me appraisingly as he licks his spoon clean. "But I would like it best if Father came to live here. We can have our own tepee. Living with the Indians is more fun than living at the agency."

His words astonish me so much I sit back on my heels. "Jimmy, the last time we rode in a wagon together, you said you wanted to escape."

"I know." He cocks his head. "But I have many friends now. And Ina says that someday Chaska will teach me how to hunt."

"Oh, son." *Another casualty of Sibley's shilly-shallying. Thanks to him, my boy is more than half Indian already.*

I reach for my bowl. Even though my gruel is cold, I will eat it because I'm not sure what other food we'll have today.

Not long afterward, Chaska rides up on Lady. He wears war paint and carries his rifle crossways in front of him. Stopping the mare directly in front of me, he says, "Remember what I told you. Stay with my mother."

I stand to face him directly. "I will."

The noise of riders gathering at the edge of camp grows louder. Chaska glances over his shoulder and then back at me. "Do not talk to white women. Do not go to friendly camp," he repeats in a stern tone. "If you do, you will be killed."

"What do you mean?"

"I cannot explain now. Promise me."

"I promise."

He nods once and gallops off.

Because we are confined to the tepee, the morning passes slowly. Jimmy whines that he wants to play with his friends. Nellie is so irritable I fear she is about to have another relapse of illness. To keep them distracted, I tell stories as I sew, talking without ceasing until my voice grows hoarse.

About midday, we hear yelling and the sound of horses riding into camp. A gun fires. Then a man calls in English, "I am Paul of Hazelwood Mission. I come to lead the captives to the friendly camp." He repeats the announcement in Dakota.

Shouts of protest greet his words, and Ina hurries to look outside.

She whispers back to me, "Mazakutemani is here with several Wahpeton and Sisseton. Some old men oppose them, but the old ones can do nothing against fighting men."

"What about the captives?"

Ina watches a minute before saying, "White women come out to the clearing."

"What should I do?" I ask her.

She turns to stare at me. "My son said you must stay here."

"But why? He did not tell me why."

Ina shrugs. "He is a man. He does not need to explain."

"He needs to explain to me," I insist. "I am not a child"

We glare at each other. Little Paul calls from outside our tepee, "Mother of Wicaŋḣpi Wastedaŋpi, it is Mazakutemani. I must talk to the doctor's wife. I have come to take her to safety."

Ina gives me a questioning look, but indecision paralyzes me. More than anything else, I long to go someplace where my children and I will be safe from danger. But to leave would mean disobeying Chaska. How can I disregard his warning, especially since I have never seen him as worried as he was this morning? Then too, if I leave now, how will I find out if he survives the battle against Sibley? That last thought settles my wavering mind. "I will stay here."

The old woman nods and goes to send Little Paul away. They argue for several minutes, but she does not allow him into our tepee. Eventually, he leaves to round up other captives.

I expect Ina to reenter the tepee, but she does not return for more than an hour. When she does, she says, "The other captives are gone. I followed them until they reached the friendly settlement. Once the captives arrived, the people began to dig ditches around the camp."

"They expect to be attacked."

"I think it is so." She sits down to sew again, apparently unconcerned about whether the so-called friendly camp is in danger.

Not long afterward, one of Chaska's younger cousins comes to our tepee, carrying a string of four walleye he speared in the river. The fish range from fifteen to twenty-four inches long. He hands the catch to Ina, who takes them outside to clean.

The young man goes by the Christian name Timothy because, like the saint in the New Testament, he is the son of a mixed marriage; his mother is Chaska's aunt and his father is a white trader. He turns to me and says in English, "I hear only three white women remain in this camp. I am glad to see you are one of them. My cousin was anxious for you to stay away from the friendly Indians."

"Did he tell you why?"

Timothy sits cross-legged on the men's side of the tepee near the door. "If Little Crow is victorious over the white soldiers, he plans to attack the friendly camp when he returns. He will destroy everyone."

"Then the other women should not have gone! Why did no one warn them?"

Timothy scratches his temple. He is a good-looking young man, with large, dark eyes and shining black hair cut as short as a white man's. A half smile plays about his lips. "Do you think they would listen to one such as me? Or to my cousin? They would claim we were setting a trap."

"I suppose you are right."

Gazing out the open *tiyopa,* I see Ina building a campfire so she can grill the fish over glowing coals. "Do you think it is safe for me to go outside and help Chaska's mother cook the meal?"

"I think it will be safe if I show my presence outside the tepee."

I stand. "Of course, you must eat with us. There is too much fish for two women and two children to eat."

He grins broadly. "I can help solve that problem."

No word comes all day. Finally, long after dark has fallen, I lie down on my pallet to sleep. Ina remains outside, smoking by the embers of our fire. I suspect she will spend the night worrying and waiting for Chaska. Recalling how I felt when I was separated from Jimmy, I pray that her son will return safely to her.

In the morning, I rise, fetch water, and wake my children. Ina makes coffee, and we all sit down to a meager breakfast of crackers and leftover fish.

While I am busy using a knife to flake apart the flesh and remove any bones before feeding my daughter, we hear the muted crack of distant gunfire. To begin, just a few shots followed by a sudden flurry that reminds me of the way corn pops, slowly at first and then all at once. At the sound, Ina puts down her tin mug and stares into the distance. A lull follows the initial exchange, and she chews her lower lip. After a few minutes, a heavy volley of shooting starts up again.

Ina moves her dish from her lap to the ground, stands, and walks toward the edge of camp. Going out into a meadow, she stands there, gazing down the valley with her hands clasped beneath her chin.

"Mama, what—" Jimmy says.

"Shhh. I told you there was going to be a battle. Now be quiet and eat."

"But what's the matter with Uŋci?" he persists, making the concession of lowering his voice to a whisper.

"She is scared for Chaska," I whisper back. "I need you to be especially good today so you don't upset her. Do you understand?"

"Yes, Mama."

We finish our breakfast in silence. As I gather up the fish bones to keep them away from the dog, a dull, rumbling, concussive noise begins. *Cannon fire.* At this new sound, Ina wraps her arms around herself and sways back and forth.

I go and put a hand on her arm. "Come to the tepee. We will wait together."

"No, I will stand here."

How can I quarrel with her desire to position herself where she will be most likely to hear the first news? If Jimmy were at war, I would no doubt do the same.

I stand with Ina a few minutes longer until she pats my hand. "Go back to your children. Your place is with them."

Nodding, I turn back. The autumn day is chilly, which is more noticeable here in the field away from our fire. When I return to the tepee, I duck inside and find Ina's shawl. It is about five feet wide and six feet long, made of yellow wool trade cloth with a rainbow-striped selvage. I tell my children to stay where they are until I return, then carry the shawl to Ina, and drape it around her shoulders. "Thank you, my daughter," she murmurs but never takes her eyes off the horizon.

The sounds of the battle continue about two hours, then silence falls. Midday comes and goes. Timothy stops by the tepee, bringing six eggs he took from who knows where and a sack of potatoes foraged from an abandoned garden. I roast a few of those for our midday meal. Ina remains standing in the field as still as a sentinel. When I carry her a warm potato, she shakes her head. "I cannot eat."

In the early evening, the men begin to return. Chaska is one of the first, and as soon as he sees his mother, he dismounts to speak to her. The two of them walk together into camp, with Chaska leading Lady by the reins. Ina, whose face is drawn and weary, nods to me and goes into the tepee. I ask Chaska, "Who won the battle?"

He lifts his hands palms upward. "I was near the back. A warrior told me we killed 150 white soldiers, and they killed only two Indians."

My heart sinks. How could a band of fewer than a thousand Indians defeat a militia of 1,600 soldiers? In an instant, the results of such a disaster play out before me. The soldiers will retreat; Sibley will grow as indecisive and fearful as former General-in-Chief McClellan, and it will be weeks before he commits his force to battle again; by then, Little Crow will have slaughtered all the captives, and if by some miracle, I survive, I will have to flee to the Dakotas with Chaska and Ina.

"God must be on your side," I say bitterly and go into the tepee.

Once inside, I pour Ina some coffee, which I've kept warm over the tepee fire. The poor woman is exhausted from standing watch all day, so I tell her to rest while I cook the eggs for our supper.

Chaska returns. As we eat, the sound of a keening woman rises somewhere outside. Soon other women begin to lament, and by the time it is full dark, hundreds of women are wailing throughout the camp. Why such widespread grief if the Indians lost only two warriors? I shoot a questioning look toward Chaska, who rises and heads outside.

He returns about three-quarters of an hour later. "You must lie down," he tells me. "Your shadow shows on the tepee cloth. I fear someone will shoot through it and kill you. The Indians are very excited."

"What happened?" I ask, lying on my side on my pallet and gathering my children close to me. Chaska damps down our fire so it won't glow so brightly.

"We did not win the battle. I went to the center of camp and heard Little Crow address the people. He is very angry. He says that cowardly whites should not have defeated seven hundred picked warriors. He claims traitors are in our midst."

I clap my hand over my mouth. Little Crow will want to take vengeance on someone, and only a handful of captives remain within his power. "What is he going to do?" I whisper.

Chaska glances at the door. "He has called a council. I must go. Stay here and do not let anyone see you."

As soon as he is gone, I ask Ina, "Will they come for me and my children?"

"Be quiet," she snaps at me. "I will sit outside the tepee. If anyone comes for you, I will say you ran away this afternoon."

She leaves us alone in the now-dim tepee. Squeezing my eyes shut, I whisper fervently, "Dear Father in Heaven, please keep us safe. Do not let us be killed now after you have protected us in the enemy's camp for five long weeks!"

My stomach clenches in fear. Oh, surely God would not have kept us alive this long only to let the Indians murder us at the very end of the conflict.

Chaska is gone for hours, and the whole time, the mournful caterwauling continues. Ina remains on guard outside, but to my relief, no one accosts her with a demand to know my whereabouts.

Finally, Chaska returns. Sitting cross-legged upon his pallet, he stares across the tepee at me. "The chiefs have decided to give up all captives. They will send a letter to Sibley in the morning to ask him to come get you."

Forgetting all thought of danger, I sit up and clap my hands. *Thank God. My ordeal is finally over.*

CHAPTER

27

EARLY IN THE MORNING, INA STARTS WRAPPING HOUSEHOLD GOODS IN cloth bundles.

"Why are you doing that?"

"We are going to cross the Red River," she answers, continuing to pack.

I move closer to her. Jimmy and Nellie are still sleeping, so I whisper, "But you cannot leave now. Chaska said Sibley will come for us today."

"Talk to my son."

I head outside and find Chaska offering a bucket of water to Lady. Travois poles lie on the ground next to her. "What are you doing?" I demand. "You cannot leave me here by myself. You said you would give me up to Sibley when he comes."

Chaska lifts the poles to lay them across the mare's back. "I cannot stay. I asked five mixed bloods to take you and your children to Sibley's camp."

I stare at him aghast. "I will not go with them. The minute I leave this camp, Little Crow's soldiers will kill me. I am only safe with you."

Chaska stops what he is doing to stare at me. "Do you mean what you say?"

"Yes, I want to remain with you."

He frowns and shakes his head. To forestall an argument, I cross my arms across my chest and say, "I have made up my mind."

274

Shrugging, Chaska drops the poles, crosses to the *tiyopa,* pokes his head inside the tepee, and speaks to his mother. Then he walks back to the mare and places the poles upon her back.

"Why are you doing that?"

He shoots me an irritated look. At that moment, Ina hurries out of the tepee, passes between us, and uses a stick to extract some potatoes she had been roasting in the ashes of the fire. "Wake your children. You must eat now. Once we cross onto the plains, we will not be able to find food."

"What?" I stare at her in befuddlement and then look at Chaska, who is now running a strap beneath the mare to hold the poles in place.

He fastens the strap, brushes off his hands, and speaks in the tone of exaggerated patience he sometimes uses with Jimmy. "My mother says you must eat. We leave soon. We will not eat again until night."

"Leave?"

"Yes." He makes a sweeping gesture to encompass the whole camp, and I notice that all around us tepees are coming down and wagons are being loaded.

Ina glances up from where she is dowsing the embers of the fire. "My son said that you wish to go with us."

"No!" A powerful wave of frustration rolls over me, and I burst into tears.

Chaska and Ina look at each other. He takes a step forward. "What are you crying about?"

I wipe my face and try to speak, but all that comes out are hiccupy gasps. As I press a hand against my breastbone, Jimmy rushes from the tepee. "Mama, what's wrong?" He flings himself at Chaska. "Did you hurt my mother?"

Anxiety for my son overrides everything else. "Jimmy, no!" I shout.

But I need not fear Chaska. He kneels down and grasps both of Jimmy's arms, firmly but not cruelly. "Your mother is sad. We must ask her why she cries."

They both turn to gaze at me, and I say, "The Indians are going to leave Minnesota. I don't want to go!" Fixing my stare upon Chaska, I declare, "I told you many times. I don't want to cross the Red River."

Releasing my son, he stands and lifts his hands palms upward. "What do you want? You will not go to Sibley with the mixed bloods. All the Indians are going away very soon. You said you want to stay with me."

"Oh!" I exclaim, comprehending that we have been talking at cross-purposes. "I thought the Indians were going to stay here and make peace with Sibley."

When Chaska steps closer, Jimmy interposes himself between us. Placing a hand on my son's head, Chaska says, "The people are afraid to stay. They think the white soldiers will kill us. We are leaving, and mixed bloods will guard you."

As I rise to my feet, I push straggling hair away from my face. "You will not be killed. Sibley will treat you like a hero when he hears my story."

Chaska shakes his head vehemently. "I fought with Little Crow. I was there when Hapa killed Mr. Gleason. White soldiers will shoot me first and then ask you what I did."

"Not if we stay together. I will tell them the truth as soon as they come."

He frowns. "So *you* would become *my* protector?"

"Is that not fair?" I ask him.

He shakes his head, and anger wells up within me until Chaska makes it clear that he is not rejecting my help, only my certainty that I can protect him. "It is not safe for me to stay. You must decide if you will stay or go."

Tears fill my eyes again. "I cannot go the Dakota Territory," I say, stretching out my hands to him. "I feel in my heart that if I do, I will never come back. You vowed to protect me until you can return me to my husband."

Ina hurries forward, her face blazing with indignation. "Do you not care that my son is in danger?"

Chaska puts out an arm to hold her back. "Be quiet, Mother." He rubs his chin and ponders what to do. Just then, two chiefs approach our tepee and call to us. The older man has shoulder-length hair with a fringe cut across the forehead and two bunches of feathers sticking up in back. The younger man wears his hair in two long braids and carries a leather bag strung over one shoulder.

The elder says to Chaska, "Joe Campbell"—a mixed-blood cousin of Little Crow—"is being sent to fetch John Other Day to protect the captives."

I inhale sharply. John Other Day is the man who led my husband and the other Upper Agency settlers to safety. The thought of being moved into his custody eases the vise of fear constricting my chest.

The younger chief turns to me and says in well-schooled English, "Taŋka-Winohiŋca Wašte, we have come to ask you to do something for us."

"What?"

"We want you to write an account of the way this man treated you. When the soldiers come, we will have your testimony that the people protected you."

His request sends a prickle of uneasiness across my scalp. "I do not need to write an account. When the soldiers come, I will tell them that Chaska and his mother treated me well."

The two chiefs exchange a look, and the younger one says, "We want to have it in writing."

My anxiety deepens. Although the two men appear perfectly friendly, I am suspicious of the request. How can I be sure that they are not planning to take my testimony and then kill me and hide my body where no one will ever find it? I glance at Chaska, who watches solemnly but does not seem inclined to tell me what to do.

Seeing my reluctance, the younger chief says, "White people set much store by writing. If you write your account, we will have your testimony even after you go back to your people."

"True." Expelling a sigh, I decide I might as well trust them. If they're planning to kill me anyway, refusing to do what they ask will not save me. And after all, they're only asking me to tell the truth. "I will do it. But I do not have any paper."

The younger chief slides the bag off his shoulder, pulls out several sheets of stationery, and hands them to me. I gaze in wonder at these ghosts from another world. The sheets are made from watermarked, pale blue paper whose quality is evident from its finely ridged texture. This is a laid paper, made by hand from linen pulp, not cheap, machine-made paper. Stationery like this rarely makes its way out to the frontier, and I wonder how it got here.

The young man holds out a bottle of ink and a pen with a steel nib. I take the writing implements and sit on the ground. "Jimmy, bring me my satchel," I say.

He runs into the tepee and quickly returns with the bag. I set it flat upon my lap to make a writing surface. After thinking for a few moments, I write a note explaining how Chaska and Ina protected me—making sure to catalog Chaska's sacrifices, such as selling his coat for food and going without his blanket when we were cold. Once I finish, I sign my name and then hesitate. Looking up at the two chiefs, I ask, "Do you know what day it is in the white calendar?"

They both shake their heads. Absently chewing the end of the pen, I try to calculate how many days I have been a captive. After a minute or two, I write under my signature, "Sometime around September 23, 1862."

The young chief thanks me and puts my account in his bag. As the two men walk away, I breathe a sigh of relief.

Ina walks up to me. "You should put on your own dress. It would be wrong for white soldiers to see you in Indian clothes."

I glance down at my dirty clothing, permanently stained with mud and grease. "You know I don't have any white dresses left."

A wide grin breaks across Ina's face. "I saved the dress you wore the day you came to my tent."

Together we go into the tepee. From beneath a stack of hides, Ina unearths a rolled-up bundle and hands it to me. When I unroll it, what emerges are a much-wrinkled, white shirt and my fawn-colored, piqué skirt with elaborate black braid scrolled around the hem. Rust-colored stains spatter one side of the skirt, but that can't be helped now. "Where is the short coat?" I ask, looking for my favorite part of the outfit—a short, rounded jacket also decorated with braid.

Ina's face falls. "The coat had too much blood. I burned it."

"Please do not feel bad," I pat her arm. "I am grateful you saved this much."

When she leaves me alone, I strip out of the clothes I've worn for the last few weeks and wash my face, neck, and hands. Then I slip on the shirt. As I button it, I become aware of how much weight I have lost. The once snuggly fitted garment is so large that it hangs on me in draped folds like a cloth on a round table.

The skirt is even worse. The waistband is so loose that it slides down and rests upon my hips. With it hanging so low and without hoops to hold out the skirt, I am afraid I will trip over it. "Ina," I call out the doorway, "do you have pins?"

The old woman bustles into the tepee and stops short when she sees me. She giggles and her hand flies to her mouth. Ina walks around me with a wide-eyed expression. "The people can no longer call you *Large* Good Woman!"

Her comment surprises me so much that I hoot with amusement, and within seconds, we are leaning on each other, weak from laughter.

"I am sorry. I do not have pins," she finally says.

Frowning, I bunch together one side of the waistband and wonder how to take up the excess fabric. The only thing I can think to do is to move the eyes of the hook-and-eye fasteners to make the closure overlap. "Bring me needle and thread," I say. Together, the two of us work to move the fasteners—a tricky task to perform with the clothing still on my body. I no longer possess undergarments of any kind, so I refuse to take off the skirt in front of Ina.

At last, the eyes are repositioned, and Ina refastens the waistband. This time it stays up where it belongs, although it remains so loose that I can tuck both hands into it. I am, if not exactly well dressed by white standards, at least no longer mistakable for a Sioux. After I take one last look around the tepee and retrieve my satchel, Ina and I go outside where Chaska and my children wait. Chaska's cousin Dowonca stands with them, as do some of Ina's women friends.

"My cousin and I will take you to where the council meets," Chaska says. "We will ask them if you and your children may go to the friendly camp."

The plan sounds risky, but I don't know what else we can do. I refuse to cross the prairie to Sibley's camp with strangers, and I understand why Chaska is reluctant to stay here after the rest of Little Crow's band leaves. I nod in agreement.

A hand plucks my sleeve. I turn to see Ina, her face puckered with the effort to hold back tears. She pulls me down to kiss both my cheeks.

"You will go where you have warm houses and plenty to eat. We will starve on the plains this winter. Oh, Little Crow is a bad man to bring this trouble on his people."

Impulsively, I hug her, and she begins to cry. "I wish you could come with me!" I exclaim. "You are like my mother."

Ina pulls away and holds her clasped hands up near her face. "Tell your people my son protected you. Maybe they will let us come back to the land of our ancestors."

Turning to Chaska, I gaze at him beseechingly. "Are you sure you will not stay? I swear I will speak only good of you to the white authorities."

His expression is as hard and cold as iron. "I believe you, Taŋka-Winohiŋca Waŝte. But I do not trust the white soldiers."

Jimmy moves close to me. "Mama, are we going to leave the Indians now?"

"I don't know. We are going to ask the chiefs if we can go."

To my astonishment, Ina's friends wail. One of them hurries over to us and lays her hands on Jimmy's shoulders. "Please, do not take the white-haired boy. We have come to love him. Let him stay with us."

For a moment, I can think of no reply to this audacious request. After casting about desperately for an answer they will respect, I say, "I cannot leave him here. The boy's father would be very angry if I gave away his son."

"Ahhh," they murmur and nod in understanding. One of them reaches into her buckskin bag and pulls out a small knife in a beaded sheath.

"Please take this." She gives it to Jimmy. "When you are a man, remember us."

"Thank you," he says and quickly puts it into the bundle that contains his slingshot so I will not confiscate it.

After I embrace Ina one last time, we set out for the center of the hostile camp. I carry Nellie, Dowonca carries Jimmy, and Chaska leads Gleason's dog. When we reach the area where Little Crow's tepee stood, we find it empty of dwellings. A large American flag flies from a pole, and I take that as a sign that the conflict is truly over at last. My children and I sit on the ground at its base. The Stars and Stripes flaps noisily in the breeze, as though symbolically waving away the life I have lived the last six weeks. *I will never see these people again.* My heart squeezes. Chaska, Ina, and I have been through so much danger and difficulty together that it seems wrong to go our separate ways without any hope of ever learning how each other fares.

A few remaining leaders in camp gather at Chaska's request, among them the elder chief that we spoke to yesterday and Joe Campbell, the mixed-blood translator who is planning to fetch John Other Day. Chaska explains that we wish to cross to the friendly camp in safety.

"The doctor's wife may go in peace," says the chief with two bunches of feathers. "We are leaving for the plains and do not want extra mouths to feed."

"Some young men are angry and may harm her," Chaska replies. "She needs an escort."

"You take her."

"I cannot go to that camp. The Sisseton may take me prisoner and give me to white soldiers to gain favor. My sister's husband killed a white man, and I was there when it happened."

"But I was there too!" I exclaim, interjecting myself into their conversation. "I will swear that Hapa did it."

Whirling to face me, Chaska makes an abrupt horizontal gesture to quiet me. Then he turns back to the chiefs. The oldest one says, "None of our warriors will go near the friendly camp. Many have more reason to fear the white soldiers than you."

"This is ridiculous!" I exclaim in English, but no one pays me any attention.

Another chief says, "We will ask the mixed bloods to take the doctor's wife to the other camp. They have little reason to be afraid."

"No!" I shout. The men continue to talk among themselves, and panic squeezes my throat. "I will not go anywhere with men I do not know!"

The men turn to me with irritation plain upon their faces. I feel as if I want to attack them all, scratching them and kicking their shins. The pent-up fear of the last six weeks transmutes into rage, which boils over like coffee on a too-hot fire. "How dare you talk about protecting yourselves! What kind of men are you? My children and I have been held captive and endured death threats. It is your duty to take us safely back to our people." I fall silent, panting in indignation.

Before anyone else can react, Chaska stretches out an arm to hold the other men back. "Please go over there. I will talk to her alone."

Dowonca picks up my daughter, takes my son's hand, and leads him about fifty feet away from the flagpole. After a moment, the other men follow.

Taking a few steps toward me, Chaska asks gently "Why do you act this way? You talk like one who is crazy. What good do you do by shouting at chiefs?"

I stare at him, taking note of his steady gaze and the firm set of his lips. He looks older than he did when the war started, with more crow's feet at the corner of his eyes and deep creases from his nose to mouth. "I do not feel safe with any Indians but you," I admit. "Some of the others do not want white captives to go back where they will have food and comfort."

"Do you believe this of me?" he asks with an edge to his voice.

"No, I trust you. That is why I ask you to stay with me until Sibley comes."

"Would you have me die?" He lifts his hands. "Hapa spread the story that I killed Mr. Gleason. Now he has fled to the plains. The soldiers will not care if his story is true. They want to hang someone for Mr. Gleason's death."

"But I will tell the truth. Do you not trust me?"

He looks away and swallows so hard that his Adam's apple bobs. "I trust you. But where can we both be safe? You are afraid of all other Indians but me. I am afraid of all other whites but you."

"Oh," I say in a small voice, stunned to hear Chaska admit fear. How extraordinary our friendship is. We have stood together on a middle ground between two warring nations, holding out our hands to each other to build a bridge between our peoples, but we have failed. "What should we do?"

He smiles sadly. "You say you are a fearful woman, Taŋka-Winohiŋca Waŝte. But I have seen you act brave. Can you do that again?"

"I want to be brave. Then the fear comes. It feels like a rope around my neck, cutting off my air. I cry and shout even when I do not want to."

Chaska nods. "Yes, that it how it is." He glances downward, and when I follow his gaze, I see that his hands are trembling. "I will take you to the friendly camp if you ask it," he says quietly. "But is there no one else you can trust?"

"Is your cousin Timothy still here?"

He shakes his head. "No, he is gone."

Biting my lip, I try to think of another escort. "I do not know who else to trust. But I do not want to endanger you." Tears fill my eyes. "I am sorry that my children and I are a burden."

"I am not sorry. I hope your God will remember I protected you and not be angry about Mr. Gleason."

In a vivid flash of memory, I recall how swiftly Hapa fired his gun that day. There had been no warning at all, and once poor George Gleason was shot in the gut, he could not survive. "You are not guilty. You could not save him."

Chaska blinks and nods. "Come. We will tell the others that I will take you to the camp."

"Oh dear," I murmur in English, and he looks at me quizzically. Switching back to Dakota, I say, "If you are hurt because of me, I will feel bad."

Chaska lifts his hands and shrugs. "We face three paths. The first is for you to stay with me and go to the plains. But you will cry for your husband. The second path is for us to part and for you to walk to the friendly camp with others. But I will worry for your safety. The third path is for me to take you to the camp myself. I made a vow to protect you, so I will keep my word."

I bite my lip again, trying to work up the resolve to release him from that vow. But God help me, I am too frightened.

Turning, we walk toward the others, who meet us in the clearing. Before we can speak, Joe Campbell says in English, "Mrs. Wakefield, you can stay with my wife while I go get John Other Day. She is a white woman, and you will be safe with her. When I return, Other Day and I will take you to the friendly camp ourselves."

The sudden switch in plans is almost too much to take in. I look at Chaska, who tries to maintain an impassive expression, but relief lurks within his eyes. How can I risk this good man's life when a reasonable alternative has presented itself?

"All right," I say slowly. "Thank you, Mr. Campbell. I accept."

CHAPTER
28

WHILE I WAIT FOR MR. CAMPBELL, CHASKA AND HIS MOTHER BID ME farewell. When they head back to their tepee to load the travois on Lady, my chest aches with sorrow. It hurts as though I have been orphaned a second time.

Joe Campbell returns, and we set out for the friendly camp a couple of miles away. It is located on a bluff just east of a bend in the Minnesota River, not far from the place where the Chippewa empties into it. I carry Nellie against my shoulder in the manner of white women, and Jimmy walks by my side, leading Buster the dog. My son is dressed in the buckskin clothes Paul's wife made for him, the only clothes he has.

In spite of the adjustment Ina and I made to the waistband of my skirt, the hem drags across the ground. To keep from tripping, I have to reach down and lift the fabric, but I can't hold it up for long because Nellie is too heavy to carry with only one arm. If she were not still debilitated from weeks of diarrhea, I would make her walk, but I'm afraid of exhausting the poor mite and bringing on a relapse.

As we climb up the rise of land, I see a sprawling camp of at least 150 tepees. Several mixed-blood men work at shoveling defensive ditches along the lengthy perimeter.

"There are over 200 prisoners here. Too many captives to take to Sibley's encampment," Joe Campbell says. "Some chiefs fear that Little

Crow might attack. This morning, some mixed bloods left on horse-back under a white flag. They carry letters to tell Sibley of the captives' plight and ask him to come quickly."

Halting, I tighten my hold on Nellie. "I thought Little Crow already fled the state."

Mr. Campbell scratches his nose. "Well, now, he's a tricky one," he drawls, and I recall that he is related to the chief. "I wouldn't put it past him to fake a retreat to put the friendlies at ease, so he can launch a surprise attack against those he views as traitors."

"Dear God! Will this terrible conflict never end?"

Mr. Campbell runs a hand through his hair and clamps his hat back on. "Now, don't fret, Mrs. Wakefield. Colonel Sibley is bound to come as soon as he gets them letters, and then it will all be over."

We cross the trench by way of a rickety, wooden-plank bridge that looks like it was once the side panel on a high farm wagon. Worried about my feet getting tangled in my skirts, I ask Mr. Campbell to carry Nellie. Next Jimmy follows, leading Buster on a rope. Finally, I pick up my skirts with both hands and carefully set one foot before the other. The bridge wobbles alarmingly beneath my weight, but I manage to cross safely to the other side.

Nellie holds out her arms to me, but I tell Mr. Campbell, "Set her down. We're almost there, and she can walk." I ask him to guide me to Bit-Nose, but he claims not to know Chaska's cousin. "I've been instructed to take you to Mrs. John Renville."

"By whom?" I demand, but he ignores the question and makes his way down a path between the tepees. Sighing, I follow him.

The Renvilles are an important family in our part of Minnesota; Joseph Renville, a mixed-blood trader who married into Little Crow's family, built the stockade at Lac Qui Parle, welcomed missionaries there, and helped them translate the gospel into Dakota. Joseph's youngest son, John, went to college in Illinois and, while there, married a white woman about my age named Mary Butler. Together they came back to teach at the mission.

Entering Mary Renville's tepee now, I am shocked by her appearance. Her hair is falling out of its bun, her eyes are red, and her skin is pale with smudges beneath the eyes. Wondering at her apparent distress, I greet her: "Thank you, Mrs. Renville, for sheltering us until Sibley's men come."

Her eyes widen, and she holds a finger to her lips. Moving very close, she whispers, "Be careful what you say. Little Crow's spies are everywhere."

I jerk back in surprise. This is the friendly camp, not the hostile camp where my children and I have been living. Why is she so afraid?

The Renvilles' daughter Ella, who is about a year older than Nellie, sits on a pallet staring at us. She has dark hair and eyes, but her skin is nearly as pale as mine. I give my daughter a gentle push in the other child's direction. Nellie puts three fingers in her mouth and looks at me timidly. "Go play with the nice little girl," I say.

Jimmy tugs my arm. "Mama, can I go outside to look for Opa and Bit-Nose?"

"Keep the boy here," Mrs. Renville says, stretching out a hand toward him.

Once again, her tone is fearful, so I tell Jimmy, "Stay with me a little while."

"All right," he says, but a scowl darkens his face.

Squatting before him, I say, "Can you do me a favor? Will you teach Ella and Nellie how to play together?"

Jimmy's brow lowers even more. "I don't know any girls' games!"

I smile at this display of indignant masculine pride. "Of course not. But do you remember how we used to play pat-a-cake when you were a baby? I haven't had time to teach Nellie that game because of the war. Would you do that for me?"

He gives me an exasperated look reminiscent of his father. Then he hands me Buster's rope and walks to where the girls sit watching each other warily. Positioning himself cross-legged in front of his sister, he says, "I bet you can't do this," before proceeding to make the hand motions of the game.

I smile at Mrs. Renville, who shocks me by pointing at Buster and saying, "Tie that animal outside. Tepees get crowded enough without bringing a dog in here."

Rising to my full height, I stare at her coolly. Mary Butler Renville has never quite fit in with the other white women on the reservation, what with her college education and her decision to marry outside her race. In the past, I've defended her—who knows better than I do how unfair gossip can be?—but that doesn't mean, I'm willing to be given orders like a servant.

"I'm sure you remember Mr. George Gleason," I say.

She cocks her head in surprise at the non sequitur. "Of course. He was a nice young man with pleasant manners. Such a favorite at Redwood."

"Maybe you haven't heard that I was with him when he died."

Her voice drops. "I heard."

"In fact, this is his blood that stains my clothes."

Mrs. Renville puts a hand to her mouth as though she feels sick. "This dog was Mr. Gleason's dear companion," I go on relentlessly, "and my boy adopted him. If the dog isn't welcome here, I will go find someone else to take us in."

Two spots of red color burn on her cheeks. "Mrs. Wakefield, forgive me. I didn't mean to sound inhospitable." She stretches out her hands, and when I don't respond in kind, drops them to her sides. "I confess that I haven't ever accustomed myself to living in these cramped and filthy tents. Don't you find it a hardship?"

I look around me at the stack of buffalo robes and blankets, the two woven backrests, and the pile of cooking utensils, and I realize how familiar such surroundings have become to me. Shaking my head, I say, "Living in a tepee has been the least of my difficulties."

"Oh." Mary Renville lowers her gaze and says wistfully, "I miss my stove. And my rocking chair."

I stare at her incredulously, reminded of the German woman who grieved for her featherbeds. Why do some women grow so obsessed with comfort? "Perhaps that is because you have never had to wonder whether your husband was a victim of the massacre."

"No. No, I haven't." Shamefaced, she twists her hands in the folds of her calico skirt. "Please, Mrs. Wakefield, how can I make amends for my poor welcome?"

Seeing her obvious contrition, my anger seeps away like water from a leaky bucket. My own anxiety is no reason to be rude to her. "Don't trouble yourself about it." I sit down on the ground. Pulling Buster onto my lap, I rub his ears for comfort. He leans heavily against me as though he needs reassurance as much as I do. "We've all been under a terrible strain."

Using both hands, she combs the straggling hair away from her face. "I wish I could offer you coffee, but we ran out of supplies two days ago."

"You have no food?"

She shakes her hand wordlessly.

My heart sinks, and I fear that my stomach will growl in protest. Mrs. Renville and I fall silent and sit listening to the sound of hands clapping and childish voices saying, "Pat-a-cake, pat-a-cake, baker's man. Bake me a cake as fast as you can." *Cake!* I think ruefully. *I should have picked a different game.*

Then the flap to the tepee is pulled open, and John Renville enters. He has a long, narrow face, unusual for the Sioux, and a large, aquiline nose. "Mrs. Wakefield. Thank God that you and your children made it safely to our camp."

Mary fixes her gaze intently upon her husband's face. "Any word of the soldiers yet, Johnnie?"

He shakes his head. "Not yet." Then he lifts his eyebrows as if he's about to impart astonishing news. "There are reports that some of the Indians from the other camp have changed their mind about leaving for the Territory. Many have requested permission to pitch their tepees with us."

"Why?" I ask.

John Renville shrugs. "I'm not certain. Perhaps they think that if they run away, the government will forever brand them as enemies."

"But many are not," I say. "The angry young men in the hostile camp tried to force everyone to make war, many against their will."

John Renville rubs his chin. "You surprise me, Mrs. Wakefield. Most of the captive women I have spoken to express great rancor toward their captors."

"The family I have been staying with are good people, Mr. Renville. They took care of me as though I was a relative."

He nods and holds up one hand, palm upraised. "Praise be to God. He raised up a protector for you."

Mrs. Renville looks at me doubtfully and passes me a cup of water, all she has to offer. I chew my lip and wonder who decided we should stay with a family that has no food. Hours have passed since I ate my roasted potato, and I am famished.

For the next hour or so, the Renvilles and I compare our experiences of the war. John Renville confirms that Mrs. De Camp and her children were able to escape, led to safety by a Christian Indian named Lorenzo Lawrence.

As we converse, a man outside the tepee calls a greeting. Mr. Renville excuses himself and goes outside, but in a few seconds, he returns. "Mrs. Wakefield, there is an old Sioux gentleman out here who wants to speak to you."

I get to my feet. Mr. Renville says, "I don't think he speaks English. Do you want me to come with you?"

For some reason I don't fully understand, his solicitude annoys me, and I have to take a deep breath before answering, "If you like. I probably know enough Dakota to converse with him, but I'd be glad to have you by my side in case he means mischief."

I go outside and see Chaska's bent, silver-haired grandfather standing before me. "Eagle Head!" I exclaim in delight. "Why are you here?"

"My daughter and her son have turned back."

"That is good news!" I turn to Mr. Renville and explain in English, "This is the old grandfather from the family who protected me."

"You had better come back to my daughter's tepee," Eagle Head says. "My grandson has decided to camp with the friendly Indians. He will feel safer if you are there to speak for him to the white soldiers."

"Yes, I will!" I say without hesitation. This is what I wanted after all, to wait for Sibley with Chaska and Ina. "Let me get my children."

Mr. Renville takes hold of one arm. "Mrs. Wakefield, I don't think you should go," he says in English. "Stay here with us. Or if you don't want to remain in our tepee, you could stay with Little Paul."

"No, not him!" I say, recalling Paul's bigamous designs on me. I remember too that, at one point, Paul convinced the Renvilles to write and urge me to come to the friendly camp. Perhaps that is why I distrust them.

Mrs. Renville bursts out of the tepee, so agitated that she cannot control herself. "Mrs. Wakefield, please listen to my husband. Think of your children."

Eagle Head speaks again, and I pointedly turn away from the Renvilles to listen to him. "My daughter's tepee stands there." He points, and I spot the familiar clean canvas about fifty feet away. Eagle Head's tone grows scornful. "Little Crow might still come back. You will be safer with my grandson than with a half-breed who pretends to be white."

"How dare you say such a thing!" Mary Renville exclaims. She grabs my other arm, so that the two Renvilles hold me between them. Pushing her face close to mine, she says, "You must be crazy to think of going with them. He will kill you."

Jerking free of her grasp, I say, "Neither Chaska nor his family would hurt me. They have already made many sacrifices for us."

"But they are not Christians," she says, and the last word comes out in a hiss.

"Chaska has been more Christian in his actions than anyone else I know," I retort and duck into the tepee to get my children and the dog.

When we come back outside again, Mrs. Renville clasps my hands. "Please reconsider. I want you to go to Little Paul's tepee. He has no one to release to the soldiers; they might not believe that he worked so hard on the captives' behalf."

"Why should I help him rather than the Indians who saved us from danger?"

She clucks reproachfully. "But Paul is a good man."

Oh, how I long to expose Paul's faults to this woman, but to what end? We are supposed to be on the same side, and I need to focus on what is important. "Chaska is a good man too," I declare, "and he has no one to defend him but me."

Pulling away from her, I say to Eagle Head in Dakota, "Let us go."

As we walk away, I glance back over my shoulder and see John Renville pull his wife into a comforting embrace. She looks so fragile that I feel sorry for her, even though my time in her tent was uncomfortable for both of us.

We reach Ina's tepee in a couple of minutes, and my friends rush out to greet us. "Why did you come back?" I ask.

Chaska evades the question by saying, "I must go ask if the mixed bloods have come back from Sibley's camp." He hurries away.

Ina gestures that I should come into her tepee. Once we are seated, she takes out her pipe and fills it. "My son is worried. He did not cross the Red River when Little Crow told his people to go. Now the chief is angry. If we come upon Little Crow's people on the plains, they might shoot us. My son decided it was safer to come here because you said you would speak for him."

"I will," I pat her on the arm. She lights her pipe and passes it to me.

The mixed-blood messengers return in the early afternoon and say that all went well at the white soldiers' camp. Sibley promised to rescue the captives as soon as possible. He sent word that we are not to leave this place. One of the mixed bloods estimates that the troops are no more than twenty-five miles away.

Over the course of a long afternoon, the friendly camp grows increasingly tense. One by one, white women come out into the open, staring in the direction from which we expect Sibley to come. The horizon remains empty without even a wisp of dust to signal a marching army. Trailed by my son, I walk up to a group of three women and say, "What is keeping Sibley so long?"

"I cannot imagine," says an acquaintance from Shakopee who is in her forties.

Another, younger woman turns to stare at me. "I see you are dressed properly again. Someone told me you decided to escape west with your Indian husband rather than return to white society."

"He isn't my husband," I say, trying to keep my voice calm despite my rage that she would say such a thing in front of Jimmy. "Chaska told his brother-in-law that to stop him from hurting me. It was a pretense."

"You put on a good act," she replies caustically and turns to scan the horizon.

Jimmy tugs my skirt and says, "Mama, look." I turn, hoping to see our rescuers in the distance, but my son has spotted someone else much closer to hand. A young warrior with long braids, whom I recognize from the hostile camp, strolls past us and eyes me insolently. "What is he doing here?" I whisper to Jimmy.

"Who is it?" the older, friendlier woman asks.

I bite my lip, uncertain if I should say, and then answer, "One of Little Crow's brothers." Without another word, I hurry back to Ina's tepee to warn Chaska that Little Crow has sent spies among us. The news does not surprise him, but it does send him out into the camp to inform the chiefs.

Restlessly, I go back outside. Hours have passed since the mixed-blood messengers returned, but the soldiers do not appear. As daylight fails, the captives grow agitated. "What can be the matter? Why doesn't Sibley come?"

A scouting party rides into camp and reports that Sibley's troops turned back toward Fort Ridgely because they thought their force was too small. I track the progress of the news as cries of outrage spread across the camp. A second scouting party arrives half an hour later and contradicts the report of the first. Sibley has not retreated, but he has not broken camp to come for us either.

Standing there, wondering what to believe, I see Ellen Brown walking toward me. I wave and exclaim, "I'm so glad to see you." Impishly, I add, "Although I would be much happier to see Sibley and his men."

She laughs but quickly grows sober again. "Isn't this dreadful? Where can they be?"

"Surely, after all the communications he's received, Sibley must know we are in danger of being attacked any instant. Maybe he doesn't believe much of a threat exists, but...," I pause before bursting out, "how can he doubt it? He may come at last only to find a field of blood. Even then, he will probably blame his failure on poor roads or inaccurate maps."

"Mrs. Wakefield!" Ellen Brown lays a hand on my arm. "Please, don't give way to bitterness. Remember that God's eye is on the sparrow. I know He watches us."

I nod, too indignant to answer calmly.

Chaska returns from his conference with the leaders and walks up to Miss Brown and me. His hands are trembling. "I think Little Crow's brother will tell him Sibley does not come. We are in danger. I want you to go back with the Renvilles. Take my mother with you and keep her safe. I will go to the plains."

Dear God, no, I think. *I'm tired of being bounced back and forth like a child's ball.* Swiftly casting about for an argument to change Chaska's mind, I demand, "Will Little Crow have you? Or will his people kill you because you stayed behind?"

He shrugs. "I do not have to go to Little Crow. Maybe I will find a village somewhere that will let me live with them."

"But why must you go? You said you would stay in the friendly camp as long as I promised to speak for you. Do you doubt my word?"

Chaska shakes his head. "It will not help. The soldiers will kill all Indians."

Ellen Brown looks from him to me, and then decides to take my side in the debate. "Sibley is a good man. He has promised to shake hands with everyone who remains and with all who give up prisoners."

Making a chopping motion with his right hand, Chaska says, "No, I must go. Many in the friendly camp hate me because I was with Little Crow. And many in Little Crow's band hate me because I sheltered a white woman." He stares off at the horizon before turning to me with a pleading expression. "I must go if I want to live. Please care for my mother."

"I love your mother and will look after her," I say to reassure him, but then my fearful emotions get the better of me. "But if you go to the plains, you will starve. Stay here, and let me talk to the white soldiers for you."

Chaska steps closer to me. "Taŋka-Winohiŋca Waŝte, you must let me listen to my heart."

"I think your heart is wrong," I say quietly. "I believe that you will be safer here. Or are you ashamed to accept help from a woman?"

His face flushes dark. "I am not ashamed."

Chaska's own words come back to me, and now I use them to persuade him. "You told me once that we are the same. We help each other. Is it not so?"

Chaska lowers his brow and then grudgingly nods.

I hold out my hands toward him, palms upward. "Why should we do different now? I think we are both safer if we stand together."

Turning his face away, he stares into the distance once more. After a moment, his shoulders slump. "Since you wish it, I will stay. But if I am killed, I will blame you for it." Turning on his heel, he stalks away.

CHAPTER

29

Chaska declares that he will stay awake all night in case Little Crow attacks. He sits in crossed-leg position facing the *tiyopa,* holding his rifle in his lap.

I lie on my pallet, listening for war cries and screams in the night, but the camp remains quiet. No feasting, singing, storytelling, or dancing. Only occasional barking. Even though all is calm, icy fear encompasses me like a skin I cannot shed.

Dawn finally breaks. As daily life gets underway, everyone asks, "Where is Sibley?" All morning, captives and Indians wander to the western edge of camp to stare at the horizon. The question *Why doesn't he come?* possesses us all.

Before breakfast, I go to fetch water and find myself wishing I was wearing Indian dress. My full, floor-length skirt is more cumbersome than the shorter gowns of the Sioux, and I have to hold it up, which means I can carry only one pail at a time. As it is, the hem is already muddy and torn from dragging along the ground.

On my way back from the river, I pass a group of gossiping Sioux. "The white chief gave his word he would come for the captives," an old woman says. "We cannot wait here anymore. Little Crow will come back and kill us all soon."

"My husband says Sibley is afraid of Little Crow."

"If he does not care about the white captives," the first woman says, "why should we? We should pack up and go to the plains. Leave the captives here."

Seeing me, they fall silent. I walk on toward Ina's tepee.

Later, when Jimmy asks why the soldiers don't come, I answer with more reassurance than I really feel, "I am sure they will be here soon. Maybe something happened to delay them."

In the afternoon, I join several white women in the clearing at the center of camp. "How can Sibley just leave us here?" a young mother exclaims as she rocks a fussy babe in her arms. "Even if there is a risk that Little Crow might ambush his men, isn't the danger to us greater?"

A short, hard-faced woman with grey hair coiled at the nape of her neck crosses her arms over her ample chest. "Well, Sibley might have other reasons for being reluctant to fight. Maybe he's worried he'll have to fire upon his relatives. You know, he once had an Indian wife and daughter."

"No!" the young woman exclaims.

To bring the conversation back to the main point, I say, "It's ineptitude, plain and simple. Sibley's a politician. What the devil does he know about leading militia?"

A few of the women tut disapprovingly over my use of the word *devil,* so I glare at them and walk away.

When I get back to the tepee, I find my children there alone. "Where is Ina?"

"I don't know," Jimmy answers. "She said she had to find something."

I duck back through the *tiyopa* and gaze around the camp but do not see her. Uneasiness takes hold of me. I am used to Chaska's comings and goings, but Ina usually stays close to the tepee, especially if my children are alone.

Sighing, I go back inside and find scissors, needle, and thread. Then I sit on my pallet and stare at my bedraggled skirt. I could cut four inches off the bottom, turn up the fabric, and sew a new hem, but such a short skirt—which would barely reach my ankles—would scandalize the other ladies. And how long would it take me to effect such a repair? The skirt's circumference must be nearly four yards and would take at least half a day to stitch even if I don't worry about making the hem even. What will I do if Sibley comes to rescue the captives while I'm in the middle of sewing?

Ina enters the tepee carrying some rolled-up cloth. I glance her way and then stare more intently at the bundle. It is made of calico with a coral background and a green trellis pattern surrounding cream rosebuds. I know it well.

"Where did you get that?" I cry as she holds the bundle out to me.

"Your skirt is bad. I went to find a white woman's dress you could wear."

With trembling hands, I shake out the garment. It is the very dress I sewed for Susan Humphrey the week we stayed at her home. My heart thumps painfully, and my skin grows cold as I wonder what chain of events brought it here.

Noticing my expression, Ina says, "What is wrong?"

"I made this dress," I tell her. "I sewed it for Mrs. Dr. Humphrey. But she isn't here with the other captives. Where did the women in this camp get this?"

"They took things from houses after white people left."

"Or were murdered."

Ina shakes her head. "The woman said the doctor's family ran away."

I shake my head, trying to dispel the horrific images of massacre my mind has conjured. Then I hold the dress against my body. "I think this will fit me. The skirt might be short."

"That is good," Ina says pragmatically. "You will not fall."

She bustles my children out of the tepee, leaving me alone to change. The thought of putting on this dress disturbs me, as though to appropriate it would make me complicit in whatever Susan's fate has been. *Ina said they ran away,* I reassure myself. *And besides, Susan would want you to benefit from her things.*

As I button up the bodice, I am amazed at how well the dress fits. I must have lost almost forty pounds. Running my hands down the front to smooth out wrinkles, I feel how much more pronounced my waistline is than it used to be. If I stay this size, I could wear stylish clothes without being embarrassed that they look foolish on me. Is it frivolous to have such thoughts when so much evil has happened?

My hairpins are long since gone, so I put my hair in a single braid that hangs down my back. Then I slip on the moccasins that are my only footwear. When I walk outside, my son claps his hands and says, "Mama, you look beautiful."

Ina nods. "You look like doctor's wife again."

I gaze toward the edge of camp. "Do we know where Sibley is?"

"My son went to ask if anyone has news."

She motions me into the tepee, walks to the place near the *tiyopa* where she keeps her stores, and pulls out one of the pouches of dried food that we prepared.

"You need that for winter," I say, pitching my voice low so my children won't hear me through the canvas.

Ina shrugs. "We could die tomorrow. Your children are hungry now." She puts several handfuls of dried potatoes and carrots into a kettle, adds water, and sets it on the fire.

I press my lips tightly together to stop them from trembling. These people are in danger of losing everything they own, yet Ina worries that my children might go to bed with empty stomachs. I have rarely known such generosity.

For the next hour, I sit outside pounding dried corn kernels with a large pestle to break them into smaller pieces. It is tiring work, and I am glad to take a break when Chaska returns. "What did you learn?" I ask him.

"A scout arrived. Sibley's men marched only until the sun was high. Then they stopped to camp and began to dig trenches."

"They stopped? They will not come today?"

He shakes his head with a disgusted expression.

"How many miles did they come?"

After considering a moment, Chaska says, "The scout said the distance they walked is half as far as the distance they still have to come."

So they came a third of the way, only eight miles out of twenty-five.

"A day and a half has passed since the mixed bloods took him our message!" I exclaim. "The militia could be here by now if they kept marching." As I gaze at the horizon that we have watched with such hope, tears fill my eyes. "Do you think he wants us to die?"

The corners of Chaska's mouth turn down, and his forehead wrinkles. "I do not think so. But we heard that Little Crow's warriors will attack tonight. I think the white chief fears Little Crow will turn on his army and war will start again."

Staring morosely at my pile of still-too-coarse corn pieces, I say, "I thought Sibley would hurry to help us. I am sorry I told you to stay here. If you had gone away, you would be safe."

"I think no place is safe now."

Sadly, I realize that Chaska is right. Picking up my pestle, I go back to grinding the dried kernels—this time using a circular, pressing motion to break down the coarse pieces. When the cornmeal is as fine as I want, I add a little grease, water, and salt. I pour the batter into a greased iron skillet and place it atop the glowing embers of our outdoor fire.

When dinner is ready, Chaska refuses to eat with us. He says something quietly to his mother, who nods her head. A few minutes later, Dowonca and a few other men approach us. They pass by without a word and enter the tepee.

"What is happening?" I ask.

"Dowonca is going to humble himself and call upon *wakaŋ* beings," Ina answers in a whisper.

Chills run down my arms at the thought that the men will be conjuring spirits. "Why?" I whisper back.

"They seek to know if white soldiers will hurt them."

"Oh, they want to see the future."

Ina shakes her head vigorously. "It is a man's rite. I cannot talk about it."

"How long will it take?"

She shrugs. "Maybe all night. We must sit out here. Women are not allowed to watch."

I let out a sigh of exasperation. "They could have warned us so we could get our blankets."

Ina laughs as though I have said something funny. "They do not concern themselves with such things."

Together we build up the campfire so we can stay warm through the night, and I call my children to come sit with me. Night falls, the temperature drops, and I put my arms around Jimmy and Nellie to hold them close to my body. For the next several hours, we hear the muted sounds of chanting, rattles, and drums through the tepee cloth. Except for that, the camp is quiet. Everyone expects Little Crow to fall upon us at any moment, so all are watchful and wary.

To our great relief, the night passes without attack. The next morning, the horizon remains empty, and the women at the river say, "We will go. There is no use waiting any longer. The white soldiers have turned back to the fort."

What will happen to me? I wonder but keep silent.

As I draw water, the women continue to discuss the situation, pounding away at the same points over and over again as if they are grinding corn. Weary of the subject, I trudge back to camp with my pail. Our outdoor vigil of the night before has left me exhausted and close to tears, and I fear I will lose control of myself if Chaska declares that he and his family must flee for the Dakota Territory.

Over breakfast, he says nothing about leaving, and I am afraid to ask about his plans in case my doing so pushes him to make the very decision I fear.

After a meager meal of leftover corn pone, I tell myself to take a nap to make up for sitting outside all night, but my fear won't let me rest. Instead, I walk to the edge of camp and pace back and forth, staring at the horizon. Several other white women join me, and as the morning wears on, we convince ourselves that the militia has fled back to Fort Ridgely to ask the governor to send more troops.

Then, as the sun is climbing to its zenith, one of the youngest women cries out, "There! Isn't that dust?"

We follow the direction of her pointing finger. For a terrible moment, I see nothing at all. Within seconds, we all discern the unmistakable signs of an army on the march.

"Thank God!" the other women cry and burst into tears. "We're saved at last!"

Instead of the joy I hear all around me, I feel scalding rage. As the militia comes into view, I estimate the force at perhaps 2,000 men.

With that many troops, Sibley should have hurried ahead to rescue us. I will never forgive him for leaving us in peril three days longer than necessary.

As word spreads, more captives come out to watch the marchers. The excited babble of jubilant women shreds my threadbare patience, so I return to the tepee. "Sibley is coming," I tell Ina and her parents, who have joined us for the wait.

She nods. "My son heard the news. He has gone to see what he can learn."

The soldiers march to within a quarter mile of our camp and begin to set up their tents. Sibley sends a messenger to announce that we captives should remain where we are; he will come over to talk to the chiefs after he has eaten dinner. *Dinner!* I think hotly. *Once again, he puts his needs before ours.*

Although I have long anticipated the moment of rescue, when I sit down to my final meal with my Indian friends, my heart is so heavy I can barely eat. Looking up, I see Ina picking at her food. Our eyes meet, and we exchange quavery smiles.

At last, the camp crier walks up and down the paths between tepees shouting, "The white war chief says that any Indians who have prisoners must come and give them up now."

We all rise and leave the tepee. Chaska and old Eagle Head will accompany my children and me. I turn to kiss Ina good-bye, but she holds up her hand. "Wait!" She rushes back inside. I look inquiringly at Chaska, who shakes his head.

After a moment, Ina comes back outside carrying her yellow wool shawl. She has torn it in half, so that it is still six feet long but now only two-and-a-half feet wide. "The nights are cold," she says. "You must have this."

"Pidamaya ye, Ina." Tears trickle down my cheeks.

We embrace once more, and then I turn to Chaska. To my astonishment, he is trembling. His pupils have dilated with fear so that his eyes look completely black. "You are a good woman," he says in a rush. "You must say good things to your white people, or they will kill me."

"Do not fear. I will tell Sibley of your kindness. The white soldiers will not injure you. I will not let them."

He presses a fist to his mouth and nods. I pick up Nellie, Jimmy puts a rope on the dog, Chaska takes Jimmy's hand, and together with Eagle Head, we join the stream of people walking toward the central clearing of the camp.

As we draw close, I see Colonel Henry Sibley, the Reverend Stephen Riggs—the missionary from Hazelwood—and a few other officers standing to receive the captives one by one. Both Sibley and Riggs are about fifty years of age. Sibley wears a blue uniform with a double-breasted tunic. He has an oval face, a receding hairline, a full mustache whose corners stretch down past his mouth, and a small tuft of hair below his lower lip. Riggs is dressed in a black suit, a shirt with a stand-up collar, and a black silk cravat. He has wavy hair combed straight across his head from a low side part, a long face, kindly eyes, a large nose, and a wide mouth.

Because of the great number of captives—there must be more than two hundred white and mixed-blood prisoners milling about the clearing—my children and I wait a long time to introduce ourselves to those in charge.

Nellie squirms in my arms and whines that she wants down. I set her on the ground and ask Jimmy to walk her about. "But stay where I can see you."

Many of the soldiers who are not on guard or some other duty leave their tents to come watch the proceedings. The blue-uniformed men form a thick wall—six or more men deep—around the perimeter of the circle. They murmur among themselves, passing news to those who stand in back as each new captive approaches Sibley and tells her tale.

Chaska, standing beside me, begins to shake. "Do not fear," I whisper. "I will do as I promised."

More than an hour passes. After most of the other captives have spoken to Sibley, a private beckons me. I call Jimmy, pick up my daughter, and step forward into the clear space. Immediately, Stephen Riggs says, "Mrs. Dr. Wakefield, I am so relieved to see that you are well."

"Mr. Riggs, have you seen my husband? Do you know if he is alive?"

"I have seen him at Fort Ridgely. I don't know if he is still there, but I can assure you that we will do everything within our power to reunite you with him."

So he is alive. Relief makes me weak as I say, "Thank you."

I turn to Sibley, intending to demand why he delayed his arrival for so long, but Nellie complains in my ear, "Mama, put me down."

"Shhh," I say and bounce her up and down.

Sibley says to me, "Mrs. Wakefield, do you have anything you wish to tell us about your captors?"

Nellie continues to squirm. Shifting her to my hip, I briefly recount the story of how my husband hired George Gleason to drive us to safety and how two men waylaid us, one of whom killed Mr. Gleason. "The other man took my children and me under his protection. He saved us from many threats and provided us with food and shelter throughout the war. He asked nothing in return but only wanted to make sure that we would be returned to my husband safely."

"Well, well. Where is this man?" Sibley asks in a booming voice.

I turn my head and call Chaska, who inches forward. Both Sibley and Riggs shake his hand; Sibley thumps Chaska on the back. "You are quite a hero, man. If what Mrs. Wakefield says is true, you deserve a reward."

"I do not ask for money," Chaska says.

Just then Nellie kicks her heel into my stomach. I smack her on the bottom, and she screams. Henry Sibley looks crossly at us, and I say, "Excuse me, gentleman."

Carrying my daughter off to the side, I set her down and shake my finger in her face. "Stop this right now. Mama was talking to some important men."

Nellie rubs her eyes and sticks out her lower lip. "Noo noo?" she pleads.

"Oh, Nellie." I run my hand through her hair. "If you will be quiet and wait a little longer, then Mama will nurse you."

"No," she says and bursts into tears, a sure sign that she is overtired.

Glancing about, I notice a vacant tepee twenty feet away. Taking Nellie within, I sit down and give her my breast to restore her good humor. As the minutes pass, I wiggle my foot and strain my ears to learn what is happening outside, but all I hear is an indistinct drone of voices followed by a sudden increase in rustling, shuffling, and thudding noises. Panic seizes me, and I cry out, "Don't leave without us!" but no one hears me. I try to disengage from Nellie, but she grabs the fabric of my dress with both hands and sucks with greater determination than ever.

About five minutes later, my daughter releases my nipple and lies back contentedly in my arms. I struggle to rise without disturbing her. Then I go outside.

None of the white captives remain in sight, and only a few soldiers walk about the area. Two officers lounge against a tree a few feet away from me, one of them smoking a clay pipe. My son stands near them, holding Buster by his rope.

When Jimmy sees me emerge from the *tiyopa* with his sister, he runs up to us. The dog barks from excitement and leaps against my knees. Jimmy says breathlessly in Dakota, "Chaska and Eagle Head had to go back to Ina's tepee."

The two officers—revealed to be corporals by their two-bar chevrons—exchange wary looks when they hear my son speak the Indian tongue.

Ignoring them, I ask Jimmy, "Did he leave me a message?"

"Yes. He told me to thank you for what you said to the white men."

I look around the clearing as though I might see some trace of Chaska. Tears sting my eyes at the thought that he left without a final good-bye. *If only I had thought to ask for some small memento. But no, he would think that was foolish.*

The man with the pipe taps its contents out onto the ground and grinds them with his boot heel. He stands up straight. "Ma'am, I am Corporal Henderson. Corporal Archembault and I have been assigned to escort you and your children to the militia's camp."

This is it? Just like this, with so little fanfare? Everything has happened too quickly, and now I feel utterly disoriented—as though I have one foot upon a train car and the other on a platform at the very moment that the engine starts to move.

After a moment, I ask, "What date is this?"

"Madame," says Corporal Archembault, speaking with a French-Canadian accent. "Zis is Friday, ze twenty-six day of Septembre."

"September 26." I count out the weeks in my head. "This was our fortieth day of captivity." Forty days, as the Israelites wandered for forty years in the wilderness. I wonder if the coincidence means anything.

"Zat is a long time, madame," Corporal Archembault says sympathetically. "You must be rejoicing that your ordeal, she is finished."

"Yes, I suppose I am," I reply, although in truth, I feel dazed. Our ordeal, as he put it, does not seem to be finished at all and won't until I am reunited with John. Still, I muster a smile. "All right, gentleman. My children and I are ready to go."

CHAPTER

30

As we enter the soldiers' camp, several men gape at me and murmur to each other as I pass. God alone knows what ignorant speculation they are spreading. The corporals escort us to a field where ten large tents stand in two rows, their openings facing onto a common lane. Each tent looks to be about fourteen feet across and slightly deeper than it is wide.

"These were designed as hospital tents for the Union Army," Corporal Henderson says. "Colonel Sibley had to send for them before we could leave on our rescue mission. If you ask me, we could have used a few more." At last count, he adds, more than 250 captives have arrived at what is now being called Camp Release.

Henderson directs us to the last tent on the right. When we enter, I see that it is full to bursting; a quick count reveals twenty-one other women and children already there. A layer of straw has been strewn over the floor except in the center where a shallow fire pit has been dug. The canvas roof above has a hole for a chimney pipe, but no stove has been provided, nor do we have cots.

My children and I pick our way toward a free space along the side, and only after we claim it do I realize why others have shunned this area. The woman to our right, who has been lying down with a shawl over her head, sits up; she is Harriet Adams, the scorned girl who had to leave our camp because she caused jealousy between a man and his wife.

"Good afternoon, Mrs. Adams," I say warmly. She smiles, nods, grows teary-eyed at the sight of my children, and lies down again with her back to us.

Two privates and a corporal come to our tent. Each private holds a pile of blankets, which the corporal passes out. Too few have been gathered, and I must harangue the corporal into giving me two blankets rather than just one for the three of us.

One of the older women calls out, "Where are our cots?"

The corporal tips his cap to her. "Ma'am, there ain't any."

"You expect us to sleep on the ground?"

He swallows so hard that his Adam's apple jerks up and down. "Yes, ma'am. I'm sorry, ma'am." An angry murmur fills the tent.

"The nights are cold," says the same woman. Although I don't know her, I recognize her type—the kind of woman who seizes control of any committee on which she serves. She is short and rail thin, but her eyes are sharp and her voice is as raspy as the cry of a red-tailed hawk. "Why don't we have a stove?"

"I don't know, ma'am. But we was directed to bring you a cord of firewood after passing out blankets. You can build a fire in that there pit."

At this, the wasplike buzzing of ire grows even louder.

The corporal raises his voice and says in a determinedly cheerful voice, "Our sergeant bid us tell you that we will bring you a cooked supper shortly. Tomorrow, you will be given food to fix your own meals, but tonight, you are our guests."

"How long will we be kept here?" I call.

The corporal fiddles with a button on his tunic. "I'm sure I couldn't say, ma'am. If you like, I can ask the captain to come talk to you."

"You do that," says the overbearing woman.

The soldiers hurry out of the tent. Minutes later, a private brings us wood and a flint. Two women build a fire, and I set about piling up straw to make as comfortable a sleeping area as possible. As I do so, Jimmy opens his pouch, looks through it, and exclaims, "Where's my knife? Mama, did you take it?"

I look up. "No. Why isn't it in your pouch? I told you not to play with it, that it wasn't a toy and I'd take it away from you if I saw you handling it."

"I didn't." Suddenly, he claps his hand over his mouth.

"What is it?"

He tugs at the fringe on his buckskin shirt. "When Chaska said Little Crow was going to attack last night, I put it by my bed so I could grab it."

"You mean, you left it in the tepee."

Jimmy nods.

"Well, that's it. You've lost it."

I don't mind this turn of events as I think him too young to have a weapon, but tears fill my son's eyes. He brushes them away angrily. "Mama, please, that was my special gift to remember the Indians. Let me go get it."

The thought appalls me. "Absolutely not. There are still too many dangers for a little boy to go wandering about alone."

"Then will you take me?"

"No, it's too close to dark."

"Can we go tomorrow?" His voice takes on a desperate, begging quality.

"I will take him if you like," says Harriet Adams behind me. I turn and see her staring at my son with eyes that bleed tragic longing, and I realize that she wants to ease Jimmy's unhappiness as a way to appease her guilt over her own son's death. "We will all go together," I tell her gently. "There is more safety in numbers."

She presses her lips together and nods.

About an hour later, an officer comes to our tent. He is a tall man with a neatly trimmed mustache.

"Ladies, I am Captain Saunders. I understand you have questions about Colonel Sibley's plans. He hasn't yet finalized the arrangements for returning you to white society, but I have been authorized to share some important news. The day after tomorrow, we will begin to try the Sioux men who committed crimes during the war. The trials are likely to continue for some days. Many of you will be asked to testify. Tomorrow, some of our senior officers will come around to question you and decide who should be witnesses. I know that you are anxious to—" He stops and clears his throat. "To return to as normal a life as is possible after your ordeal, but I am certain you will want to assist us in bringing the miscreants to justice."

The cries of vengeful affirmation that erupt throughout the tent fill me with fear for Chaska's safety. When the officer departs, I rush after him. Emerging outside, I see him approach a neighboring tent. "Captain Saunders, please wait."

He turns, and even in the waning light, his inquisitive expression is visible. "My name is Mrs. Wakefield. My husband was the doctor at Yellow Medicine."

"Oh, yes?" His sharp tone makes me think he has heard something about me.

"Yes." Once more, I launch into the story of how Chaska saved my life and protected us during the war. "Surely, he will not be charged with anything."

"I couldn't say. I believe the plan is to try everyone we capture to make sure justice is done. If you testify to this man's kindness to you and your children, the court will likely pardon him."

"Thank you, sir!" I impulsively shake his hand. "You have eased my mind."

"Indeed." Captain Saunders gazes at me, using one index finger to smooth his mustache. "Good evening." He turns and calls out a request to enter the next tent.

The hole in the top of our tent does not draw smoke as well as the ventilation flap of a tepee, so as soon as the fire is lit, the interior grows smoky. Several of the other women and children have colds, and as the air grows dense, the tent fills with the sounds of sneezing and coughing.

"Goodness," I say to Jimmy. "This is far more uncomfortable than a tepee."

"You would rather be back in a tepee, would you?" exclaims the middle-aged woman to my left.

"I didn't say that," I retort. "I am as happy as anyone to regain my freedom. But the tepees I stayed in were far more comfortable than this ill-designed tent."

She answers with a loud harrumphing noise. "If these tents are good enough for our gallant soldiers, they are good enough for me."

After drawing Nellie next to my body and directing Jimmy to sleep on the other side of her, I press my face into the straw and pull the blankets over our heads so the smoke won't suffocate us. Even though a fire burns at the center of the tent, it is small. Cold seeps through the canvas wall near our heads. My children fall asleep right away, but I have trouble calming my agitated mind.

As soon as my children, Mrs. Adams, and I reach the Indian camp the next morning, we are invited to a Dakota prayer service being held in the largest of the chiefs' tepees. We arrive as Paul Mazakutemani begins to read from a Dakota translation of the Bible, so we quickly find seats just inside the *tiyopa.*

A few minutes later, someone touches my hand and points to the open doorway. I turn to see Chaska standing outside, gazing in at me. He beckons and I nod. After whispering to Jimmy to stay there with his sister, I duck outside.

Chaska walks about two yards away, rubs his face, and paces back and forth. "Soldiers came to arrest two men in our camp today. They asked my name and wrote it in their book and went away." He whirls around to confront me. "If they arrest me, I will know you told falsehoods. Then I will lie too, and they will think you are a bad woman."

I wave away the threat because Chaska often blurts out rash assertions when he is angry or frightened and retracts them later.

"I have not lied. You heard what I told Sibley yesterday. Last night, I spoke to another officer and told him all that you did for us. The captain said that you should be pardoned on account of your kindness to my children and me."

Chaska lets out a deep sigh and rubs his forehead. "Do you swear by your God that this is true?"

Holding up my right hand, I say, "I swear it."

He nods and gazes at the ground. "I know you are a good woman. You will do what you can for us, but..." Looking up, he shrugs. "The soldiers will do what they want, no matter what you say."

"I promise I will talk to everyone again and again until they believe me. I will not let anything bad happen to you."

Chaska smiles, but it is a sad, resigned smile that chills my heart.

Gesturing to the tepee, he says, "Go back to pray now."

"No, I will disturb the others. I came to camp today because Jimmy left his knife in Ina's tepee. He asked me to fetch it."

Chaska nods and sweeps his arm forward to indicate that we should walk together. "You also left something. I was going to bring it to you later."

Reaching into his pouch, he extracts the flask that I carried in my satchel, the one that contained medicinal brandy. It is sterling silver, slightly tarnished, and engraved with my husband's initials: JLW.

I say, "This is valuable. You could keep it to sell for money."

He halts and frowns at me. "The white traders will say I stole this thing. They will tell the soldiers I am a thief. If I keep it, I will be arrested."

I sigh and accept it from him. "You are right."

"You have a good heart, Taŋka-Winohiŋca Wašte."

"Chaska—" Embarrassed, I bite my lower lip. I want to ask him if he knows my white name. Just once, I want to hear him call me *Sarah,* and I want to call him *Wicaŋhpi Wastedaŋpi,* which I think means "Good Little Stars." But the Sioux are private about their names, and perhaps he would find such a request immodest.

He stares at me with a questioning look, and I shake my head. "I should hurry. My children and I must return to the soldier's camp."

We walk to his mother's tepee, where I find the sheathed knife under the edge of my son's pallet. Ina also hands me the cornhusk doll she made for my little girl. "Thank you. Nellie will be glad to have this."

Shortly after I return to the army camp, a fresh-faced lieutenant comes to fetch me and some other women. "Are the trials beginning?" I ask, feeling a spark of hope. Surely, they will not start the trial until they have arrested all their suspects. Since Chaska is still free, perhaps they don't intend to charge him with anything.

"No, ma'am," the lieutenant answers, plunging me back into the scalding cauldron of worry. "This is an inquiry to help them decide who should be arrested."

He leads us to a tent, where eight men sit behind a long table. They are introduced as Colonel William Crooks, Lieutenant Colonel William Marshall, Captain Hiram Grant, Captain Hiram Bailey, Lieutenant Rollin Olin, attorney Isaac V. D. Heard, Reverend Stephen Riggs, and interpreter Antoine Frenier. Riggs is the only one I already know. We witnesses are directed to sit in three rows of chairs near the entrance. A screen blocks off an area at the right side of the tent.

My name is called first, and the young lieutenant directs me to sit in a chair placed at the left, sideways to the table. Under questioning, I relate how my children and I were taken captive and how Chaska protected us during the long weeks that followed. I emphasize the many times he saved my life and the sacrifices he made for us. As I speak, attorney Heard takes notes.

When I finish, Colonel Crooks says, "Let us return to the day you were taken captive." He proceeds to ask several detailed questions about George Gleason's murder, about who fired at him, how many shots were fired, and which of those shots actually killed him.

Once Crooks completes his interrogation, Lieutenant Colonel Marshall says, "Mrs. Wakefield, if you have anything of a more private nature to relate, you may step behind the screen and communicate it to Reverend Riggs."

I glance at the screen and then at Mr. Riggs, who wears a professionally sympathetic expression. "Gentlemen, I don't know what you mean."

Marshall clears his throat and looks to Colonel Crooks, who leans forward and gestures to Mr. Riggs at the far end of the table. The clergyman says, "My dear, if you have any crimes against your honor to report, I will hear those privately."

"There is nothing. Chaska treated me as honorably as any white gentleman would."

The officers lift their eyebrows in frank disbelief. Colonel Crooks says, "Mrs. Wakefield, we are astonished that you could have been held captive for six weeks and not have a single complaint to make."

I start to retort that whether they believe it or not, it's the truth, but I quickly realize that they will find me more credible if I play to their expectations. "There were Indians who mistreated me, the man Hapa and his wife, but when they heard the army was coming, they fled to the Dakota Territory. As far as Chaska and his mother are concerned, I have no complaints to make."

"None?" Marshall asks, his voice dripping with skepticism.

"None at all."

Restive muttering breaks out in the audience. Crooks pounds a gavel on the table. "Silence. This may not be a trial, but it is still an official court proceeding."

The murmuring dies away. The colonel turns to me and says, "Thank you, Mrs. Wakefield, you may go. The trial will start in the morning."

As I walk past the rows of chairs toward the exit, the hiss of subdued but spiteful whispering follows me.

Once outside, I walk quickly toward the Indian camp to tell Chaska what happened. I keep remembering the derisive looks of the officers and hearing their disbelieving tones, and I find myself arguing with them in my mind. By the time I reach the edge of the friendly camp, my breath is short and my chest aches as though I have been running.

Seeing the tepee of Julia LaFramboise, I stop to see if she is at home. She is, so I ask her to send someone to fetch Chaska as I am too spent to walk farther. She goes to find a messenger, then returns, and asks, "What is the matter, Mrs. Wakefield?"

"I was questioned by the army officers, and I think they doubt my story. I thought that Chaska ought to know what is happening."

She nods thoughtfully and sits across from me. "Sibley and his officers must be under great pressure to prove that they did not endanger the captives by delaying so long. I hope they do not take vengeance on innocent prisoners just to demonstrate that they are tough on Indians."

"What a terrible thought!" I exclaim. "Stephen Riggs is taking part in the trials, and he is a man of God. Perhaps he will restrain their thirst for blood."

She nods. "Let us hope so."

Chaska arrives. Julia will not leave us alone because of her concern for my reputation, but she moves to the back of the tepee to give us privacy.

In the few hours that have passed since I saw Chaska, he has grown pale and the lines that run beside his mouth seem to be etched more deeply. Quietly, I tell him about what happened at the inquiry.

He nods but does not look surprised. "The white men are not doing what they promised. I know they will kill me."

"So leave before the soldiers come. Take your things and run to the west."

He stiffens his spine. "No, I am not a coward. I am not afraid to die. All I care about is my mother. Who will care for her when I am dead?"

"Maybe I can take care of her."

Anger flares in his eyes. "Do not promise what you cannot do. Your people are angry about the war and will not let an Indian woman live in their towns."

My cheeks grow hot with shame over my helplessness. "I am sorry."

My apology does nothing to blunt his fury. Chaska crosses his arms in front of his chest. "I am sorry I let you tell me to stay. My mother and I could be safe on the plains. My mother is very angry too. She blames you that I am in danger."

"That is not fair!" I protest. "I agreed that you should go, and you left, but you came back. I did not force you to do so."

Chaska opens his mouth to argue, but then snaps it shut again. "What is done is done," he growls.

"I believe that all will be well," I say, with more certainty than I really feel. "If they arrest you, I will speak at the trial and tell them that you are a good man."

He shakes his head sadly and rises to leave. "Do what you must. *Wakaŋ Taŋka* will decide my fate."

By the time my children and I return to the militia's camp, it appears that a party is taking place. Most of the captives have gathered outside near campfires, and I smell the aromas of coffee, beef stew, and beans cooked in brown sugar. The air is filled with laughter, and a trio of soldiers play popular dance tunes on fiddles.

Some of the officers have come to visit; Captain Grant and a lieutenant I don't know are speaking with women from my tent. As I approach them, the lieutenant remarks, "We have arrested seven Indians."

The ladies cluck approvingly, and Captain Grant adds, "Yes, we have seven of the black devils, and before tomorrow night they will hang as high as Haman."

I speak up, "Surely you did not arrest the man who protected me?"

The captain stares at me coolly. "Yes, we did, and he will swing with the rest."

"Captain Grant! If you hang that man, I will shoot you if it takes me twenty years."

The women gasp and babble in shocked protest. Among their whispered phrases, I hear the words *Indian lover* and *paramour.* The two soldiers stare at me with disdain, and I realize I have made a terrible mistake. My impulsive expression of outrage has worsened Chaska's situation because it has convinced my listeners that our relationship was as improper as everyone suspects.

To soften that impression, I pretend that I was joking and say with a forced laugh, "But first you must teach me how to shoot, for I am afraid of a gun even if it's unloaded, and I don't know how to use one."

Captain Grant raises his eyebrows, and a malicious gleam enters his eyes. "Now that is a novel request. This is the first time anyone has asked me to teach her how to shoot so she can take her revenge on me. Madam, do you think me such a fool?"

I try to giggle flirtatiously, but my laughter holds a note of hysteria. "Certainly not, Captain. That is just a rude, impulsive way I have of speaking, and I beg you not to take it seriously."

He turns his back on me, and the other women move away, leaving me outside the circle.

CHAPTER

31

THE TRIALS OPEN THE NEXT DAY, SUNDAY, SEPTEMBER 28, EXACTLY SIX weeks after the massacre at Acton that sparked the war. The officers tell me I must attend because Chaska will be one of the first defendants, so I leave my children with Harriet Adams and make my way to the tent where the inquiry was held yesterday.

The interior is set up as it was before except a small table now faces the officers. Colonel Crooks, a man with a receding hairline, a bushy mustache, and chin whiskers, introduces himself as the president of the commission. Officers Marshall, Grant, Bailey, and Olin are the other commission members, and the five of them together will decide the fate of the prisoners. Olin will also act as the judge advocate, or legal advisor, even though he is younger than the other men and has the lowest rank. Attorney Heard will take notes.

The first defendant to be tried is not an Indian but a colored man named Joe Godfrey, who escaped from slavery years ago, came to live with the Sioux, and married the daughter of Wakpaduta. Although Godfrey is said to have a French father, he is almost entirely Negro in appearance. He has dark skin, springy black hair, a mustache and short-cropped goatee, and slightly crossed eyes.

The prisoner's hands are tied in front of his body, so a guard leads him to the witness chair. Two charges are brought against Godfrey, that on the 18th of August, he joined a war party and with his own hand murdered seven white citizens of the United States, and that at various other places and times, he participated in murder and massacre on the Minnesota frontier. After the charges are read, Godfrey is allowed to make a statement. He speaks very broken English, so the commissioners often interrupt him to ask for clarification. In such cases, he usually repeats what he said in French, which Frenier translates for the court. Impatiently, I wonder why Godfrey doesn't give all his testimony in French, but for some unknowable reason, he insists on trying to defend himself in a language other than his own.

He relates that on the day of the massacre at Redwood, he was mowing hay when an Indian rode up, cocked his gun, and demanded that Godfrey join the Sioux in killing whites. Godfrey demurred, but the Indian said 200 warriors were close behind him and Godfrey would be killed if he didn't join the war party. So he did. He admits that on that first day, he struck an old man from behind with the blunt side of a hatchet, but he swears that was the only person he attacked. Godfrey claims that each time he participated in other raids, warriors forced him to go along, but he managed to avoid killing anyone.

To me, Godfrey's testimony sounds plausible, but the other people in the courtroom shutter their faces with disbelief. I dig my fingers into my palms as I worry that these people do not seem disposed to consider defendants "innocent until proven guilty."

After Godfrey speaks, a guard leads him to the small table facing the officers. Then the commission calls its first witness: Mary Woodbury, a part-Sioux woman married to a white soldier, who was taken captive with her children. She testifies that Godfrey was "willing to go, he was whooping around, he was very happy with the Indians." She says she heard Godfrey claim to kill seven people.

The spectators in the courtroom buzz, and I sense anger rising as palpably as floodwaters. Godfrey lifts his bound hands, shrugs, and calls out, *"Je ne le comprends pas,"* but no one translates Mrs. Woodbury's testimony for him.

By now it is late afternoon, and after glancing at his gold pocket watch, Colonel Crooks announces, "We will not be able to get through all the witnesses for this case today. Let us adjourn and reconvene on the morrow."

"Whoever thought it would take this long," a woman ahead of me murmurs as we witnesses make our way out of the tent. She is about forty and has a grey streak running down the middle of her dark hair.

Her companion, a younger blonde, replies, "A waste of time, if you ask me. We know they're guilty, so why not pronounce sentence and get on with the hangings?"

"That wouldn't be right!" I exclaim, unable to refrain from injecting myself into their conversation. "Everyone has the right to a trial."

The blonde shoots me a withering look. "These savages are not citizens. Such rights are not for them."

The grey-streaked woman takes her companion's arm. "Don't pay her any mind. That's the doctor's wife."

"Oh." The blonde's eyes open wide, and she looks my figure up and down before hurrying away with her friend.

I halt, bite my lower lip, and wait until everyone else has gone before I exit.

Back at my tent, I learn that both my children have come down with severe colds. Mrs. Adams has tended them faithfully, keeping them wrapped in blankets and feeding them broth she prepared over the fire.

"It's this horrible tent," I murmur as I kneel down to feel my daughter's hot forehead. "It is too cold and crowded, and the air in here is bad."

Sitting back on my heels, I turn to look at Harriet. "Mrs. Adams, I am sorry to impose on you, but I must ask if you will look after my children tomorrow too."

She lays a hand on my arm. "I am only too happy to help," she says softly. "Knowing that you trust me with their welfare—"

When I reply, "I do not know of any reason *not* to trust you," tears roll down her cheeks.

Lieutenant Colonel Marshall calls the trial to order, and I jerk my head up when he announces that it is September 29th. Today is my thirty-third birthday. Worry has completely driven that fact from my mind.

Swiftly I think back to a year ago when John gave me the gold-and-amethyst earbobs and Jimmy drew a picture of something resembling a burlap sack of rice topped by a smiling face, proudly labeled "Mama."

This year I will receive no cake, no presents, not even any felicitations.

Sadness seeps through my body until I feel as though I have grown drunk on sorrow. How long will it be before I am reunited with John and we are once again living in a safe and comfortable home? Unless his family helps us reestablish ourselves, we will have no money with which to start over.

Don't think about that, I admonish myself. *Right now, the only thing that matters is saving Chaska.*

I look up when they call the day's first witness, Mary Schwandt. When she approaches the chair, I recognize the round-faced German girl who was with Winona's friend Maggie Brass—the girl who spat the word *whore* at me. She testifies that Godfrey was one of a party of forty warriors who captured her and killed several of her companions. Although Godfrey drove the horses and she did not see him commit any acts of violence, she believes he went with the Indians willingly.

Four other witnesses follow. None of the testimony is translated for Godfrey, nor is he given the opportunity to question the witnesses. No lawyer has been assigned to his defense, and I grow increasingly uneasy about the way the trial is being conducted. Who is here to speak on behalf of this man, who scarcely comprehends the legal machinery that has him in its grip? No one. The witnesses state their observations and then answer whatever questions the commissioners care to ask.

After the last one is dismissed, the officers clear the courtroom so they can deliberate the case. They sternly order all potential witnesses to remain nearby.

Outside, the sky is grey, the air has grown chilly, and a brisk breeze tears brown and yellow leaves off trees with the glee of a naughty child. I draw my shawl closer around me. The other women, huddled together in clusters of three and four, conspicuously avoid my gaze. I walk a ways off and stare into the distance.

Nearly two days have passed, and we are still enmeshed in the first trial. How long does Sibley intend to remain here holding court? The day the militia arrived at Camp Release, rumors placed Little Crow and his warriors less than ten miles away. Why has Sibley decided to stop here to try those Indians who willingly surrendered? He could have easily left a small force to guard them and led the majority of his troops in pursuit of the real villains. It hardly seems like a good strategy to let the most violent enemies escape in order to punish men who are no threat.

After a mere fifteen minutes, the guards call us back into the tent. Lieutenant Olin announces that Godfrey has been found guilty and sentenced to be hanged by the neck until dead. Frenier translates this for the prisoner, who covers his face with his hands and weeps.

Colonel Crooks pronounces his name sternly. Joe Godfrey wipes his face on his sleeve and looks up. "The court may be disposed to offer you leniency," the colonel says, "if you agree to testify against other prisoners."

"Monsieur?" Godfrey asks in bewilderment.

Frenier translates what the colonel said, and Godfrey nods his head eagerly. *"Oui, monsieur, oui, oui."* Two soldiers lead him out of the tent.

Colonel Crooks announces that the trials will resume on the morrow.

I walk away from the tent in a daze. Chaska speaks more English than Godfrey does, but I doubt if he knows anything about the judicial process, nor do these trials match what I have been taught about our legal system. A terrible burden presses upon my heart as I realize fully that I am the only one who can save his life.

Captain Grant stops me and tells me I must attend the next day because they will hear the case of "my Indian." I nod, and the weight in my chest grows heavier.

The third day begins with the trial of Tihdonica, a warrior accused not only of killing settlers but also of ravishing a white woman. I bite my knuckle when I hear this. The whole time I was in the camps, I heard of only two white women who were violated. Why do they have to try one of the rapists on the same day as Chaska? It will only inflame people and predispose them against all Sioux men.

Tihdonica's trial goes quickly as he himself admits to "sleeping with" the woman. As before, the commission sends us outside while they deliberate, but they take only five minutes to reach a verdict of guilty and decide on the death penalty.

After he is led away, the guards lead in Chaska. Seeing him with his hands tied like a common criminal makes me want to weep. I try to catch his eye as he walks past me to the witness chair, but Chaska keeps his gaze upon the ground.

Lieutenant Olin reads out the charges: "In this that the said We-chank-wash-to-do-pee, Sioux Indian did, on or about the 18th day of August 1862, kill George H. Gleason, a white citizen of the United States, and has likewise committed sundry hostile acts against the whites between the said 18th day of August 1862 and the 28th day of September 1862. This near the Redwood River, and at other places on the Minnesota frontier."

Olin sets down the paper and addresses Chaska directly, "How do you plead?"

Chaska frowns. "What do you ask?"

Speaking with exaggerated slowness, Olin says, "We say you murdered George Gleason. Are you guilty or are you not guilty?"

I know Chaska so well that I can see resentment flare in his eyes at the condescension. "I am not guilty of murder," he says, equally slowly and clearly.

"Were you not one of the two men who attacked George Gleason as he drove Mrs. Wakefield and her children to Fort Ridgely?"

"I was by the road with my sister's husband. The other Indian shot Gleason, and as he was falling over, I aimed my gun at him but did not fire."

Captain Grant leans forward. "Why did you aim your gun if you did not mean to kill him?"

"I wanted to be ready in case he shot at us."

Olin asks, "Do you deny that you took a white woman and children captive?"

Chaska shakes his head. "I have had a white woman in my charge, but I could not take as good care of her as a white man because I am an Indian. I did the best I could. I kept her with the intention of giving her back to her husband."

Lieutenant Colonel Marshall declares, "But you took part in other hostile acts against citizens of the United States."

At this, Chaska shakes his head more vigorously. "Don't know of any other bad act since Gleason was murdered. I moved up here with the friendly Indians. If I had done any bad act, I should have gone off with Little Crow. But I stayed here to keep the white woman and her children safe."

"Weren't you part of the large raiding party that attacked the Lower Agency before you killed Gleason?" asks Captain Bailey.

Chaska glances briefly at me. "No. There were two in my war party. The other Indian was not a blood relative of mine. The other Indian fired twice. He said, 'Brother-in-law, let's shoot him.' He had already shot him when he said that. I aimed at Gleason because I was told I must kill whites to save myself. I have been in three battles, but I have not fired at any other white man."

"Come now, didn't you and the other Indian both shoot George Gleason?"

"No, I wanted to stop the other Indian from shooting. I stopped him from killing the woman and children. The other Indian told me I must help kill whites, so I shot over Gleason when he fell. This was the third shot. I afterward snapped my gun at him when he was dead on the ground."

"So you did shoot at Gleason!" Captain Grant exclaims.

"No. I shot in the air above him, but I did not kill him. The last time, when I snapped my gun at him, I wanted to put him out of pain. It was too late to save him."

"So say you," mutters Heard as his pen races to transcribe the testimony.

Colonel Crooks tells Chaska to step down, and the guard leads him to the small table. Then they call me to the witness stand.

My knees tremble as I walk to the front of the courtroom, and my throat goes as dry as dust. "May I have a drink of water?" I croak. Colonel Crooks pushes forward the glass of water that sits before him, and the guard hands it to me. I gratefully drink it down and return the glass. Lieutenant Olin swears me in.

"Mrs. Wakefield, please tell us in your own words what happened to you on August the 18th."

I nod, straighten my posture, and fold my hands in my lap. Looking at the table full of officers, I say, "I was with Mr. Gleason when he was killed. My two young children and I were riding with him. There were two in the party who attacked us, the prisoner and his brother-in-law, Hapa. The other man shot Mr. Gleason; this man tended the horses. When the shots were fired, the horses ran, and this man caught them. The other Indian, Hapa, was near the wagon when he fired. He shot both barrels and loaded up while this Indian ran after the horses."

Lieutenant Colonel Marshall interrupts me: "How can you claim that it was all Hapa's doing? The prisoner admits that he shot his gun at George Gleason."

I glance at Chaska, who stares ahead with a stoic expression. "When Mr. Gleason was in his death agony, this Indian snapped his gun at him, but it did not fire. He afterward told me it was to put him out of his misery."

"Then what happened, Mrs. Wakefield?"

"I saw this Indian endeavor to prevent the other Indian from firing at me. Hapa raised his gun twice to do it, but this man stopped him."

"So you claim that he saved your life."

"He did save my life," I retort hotly. "The other Indian wanted to kill my children, saying 'they were no use' and this man, Chaska, prevented it. When we got to the village, he took my babies and me from a tepee where it was cold to one where there was a white woman and a warm fire.

"Since then he has saved my life three times. His mother took me in the woods to hide when my life was threatened. They hid me under robes when I was in danger. And he saved my life when another man in his band tried to kill me."

"That's all well and good," says Captain Grant, but I interrupt him.

"I have not finished, sir. This Indian has no plunder in his tent. They are very poor, he and his family. They had to beg victuals for me, and he has given his coffee and food to my children and gone without himself. He gave us his blanket, and he sold his coat to buy food for us. He is a very generous man."

Captain Grant drums his fingers on the table and glares at me. "May I speak?"

Pressing my lips together, I nod.

"What can you tell us about the other charges, that he committed hostile acts against white settlers?"

I take a deep breath to steady myself. "I have never known him to go away but twice. He went only when he was forced to go and expressed great feeling for the whites. He did not want any part of this war. Ask others about his character. Joseph Reynolds knows him very well and considers him a fine man."

Finally, they dismiss me. When I rise, my legs feel even wobblier than they did before. On my way back to my chair, I meet Chaska's gaze. Not a muscle of his face moves, and yet somehow his eyes convey gratitude.

They call one more witness, Andrew Robertson, father of Thomas Robertson, one of the two Toms who carried messages between Sibley and Little Crow. He testifies: "I heard the prisoner say that he fired the third shot at Gleason. His brother-in-law wanted to kill Mrs. Wakefield and her children, but he prevented it. He said his shot didn't kill Gleason. This Indian is a very good Indian. His conduct has been uniformly good toward Mrs. Wakefield and her children."

This time, the officers do not clear the courtroom, but rather whisper among themselves. I clasp my hands tightly before my bosom. My heart hammers with hope that Chaska is so obviously innocent they don't need to consult privately.

After two or three minutes, Lieutenant Olin rises. "We find the prisoner guilty of the charge of murder. He is to be hanged by the neck until dead."

"Nooo!" I rush the officers' table. Colonel Crooks bangs his gavel and calls for order, but the magma of righteous indignation surges through me. I press my palms against the table and lean over it. "Chaska did not kill anyone. He saved our lives. How can you convict him when he is the only reason I stand before you today?"

"Guards!" Colonel Crooks pounds his gavel. "Remove this woman from the courtroom!"

Two soldiers come grasp my arms and pull me away, but I strain forward to get closer to Crooks. "Colonel, this is unjust! I was there. You must listen to me."

The colonel points his gavel at me in such a forceful gesture I fall silent. "Madam," he roars, "if you do not bring yourself under control this instant, I will have you arrested. And who will care for your children then?"

I freeze in horror, but then scalding rage bubbles up again. *How dare he try to muzzle me with such a threat?* I open my mouth to protest, but the unyielding look on his face silences me. The two guards lead me from the tent.

I will not let this injustice stand. All day, every day, the military commission conducts trials, but in the early mornings and the evenings, I stalk the camp looking for men I can petition. First, I go to Stephen Riggs. "You must help me convince Colonel Crooks to overturn Chaska's conviction."

He crooks his index finger before his wide lips and gazes at me with a kindly melancholy. "Mrs. Wakefield, I have no authority with the commission and cannot interfere with their verdict."

"But you can ask Colonel Crooks to reconsider this case. They decided too hastily." I strike my breastbone. "I am the only eyewitness to what happened that day, and I swear to you that Chaska did not murder George Gleason. It was the other Indian, Hapa."

"My dear woman, your Chaska admitted that he fired his gun at Mr. Gleason. The commission could not let him go free."

"No, no, no!" Panic rises in my throat like regurgitated bile. "He explained all that. He was only trying to put Mr. Gleason out of his misery. The poor man was gutshot and could not have lived. I heard Chaska say, 'Do not leave him to suffer.' And even then, his gun failed to discharge. He is not guilty, I tell you."

Stephen Riggs clears his throat and rubs his fingers across his chin. "Mrs. Wakefield, are you sure that you are entirely objective in this matter? You appear to be quite—taken with this man."

I wag my finger at him. "Reverend Riggs, a man of God should not listen to gossip. I am a faithful wife. If I am passionate about this Indian's defense, it is only because God raised him up to be a protector for my children and me. Surely, that is reason enough for me to champion his cause."

Riggs inclines his head in acknowledgment. "I will look for an opportunity to speak to Colonel Crooks, but I cannot promise it will do any good. They have many men to try and are not likely to revisit those cases that are already closed."

Next, I take my two children with me to confront Colonel Sibley. His aide makes us wait outside for an hour before we are admitted to headquarters, and during that time, I pace back and forth, planning a well-reasoned argument.

As soon as we are admitted to his presence, however, my emotions get the better of me. Holding my daughter out before me, I blurt, "Look at my babies, Colonel. You are a father and know what it is to love a child. I swear to you before God that if it were not for Chaska, these two children would be naught but bones on the prairie. He risked his life to protect us, incurring the wrath of Little Crow's people. When I first told you about his deeds, you hailed him as a hero. Yet now he is sentenced to hang. What kind of reward is that for noble deeds?"

Sibley, who is seated at a desk, presses his hands on the surface and stands. Coming around to us, he lays a hand on my arm. "Mrs. Wakefield, you know very well he is not convicted for his kindness to you but for murdering George Gleason."

"He did not murder Mr. Gleason. We both explained that at the trial."

"Believe me, I understand your distress," Sibley says, using a vexingly placating tone. "But please understand. This is a fine point of law. Even if he did not fire the fatal shot, he was a participant in the crime. In the eyes of the law, that makes him an accomplice and as guilty as the actual murderer."

"I don't care about the fine points of the law!" I shout, wishing I could shake Sibley until he sees sense. "I care only about Chaska. He is no killer. He was our savior, and you are going to martyr him for it."

"My dear Mrs. Wakefield, I know you have been through a terrible ordeal, and I am sorry to say that I fear it has affected your reason. Are you sure that you are not motivated by—love of something other than justice?"

Pulling Jimmy close, I say through clenched teeth, "Colonel Sibley, such an imputation does not deserve an answer." Turning sharply, I march from the tent.

Once we are outside, Jimmy says, "Mama, will the soldiers hurt Chaska?"

"Not if I have anything to say about it."

The trials begin to go more quickly with four or five conducted in a day. Near the end of the week, an Indian named Wakiŋyaŋtawa is put on trial for the murder of George Divoll, a clerk who worked for the trader Andrew Myrick. I do not attend the proceedings, but I learn about them soon enough. The court finds him not guilty, ostensibly for lack of evidence, but it soon becomes manifest to me that favoritism has come into play. The day after Wakiŋyaŋtawa is acquitted, he is celebrated as a hero because he rescued George Spencer, who was shot at Forbes's trading post at Redwood. Wakiŋyaŋtawa carried Spencer to camp and protected him for the remainder of the war.

When I hear about this, I decide to confront Colonel Crooks with the inconsistency of the commission's findings. I make my way to the tent where the trials are being held and stand outside until the end of the day. The moment Colonel Crooks exits, I accost him.

"Colonel, I must speak to you once again about the fate of my Indian."

His face registers distaste, and he gestures for guards to remove me from his path.

I set my feet wide and place my hands on my hips. "We are not in court now, sir, and I have as much right as any to speak here."

He sighs and waves off the guards. "Mrs. Wakefield, the commission has reached its verdict. There is no mechanism for you make an appeal."

"Sir, I beg you to hear me out."

Crooks folds his arms before his chest and cocks his head slightly. "Do you have new evidence to bring to our attention?"

"No. I want to know why the murderer of Mr. Divoll is lauded to the skies and feted as a hero for saving George Spencer, when the Indian who did the same for me and mine remains in prison with the threat of a noose above his head."

"Wakiŋyaŋtawa was found not guilty of the Divoll's murder, Mrs. Wakefield. If someone told you otherwise, that man was misinformed."

"And you never proved that Chaska killed George Gleason. My children and I are the only eyewitnesses, and I tell you he didn't do it."

Crooks steps close to me, tilts his head forward, and lowers his voice. "I am sorry to be blunt, Mrs. Wakefield, but your testimony was judged to be unreliable."

"Why, because I am a woman?"

"No, because you have shown yourself to be infatuated with your captor."

I clench my fists at my sides. "That is untrue, Colonel Crooks, and it is unbecoming in an officer to cast such an aspersion on the character of a lady. I want to know why the commission values the life of George Spencer so much more than it values my life and the lives of my children."

He steps back but does not take his eyes off my face. "You are not well, Mrs. Wakefield. Your judgment has been impaired by the trauma you experienced. Allow me to ask one of our physicians to attend you."

"Do not trouble yourself, Colonel. I am quite as sane as you are, and I assure you that I know exactly what is going on."

CHAPTER

32

TRYING TO FREE CHASKA IS LIKE DIGGING IN SOFT SAND; FOR EVERY shovelful I fling from the bottom of the hole, an equal number of grains slide down the walls of the pit and form a soft pile in the center that mocks any hope of making progress.

I lie awake at night cautioning myself, "Be calm, Sarah. Be sweet and respectful. Appeal to the officers' better natures. Do not fly into a rage."

Yet each time I plead Chaska's case, no matter how carefully I have rehearsed my speech, sarcasm and invective fly from my lips, and whichever officer stands before me turns as cold and deaf as a marble statue. I cannot help it. I have always been a person of great sensibility, and the more deeply I care about something, the harder it becomes to suppress my emotions.

One afternoon, after another failed interview, I return to our tent to find Reverend Riggs and the thin, elderly woman with a hawk's voice confronting Harriet Adams, who stands with her arms protectively around my children. *Good lord,* I think. *Why are they picking on her now?*

But Harriet is not the reason for this day's wrath. "There's the hussy," the grey-haired woman shouts as I enter. "We demand she be moved out of here."

I appeal to Reverend Riggs. "What is this about?"

"The other women have requested that you be housed in another tent."

"Not me!" Harriet exclaims. "I want no part of this shameful petition."

"And why would you?" the older woman snarls. "You're as bad as she is, if not worse. At least, she didn't take her own child's killer for a lover."

"Ladies, enough!" Reverend Riggs rubs his chin as he glances from one woman to another. "Mrs. Campbell, the camp is overcrowded, and there is no place else for Mrs. Wakefield to go. These petty recriminations do no good."

"Petty!" she cries, and he holds up his hand to silence her.

"Exercise Christian forbearance, and do not concern yourself with what other women might have done. Colonel Sibley has announced the trials are going to move to Redwood in a week or so. Surely, you can tolerate this situation that long."

The old woman narrows her eyes. "I will tolerate it, but I do not like it, sir." She returns to her own side of the tent and whispers to another woman.

Reverend Riggs shakes his head in mute disappointment. "Mrs. Wakefield, may I speak to you privately?"

We step outside and walk a few yards away from the tents. Staring toward the woods beyond Camp Release, he says, "My dear woman, will you allow me to offer you some pastoral guidance?"

"And what might that be?" My tone is sharper than I intend, and I pull my shawl tightly around me to hold in my emotions.

He steps close. "I have meditated upon our last conversation and endeavored to take you at your word that your only motive is to win justice for your protector. But surely you must realize that your impassioned pleas have conveyed quite the opposite impression. The general consensus is that you love this man, and if not for your children, you would have eloped with him to the Dakota Territory."

I snicker to show the absurdity of such beliefs, yet my laughter sounds brittle. "Reverend Riggs, if I were in love with Chaska, I would have taken my children, and the four of us would have been long gone from this place before Sibley arrived."

Leaning closer, I add, "But I did not. I would never let myself love an Indian in that way. At one point, Chaska told his brother-in-law that he would take me as wife, but that was merely a ruse to protect me from the worst sort of violation. That kindness is the origin of these rumors. As God is my witness, we lived together as chastely as brother and sister."

Riggs removes his hat and, holding it by the brim, turns it around and around in his hands. "Would that you had conducted your campaign more moderately. I fear your too-fervent arguments have set people more strongly against him."

I touch his arm, and the hat twirling ceases. "If I have been over-zealous, it is only because I feel so desperate. You have witnessed the trials, Mr. Riggs. Can you honestly say you believe these poor wretches are receiving a fair hearing?"

Riggs hesitates before shaking his head. "I myself would not want to come under this tribunal's judgment."

"I spoke reasonably when they called me to the witness stand, but they paid me no heed. The commission is bound and determined to convict as many Indians as they can. For that reason alone, I dare not relent."

He puts his hat back on his head. "I commend your motives, Mrs. Wakefield, but I retain the gravest doubts about your methods."

"I would rather go to my grave knowing that I tried too hard rather than not hard enough," I reply and march back to my tent.

The next evening Captain Saunders comes to tell us that the captives who have already testified will soon be sent to Fort Ridgely. The news steals my breath away. I may be reunited with John in a few days.

But what about Chaska? How can I leave when he remains under sentence of death? My conversation with Mr. Riggs echoes in my mind, forcing me to admit that the authorities are so heartily sick of me they would probably not allow me to stay even if I ask. Perhaps, once I leave, the officers will be able to swallow their anger and consider what I have said.

Before that happens, however, one thing remains for me to do. Since the day of the trial, shame over my failure to protect Chaska has kept me from visiting Ina. But I cannot slink away from camp as though I have done something wrong. First thing tomorrow, I must see her and explain how I've tried to save her son's life.

Mindful of Mr. Riggs's warning about my tarnished reputation, I ask Ellen Brown to accompany me. She too testified at one of the early trials—in her case, in defense of a half uncle, who unlike Chaska was acquitted. *It helps to have influential relatives like Joseph Brown,* I conclude, but refrain from expressing that bitter thought. Instead, I ask, "What will your family do now that the war is over?"

"I don't know. There has been some talk that Father might go with the army when they head into the Dakota Territory after Little Crow."

"So Sibley plans to finally take care of that little detail, does he?"

Miss Brown glances sideways at me. "You do not think Colonel Sibley has conducted the campaign well?"

Her sharp tone reminds me that the colonel is her father's friend, and I rebuke myself for the way my impetuous tongue keeps getting me into trouble. "Well, I admit I know little about military strategy, but it does seem Colonel Sibley exercised undue caution moving up the Minnesota Valley. Had the troops arrived sooner, they might have caught Little Crow's warriors before they escaped."

"And they might have precipitated a mass slaughter of the captives."

"Perhaps," I reply, although I remain unconvinced. It will profit me little to provoke an argument with Ellen Brown, so I remain silent as we reach the clustered tepees of the Indian camp.

Ina is sitting outside her tepee, hugging her knees to her chest, rocking back and forth, and keening softly. The instant she sees me, she lets out a heartrending wail, scrambles to her feet, and throws her arms around me. "My boy! My boy! They will kill him!" She gazes up at my face, tears flowing from her eyes and cascading down her wrinkled cheeks. "Taŋka-Winohiŋca Waŝte, why don't you save him? You promised to speak for him. He saved your life many times. You have forgotten your Indian friends now your white friends have come."

"No, Ina! I spoke the truth, but other people lied. They swore Chaska killed Mr. Gleason even though none of them were there to see it. I could not make the soldiers believe me." Now, I too am weeping, and

I rub the back of my hand under my runny nose to keep snot from dripping onto my upper lip. "Since the trial, I have pleaded with every officer in camp."

I glance beseechingly at Ellen Brown, who steps forward. "It is true. She is fighting for your son's life as though he were blood kin."

Ina slumps and rests her forehead against my bosom. "He is my only son, and they will not let me see him. I walked there to carry him bread, but the soldiers laughed at me."

"That is not right!" I cannot believe they would be so heartless as to keep a mother from her son. There is no ban on visitors. I know former captives have been allowed into the prisoners' tent because some have told me they taunted Chaska with the fact that he would hang. The hypocrites. Some of those very same women partook of the feast after he shot the deer and played cards with him during the all-night gatherings. Now they goad him when he is condemned.

Ina grasps my arms. "Will you go to him and see if he is well?"

"I—" My voice fails, and my lungs feel as though a vortex has sucked all the air out of them. I have not visited Chaska yet because I know it will make me feel sad and helpless, and what good will a visit from a weeping woman do him?

Ellen Brown says, "Of course, we will. We will go today."

Her voice assumes a brisk heartiness to raise Ina's spirits, and I hear myself adding, "Yes, I will go. Do you want me to take him bread?"

"Thank you!" Ina squeezes my hands before disappearing into her tepee.

Turning to my companion, I lower my voice and switch to English. "I am worried about her. What will become of her if I cannot save her son? Do you think the authorities will allow me to take her with me when I leave?"

Ellen Brown's shakes her head emphatically. "Do not even attempt it. If you bring her into a white community, both she and you will incur great wrath. I've been told that the authorities intend to expel the Sioux from Minnesota."

"But I owe her such a debt."

She cocks her head and regards me quizzically. "You surprise me, Mrs. Wakefield. Most white captives speak of being owed reparations for their troubles. Yet, you seem wholly concerned with what you owe your captors."

"I do not blame them for my captivity. I blame Hapa, who murdered George Gleason. On his own, Chaska would never have instigated violence." Speaking of the murder recalls my first days in the Sioux camp, and the faces of other captives rise in my memory. "Some of the other women lost husbands and children in this war. I have not had that sorrow. If I had, I might be more bitter."

"Perhaps, but I think you may be a better Christian than you know."

Ina comes out of the tepee carrying a cloth bundle. "I wrapped up bread and *wasna* in a shirt. Promise you will give this to my son."

"If the soldiers allow it, I will put it into his own hands."

"Tell my son my heart goes with him. I am proud to be the mother of a good man. If he must go to our ancestors, they will receive him with honor."

My eyes tear up again. "I will tell him."

We hug once more, and then with a sore heart, I leave.

Back at Camp Release, we request permission from Major William Cullen to visit the prisoners' tent. "I'm walking that way myself," he says. "I'll accompany you."

Cullen, the Superintendent for Indian Affairs in Minnesota, is a middle-aged dandy with dark blond hair, a waxed mustache, and highly polished boots. He chats about inconsequential things as we stroll, and I want to swat him into silence as though he were a buzzing mosquito.

Two soldiers stand on guard outside the tent. Major Cullen says, "I have given these ladies permission to visit—" He turns to me. "Which prisoner was it again?"

"Wicaŋhpi Wastedaŋpi. Case number three."

"That's it. Private Cummings, accompany the ladies. And make sure there is no contraband in the bundle they brought the prisoner."

The private, a young lad with dark hair and angry red pimples, holds out his arm, and I hand him the bundle. He opens the tent flap and gestures for us to enter.

The first thing that strikes me is the smell, a wretched miasma of sweat, human waste, and stale grease. The interior is so dim I see only indistinguishable figures sitting in a line that snakes around the tent walls. I move forward uncertainly, peering at each face. Gradually, I make out that twenty-one Indians are being held in that tent, with thick rope binding their ankles together.

"Chaska?" Then I find him. He is near the far end of the line. He keeps his head down with his chin upon his chest as though dozing, but something about the tension in his posture belies the pose.

I cross the tent but stop about four feet away from him when Cummings makes a warning noise. "Chaska, why are you acting so unfriendly?" I say. "Will you stand and shake my hand?"

He stands and launches into a tirade: "You told falsehoods to the soldiers. That is the reason I am tied up in this dark place. I took you into my mother's tepee. I protected you from bad men. I sold my coat to buy food. I went without a blanket so your children would not be cold. How could you forget all my kindnesses?"

Each sentence strikes me like the stinging lash of a whip. I clench my fists and lift my chin, but still begin to cry.

"That i...is not so. You heard what I said in court." Which is true, but I suddenly recall that Chaska's English is not as good as my Dakota. He may not have understood all of my testimony.

I switch to his language. "All that you say now, I said in the trial. And I have said it to many officers and begged them to save your life."

Chaska blinks, and the hard mask of anger he wears slides away. "Do you speak the truth?"

"Yes! I have lost all my white friends because I tried to save you. It is very wrong for you to blame me for what has happened. I do not want you to die."

I choke on that terrible last word and weep, covering my face with my hands. Ellen Brown puts an arm around my shoulders. "Mrs. Wakefield speaks the truth. She has fought for your freedom every day."

"I thank you," Chaska says quietly.

Nodding, I wipe away my tears. Because I am staring downward, I see that Chaska wears the moccasins I made. "Oh!" I cry. Grief threatens to overpower me again, so I squeeze my eyes shut to push it back down.

After a moment, I say, "Miss Brown and I visited Ina. She is well.

She asked us to say she knows you are a good man and she is proud to be your mother."

Chaska presses his lips tightly together and nods.

I turn to Cummings. He has already untied and inspected the bundle, which he hands to me. I give it to Chaska. "Ina sent you food and another shirt."

"Thank my mother. Tell her I am not afraid. I go to my ancestors."

I nod. "She believes this. She told me so."

As Chaska sets the bundle on the ground, I ask, "Will you not say good-bye to me in friendship?"

He extends his arm, and I step forward. We clasp hands. "You are a good man, Wicaŋhpi Wastedaŋpi. I will remember you always, and I will pray to my god that your spirit rests in peace."

"Do not feel bad, Taŋka-Winohiŋca Waŝte. You tried to do what is right. But a big storm came, and we were not able to run away from it."

We fall silent. As we gaze into each other's eyes, my awareness of the other people in the tent falls away, and my spirit fills with the certainty that this greathearted man bears me no ill will. *You would do it all over again, wouldn't you?* I think.

Chaska nods as if he has heard me.

Private Cummings clears his throat, and Chaska and I release each other. Ellen Brown takes my arm and leads me from the tent. As we step outside into the late afternoon, I murmur, "No matter what happens, I have been privileged to know such a generous, honorable man."

"Greater love hath no man than this, that he lay down his life for his friends," Ellen murmurs.

I stop and stare at her as the Bible verse she quoted lays the balm of hope on my sore heart. Chaska may not be baptized, he may not have formally converted to Christianity, yet his life is more Christian than many of those who publicly espouse the faith. He has *lived* the gospel. Surely, the great Judge who looks into men's souls will see that and accept Chaska into the Kingdom.

The emotional strains of the day have exhausted me so that all I want to do is to fall upon my pallet, but when I enter our tent, I notice that a change occurred in my absence. Several women are gone.

When I query Harriet Adams, she says, "The officers sent a train with forty wagons, a number of prisoners, and an escort of eighty soldiers to the fort today."

"Oh," I say, cast down by the news. "I thought I was to go too."

"Captain Grant came looking for you. He said he'd return just before supper."

"All right." Turning, I check on my children. Their colds are almost gone, but a slight cough still lingers, so I am not prepared to pronounce them well. When I sit on the pallet near them, Nellie climbs on my lap to snuggle, but Jimmy, in the first flush of renewed energy, wants to get up and run around.

"You must rest this evening because we're supposed to take a journey soon."

"I feel fine, Mama!" he insists, but then he promptly coughs for nearly a minute until he brings up a clot of phlegm.

"See," I say, wiping his chin. "You're not as well as you think."

He scowls and lies back down. To distract him, I tell both children Aesop's fable about the fox that uses flattery to trick a crow into dropping the piece of cheese it holds in its beak.

Jimmy laughs loudly at the end. "Tell us another one!"

Soon after I begin the tale of the ant and the grasshopper, Captain Grant comes and asks me to step outside. "I'll be right back," I say to my children and go to speak to the officer.

Captain Grant stands with his legs wide apart and his hands behind his back. "Mrs. Wakefield, I wanted to let you know that we will be sending you and three other ladies to Fort Ridgely in the morning."

"Thank you, Captain. Who will I be traveling with?"

He names three women I do not know.

"Only four of us, you say?"

He nods curtly. "The road should be safe. We sent a large convoy this morning, and they will have cleared out any troublemakers."

"I see," I murmur, thinking how little he knows of the Sioux's ability to move swiftly across country. But as long as we have an armed escort, we should be fine.

Captain Grant brings his left hand to his chest and clutches the edge of his tunic. "There is another reason I wished to speak to you in private, ma'am."

"Yes?"

"I have it in the strictest of confidence that the prisoner you have been petitioning for—what is his name?"

"Wicaŋhpi Wastedaŋpi," I reply, wondering why none of these officers can trouble themselves to learn their prisoners' identities.

"Yes, well, I have it in the strictest of confidence that his sentence will be commuted to a term of five years imprisonment."

"Oh, Captain Grant!" My hands fly up to my cheeks and I gape at him in astonishment. "Can it possibly be true?"

"Please, Mrs. Wakefield, lower your voice." He glances from side to side. "The negotiation to bring this about is still at a delicate stage, and if you say anything about it, anything at all, you will ruin his chances. You must not say a word to anyone. Do I have your word on that?"

"Yes, of course." I nod for emphasis. "But who is negotiating on his behalf?"

"I cannot tell you. I could be court-martialed for saying as much as I have."

"Thank you, Captain." I exhale, and a large boulder of worry rolls off my back. I reach out to take Captain Grant's hand, but he does not reciprocate the gesture. Lowering my arm awkwardly, I say, "I am more grateful than I can say."

He watches me with a slight smile playing about his lips. Then he nods, tips his hat, and after turning smartly on his heel, strides away.

CHAPTER

33

IN THE MORNING, MY CHILDREN AND I WALK TO THE AREA WHERE THE militia's horses are corralled. I take only my satchel, as the blankets we have been using must be returned to the soldiers they were requisitioned from.

A three-seat farm wagon stands waiting for us with three other women already in the backseat. I am surprised to see a single teamster, wearing an oilskin coat and a dirty felt hat, in the driver's seat. Captain Saunders stands nearby to oversee our departure. I ask him, "Where is our military escort?"

He smooths his moustache. "No escort will be necessary. We sent a large wagon train down the road yesterday, which will have scared off any hostiles."

I place my hands on my hips and shoot him a look of blazing incredulity. "Captain Saunders, do you have any conception of the foe we are dealing with? Whereas your men traveled seven or eight miles a day on their march to Camp Release, I myself have covered sixteen miles a day in a caravan of Sioux women and children. Their warriors can cover far more territory than that, and they know this region as you could never hope to do. To imagine a single wagon train could secure the territory is foolhardy in the extreme."

The captain shakes his head. "I assure you we have pacified all the

Indians remaining in Minnesota. Our scouts would have alerted us if any hostiles had returned from the Dakota Territory."

"That is precisely my point, Captain. You would not know because they are skilled at moving with both stealth and speed."

His voice hardens. "Colonel Sibley would never willingly endanger civilians."

I snort. "He risked our lives every single day he dawdled his way up the Minnesota Valley."

"Mrs. Wakefield, we have prisoners to guard and cannot send troops to accompany every single wagon. I regret that you feel unsafe. Had you been in your tent yesterday, you could have traveled with the train, but as it stands, this is the best we can offer. Now please get in the wagon."

I feel as though I am reliving the argument I had with Mr. Gleason on that fateful day two months ago. This time, I will not allow any man to force me to go against my better judgment. "I have my children to think of, Captain. You are sending us down the very road where we were taken prisoner. You have no right to send us back into danger without armed escort."

Captain Saunders snatches off his hat and runs his fingers through his hair. "The danger is all in your mind. Besides, your driver *is* armed."

"I was told that once before, sir, but it was a damned lie just to placate me."

Saunders's eyes widen when he hears me swear. He calls to the driver, "Mr. Philpotts, will you please show the lady your weapon?"

The teamster stands, turns to face us, and pushes back his coat to reveal a holster with a pistol. He smiles, showing crooked teeth stained brown from tobacco. "I also got a rifle under the seat, lady. You wanna see that too?"

"No." I swiftly consider my options. The driver is armed, and from what Saunders said, I don't think we will get much more protection than that. Turning back to the officer, I say in an undertone, "We will go. But if anything happens to either my children or me, our blood will be on your head and on that of Sibley."

"I'm not worried," he says as he lifts Jimmy and the dog into the wagon, "and neither should you be."

I ask the officer to hold my baby and then climb up beside my son. As Saunders hands Nellie to me, Jimmy leans close and says, "Don't be afraid, Mama, I have my knife. I'll keep you safe."

My first impulse is to rebuke him with the reminder that he is a child, but one look at his earnest expression stops my tongue. Our time with Chaska has taught my little boy what kind of man he wants to be, one who protects the people within his care. Who am I to discourage such a worthy ambition?

The three women behind us offer no greetings. From the frenzied whispering going on back there, I assume they are picking over the juiciest morsels of gossip about me, so I determine to ignore them.

Not long after we set out, my baby starts to fuss. A quick examination reveals that her fever has returned. The October day is chilly. All Nellie has on is the yellow calico dress I made her and a diaper, no shoes or socks or any outer garment. Holding her close to my bosom, I wrap my narrow shawl around both of us.

I had expected to relish the journey toward John, but each mile we travel evokes a hideous memory. A bluff across from the mouth of the Chippewa River is where Red Iron refused to let us pass and where we consequently lived in fear that Little Crow would slaughter us. A few miles farther on, a trampled meadow marks the campsite where the warrior boasted about baking a baby in an oven. Then comes the turnoff to Hazelwood Mission, where the Williamsons' fine home was ransacked and later burned.

By late afternoon, a veil of black despair settles over me, causing me to see everything in the gloomiest possible light. As Nellie wheezes in my arms, I fear that our deprivations have permanently damaged her constitution. When the blackened timbers of traders' stores at Yellow Medicine come into sight, I wonder if the reports of John's survival are true or if his bones lie undiscovered on the prairie.

We drive into the burned-out area where the traders' homes once stood. There, Major Galbraith sits astride a horse, overseeing a work party of Indians who dig for potatoes in the abandoned gardens. When Mr. Philpotts halts our wagon, Galbraith rides up to us. He tips his hat and says, "Mrs. Wakefield, words cannot express how glad I am to see you. Are you on your way to your husband?"

"So they tell me. Have you seen him? Has he truly survived?"

"He has indeed." The major turns to Mr. Philpotts. "If you're trying to catch the wagon train, you'll find them on the far bank of the Yellow Medicine River. They're planning to head to Wood Lake and camp there tonight."

"No, sir, I was fixing to drive on down to Redwood this evening."

"Man, you've thirty miles to go! Darkness will fall hours before you get there."

Horror fills me at the thought of passing the spot of poor Mr. Gleason's murder at night. "Oh no!" I exclaim. "I refuse to let you take us down that road in the dark. We should camp with the wagon train."

The driver spits a brown projectile onto the dirt. Then he pushes his stained hat back on his head, revealing oily strands of hair that lie flat against his scalp. "Ma'am, if you'll recollect, Captain Saunders already told you the road is plenty safe. There's no Indians within a hundred miles of us save those at Camp Release."

"I don't believe that, and I am not going to let you browbeat me into going on when every fiber of my being tells me that danger lies ahead."

"We agree with her!" shouts one of the women behind me.

Galbraith puts his hand to his mouth to hide a smile and says, "Looks like you're outvoted, man. Do as the ladies ask."

Philpotts spits again and urges his team forward. As we near the river, we pass a cluster of tepees and army tents belonging to the work party. We cross the ford and see the tail end of the wagon train ahead of us, driving to Wood Lake three miles south. "Once we reach that camp," Philpotts calls back, "I'm gonna leave you ladies there and be on my way. I've got business down to Redwood and can't be moseying along behind no oxcarts."

"Best see what the officers say first," I reply.

When we pull into camp, I beckon to Captain McLaren, a bearded officer I recognize from Camp Release. He approaches, and I explain our situation.

"I am certain we can make room for you ladies." He helps me climb down. "Go to the center of camp. You'll find soldiers passing out tents and supper rations."

As we walk that way, I see a heavily pregnant Marion Hunter, the daughter of Andrew Robertson, walking ahead of me. We knew each other before the war, and she and I were in the same camp my first days of captivity. Part Sioux on her mother's side, Mrs. Hunter was married to a carpenter at the Lower Agency. The poor girl saw him shot to death as they fled toward safety.

"Mrs. Hunter!" I say as I catch up to her.

She impetuously hugs me. "Mrs. Wakefield, I am relieved to see that you and your children are safe."

I smile. "How are you?"

"Physically I am well." Placing her hands on her belly, she adds, "And grateful that my husband left me this consolation."

"If you're willing, let us see if we can be housed together."

For efficiency's sake, we divide up, with Mrs. Hunter going to get food and me going to get shelter. After standing in line half an hour, holding my baby girl against my shoulder, I am shocked to learn that my children, Mrs. Hunter, and I must sleep in a small, two-man tent without benefit of fire or bedding, even though the evening air already has a nip of frost.

"Have you no blankets for us?" I ask the corporal who hands Jimmy a bundle of canvas and stakes.

"Sorry, ma'am. This is all I can offer."

Turning away, I walk over to Mrs. Hunter, who is still in line for rations, and report what the corporal said. Nellie whimpers, and I pat her back soothingly.

The line inches forward, and we shuffle along with it. "I have an idea," Mrs. Hunter says. "Did you notice the tepees near the Yellow Medicine? One of them belongs to my uncle John Mooers. We could go back and stay with him tonight."

I glance doubtfully at the sky. The sun has sunk nearly to the horizon. "It's already so late. It isn't safe to walk back there in the dark."

"Maybe they'll let us take a wagon. As long as we return before the train leaves in the morning, what difference will it make?"

When I consider Nellie's health, a tepee certainly seems preferable to one of these inadequate tents. "Let's ask Captain McLaren."

We've reached the head of the line, so Mrs. Hunter collects our rations of salt beef and hard tack. Then we go in search of McLaren. When we find him and make our plea, he shakes his head. "Ladies, it's far too dangerous for you to go off like that."

My patience snaps. I am sick to death of men thinking they know what is best for me. "My child is ill and in danger of developing pneumonia, Captain. You wouldn't want that on your conscience, would you?"

McLaren rubs the back of his neck.

"If we are going to go, we need to set off right away to get there before dark," I add forcefully.

The captain heaves a sigh. "Wait here."

He returns in ten minutes driving a small wagon pulled by two elderly horses. A private on horseback accompanies him. "Ladies, Private Cooper will accompany you to the camp. Private, head right back here when they're settled."

"Yes, sir." The private salutes.

McLaren jumps down. "We will wait for you in the morning, but see that you are here by eight."

I nod and load my children and the dog into the back of the wagon, telling Jimmy to hold onto his sister. Mrs. Hunter sits beside me on the driver's seat.

At the Yellow Medicine River campsite, John and Rosalia Mooers welcome us into their tepee. They have a fire going, so the shelter is warm and dry. It feels homey and safe, and soon my children and I fall asleep.

Mr. Mooers wakes us as soon as the sky starts to lighten, and we hurry outside without taking any breakfast. As Mooers leads the first horse to the wagon, Major Galbraith exits his tent a few yards away. He stretches, yawns, and then notices us. "Mrs. Wakefield! What are you doing here?"

I quickly explain why we thought it was better to stay with the Mooerses. Galbraith nods. "But surely you don't want to cross the prairie unescorted."

"I can go with them," John Mooers says.

Galbraith shakes his head. "I'll send Captain Kennedy and one of the privates with the ladies."

Accompanied by our mounted escorts, we set off when the sun is a few fingers above the horizon. About three-quarters of an hour later, we reach the field where the wagon train stopped last night. To my astonishment, every last vestige of the camp has been cleared away.

"They've gone!" Turning to Captain Kennedy, I ask, "What time is it?"

He pulls out a pocket watch and replies, "7:13, ma'am."

"Captain McLaren said he'd wait until 8:00. How could they be gone?"

I gaze about the area, seeing the ashes from numerous campfires and the places where tent stakes pockmarked the prairie sod. How are my children and I supposed to get to the fort nearly fifty miles away? Galbraith gave Captain Kennedy and Private McKimson strict orders to return to the work party as soon as we reach Wood Lake, and without them, we will be in danger every mile.

A terrible sense of betrayal fills me. How I wish we were still in Chaska's care. He would never have abandoned us like this. The longing to see him again is so fierce that I feel as though someone has kicked me in the ribs.

Finally, I say, "What can I do? I must get to the fort to find my husband."

Captain Kennedy tugs at his stand-up collar as though it is too tight. "It's a violation of our orders, but I cannot in good conscience send unprotected women over the prairie. McKimson and I will accompany you to the fort—or until we catch up with the wagon train."

Marion Hunter and I exchange questioning glances, each face mirroring the other's terror. We are heading straight for the region where the initial war councils were held, where my children and I were captured, where her husband and George Gleason were killed. If we are to reach the fort, we have no alternative but to take this route—and as things now stand, this small military escort is the best protection we can hope for. I nod. "Thank you, gentlemen. Let's be on our way."

If yesterday passed under a haze of gloom, today is spent in the iron manacles of terror. I am certain that some of Little Crow's renegades remain at large. Each time we pass a clump of bushes or a stand of trees, Mrs. Hunter and I swivel our heads from side to side, looking for signs that we are being stalked. Whenever we hear an especially loud birdcall, we jump. The soldiers laugh at our "vapors" and say, "You are frightening yourselves over nothing."

"That's what Mr. Gleason said as we traveled over this road, and now he is buried by the side of it."

The soldiers' scorn angers me, but how can I expect them to understand? To them, the brown ribbon that unspools before us is a road like any other. To me, it is a highway of death, haunted by specters. As we pass the old Indian mound where Mr. Gleason and I argued, they see a jewel-bright blue sky, but I see a phantom column of smoke on the horizon, the first sign that Redwood was burning. To the soldiers, the woods are simply trees with a few red and yellow leaves clinging to bare branches, whereas I still see how dark green the foliage was the moment two armed figures stepped out from its shadow. As we drive by the spot where Mr. Gleason was attacked, the soldiers see only the mounded dirt of a recent grave. For me the scene is overlaid by the ghostlike image of a man lying on the ground, calling my name in agony, and clutching his belly as his lifeblood oozes through his fingers.

After several hours, we ascend the crest of a hill and catch sight of the wagon train several miles ahead. But the old horses drawing our wagon walk scarcely faster than oxen, and I doubt we will catch the train before it reaches the fort.

By late morning, we come to Little Crow's abandoned village. The buildings, including the chief's government-built house, still stand, but the settlement has a forlorn air as though it knows its inhabitants will never return. The cornfields next to the village are brown and sere, with many toppled stalks.

Captain Kennedy signals for me to halt the wagon. When I do, he says, "Ladies, we must stop here for a while. Private McKimson and I had to leave this morning without feeding our horses. We're going to forage in that barn over there"—he nods toward the west—"to see if we can find some corn."

Without waiting for an answer, they spur their horses in that direction. Mrs. Hunter and I exchange worried looks. We need no words to know each other's fears.

The area is unnaturally silent. Not only are there no noises of human habitation, but even the birds have gone ominously mute. I dislike sitting in the open. A sensation of being watched comes over me, and I have to press my lips together to keep from saying something that might frighten my children.

Keeping my eye on the soldiers, I see them wave to indicate that their mission to find corn was successful. Each man pulls a feedbag from his knapsack and tends to his animal. As the horses eat, the men roam the gardens. McKimson stoops among what look to be tomato plants. "Anything he finds is likely to be mush after the frosts we've had," I remark to Mrs. Hunter.

"They must be city folk."

Somewhere to our left, a dog barks and Marion Hunter cries, "Indians!" She scrambles down, lifts her skirts, and races for the cover of the cornfield, supporting her belly as she goes. Scanning the area, I see two Sioux warriors bending low and running from the cover of bushes to a stand of trees not fifty yards away.

"Captain Kennedy!" I call and point to the woods. "Indians!"

The two soldiers whip the feedbags off their horses, mount, and gallop toward us. As they draw near, Mrs. Hunter runs out of the cornfield and places her foot upon the wagon step. I grab her hand and pull her into the seat.

Captain Kennedy rides by our side with his pistol drawn, but Mc-Kimson races down the road to alert the wagon train ahead of us. When we reach a spot where the road curves to the left, following a meandering curve of the river, Captain Kennedy orders, "Go straight across the land. It'll cut off several miles."

I obey. Instantly, the wagon begins to judder and jounce as we bump across the rough prairie. By my side, Mrs. Hunter cradles her abdomen and groans.

Ahead of us looms a long belt of trees, and I veer left to go around it. "I don't think we're saving any time," I mutter. Mrs. Hunter does not answer.

As the wagon rounds the end of the woods, we see five warriors running at us. Even though they are still about twenty yards away, I can see that their faces are distorted with hate. Two of them raise rifles, and one prepares to throw a tomahawk. I shriek. Captain Kennedy fires at them but misses.

Several answering shots come from our left. We are now within sight of the road, where a party of white men on horseback gallops toward us. The Indians turn and sprint toward the woods.

I halt the wagon and sit panting. A sharp vinegary smell assails my nostrils. Glancing at Marion Hunter, I see her sag in her seat with her chin on her chest. She is weeping. "Don't cry. We're safe now, Mrs. Hunter."

She leans on my shoulder and whispers, "I wet myself."

Impulsively, I kiss the top of her hair. "That's no reason to fret. It's as much because of the baby as from fear. Hold up your head, and the men will never know."

She presses her trembling lips together and straightens her back.

Once our wagon is safely incorporated into the wagon train, Captain Kennedy and Private McKimson tell us that they are heading back to their camp.

"God protect you on your journey," I tell them,

Captain Kennedy nods soberly and tips his cap before riding away. The cocky young men of this morning, so sure our fears were feminine hysterics, now know what a dangerous journey lies ahead of them. I pray for their safety.

We arrive at Fort Ridgely about five o'clock. The so-called fort is a collection of buildings arranged around a square of brownish grass. A long barracks building makes up the northern side; on the east and west sides stand several buildings comprising officers' quarters and a mess hall.

I ask the first officer we meet if my husband is at the fort and learn that he has been there helping the surgeon with the wounded, but he went to Shakopee on business a few days earlier. "I'm sure he will return soon," the officer says.

Most of the former captives who came in the wagon train will be housed in the enlisted men's barracks, necessitating that the troops camp outdoors. Because of John's relationship with Dr. Muller, Mrs. Hunter and I are taken to the surgeon's quarters at one end of the hospital building, the only structure that stands to the south of the square. There, Mrs. Eliza Muller greets us. A short, dark-haired woman about my age, she has an oval face with small eyes and a full bottom lip. She speaks with a German accent because she and her husband are from Switzerland.

"Welcome, ladies. You have had quite a time, I am certain, but now I must not ask you questions. First things first. A bath you would like, *ja?*"

"A bath." I blink, stupefied by the idea. "In a tub? With hot water?"

"Of course. A good wash will make you new women, *ja?*"

At that, I laugh, and Marion Hunter cries, and we hug each other to keep from collapsing with giddiness. I fear Mrs. Muller will think us mad, but she simply stands there wiping her hands on her apron and murmuring, "Poor things, poor things."

While Mrs. Hunter bathes, Mrs. Muller and I lead my children into the kitchen and wash them in the tin laundry tub. The room is filled with the aromas of baking bread and savory chicken stock, and as I scrub my son, he says, "Mama, I'm hungry."

"Shhh," I whisper. "We will eat soon." Mrs. Muller laughs and gets a plate of molasses cookies for us. The cookies are crispy, but once in the mouth, they melt on the tongue. They remind me of my grandmother's baking, and for a brief moment, I remember the security and love I always felt at her table.

A short while later, I enter a small room that contains a tin bathtub, a straight-back chair, and a dressing screen in the corner. I take off Susan Humphrey's dress and examine it with regret. After three weeks of wear, the garment is torn in places and stained beyond redemption. I drape it on a chair and get into the tub.

The warm water slides over my skin like a caress, and I lean back and sigh. After several minutes of blessed calm, I soap myself. The suds that run off my body are grey with dirt, and within minutes the bathwater is as murky as a silted pond. Too late I realize that I should have washed my hair first. Even so, I dunk my head backward in the bathwater and rub lather into my scalp. A pitcher of clean water stands on the floor next to the tub, so at least I can rinse my hair properly.

When the water cools, I climb out of the tub. Examining myself, I note that grime is still embedded in the creases of my skin. It will take more than one soaking to get clean again. I pat myself dry gently, not wanting to stain Mrs. Muller's towel.

A knock sounds on the door. "Mrs. Wakefield, may I come in?"

Swiftly, I wrap the towel around myself and call, "Yes."

Mrs. Muller enters with a blue gingham dress draped over her arm. "I took the liberty to ask my neighbor if a clean dress she could provide."

"Oh, thank you." I discover with gratitude that she also brought a pair of white cotton drawers. The simple act of wearing undergarments will go a long way toward making me feel civilized again. Holding up the dress, I say, "This should fit."

Mrs. Mueller picks up the filthy coral calico. "Shall I burn this?"

"Might as well. It was a new dress, but it will never look nice again. I made it for Mrs. Dr. Humphrey; the Sioux stole it from her house after the family escaped."

Mrs. Muller gasps. "Don't you know? The Humphreys—"

"No!" I grab the rim of the bathtub for support. "All of them?"

"Only the oldest boy, Johnny, escaped."

I cover my mouth as I remember my promise to Jimmy that we could go back to visit Jay. Then I meet Mrs. Muller's eyes. "What happened?"

"Perhaps I should not say."

I want to laugh at the idea that this good woman thinks she can protect me from horror. Instead, I gather up the clean clothes and walk behind the screen in the corner. "Mrs. Muller, I need to know. She was my friend."

"They were trying to get away from the agency, but they missed the wagons and had to walk. Mrs. Humphrey was very weak. Some recent illness she had."

"Yes." I raise my voice as I pull the dress over my head. "She had miscarried."

"*Ach,* the poor woman. They got to an abandoned cabin. Mrs. Humphrey was faint, so they stopped to rest. The boy Johnny went to fetch water from a spring. As he returned, he heard voices and wisely hid. Several hours later, he went back to the cabin and found in the yard his father dead, a bullet through his forehead. The cabin with the rest of his family had burned to the ground."

I clench my jaw to keep from crying out as visions of Susan's death engulf me: the choking smoke, the biting flames, the helpless terror of knowing she could not save her children. My gorge rises, and I bend over and breathe deeply to stop myself from vomiting.

After a minute, I button up my bodice and come out from behind the screen. "What a dreadful way to die. Did you know Susan? She was such a kind, Christian woman."

Eliza Muller nods. "That she was. She is with our Lord and savior now."

That knowledge is some comfort, yet the news of Susan's death leaves me bone weary. How many more of these stories will I hear in the coming weeks? What other acquaintances have I lost without knowing it?

My head pounds. Lifting a hand to my forehead, I say, "I don't know why I should be so lucky that all my family survived when so many others didn't."

Mrs. Muller puts her arm around me as we walk from the room. "There are no answers to such questions."

I halt. "And Johnny? Where is here now?"

"He has gone to live with an uncle in St. Paul. Thank the good Lord, he still has some family."

CHAPTER
34

As we sit at the Mullers' dining table devouring sausage, eggs, biscuits, and jam—the type of breakfast I used to take for granted but which now seems like a feast—Jimmy glances outside and cries, "There is my father!"

I set down my cup, rush to the window, and stare out the glass. There, halfway across the square, comes John, looking tall and unusually tan, wearing his everyday brown suit and a hat I've never seen. His gait is purposeful.

Lifting Nellie into my arms, I say, "Come, Jimmy." We hurry through the archway into the parlor and out the front door.

"Father!" Jimmy runs to him, arms outstretched.

Delight breaks across my husband's face. He kneels on the dirt and embraces our son. "Jimmy! My boy, my boy!" He ruffles Jimmy's white-blond hair and kisses the child so hard that his own hat falls off backward. Then John gazes over Jimmy's head toward the porch where I stand with Nellie in my arms. Tears stream down his face. When he wipes his cheeks with the back of his hand and rises to his feet, he is unsteady. "Sarah." He takes a step toward us.

Jimmy grabs his hand, not yet ready to relinquish his father's attention. "We have a dog! His name is Buster."

"What?" Startled from his thoughts, John looks from our son to me. "A dog?"

"Mr. Gleason's terrier," I answer, finding it odd that these are the first words we exchange. "We adopted it after he was killed."

John flushes at the mention of the murder. I hope that means he bitterly regrets the decisions he made that day.

And what do I feel? Certainly not the pure, unadulterated bliss I thought would flood my soul at our reunion. I am happy enough, but other spices add discordant undertones to the sweet syrup of elation. Tempering my joy is the bitter rind of grief; how can I take unmitigated pleasure in our survival when so many fine people have perished? Deeper still, I detect the peppery aftertaste of anger toward this man who sent me on the foolhardy drive that resulted in our capture.

I cover my mouth to hide the resentful set of my lips. John walks two more paces and stops in front of the porch steps.

He cannot disguise his shock as his gaze sweeps over me. Bringing his eyes back to my face, he tries to muster a flirtatious smile. "Why, if it isn't Sarah Brown."

"The name is Wakefield, sir." I cannot imbue that answer with the necessary playfulness, so I hold out Nellie to him. "Say hello to your daughter."

John's smile falters as he takes her into his arms. Noting her red eyes, flushed cheeks, chapped nostrils, and dry lips, he says, "She's ill."

"There was a lot of sickness at Camp Release. This is a cold, but she also had a lengthy bout with bowel complaint a few weeks back."

John's physician's demeanor asserts itself. He hefts Nellie. "She doesn't seem to have grown much. I thought that in two months—"

He meets my eyes.

"We didn't have enough to eat."

He flinches again. "You've lost weight. And your hair— Were you sick too?"

I shake my head. "No. Just underfed and marched nearly the whole length of the Minnesota Valley. We moved camp often, fleeing one danger or another."

John climbs the three steps to the porch, hands me our baby, and puts his arms around me. "You're safe now."

The instant I hear those words, I melt against his shoulder. "You don't know what it was like to worry about the children's safety every hour of every day, with no one to share the burden. Worrying I would do the wrong thing and get us all killed. The strain never eased, not even after the militia arrived. Only yesterday, we were nearly attacked on our journey down here. I tried to warn the soldiers that the road was dangerous, but they wouldn't listen. I couldn't trust anyone but myself."

I fall silent, appalled at the lie I told him. Although it is true that I learned not to trust the judgment of other whites, I did trust Chaska. I trusted him more than I have ever trusted John, more than I have ever trusted anyone except my father. And that is a truth I can never tell my husband.

John turns away and pounds the porch pillar. "I've cursed myself for sending you off that day. I thought it was the right thing, but—"

I sigh. Even though I know how difficult it is for John to apologize, I find myself struggling to grant him absolution. Try as I might, I cannot forget how he refused to tell me what was happening that day and how his judgment failed us.

From the corner of my eye, I see my son pick up John's hat from the ground and carefully dust it off. That loving gesture reminds me that more than my happiness is at stake. Choosing my words carefully to make sure I don't express more forgiveness than I really feel, I say, "You couldn't see the future. Even in the worst moments, I always knew your intention was to keep us safe."

John faces me again. "Gleason died."

"He never had a chance. He lied about having a gun, and anyway, Hapa shot him without warning."

John frowns. "Hapa? Was he the one you—" His voice falters.

"No, his brother-in-law. Two men stopped us on the road. One was drunk and violent. The other one, Chaska, was reasonable and kind. He talked Hapa out of shooting us, and he's the one who protected us for the rest of the war."

My husband's face hardens almost imperceptibly. "What does that mean, exactly?" he demands. "Did he—were you two?"

"John, I will tell you anything you want to know, but do we have to discuss it out here in the public square?"

He doesn't answer. His stare grows stony.

"No one abused me." My voice rises with anger. "No one compromised my honor. Chaska made a vow to return me to you exactly the way he found me, and he kept that vow. It may cost him his life, but he kept it."

"I'm sorry, but I had to ask." My husband holds out his hands palms upward and adds in an apologetic tone, "A man has a right to know."

I set Nellie on her feet and put my hands on my hips. "Do you? And would you have refused to take me back if I were 'spoiled goods'? Even if submitting were the only way I could keep your children alive?"

Anger flashes across John's face, doused quickly by contrition. "Of course not. It wouldn't matter, not really. But can't you see that I have to know?"

At that moment, Jimmy climbs the steps and takes his father's hand. In his right hand, he carries John's hat. Anxiety clouds his face. "Mama, why are you angry? Aren't you glad to see my father again?"

For his sake, I manage to smile. "Of course, I am, darling. Your father and I had a little misunderstanding. But it's all settled now. Isn't it, John?"

He looks at me warily and nods. "Yes. We're both happy."

"Let's go back inside and finish breakfast. It's probably cold by now, but God knows we've eaten worse."

John steps forward and opens the door for me. "I rented a place for us in Shakopee. I thought we could be on our way this afternoon."

Jimmy pushes past us to run ahead into the dining room and Nellie toddles after him. John takes my arm to hold me back. In a low voice, he says, "Please put other clothes on the children before we leave. They look like little savages."

I gaze at him, astonished by his request. "We have no other clothes. Everything was stolen. I'm wearing a borrowed dress."

"Couldn't you borrow something else for Jimmy, at least?"

Much of my thought has revolved around how to make our marriage better if we reunite, but now my compass needle swings back toward the one lodestone that has controlled my direction these last two months: protecting my children. "So you could throw away his Indian clothes? He would never forgive you. You may not like this, but Jimmy loved his time with the Sioux. He didn't want to come back. The only thing he missed was you. Don't make him resent you for taking away his treasures."

John jerks his head back. "You've changed."

I laugh. "You show me someone who lives with the fear of death for six weeks without being changed, and I'll show you an imbecile."

The distance from Fort Ridgely to Shakopee is seventy miles by direct route, but when John proposes going that way, I object: "Few towns lie along that road. Did you find safe places to stay overnight when you drove down from Shakopee?"

John, who is using a pocketknife to cut the end of a cigar, shrugs. "I pulled off to the side of the road and slept in the wagon."

The image of the warriors who came so close to attacking us yesterday leaps into my mind. My hands tremble.

As John reaches into his pocket for his box of wooden matches, he notices my distress. He sets both matches and cigar on the table. "What's wrong?"

"I will not risk sleeping out in the open, John. I'm too frightened."

He points a finger at me. Rather than let him make the inevitable accusation that I am being silly, I lean forward and say, "Listen to me. Five warriors came within ten yards of our wagon yesterday. If a rescue party hadn't come barreling down the road, the children and I would never have made it as far as Redwood."

Blood drains from John's face. He blinks twice. "But we'll be driving north and east, away from the reservation."

"Acton is north of here," I say, referring to the location of the first massacre. "It's farther north than Shakopee."

John goes through the complicated routine of lighting his cigar without letting the flame touch the tobacco. Once it is burning to his satisfaction, he concedes, "All right, we'll drive to New Ulm tonight and then northward tomorrow."

As we travel, I tell John our story, episode by episode, in as close to chronological order as I can manage. Our captivity is very painful to talk about, and I often have to fall silent to keep from weeping. To give John credit, he makes small, encouraging noises whenever that happens, showing far more patience with me than usual.

But after I describe the night in the ravine, he frowns. "I don't understand. It sounds like you were in more danger than the other captives."

I shake my head. "Yes and no. All the prisoners were at risk of harm. It's hard to explain how complicated it was, John. The mood among the Indians was unstable, and we could feel perfectly safe one minute and threatened the next. At times, I did fear that Little Crow singled me out for particular enmity. He had hoped to capture the Galbraiths, and I was the only white captive from Yellow Medicine, so we feared he wanted to punish me in their stead. But, even if I was in more jeopardy, I also had the advantage of having better protectors than most. Whenever there was the least hint of danger, Chaska and Ina hid me or moved me."

John nods slowly and reaches out to squeeze my hand. Expelling a sigh, I resume my story.

Toward evening we reach New Ulm, a pitiful remnant of its former self. Only the innermost center of the town still stands with a wide, scorched doughnut around it. At the Union Hotel, the proprietor tells us that the town's defenders herded women and children into brick buildings for safety and then erected defensive barriers in the streets. Everything outside the perimeter, nearly 200 buildings, burned. The hotel itself served as a hospital. "Things aren't yet restored to the way I want them, but I'll give you the best rooms I have."

"We lived with the Sioux!" Jimmy declares as the proprietor leads us upstairs.

The man stops and glares at my son in his buckskin garments.

"My children and I were held captive for six weeks," I say quickly. "We've only recently been released and reunited with my husband."

"My sympathies, ma'am." The proprietor's gaze turns avidly curious. "I heard the army is trying those red devils. Is that true?"

My throat tightens as I think of Chaska, and all I can do is nod.

"Waste of time, if you ask me," the man declares, starting to climb the stairs again. "They ought to hang every man jack of them."

During the second day on the road, I narrate the middle part of our captivity. As I describe how hard it was to adapt to Sioux ways, John's attitude grows less sympathetic. He interrupts to ask questions like "Why did you do that?" or "Why didn't you spend more time with other captives?" or "Don't you think you should have...?"

By the time we stop to eat lunch, I feel as though I have been called before a tribunal every bit as judgmental as the one that condemned Chaska. I tell Jimmy and Nellie to take Buster for a walk. When John and I are alone, I take a deep breath and say, "Could you listen instead of interrogating me? I know you would have done things differently, but you weren't there."

He flushes. "I'm not criticizing you, Sarah."

"You question nearly everything I did."

John folds his arms across his chest. "I'm trying to understand. As you say, I wasn't there. I need to know what happened."

I reach for the cloth bundle holding the lunch we bought at the hotel and unwrap bread, cheese, and hard-boiled eggs. "All your questions have only one answer. Every time I had to make a choice, I did what I thought gave us the best chance to stay alive."

"Yes, but why adopt Indian customs? They're our enemies."

I stare at him and wonder if he has heard a single thing I said. "Chaska and Ina were not my enemies. Neither was Mother Friend or Eagle Head or Opa. They were my friends and protectors, and I respect them."

"Respect! What is there to respect about savages who slaughter innocent people? Don't you know what they did? Have you heard about the Humphreys?"

"Yes, I heard." With great effort, I keep my voice calm. "Do you really think you know more about what this war did to people than I do?"

John flushes. "Dammit, I don't understand you. How can you forgive them?"

I step closer and touch his face. "I don't forgive the murderers. I want them to hang. But many Sioux opposed this war. Some of them worked hard to stop the hostiles from slaughtering us captives. They should be honored."

John swats my hand away. "The state is in no mood for such fine distinctions. People are outraged and want blood."

"All the more reason for someone like me to testify to what really happened."

He shakes his head. "Don't do it. People won't thank you for preaching about brotherhood if they lost loved ones in this war. You'll only make trouble for us."

His bitterness saddens me. When we are driving again, I change the subject and ask John about his wartime experiences. Still peeved, he makes short work of his answer, and the account of his escape adds little to what Chaska already told me. "After I arrived at Fort Ridgely," John concludes, "I remained to help Dr. Muller and get news of you. Until Mrs. De Camp arrived at the fort, I had no idea if you and the children were alive. Even then I couldn't be certain you remained safe until a messenger arrived with a list of people freed at Camp Release."

"That must have been dreadful. I remember how horrible it was the first few weeks when I kept hearing rumors that you were dead."

He turns to me in surprise. "You did?"

I nod. "One woman went so far as to tell me that your head had been cut off. I nearly lost my mind. At one point, I decided to kill the children so they wouldn't be raised as savages. But thank God, Ina's friends stopped me."

John's mouth drops open in shock, and he glances back at Jimmy. Then he shakes his head as if to ward off the terrible images. "Thank God, indeed. How did you find out I was alive?"

"Chaska told me."

"Of course. *Chaska.* I should have known." He pronounces it *Chaskuh,* even though I have been saying *Chas-kay* for two days. I think he does it to needle me.

Jimmy stands up in the wagon bed and grasps the back of our seat. "Do you know what else Chaska did, Father?"

John's jaw tightens. "No. What?"

"He said he would teach me how to hunt when I got older." Jimmy's voice grows sad. "But now he's in jail."

"Where he belongs," John mutters under his breath.

By digging my fingernails into my palm, I keep myself from rebuking him for that uncharitable sentiment. Instead, I say, "I still haven't told you about the end of the war." I proceed to describe our move to Yellow Medicine. "I saw them burn our house, but there wasn't much left in it anyway."

John grunts. I go on to describe the confusion of the final weeks, the conflict between the friendly and hostile Indian camps, the fear that we would be carried off to the Dakotas, and my anger that Sibley took so long to execute his rescue mission.

"By then it was cold, and our supplies were lower than ever. Chaska sold his one good coat to buy food so the children wouldn't go hungry."

"I wonder he didn't just feed the five thousand," John snipes.

"There's no call to be sarcastic. Why aren't you grateful for all Chaska did?"

John snatches the cigar from his mouth and speaks with such venom that spittle flecks my face. "Grateful! You want me to be grateful that my wife and son can talk of nothing but the brute who took them captive? He kidnapped you, but you describe him as though he were a saint!"

His remark so upsets me that I grip the edge of my seat. "He did *not* kidnap us, John. He took us into custody to protect us from the hostiles."

"Tell that to George Gleason!"

"Chaska would have protected Mr. Gleason, but Hapa acted too swiftly."

"That's ridiculous. The two of them were in cahoots."

"You don't know that. You weren't there. You're as bad as the tribunal. They refused to believe me when I testified at Chaska's trial."

With the speed of a striking cobra, John grasps my wrist so tightly that I yelp. "You testified on his behalf?"

"Yes!" I pry his hand loose and rub my wrist. "I only told the truth. He saved our lives. I had to try to save his."

John closes his eyes and squeezes the bridge of his nose. His facial muscles quiver with suppressed rage. Finally, he says, "That was very foolish, but it can't be helped now. You said the tribunal sentenced him to hang anyway, didn't you?"

"Yes," I reply, sick at heart that John could support such an outcome. For a second, I consider saying that Chaska's sentence might be commuted to imprisonment, but Captain Grant made me promise faithfully not to tell anyone.

In the heat of the conversation, I forget that Jimmy is standing behind us. Now he says, "Mama tried really hard to save Chaska. After the trial, she argued with Colonel Sibley and the preacher and lots of officers."

John eyes widen. He glances over his shoulder at the bright-eyed innocence of our son and then back at me. "Tell me you didn't. How could you be so stupid?"

I scoot away from him and look out at the passing scenery. Hurt makes my voice thick as I say, "You must not value our lives very much if you have so little concern for the man who protected us."

"What concerns me is our future. We're going to have to live with the very people whose lives were ruined by this conflict."

"As ours were."

He waves his cigar in my face. "Indeed, but whatever sympathy that might have garnered us will be undermined by your advocacy for this Chaska. People will run us out of the state if they think you took the wrong side in this war."

"That's preposterous. I'm a victim of the war."

John shakes his head. "Sarah, you've been isolated. You have no idea how enraged people are, how they demand vengeance against every last Indian."

"Even the ones who opposed the conflict?"

"People don't believe that any Indians opposed the war. They think it's a ruse to escape the consequences now that the Sioux have lost."

"Don't you see? That makes it even more important for me to tell the truth."

"No, Sarah." He points his cigar at me again. "That makes it imperative for you to keep quiet."

In the late afternoon of the third day, John stops our wagon in front of a small house in Shakopee. "I will show you around, and then I have to take the wagon and team back to the livery stable."

I climb down and gaze at the one-story, white clapboard structure. "How can we afford this? I thought we'd lost all our money."

"The government continued to pay my salary because of my work at Fort Ridgely, and my brother James loaned us some money to get reestablished."

He takes me through the four rooms: a parlor, a kitchen, and two bedrooms. The house contains minimal furnishings: a stove, a kitchen table, a plain dining room set, a sofa, a chair, and two beds. "We'll have to buy new dishes, pans, linens," I say. "We're starting over from nothing. It will take years to make a comfortable home."

"Maybe not. I forgot to tell you we can file a depredation claim for the property that was destroyed. The state legislature has asked the federal government to pay it out of the Indian's annuity money, which they forfeited by going to war."

"Oh." I turn away, so he won't see that the thought of taking the Indians' payments distresses me.

"Tomorrow I want you to list everything you can think of that we lost. I'll do the same, and we'll compare lists to ensure that we report everything."

"All right. The other thing I must do is to sew clothes for the children and me. Remaking our wardrobes will take weeks."

"We can go to the general store tomorrow, so you can buy fabric and essentials for the kitchen. And I'll pick out lamps and other sundry items we need. Any fripperies will have to wait."

John kisses my forehead and leaves. Walking through the strange house, I feel lost and uncertain. Everything I did to create a pleasant home at Yellow Medicine has been reduced to ashes. Do I have the stamina to do it all over again?

Turning to my children, I cluck at their dirt-stained faces. My mood lifts with the knowledge that I have an obvious first task. Much to my relief, I find a large kettle in the kitchen. After filling it at the backyard pump—a luxury after all the hauling I did this summer—I heat up water to bathe my children.

Walking into the general store is overwhelming; I find it difficult to comprehend that so many things are available for purchase. Was it always like this? As I walk down an aisle, a white porcelain washbasin and ewer painted with pink roses captures my attention, and I pick up the jug. It has been so long since I held something this pretty. Catching John's sleeve, I say, "We need one of these sets."

He glances at it. "Yes, all right, but remember to limit our purchases to necessities." Leaving me, he crosses to where oil lanterns are displayed.

After running my hand along the smooth glazed surface one more time, I set the ewer down and look for the children. Jimmy has strict instructions not to let go of Nellie's hand. They have moved over to gape at the jars of candy sticks on a high shelf. I walk up behind them and say, "If you stay right here and don't touch anything, I will buy you each a treat when we finish shopping."

"Yes, Mama," Jimmy says.

Nellie points up at the jars. "Caddy!" she cries.

"Candy," I correct her. "You can have one later if you're good."

I walk over to a table that holds bolts of fabric. Two other women are there before me, so I say, "Good morning." When they glance up, I recognize an acquaintance from when we lived here before. "Mrs. Mason! How good to see you."

To my surprise, she stiffens and does not answer. Her companion shoots her a questioning look, and she says quietly, "Mrs. Dr. Wakefield."

Puzzled but determined to be friendly, I pick up a bolt of forest green calico printed with bunches of cherries. "Isn't this lovely?"

The two women exchange another glance, and then Mrs. Mason raises her voice to call to the storekeeper, "Mr. Magnusson, please hold the items I already selected. I will come back to purchase them at a more congenial time." Tossing her head, she takes her companion's arm and flounces out of the store.

I stand there, cradling the bolt of fabric, stunned into silence by the snub. In an instant, John is at my side, hissing in my ear, "See? What did I tell you? You're going to be a pariah in this state because you defended that man."

"Don't be silly," I whisper. "We just got into town last night. How could the news have gotten here before me?"

He flings the bolt onto the table, takes my arm, and pulls me closer to the exit. "Sarah, you have no conception of what it has been like while you were gone. For the last two months, the state has buzzed about nothing but the war. Any little piece of news spreads like wild-fire. How long ago did you testify?"

I consider for a moment and say, "A little over two weeks."

"That's more than long enough for word to get back here. Obviously, that woman has heard about your antics, and she doesn't approve."

Ignoring his use of the demeaning word *antics,* I say, "You don't know that. She could be mad about something that happened two years ago."

"Don't be naive." He leans in closer. "When I arrived at Fort Ridgely and asked if you had arrived, the soldiers smirked to my face, and when I set off to find you, they sniggered behind my back. I couldn't imagine what that was about, but now I know it's because you made a spectacle of yourself."

"You're making a scene," I say quietly, "which isn't helping. What's done is done. All we can do is brazen it out. The talk will die down eventually."

"Yes, and my medical practice will die with it."

It is ten o'clock, and John isn't home. He went out this afternoon and didn't come home for supper. I assume that he is drinking in a saloon somewhere, but I'm not about to go searching up and down the streets of Shakopee. Reluctantly, I put on my nightgown and climb into bed, but I cannot sleep. I listen to the sounds that seep through the closed window—a barking dog, the cry of an owl—and wonder where Ina is. Is someone taking care of her? I wish I could have brought her with me, but those who warned against the idea were right. The bubbling anger here is so scalding that Ina would be in danger if she set foot within the city limits.

I roll over on my side, punch my pillow, and try to calm myself by praying. As I petition God for Chaska's sentence to be commuted, the front door to the house crashes open. John shouts, "Dammit!" and slams the door shut. His voice is slurred.

I sit up and light the lamp on the bedside table. Moments later, he throws open the bedroom door and stands in the doorway. His suit is disheveled and his collar is torn. "There you are, you lyin' bitch. Thought you could fool me, din't you?"

"What are you talking about?"

He steps into the room, stumbling slightly. *"Oh, John,"* he says in falsetto. *"He didn't abuse me. He protected my honor."* Leaning on his hands on the end of the bed, he glares at me. "Of course, he didn't 'buse you 'cause he didn't have to. You gave yourself to him, you whore. He was your Indian *husband.* Ever body in Minn'sota knows it but me." His voice rises to a scream. "I'm going to kill you!"

I scramble out of bed. He is standing between the door and me, so I have no escape. "John, that didn't happen. I told you the truth."

John covers his ears and roars, "Stop lying!" He rushes at me, gives me a backhanded slap that knocks me across the bed, and grabs my hair. My jaw throbs and my scalp burns as he tries to drag me from the room. I reach up and grip his arm with both hands to brace myself against the agonizing pressure.

Then Jimmy shouts from the doorway, "Father, stop! Don't hurt her."

Still grappling to loosen John's hold, I twist my head to the side and cry, "Go back to your room, Jimmy! Now!"

"No!" he cries. "I won't let him hurt you!"

John twists away from me to deal with our son, and I straighten in time to see a flash of something silver in Jimmy's hand. John's arm swings up and punches Jimmy, who goes flying and lands crumpled at the base of the wall.

I scream and push past my husband, who stands frozen with horror on his face.

"Jimmy! Say something." I kneel beside him and take him into my arms.

"Mama," he says feebly. "Mama, you O.K?"

"Oh, darling." I brush back his hair. He has a split lip and blood on the back of his head. "Yes, I'm fine. But you should have run away when I told you to."

Twisting my neck and shoulders to look behind me, I glare at John. "How could you strike a child? You could have killed him."

"Sorry." His voice is hollow with shock. "Lemme 'xamine him."

"No!" Jimmy cries and hides his face against my stomach.

John looks stricken. Our son has never preferred me to him, not ever.

I smooth his tangled hair. "Jimmy, you have to let him look at you. He didn't mean to hurt you. He was angry at me, not you. He loves you."

He pulls back and stares into my eyes. "Promise?"

I nod my head. "He won't hurt you again. He wants to make you better."

Jimmy pushes out his lower lip and shifts his gaze to his father. "You're meaner than the Indians. They never hit us."

John drops to his knees. "I'm sorry, son. Please forgive me."

Jimmy checks my face before grudgingly nodding.

John gently lifts our son to the bed. While he feels Jimmy's arms and legs for broken bones, I place my hand against the wall and struggle to my feet. My head is pounding, and my right cheek feels bruised. I take a step, and my foot kicks something. Glancing down, I see Jimmy's Sioux knife lying on the floor. When my husband bends over our son to inspect his scalp, I nudge it under the bed.

John sits on the edge of the bed next to Jimmy and raises his eyes to me. "He'll be fine. He's going to have a bump on his head, but nothing is broken."

I lean back against the wall and gaze at my husband wearily. All signs of rage have vanished from his eyes. In its place is deep shame. "John, I can't live like this. I spent the last two months in constant fear for my life. I can't sit here night after night worrying that you're going to beat me or worse yet hurt our children."

He ducks his head.

Crossing my arms over my chest, I say, "I don't know how to convince you. Whatever you heard at the saloon tonight is a lie. Chaska was *never* my lover. That's a malicious rumor spread by people who thought I was too friendly to Indians."

John rests his forehead in his hands and rocks back and forth for several minutes. Then he lowers his hands and says, "I don't know what to b'lieve. All I have is your word. If there was proof—"

"Proof!" Exasperated, I shake my head. "What kind of proof can I possibly offer? *Nothing* happened."

"I need time to think through all this. It's not wha...what I expected."

"Time." I throw up my hands in a gesture of bewilderment. "And what are the children and I supposed to do while you're thinking about whether you want to be married to me?"

A hangdog look crosses John's face. "You could go away for a while. Let the talk die down."

"If you're going to suggest that I go to Rhode Island, the answer is no."

He shakes his head. "What about visiting Julia? You and the children could stay with her."

I sigh. John's sister Julia and I have never been close, and her husband, Eli Wilder, is a pompous, straitlaced judge. But they live in Redwing on the Mississippi River, only sixty miles east of Shakopee. "All right, John. We'll go stay with Julia."

CHAPTER

35

"SARAH? YOU'RE UP EARLY. WHEN DID YOU COME DOWNSTAIRS?"

I glance up from my sewing to see my sister-in-law Julia standing in the parlor doorway. A matronly woman of forty-seven, she strongly resembles her younger brother James; they have the same oblong face, thin lips, and aquiline nose. They also have the same deep-set blue eyes and dark brown hair as John, although Julia, as the eldest Wakefield sibling, has begun to go grey.

"A rooster woke me," I lie, not wanting to admit that a nightmare image of a tomahawk raised above my head yanked me from sleep.

Julia steps into the room. "You are not sleeping well, are you?"

I keep my gaze fixed on the shirt I'm sewing for Jimmy and shake my head.

"Do you want to talk about it?"

"No, Julia, thank you."

An hour later, we gather in the dining room for breakfast: Julia, Eli, their seven-year-old daughter, my children, and me. Eli is a stout man with a bulbous nose, thick side-whiskers, and a clean-shaven chin. Because it is a Saturday, he wears tweed trousers, a tan waistcoat, and a brown frock coat, much less formal attire than the fine black suit he dons on court days.

John is not here. After driving the children and me to Red Wing, he stayed only a single night before heading back to Shakopee. His excuse was that he needs to reestablish his medical practice, but I think the Wilders noticed that we are barely speaking to each other.

As Eli takes a second helping of flapjacks and bacon, he says, "Sarah, Julia and I are hoping that you and the children will join us at church tomorrow."

The condescension in his voice causes me to bristle. "I fully intend to do so. Jimmy and I were in the habit of attending services at the missions on the reservation, and I sorely missed church while we were held captive."

Eli raises his eyebrows and nods at his wife, whereupon Julia says, "We have been considering your...um, situation."

"Do you mean the gossip?" I ask tartly, in no mood for tactful shilly-shallying.

"Well, yes, I suppose that is what I mean. Eli thinks it might remedy matters if you were to become a member of our church."

"People might see it as a good faith effort to redeem yourself," Eli adds.

I set my china cup into its saucer with a sharp clink. "Could we discuss this later, when the children aren't present?"

My sister-in-law turns to her daughter. "You've finished eating, haven't you, Ella? Take your cousins up to your room and read them a story." Julia glances at my daughter and grimaces. "On second thought, please wash Nellie's face and hands first so she doesn't get syrup on the furniture."

As soon as the children are gone, I demand, "What is this all about?"

"Do not take offense," Eli says in his best judicial voice. "We only wish to help. It has come to our attention that the general population is outraged by your behavior, a state of affairs that is injurious not only to yourself but to others."

"People won't go to a doctor if there is any scandal in his family," Julia adds. "And the rumors may harm James's political career as well."

I breathe out through my nose. When I am sure I can speak without raising my voice, I say, "The rumors are false. Chaska did not violate my honor. On the contrary, he protected it."

"That may be so," Eli says, "but it is not the only issue. People are incensed that you testified on his behalf."

"You're a judge! You of all people should be outraged by the travesty of those so-called trials. Chaska is innocent, and I want him to receive justice."

"That is hardly the point," Julia interrupts.

"Then what is?"

She holds up one hand. "I am not denying that irregularities may have occurred. But a state judge like Eli cannot interfere with a military court."

"But someone must be able to do something."

Julia opens her mouth to reply, but a look from her husband silences her. "Allow me to look into the matter," he says. "In the meantime, shall we get back to my proposal? I would like you to consider speaking to our minister, the Reverend Mr. Edward Welles of Christ Episcopal Church."

My cheeks burn hot as I admit, "I tried to join a church when we lived in Shakopee. None of the ministers I spoke to would baptize me."

Eli frowns. "You have never been baptized?"

I shake my head.

"What about your children?" Julia asks.

"They haven't been baptized either."

Her eyes widen as she cries, "Sarah, how could you risk their souls? What if they had died during the war?" Her distress is palpable, and irritated as I am, I understand the reason for it; Julia and Eli have lost two young daughters to illness.

"My dear," Eli says placatingly, "our merciful savior would have taken young James and Nellie into his bosom. They have not yet reached the age of reason."

"Still, Sarah should get them baptized."

"Gladly, if you can direct me to a willing minister."

Eli folds his hands across his belly, tucking one thumb behind his gold watch chain. "I am certain the Reverend Mr. Welles will be happy to do so. As a warden in the church, I am quite familiar with his views."

"After service tomorrow, we can invite him to call on us," Julia says as she rings the bell for the servant.

Rather than ask Mr. Welles to come to the Wilders' home, where my well-meaning but officious in-laws may intrude themselves into the conversation, I arrange to visit him at his office on Monday. The church is a mere three blocks from the Wilder home, so I walk there, having borrowed a warm cloak from Julia.

As I head northeast, Barn Bluff looms above the rooftops before me. A tree-covered bluff that extends along the southern bank of a bend in the Mississippi, it is the most distinctive feature of Red Wing's landscape.

The Wilders' tree-lined neighborhood is orderly and beautiful. Eli and Julia live in a two-story, white clapboard house on Third Street, two blocks south of the river. Many of Red Wing's leading citizens live in this residential area in homes that reflect the most popular architectural styles of our time—mostly Gothic Revival or Greek Revival, as was used in the Wilder home. Strolling past the imposing edifices, I cannot help but contrast them with the canvas tepees in which I so recently lived. Is this what God wants, for some people to live in grandeur while others barely have sufficient protection from the brutal winter cold?

Such musings unsettle me so that by the time I reach the small frame structure that houses Christ Church, I feel woefully unprepared for my meeting. Following the directions Mr. Welles gave me yesterday, I go through the side entrance and turn down the corridor leading to the rector's library. I remove my gloves, push back my hood, and after taking a deep breath, knock at the library door.

Welles is a man about my own age with a long face and narrow chin, an imposing domed forehead, brown eyes, and a full beard. He greets me courteously, shows me to the chair that sits before his desk, and says, "It is a cold day for November. Would you like some tea to warm you?"

I glance swiftly around his office but see no stove or fireplace where he could prepare the beverage. "I do not want to put you to any trouble."

"No trouble. My wife Mary and I live in a small apartment at the back of the building. It will take only a moment to step out and ask her to bring refreshments. She has been anticipating the request."

When he leaves, I examine the room, which contains plain, solid furniture and shelves filled with books. The only adornment is a wooden plaque with gold lettering: "In quietness and confidence shall be your strength. Isaiah 30:15."

The verse calms my spirit. Yesterday in church, Mr. Welles impressed me with his simple eloquence. His sermon bore evidence of careful scholarship, yet he strove to draw attention to his ideas rather than his rhetorical skill. He exhorted people to seek and obey the will of their redeemer, a message that gave me hope.

He returns to the study, sits behind his desk, and folds his hands beneath his chin. "Tell me about your religious upbringing, Mrs. Wakefield. How did it happen that you have never been baptized?"

I stare at the brass inkwell on the desk in front of me. My mouth is dry, so I lick my lips. "The reasons are complicated and some might say scandalous."

"Let me assure you," he says in a kindly voice, "that there can be nothing in your past that our Savior would refuse to forgive."

I nod but remain dubious. "My father's family, the Browns, were Quakers."

"And they don't practice baptism."

"Correct, but there's more to the story. My mother was—" I bite my lower lip as I grope for a tactful phrase. "Born out of wedlock. Her father was a sailor who passed through our port just once. The local churches shunned her mother, who eventually died under circumstances that raised suspicions of self-destruction."

"Ah, the poor woman," Mr. Welles murmured. "And your mother?"

"My father's family took her in as servant. She worked for them many years before she and my father decided to marry. He was a big, gentle bear of a man, and I think they were happy."

I briefly smile at the memory of my loving father. "So the Browns did not baptize me, and my mother had no ties to a parish. When my father died, she grew bitter against God. As a child, I often went to meeting with my Grandmother Brown, but she died when I was eleven. After that, I received no more religious instruction until I was old enough to take myself to church."

Mr. Welles nods. A rap sounds on the door, and he holds up a hand to hush me. Mrs. Welles brings a tray into the library, sets it on the desk, and serves us tea and shortbread. After she leaves, Mr. Welles says, "Why didn't you join a church as an adult? Judge Wilder told me that you sought to be baptized in Shakopee and were denied. Surely, your mother's past was not an issue here in the West."

I shake my head and swallow the bit of shortbread in my mouth. It goes down hard and dry. "No, the problem in that case was a false rumor about me."

Mr. Welles raises his eyebrows. After moistening my throat with a sip of tea, I explain how my stepfather attempted to seduce me. "My mother always resented my efforts to go to church on my own and accused me of thinking I was better than her. So she not only blamed me for my stepfather's actions, she also went out of her way to blacken my name in the town and later out here in Minnesota."

Mr. Welles leans forward to pour himself more tea. A frown creases his forehead. "As I understand it, you also claim that the current rumors about you are false. I find it difficult to believe—" Leaving his cup on its saucer, he sits back and places his folded hands below his chin. "Forgive me, Mrs. Wakefield, but you appear to have a habit of accusing other people of lying about you."

My back stiffens. "Yes, I have been unfortunate enough to have that happen more than once. Perhaps you find it impossible to believe, but it is God's own truth."

He stares at me silently, and I pick up my gloves and handbag. "It seems you did not mean it when you said there is nothing in my past that Christ cannot forgive."

"Of course, I meant it. But you must be honest in confessing your sins to receive that forgiveness."

Blood rushes into my face. "I have never claimed to be without sin! I act too rashly at times. I have a rude, impetuous way of speaking, and I do not always obey my husband. Those are just some of my sins. I will gladly confess my faults, Mr. Welles, but I will not admit to a false accusation. Surely you must know that gossip is often untrue and spiteful."

He considers my words and nods. "Let us put aside the question of your past for the moment. As an adult candidate for baptism, especially one with so little religious formation, I would need to instruct you in the fundamentals of our faith. Are you willing to meet with me several times over the next few weeks?"

"To prove that I'm worthy?"

Mr. Welles shakes his head. "No, my dear woman. I would ask this of any adult who came to me requesting baptism."

I blink and stare at his inkwell again. It is made of brass, and its stopper has a cross-shaped finial. *How appropriate,* I think. And then, *What a comfort it would be to belong somewhere. To know that I am making a fresh start in the eyes of both God and man.* Meeting his gaze, I say, "I would be happy to meet with you. What about my children? Do they need instruction too?"

"No. When we baptize a child, the adults in their lives make the commitment on their behalf. The adults also commit to teach them doctrine as they grow."

I look up in sudden understanding. "That's one reason I need instruction, isn't it? So I can teach them."

He smiles with genuine warmth. "Yes, Mrs. Wakefield."

I arrange to have my children baptized on Sunday, November 23. As soon as the date is set, I send John a letter asking him to attend the service. "Jimmy would like to see you there. He misses you," I write. My son blames himself for our separation, even though I have told him repeatedly that it isn't his fault.

The following week is full of news. On Monday after midday dinner, Eli unfolds his copy of the town paper, the *Red Wing Republican,* and reads us a paragraph stating that the trials of the Sioux are over. The condemned prisoners—303 of them—are on their way to Mankato to be hanged in December.

"Dear God in heaven! Three hundred! How could they have tried so many in a month?"

Eli gazes at me over the top of the paper. "A very good question."

I bite my lip and think of Chaska. So far, I have heard nothing about his sentence being commuted, and since I am not even supposed to know about the possibility, I dare not write Sibley to ask about it.

Eli folds up the newspaper and lays it on the table. "They say 1,700 Sioux noncombatants—mostly women and children—are being marched to an internment camp in Fort Snelling, where they will be kept over the winter."

"I wonder if Ina is there! I should like to visit her if she is."

"Honestly, Sarah, don't you realize that would further damage your reputation?" Julia snaps. "Leave it alone."

I turn to her, stunned by her indignation. But why should I be surprised? It makes sense that her first impulse is to protect the family, and her brother in particular. The Wakefields always stick together. Wearily, I say, "All right, Julia."

Two days later, Eli comes home from the courthouse with his usual copy of the *Republican.* "I think you will be interested in today's headline," he tells me. "President Lincoln thinks the number of condemned Sioux is excessive."

"As well he should!"

"He is going to appoint a commission to review the transcripts and evaluate the sentences. Then he will decide who is to hang and who will be sent to prison."

"Thank God! I have been praying for a miracle to save Chaska's life. Surely, a lawyer as canny as Mr. Lincoln will realize he does not deserve to die."

Julia purses her lips together but makes no comment.

John arrives the afternoon before the baptism, and the children race to greet him. He squats in the front hallway to hug both of them at the same time, yet his manner is subdued, and just like that, anger surges within me. I can understand why he might resent me, but Jimmy and Nellie have done nothing to deserve his coldness.

Releasing the children, he gives each of them a lemon drop from his pocket and stands. His face is drawn.

"Hello, John," I say quietly.

"Hello. How are you?"

"I'm all right. Except for having nightmares."

He nods in the way he does when listening to a patient. "I'm sure it will pass. In the meantime, I can give you morphine pills to help you sleep."

"I thought—" I pause, reluctant to disagree with him so soon after his arrival. "Haven't you told me that morphine can cause patients to have nightmares?"

"Oh," he says vaguely. "That's right."

His absentmindedness alarms me. "John, are you well?"

He wobbles his head in a way that I take as a nod. "Just tired."

As we walk into the parlor together, I wonder if he is drunk. But spirits usually make him angry and aggressive, not calm and distracted. *Be grateful that he seems to be over his rage,* I tell myself.

I have asked the Wilders to be the children's godparents, so they stand with us near the font during the baptismal service. John holds himself slightly apart from us with his hands behind his back and an unfocused look on his face. When the rector asks the customary questions of the parents and godparents, John remains silent, and again a spark of anger flares within me. I tamp it down by staring at my beautiful children as they go through this holy rite. Julia warned Jimmy and Nellie that they were going to get water poured on their heads, and I feel proud that neither of them cries.

Back at the house, we enjoy a celebratory meal of roast goose with all the trimmings and a black-walnut cake with maple icing for dessert. After the meal, Jimmy and Ella go into the parlor to play checkers, and I take Nellie upstairs for a nap.

When I come back down, I find John and the Wilders still seated in the dining room. "We need to have a family conference," Eli says from the head of the table.

Dread grips me as I take my seat. Julia passes me a cup of coffee, and Eli says, "We are happy to have Sarah and the children stay with us as long as need be, but I must say that I think you two would be making a mistake to let this separation continue much longer."

John rises from the table, moves to the sideboard behind his chair, and helps himself to Eli's port. After downing a glass, he turns to his brother-in-law. "What business is this of yours?"

Julia signals to her husband that she will answer. "John, Sarah has been here nearly a month, and the talk shows no sign of dying down. People say she must have been that Indian's lover, or you would not be refusing to live with her."

He narrows his eyes at her. "Do they now?"

Although I know perfectly well that John doubts my innocence, his refusal to defend me before his family stings like a slap. "In this one case, the gossips are right," I say bitterly. "John isn't sure of my honor."

He shoots me a look of something close to loathing. "Let's just say that I don't believe you have told me everything."

Staring directly at him, I state, "I did *not* betray you, John. My relationship with Chaska was perfectly chaste."

John sets down his glass. As he gazes at me, his face softens with a childlike longing to believe. For an instant, I think I have convinced him. Then I see his eyes grow dull as he remembers the gossip. "That's what you would say, isn't it?"

Cruelly disappointed, I shrug at my sister-in-law. "You see? There is little I can do to justify myself if he has decided I'm a liar. It's impossible to prove that something didn't happen."

Eli rubs his side-whiskers with the knuckles of his right hand. "That's true. It's why the courts operate on the principle of innocent until proven guilty."

"This isn't a court!" John spits out. "This is my marriage."

"Please," Eli says, nodding at John's empty chair. My husband resumes his seat, carrying the decanter of port with him. Eli goes on, "I must say that, after observing her closely the last three weeks, I believe Sarah's story."

I stare at him in surprise and then look at my husband. John finishes his second glass of port and pours another. "Did I ask?"

"No, but I have decades of experience listening to testimony, and it is my considered opinion that your wife is telling the truth."

A bitter smile twists John's face. "You're not the one who will have to wallow in some filthy buck's leavings if you're wrong."

I stand so abruptly that my chair screeches backward. "You have no call to talk about me in such a disgusting way." John closes his eyes and rubs his forehead as though it aches. His shoulders slump. "God knows, Sarah, I want to believe you, but when an entire state tells me I'm a fool and a cuckold to boot, what am I to think?"

Warily, I sit back down. Eli says. "John, people in this state are not thinking rationally. They don't care if their accusations are right or wrong; they only want someone to blame for the terrible carnage. Right now, we're having a witch hunt every bit as vicious as the one that took place in Salem two hundred years ago, and I very much fear that two centuries from now, people will look back and see that we were just as misled by mass hysteria."

"What are you saying?" Julia demands. "The Indians shouldn't be punished?"

"Not to the extent of hanging three hundred men. In the past, the U.S. government negotiated with the Sioux as with a sovereign nation. So if this was a war between nations, the victor has no right to execute soldiers who fought for the other side. Only those who committed atrocities against civilians deserve hanging. That is my legal opinion, and I daresay President Lincoln agrees with me, or he wouldn't have appointed a commission to review the convictions."

John rubs his temple. "A very pretty theory, but what the hell does it have to do with Sarah and me?"

"Your wife"—Eli nods in my direction—"has been fighting to prevent the execution of an innocent man, and that's why people can't forgive her. She calls into question the integrity of the trials. No one wants to hear it, not when they're howling for vengeance. As far as I can tell, she is one of the few people calling for justice."

John sets down his goblet. "I'm afraid I cannot credit her with quite as much altruism as you do."

His words sting. No one in his family knows that I was accused of immorality before our marriage. Is that what he's referring to now? Have these new rumors caused him to doubt my past? *But that can't be,* I tell myself. *He's a doctor. He could tell you had never had relations.*

Leaning toward him, I say, "I don't claim to be noble, John. To me, it's very simple. Chaska saved my life, not once, not twice, but many times. I owe him every effort I can make to save his."

"Even if you destroy my life in the process?"

I shake my head. "You're not threatened with death. You are alive and well, and you have your wife and children. There is no rope around your neck."

"But what about my livelihood? If I cannot earn a living, we will starve."

"Your family would never let that happen, Johnny," Julia says softly.

My husband stiffens. "Thank you, but I do not accept charity."

"It is too soon for this kind of talk," Eli says. "If you and Sarah would present a united front to the world, the gossip would die down. Something else will capture the public's imagination. But only if you stand together."

John looks at me piercingly. "Is this what you want? Even knowing that I may never feel the same way about you again?"

My heart feels bruised, and all I want is to find some place to hide. But I must think of my children. They will be better off if their father and I can exist together in harmony than if we live apart. "The whole time I was captive, I prayed for us to be reunited, John. Now all I ask is that you give me a chance to be a good wife to you."

He frowns. "I need to be certain that I can support us." He turns to Eli. "Is it all right if Sarah and the children stay here a few more weeks?"

Eli nods.

John faces me again. "I'll try to get reestablished as soon as possible."

"All right," I say, but I cannot muster any enthusiasm. Eli may have succeeded in brokering a reconciliation between us, but unless I am seriously mistaken, I face a cold and joyless homecoming when I finally go back to live with John again.

CHAPTER

36

GEORGE GLEASON PULLS ON THE REINS, AND OUR WAGON SLOWLY comes to a halt. On the road ahead, two armed Sioux warriors walk toward us. Hapa raises his rifle and fires—at Chaska, who falls backward, blood spurting from a hole in his chest.

I scream.

Strong hands shake me. John growls, "Wake up, Sarah! You're dreaming."

I jerk upright and collapse against his shoulder, crying. For an instant, I think we are in our bedroom at Yellow Medicine and my entire captivity was a nightmare. Then the placement of the window reminds me that we are in Red Wing. Our children were baptized today, and tomorrow John is leaving us again.

"My God, you weren't exaggerating when you said you have nightmares."

I sit back against the headboard and wipe away my tears.

"What was the dream about?"

"The day we were captured."

My husband lights the oil lamp by his side of the bed, gets up, and pads over to where his coat hangs on the back of a chair. Rummaging in his pocket, he takes out a paper packet and extracts a pill. He pours a glass of water from the carafe on my bedside table and hands it and the pill to me.

"What is this?"

"Morphine. It can hardly give you a worse dream than the one you just had."

"I suppose not." I smile ruefully and swallow the pill.

John sits on the end of the bed, facing me. "How bad was it, Sarah?"

"What? The nightmare?"

He shrugs. "Being taken prisoner, I guess."

"I never saw anyone killed before," I say. "It was horrible. The first shot knocked Mr. Gleason against me, and the next blast pushed him out of the wagon. He lay gibbering in pain on the ground. Then he called my name, but there was nothing I could do. Hapa pointed his gun at me, and Chaska had to argue with him for over an hour to convince him to spare my life."

At the mention of Chaska, John scowls, so I proceed cautiously, "But the worst part of captivity was living in fear for days on end." My words pick up urgency. "Never knowing for sure who my enemies were or who might attack me. I'd be with a group of Indians who seemed friendly enough when suddenly one of them might threaten to cut off my head or steal the children. You can't imagine what it's like to live in constant dread."

John blinks. "Yes, I can," he says hoarsely. "We felt that way when we were fleeing from Yellow Medicine. It was the worst three days of my life."

Three days. I almost laugh at the notion that our experiences are comparable. John has no idea what I've been through. Even so, he has made a rare concession by admitting he was afraid. Maybe I can use that vulnerability to make him understand why I feel so bound to Chaska. "I lived with terror almost every day for six weeks. The only time I felt remotely safe was when Chaska was nearby, and even then I had to worry about the other Indians in camp. Whenever he was away hunting or fighting, I nearly went crazy with fear."

John winces as though I have struck him. "It should have been me there to protect you. That's what you're saying, isn't it?"

"No." A wave of fatigue washes over me as the morphine takes hold. I open my eyes wide to try to stay awake. "The war separated so many families. No one blames you for not being with us."

"Not even you? You don't think me less of—" He falls silent and presses his lips together tightly.

Less of a man. That is what he cannot bring himself to say. My heart cracks with pity. The miserable truth is that my time with the Sioux taught me that there are men who have far more honor, kindness, and dignity than John does, but what good will it do either of us for me to say that?

"I've already told you. I know you made the best decision you could. You didn't know the conflict had spread from Acton down to Redwood."

He stares at me, waiting for something more, but I cannot give it to him. Finally, I say, "I'm getting very sleepy."

John nods, walks around to his side of the bed, and blows out the light. As I lay my head down upon my pillow, the thought comes to me: *Why does he carry morphine in his coat pocket?*

The days grow colder and darker as we slip into December. I sew from breakfast until bedtime to ensure that we will have enough warm clothing, and my fingers and wrists ache from the constant work. Julia offers to assist me, but her eyes are weak and her sewing irregular. I decline tactfully, saying that she bears enough of a burden, having three extra mouths to feed.

The first Friday in December, James Wakefield arrives unexpectedly shortly before supper. After a boisterous reunion with Jimmy, his namesake and nephew, James asks to speak to me alone. Immediately, I grow wary. James has never been my ally. One time in Shakopee, when John beat me so severely that I screamed from the second-story window for help, his brother stood in the street below preventing the neighbors from entering our house and "interfering in a family affair."

As the rest of the family withdraws from the parlor, James pulls an envelope from his inner coat pocket and lays it on the mantelpiece. Then he stands on the hearth, his chest pushed out and his hands behind his back—his legislator's stance, I secretly call it. He makes little effort to hide his dislike as he gazes at me. "I've been to visit John. He asked me to bring you some money so you won't be dependent on the Wilders for every little thing. It is in that envelope."

I blink, wondering why John finds charity from James preferable to charity from Julia. "Is his medical practice doing better?" I ask.

James smiles condescendingly. "Didn't you know? He's been appointed the physician in charge of medical care for the noncombatant Indians interned at Fort Snelling."

"So he's in Saint Paul," I say, hurt that John hasn't written to tell me so.

"Correct."

Although it is galling to beg James for information, I ask, "Did he give you any message for me?"

"No. None."

I sigh. Turning my mind to John's new post, I say, "Eli said there are at least 1,700 Indians interned at Snelling. That's a lot of people for one doctor to attend."

James shrugs. "Since most of them prefer their savage ways to our medicine, I doubt John will be overtaxed."

Again, worry about Ina niggles at me. "Do you think John could inquire whether someone is at the fort? I worry about the old woman I lived with."

An angry flush covers James's cheeks. "Good God, you don't learn, do you? You've already made my brother a laughingstock throughout the state, and now you want him to inquire after some old hag?"

My stomach flips over. "What do you mean, laughingstock?"

"Don't tell me you haven't heard the talk."

I shake my head.

A grudging expression comes over James's face. "Well, for all your faults, I'll grant you don't frequent saloons, and that's where this kind of gossip spreads. People say John must not be much of a man since you prefer that buck of yours."

"That's a foul lie!"

"Is it?" His voice drips scorn. "Then why did you put so much energy into trying to save him, even to the extent of threatening officers? How could you become so infatuated with a savage?"

"I'm not infatuated!" Even as I make the declaration, I have a treacherous memory of Chaska whispering in my ear the night he lay on my pallet, and I blush. James's eyes flash with triumph. Feeling caught out, I exclaim, "Wouldn't you be grateful if someone saved your life? Wouldn't you make every effort to save his in return?"

James combs his fingers through his chin whiskers. "Yes, but I wouldn't be hysterical about it. They say you've become a monomaniac."

"Oh, for God's sake! Yes, I exerted every effort, and I would do it again. Chaska is an honorable, generous man, but he's going to hang, and it's my fault because I talked him into surrendering to the army."

James narrows his eyes at me. "I wish you'd never come back from the war."

In response to the hatred in his voice, I lift my chin. "If I had died, do you think John would have ever seen his children again? The Sioux would have taken them to Dakota or Canada, and they would have been lost to your brother forever."

"Rather that than he should be saddled with a bitch like you for the rest of his days," James retorts. I gasp. Not ten minutes ago, he was laughing with my boy and exclaiming over how much he'd grown.

"You can't mean that. John loves his children." My voice grows husky. "I thought you did too."

James flushes, opens his mouth, and clamps it shut again. He scowls at me as though it is my fault he blurted out something so heartless. "Of course, I love them. In spite of their mother." After gesturing broadly as if to sweep me away, he starts to leave the room but then looks back at me. "Try not to make things worse than they already are, Sarah. Stay at home. Don't draw attention to yourself."

I stand with as much dignity as I can muster. "That's what I'm trying to do. All I've ever wanted is the chance to live quietly with my husband again."

James grunts skeptically as he walks away.

That night, the brilliant light from a full moon streams through my bedroom window, as thick and pearly as milk. Normally, I would pull the curtains shut against the intrusive moonbeams, but their beauty is strangely comforting, and anyway, I cannot sleep for remembering the conversation with James. Are people really saying I had such a passion for Chaska that I didn't want to return to my husband? Where is the logic in such a foolish idea? If Chaska and I had been lovers, we could have easily escaped to the Dakota Territory long before slow-poke Sibley reached Camp Release.

No wonder John has been in such a fury. The rumors have cast doubt not only upon my honor but also upon his manhood. *Cuckold.* That's the word he used. Poor John. Every time he stops in a saloon for a beer, he must have to face the speculative glances and hear the behind-his-back whispers.

He doesn't have much experience with having his name dragged through the mud. Oh, there was a public outcry after one of the times he beat me—a neighbor wrote the newspaper, demanding to know why a man should earn a government salary for whipping his wife. That, however, was nothing compared to this, a public mockery of John's very masculinity. Any hope that he will ever completely forgive me grows dim.

As though conjured by that thought, the light streaming through the window fades. A cloud must be drifting across the face of the moon. I pull my covers up to my chin, close my eyes, and go through a long list of prayers, ending as always with pleas for a pardon for Chaska, safety for Ina, and reconciliation with my husband.

When I open my eyes again, the room is noticeably darker. Has a snowstorm begun? I reach for the shawl draped on the bedpost and walk to the window.

Night has taken a large bite out of the moon. I cry out in shock. Immediately, I recall that I have seen this before—and not so long ago at that. It is a lunar eclipse, a perfectly natural event. Even so, my heart races with anxiety. I step backward and, not taking my eye off the window, grope for the bed behind me and sit down. As happened last June, the curved shadow of the sun encroaches upon the moon's surface so gradually that I cannot see it advance, and yet, the blackened area grows larger. When darkness covers more than half the orb, the shadowy area turns ominous orange-red.

The sight awakens some primitive terror lying dormant within me, and sobs rise from deep within my gut, bruising my throat as they elbow their way upward and bursting from my lips with the primeval roar of inmates escaping from bedlam. I double over my lap and weep uncontrollably.

The last time I saw a blood moon, I feared it was a sign that the red nation surrounding us would rise up in rebellion. That dreadful thought proved to be prophetic. What can this new portent mean? Will Little Crow come sweeping back from the plains with western tribes as allies to annihilate the remaining settlers in Minnesota? Or will President Lincoln's commission decide to hang all three hundred prisoners, causing a massacre of red men such as this country has never seen?

My eyes are swollen from crying so hard. Groping like a blind person, I crawl back into my bed, where I lie shivering until sleep finally overtakes me.

On Monday, December 15, when Eli comes home for his midday meal, he calls out as he enters the front door, "Sarah, Julia, come at once!"

We are in the parlor—I on the sofa with my sewing and Julia at the desk with her correspondence—and we exchange looks of surprise as we hurry into the hall.

"There you are!" Eli exclaims as he hangs his overcoat on the rack. Picking up a newspaper from the table, he thrusts it into my hands. "Look! President Lincoln has reduced the number of Sioux sentenced to be hanged, but I can't tell if your Chaska is named. There's a Chaskadon. Is that him?"

My hands shake as I take the paper, and my eyes have difficulty focusing on the article. Finally, I find the pertinent lines. "No! It's not him. This isn't Chaska's case number, and my Chaska was never accused of killing a pregnant woman." I scan the entire list of names but don't see another Chaska. Meeting Eli's gaze, I ask, "Are these the men to be pardoned or the men to be hanged?"

"These are the ones to be hanged. Lincoln reduced the list to thirty-nine. They will hang on December 26."

"Oh!" I drop the newspaper and clap both hands over my mouth to keep from shouting in triumph. Julia puts an arm around me.

"See, everything has worked out," she says soothingly. "He's been pardoned."

"Not exactly pardoned," Eli says. "He still has to serve a prison sentence, but the important thing is that Chaska will live. Your testimony did the trick, Sarah."

I can hardly take in the news. After two months of agonizing worry, I can finally rest, knowing that Chaska will be all right. Of course, prison will be terrible for him; he is used to living free. But anything is better than hanging.

For an instant, I close my eyes, overwhelmed by the desire to see him one more time. How I wish we could have learned this news together.

Eli pats me on the arm, and I laugh. Then I ask, "Where do you think he will be imprisoned? In Mankato?"

"Probably not. There's been talk of sending the prisoners out of state."

"Oh." Despite my elation over the reprieve, my heart sinks to hear that he will be so far away. "Do you think the army would let me write Chaska? He can't read but a few words. If I sent a letter, do you think someone would read it to him?"

Julia steps around to face me. "John will not stand for it, and honestly, Sarah, I don't understand why you want to. You have paid your debt to the man. Let it go."

Letting my head droop, I say in resignation, "All right, Julia. If you think that's best."

A week later, John writes to say that he is coming for Christmas, and he plans to bring me and the children back with him to St. Paul afterward. He hasn't given us much warning—by the time we receive the letter, Christmas Eve is only three days away—so Julia and I go into a frenzy of last-minute preparations.

When John arrives on Christmas Eve, he says very little either during dinner or in the parlor afterward. As in November, he acts vague and disconnected from his surroundings. I begin to have an uneasy suspicion. Early Christmas morning, I wake before he does and, crossing the room to where his coat hangs on the back of a chair, check the pockets. As I expect, I find a paper packet of pills that look exactly like the one he gave me in November. Since I know of no medical reason for John to be taking medication, I can conclude only one thing—my husband is using morphine to dull his unhappiness.

After putting the packet back, I sit on the chair, lean my elbows on the dressing table, and hide my face in my hands. Pity and contempt swirl through my mind. Why should John, who sat out the war in relative safety, need opiates to endure his days when I must rely solely on my own character?

Abruptly, I recall the terrible tantrums Jimmy used to have as a toddler when he didn't get his way, and my head jerks up as I see the similarities to my husband. The fact that John resorts to hitting me when he's angry proves that he isn't in control of himself. My husband is morally weak and always has been, and I've just never seen it, mistaking his bluster and sarcasm for strength.

I turn to look at John's prostrate form. He is snoring loudly—he drank too much last night—and I shudder with hopelessness. What am I going to do? Do I still want to go to St. Paul with him, knowing what I now know?

For a moment, I think about my old idea of opening a dressmaking business. Could I earn enough to support my family? Almost as soon as I pose the question, I know with a certainty that if I ever leave John, he and his family will make sure I lose the children. Given my notoriety throughout Minnesota, the courts would certainly award sole custody to John, and I may never see my darlings again.

If that happened, I would go mad. To lose my children would destroy me as the war did not. *You'll have to make the best of it, my girl,* I tell myself. *Salvage what you can of your marriage.*

I rise and pull on my boots so I can head outside to the privy. As I descend the staircase, I think, *Maybe John using morphine isn't such a bad thing. He's a doctor. He knows how much to take. If it helps calm his rage, it might be worth it.*

John does not attend the Christmas service with us. When we return to the house, I find him sitting on the parlor sofa, his head lolling against the back and a foolish smile on his face. The sight confirms my suspicions about his drug use.

As we gather around the Christmas tree, I do my best to act jolly for the children. Working late at night, I have knitted each of them a bright wool hat and mittens, and with the cash John sent me, I bought them oranges and chocolate drops.

The children's gleeful shouts rouse John. Without a word, he goes upstairs and returns laden with presents and smelling of whiskey. He gives cologne to his sister, port to Eli, a book to his niece, five carved soldiers to Jimmy, a rag doll to Nellie, and new earbobs to me: garnet ovals set in gold filigree.

"Oh, John, these are lovely." I wait until he resumes his seat next to me before whispering, "Are you sure we can afford this?"

"You let me worry about that," he answers. "I wanted to give you something to replace the ones that thieving Indian stole."

"What is this?" Eli demands, looking up from the bottle of port, whose label he has been examining. "You never told us Chaska stole from you."

"Not Chaska," I say, glancing sideways at John. To my relief, he doesn't react to the name of his nemesis. "His sister."

John nods emphatically. "Damn fine earbobs that slut stole."

"John, please!" Julia exclaims. "Moderate your language."

He claps a hand over his mouth and waggles his eyebrows. "Yes, Julia."

His sister shoots a look of concern to Eli, who responds by saying heartily, "Well, this has been a fine Christmas morning, and we still have a grand dinner ahead of us, don't we, dear?"

"Yes, I'll go check on it."

As she passes him on her way out of the room, he surreptitiously hands her the bottle of port to carry away.

"Didn't Reverend Welles give a fine sermon?" Eli asks me.

"Yes, he did," I answer, still keeping an eye on John. He has closed his eyes and leaned back against the sofa. "I regretted having to inform him that I'm leaving for St. Paul on Sunday and won't be able to have him baptize me."

"You can still be baptized. Find an Episcopal church in St. Paul. Mr. Welles could write a letter to the rector saying that you've had the necessary instruction."

"That's a good idea," I say, distracted by John's sudden snoring.

"Sarah, promise me you will do so," Eli says earnestly.

I turn to him and smile, touched by his concern for me. "I promise."

The two days after Christmas, I spend my time washing clothes and packing. On Saturday, I have the house to myself, except for the maid. Eli and Julia make calls on social acquaintances, planning to end their day by dining with a fellow judge. In the afternoon, John takes the children for a sleigh ride past Barn Bluff and along the bank of the Mississippi. By the time they return, our trunks are filled.

Sunday morning, we meet over the breakfast table before the Wilders leave for church. Dora, their maid, brings in the Saturday newspaper, which arrived yesterday while the Wilders were out, and sets it on the table in front of Eli. The headline announces the hanging of the condemned Sioux. Eli is busy explaining something about the weather to his daughter, so I turn the paper to make it easier to read. Immediately, my eye alights upon my own name.

Snatching up the newspaper, I skim the article swiftly. What I see there in black and white shatters me.

Chaska was hanged. I stare at his name, willing the addition of those three crucial letters to make it "Chaskadon," but although the print starts to swim before my eyes, the words themselves do not change. The story states clearly that Chaska, the man convicted of kidnapping Mrs. Sarah Wakefield, was executed.

"No!" I crumple up the paper between my hands. Everyone at the table looks at me. I cannot bear their scrutiny. I need to be alone, to find a way to convince myself that this report is a mistake—that such a terrible thing could *not* have happened. But my legs feel like gelatin, making it impossible to flee the room.

"No!" I moan. Julia speaks to me, but she sounds so far away. After shoving aside my plate of eggs and ham, I spread the paper on the table and smooth out the sheets, convinced that if I can just rub out the wrinkles, the words will go away.

But they don't. Chaska is dead. My vision blurs. I cover my face with my hands and shout through my fingers, "He's dead! Chaska is dead! They hanged him after they said they wouldn't."

My voice cracks. A horrible cord of sorrow and guilt tightens around my throat, slowly cutting off my air and my ability to protest. I begin to scream wordlessly. The roar fills my lungs and my throat and my ears and the room. I want the sheer volume of sound to blow the roof off this house and send a wave of fury across the whole bloodstained state. But I'm not strong enough. The next thing I know, I am bent over the table, crying like a young child.

One time when I went sledding as a young girl, my sled crashed into that of another child. I've never forgotten the sickening jolt, the splintering noise, the disorienting sense of being upended and landing face down in the snow. I wasn't really hurt, but the feelings of dislocation and shock lasted for hours.

So it is now. Julia's arms go around me, pulling me up. Eli puts a glass of brandy in my hands and insists that I drink it. I take one swallow, but the molten liquid racing down my throat makes me sick. I push the glass away. The world seems altered, as though a protective wall of glass has broken into fragments and cannot be replaced. I expel a deep breath, lift my head, and see John on the other side of the table. He hugs himself as though he is cold, and he stares at me with a terrible expression. His eyes are hollow, and he looks hurt, betrayed, and abandoned.

CHAPTER

37

I AM STILL TREMBLING FROM SHOCK AS I GO UPSTAIRS TO RINSE MY FACE. As I lean over the washbasin and splash cool water on my cheeks, John enters the bedroom and closes the door with a harsh click. I whirl around, thinking, *This is it. This time he's going to kill me.*

But his eyes hold no rage, merely a profound emptiness. He leans back against the door and folds his arms across his chest. "So now what do we do?"

I grab the towel, dry my face, and try to focus my scattered thoughts. "What do you mean? Chaska is dead, but that doesn't change anything between us."

Just like that, John's eyes spark with rage. "Let's get one thing straight. I never want to hear that man's name again."

My emotions balk—Chaska is dead; do we have to annihilate his memory?—but just as quickly, my resistance collapses. Nothing I can do will help poor Chaska now. "All right, John. So decide, do you still want me to come to St. Paul?"

"I would as soon throw you out into the street." I flinch, and a look of satisfaction skitters across John's face. Then he sighs. "But Jimmy would never forgive me. He sees himself as your champion now."

I stretch out a placating hand. Our son and I have grown close, but he needs his father too. "He's a good boy, John. You would have been so proud to see how brave he was."

"Am I supposed to thank you for that?"

"No, I take no credit for his courage. It seems to be just who he is." John rubs his forehead. "Sarah, this conversation isn't getting us anywhere."

"Where exactly do you want to 'get'? My only goal is for us to put our shattered lives back together. Do you still want that?"

"I don't know. I don't trust you anymore. But—" He sits slumped on the far corner of the bed, half turned away from me. "Julia and Eli are right. We'll never know unless we try. And maybe if we get back together, the talk will die down."

"That's not exactly a vote of confidence. Or a declaration of love."

"Love!" He jumps up to confront me. "You dare say that to me?"

"I didn't love him, John."

"You gave a pretty damn good imitation of it downstairs. I can't help but wonder if you would have wailed like that for me."

"You wouldn't ask that if you'd seen me cry when I thought you were dead." I move closer and reach out my hand again.

Ignoring my gesture, John stares stonily ahead. Then he rubs his temple. "My head is killing me." Reaching into his pocket, he pulls out a packet of pills and swallows one without any water.

"John, I—" I halt, realizing that this is not the time to confront him about his morphine use. "We have to make a decision."

He glances around the bedroom and shrugs. "Everything is packed. We might as well get back together now as later."

For a moment, I cannot respond. How cruel it seems that, after surviving weeks of terror when the only thing that kept me going was the hope of getting back to this man, the prospect of living with him now fills me with as much dread as I felt the afternoon I was captured and driven off to an unknown fate. I turn to put on my hat. "If we're going to do it, let's be on our way."

Winter is always a dark season, but this year is the bleakest winter of my life. After driving us to the frame house he has rented on Ryan Avenue, John announces that he will be at Fort Snelling most of his time—and when he does come home, he intends to sleep in the maid's room off the kitchen since we cannot afford a servant.

So I am alone with the children, stuck in a strange city with no acquaintances and no transport. I pass my days in a fog, often crying as I do my chores. Jimmy watches me with a frown on his face and tries to comfort me by making his bed unasked, drawing me pictures of dogs and horses, and keeping his sister occupied when he sees me sitting listlessly with my head in my hands.

Nightmares plague me. Either I gasp awake because of the horrifying sensation of a noose tightening around my neck, or I find myself crying out at the lurid sight of a forest hung with writhing bodies that have protruding tongues and bulging eyes, a forest in which I search in vain for Chaska.

One night after I wake up screaming, Jimmy comes into my bedroom with the dog. "Mama, I think Buster should sleep with you. He'll make you feel better."

"Won't you miss him?"

He shakes his head and stares at me with sober blue eyes.

"All right," I say.

Jimmy hoists the animal up unto my bed. "Hug him when you go to sleep, Mama. He'll keep the bad dreams away."

John won't like the idea of an animal sharing our bed, but then again, he doesn't sleep with me anymore. "Thank you, son." I coax the dog to snuggle with me. I know Buster won't keep nightmares away, but it will be nice to have his company.

After a Sunday snowstorm in mid-January, I go outside to shovel a path from our front door to the street. A horse and buggy waits in front of the house next door. Minutes later, the Andersons come outside, the wife all wrapped in a hooded cape and black shawl and the husband wearing an overcoat and a fur hat.

"Good-morning!" I call. "Where are you off to this snowy morning?"

"We're on our way to service at Christ Episcopal Church."

"Is it near? I'm looking for an Episcopal church."

The husband tells me the address and the name of the rector. Hurrying into my own house, I jot down the information. Later that afternoon, I write the minister a letter of introduction.

Three days later, he calls on me. "Mrs. Wakefield, I am the Reverend

Mr. George DuBois," he says, extending his hand when I open the door. He is about forty and has a sloped forehead and a large hooked nose. When he sets down his satchel and removes his overcoat, the elegance of his clothing surprises me: he wears a black wool Prince Albert coat, a striped waistcoat, and a black silk cravat.

"Please come into the parlor," I say, and we walk into the sitting room. He sits on the sofa and crosses his legs. "Now, your letter said that you are considering attending Christ Church?"

For the next hour, I tell him about my captivity with the Indians. When I finish, Reverend DuBois exclaims, "Of course, you would want to turn to the Lord after such a dreadful time."

He bends down to search through his satchel. Pulling out a pamphlet, he hands it to me. "We at Christ Church would welcome you into our parish. Let me give you this tract, and after you have a chance to read it, we can talk again."

I glance at it and see the title *What It Means to Be a Christian.* Laying it aside, I say, "My children and I will come to church as soon as we're able. It is difficult since my husband keeps our horse and wagon when he is at Fort Snelling."

"I understand." Reverend DuBois rises. "It has been a pleasure to meet you Mrs. Wakefield. I look forward to speaking with you again about spiritual matters."

John visits the following weekend, so I use the opportunity to drive to church, leaving the children with him. The service is much the same as the ones I attended in Red Wing, although Reverend Mr. DuBois has a more florid preaching style than Reverend Mr. Welles. After the service, as I join the line of parishioners leaving by the center aisle so they can speak to the minister, I see my neighbors and greet them.

"So you made it! Welcome," Mr. Anderson says.

"Yes, I sent a note to Reverend DuBois, and he was good enough to call on me." We take a couple of steps and halt.

"He's a wonderful man of God," says Mrs. Anderson, a plump brunette of about forty. "He started a Sunday School and confirmation class, and he leads a Bible study for those in their middle years. We're going to hate to lose him."

"Is he leaving?" I ask in surprise.

"He is an interim rector," Mr. Anderson says. "We have put out a call to a permanent rector, but he will not be able to take the pulpit until this spring."

"I see," I say slowly, wondering how this will affect me.

By the time I reach the doorway, I decide that this is not the time or place to pose such a question. When I greet Reverend DuBois and compliment him on his sermon, he smiles and calls over a pair of ladies.

"This is Mrs. Morgan and Mrs. Kingsbury. They are leaders in our ladies' aid society. Ladies, Mrs. Wakefield has expressed interest in joining our congregation."

Mrs. Morgan, a diminutive white-haired woman, nods to me and says in a high, quavery voice, "So happy to meet you."

Mrs. Kingsbury, however, glances at me appraisingly. "Wakefield?"

I stiffen. "Yes. My husband, Dr. John Wakefield, has been appointed the physician in charge of the interned Indians at Fort Snelling."

Mrs. Kingsbury's eyes narrow slightly. "And if I am not mistaken, you yourself were caught up in the recent conflict."

"Yes." My fingers curl involuntarily into fists. "My children and I were held captive for six weeks."

"How terrible!" Mrs. Morgan's dark eyes express sympathy.

"We survived with the help of Providence," I say quietly.

Behind me, Reverend DuBois booms, "Amen!"

"I am glad to have met you both," I say to the two women. "But I'm afraid I must be getting home. My husband is waiting for his Sunday dinner."

"Oh, yes," Mrs. Morgan laughs, "the menfolk do enjoy their meals, don't they? Especially on their day of rest."

"That they do."

Both ladies return my farewell nod, but as I walk away, I hear furious whispering behind me.

When John visits, he is vague and sleepy most of the time. He takes morphine openly now. Although I am uneasy about his use of opiates, I must admit that the drug seems to tamp down his rage, so I don't make an issue of it.

Over meals, I sometimes ask about his work, but it quickly becomes apparent that John hates dealing with the Sioux and does not want to talk about it. Mostly, we discuss the children or the ongoing war with the South. I have read that the Union might start drafting men into the army, but when I ask John about it, he shrugs. "I'm already working for the government. I doubt it will affect me."

When I tell him that I plan to join the church, he refills his whiskey glass. "If you think that will make you happy, Sarah. And it may help salvage your reputation."

"Perhaps, but the main thing is I want to make peace with my Maker."

"Make peace?" John's sharp tone cuts into me. "What do you need to atone for, Sarah?"

His constant probing wearies me. "Just the little ways I fail from day to day."

"If you say so," he says and walks away.

When I enter the nave of the church after two weeks away, kindly Mrs. Morgan stops short at the sight of me and scuttles down a side aisle. My eyes sting, but I keep my head high as I walk down the center aisle to an empty pew. The rejection wounds me so deeply that, as much as I love hymn music, I find myself unable to sing because repressed tears clog my voice.

After the service, I say to Reverend DuBois, "I was wondering when we might talk again. I am eager to schedule a time to be baptized and join the church."

"Ah, yes." He strokes his chin. "That isn't a decision that can be rushed. I'm afraid I have so many obligations getting everything organized for the next rector."

"Of course." I cannot keep the sound of disappointment from my voice.

The rector flushes. "Well, I will check my schedule."

To my intense frustration, I hear nothing from Reverence DuBois, and the next time I attend church, I remind him of his promise. Finally, in early March, he pays me a visit. I lead him into the parlor, where he sits on the sofa, close to the edge as though he wants to leave quickly. I take the chair. "Mrs. Wakefield, after careful deliberation, I have concluded that I am not the right person to usher you into the church. I leave in a few weeks' time, and I have so many things to do before then."

"But when we first spoke, you acted eager to welcome me."

Reverend DuBois hesitates, rubbing his knuckles on his lower lip. His easy charm has deserted him. Finally, he says, "I feel compelled to point out that when we first spoke, you were not completely frank about your situation."

"Yes, I was." As anger mounts within me, I grasp the arms of my chair. "You have been listening to gossip, haven't you? The stories are lies."

"That is precisely the issue. Because of my imminent departure, I do not have time for a thorough discernment of this situation. And I cannot make a decision that might leave my successor with an unre-solved..." The color in his cheeks deepens.

"Problem," I finish the sentence for him.

"Mrs. Wakefield, you must realize that I simply cannot ignore the questions about your character."

I jump up and cry, "Did not Christ come into this world to save sinners? Even if I were guilty of the things the gossips claim, that would be all the more reason to welcome me into the church so I might experience God's forgiveness. Why do you act as though church is only for the righteous?"

"I have never said such a thing, and you do wrong to malign my character."

"But you are allowed to malign mine?"

He presses his palms against his thighs and makes a smoothing motion along the fabric of his trousers. "Please, sit down and let us reason together."

I sit but do not soften the bitter expression of my face.

Reverend DuBois exhales heavily. "Yes, Christ came to save sinners, but He also requires them to repent. Until I am sure you have confessed and repented your sins, how can I know that you are in a proper state to receive God's grace?"

His words fill me with hopelessness. "Should I confess a sin I didn't commit?"

He looks horrified. "God forbid. All I suggest is that when the new rector comes, you discuss your desire for membership with him."

I shake my head vehemently. "Why should I want to join your church now? The ladies flee when they see me approach. They seem to believe that Christ came only to bless the already righteous and to throw sinners to one side."

He opens his mouth to protest, but I rise. "I don't think we have anything more to say to one another, Reverend DuBois. Please leave."

Mr. DuBois stands and holds out his hand. "Let us part in peace."

I put my hands behind my back like a willful child. "Good-bye."

"Good-bye. I will pray for you."

"Pray for yourself," I say as I walk him to the door, "and for those unchristian cats in your congregation."

One good thing comes out of my experience at Christ Church; anger over their rejection burns away the mist of despair hanging over me. In a paroxysm of rage, I take out my stationery and hastily compose a letter to Reverend Stephen Riggs, demanding to know the particulars of how Chaska came to be hanged.

I address the letter and lay it on the desk to be mailed the next day. Perhaps if I learn the truth of what happened, I can use it to vindicate my name. The idea occurs to me of writing a memoir to broadcast my side of the story. Narratives of Indian captivity can be very popular. Writing my tale could restore my reputation—and enable me to earn some money in case I ever need to support myself.

Satisfied with that decision, I fall asleep easily. All night, however, dreams of accusing eyes, pointing fingers, and whispered accusations disturb my slumber. The next day, I awaken in a state of indignation, certain that no one in Minnesota will lift a finger to right this terrible wrong. Driven by frenzy, I go to my desk and write to President Lincoln. After identifying myself and explaining what happened during the war, I inform him of the mistake whereby my Chaska was hanged instead of Chaskadon. I emphasize all that Chaska did to save my life and the lives of my children and then add impulsively: "I exerted myself very much to save him and many have been so ungenerous as to say I was in love with him, that I was his wife etc., all of which is absolutely false."

Realizing that I have allowed my personal feelings to distract me from the main point, I return to my theme that Chaska, who was supposed to be spared, was hanged against Lincoln's orders: "Where the fault lies I know not, but it would be extremely gratifying to me to have these heedless persons brought to justice."

Finally, I realize that one more point needs to be made—the irreparable harm done to Ina. "This family I had known for many years, and they were farmers and doing well. Now this poor old Mother is left destitute, and broken hearted."

When I reread the missive, its beseeching, almost hysterical, tone strikes me as perhaps inappropriate for the chief executive. Then I remember all the stories I have read of Mr. Lincoln's deep humanity and decide to send it as it is.

Not many days after I mail my letters, I receive a reply from Stephen Riggs:

> In regard to the mistake by which Chaska was hung instead of another, I doubt whether I can satisfactorily explain it. We all felt a solemn responsibility, and a fear that some mistake should occur. We had forgotten that he was condemned under the name We-chan-hpe-wash-tay-do-pe. We knew he was called Chaska in the prison, and had forgotten that any other except Robert Hopkins, who lived by Dr. Williamson, was so called. We never thought of the third one; so when the name Chaska was called in the prison on that fatal morning, your protector answered to it and walked out. I do not think any one was really to blame. We all regretted the mistake very much.

The letter, although written in an apologetic tone, enrages me with its feeble explanation. I cannot believe that Chaska's death happened by accident. Joseph Brown, former Indian agent, and Reverend Riggs were there to make sure that no mistaken identities occurred, and Chaska was well known to both men.

For all Mr. Riggs's consoling words, I do not believe him. The only conclusion I can draw is that the men in charge took advantage of the similarity in names to punish my Chaska for being, as they considered it, too familiar with a white woman.

That sad conclusion strengthens my resolve to write about the war. If I do not speak out, how will the truth ever be known? A hundred years from now, people will think the only victims were people like the Humphrey family, killed by hostile Sioux. Future generations will never understand that the war claimed many other victims: Chaska, who was wrongly hanged; Ina, who lost her only son; Opa and Bit-Nose who refused to fight, yet were driven from their land; and me, tarred by falsehood and tormented by nightmares. Unless I write the truth, the only stories that will survive are the ones that now dominate public discourse: the belief that all the Sioux are vicious and the white community bears no blame for the conflict.

I walk outside into the night and stare up at the cold but twinkling sky. "Wicaŋhpi Wastedaŋpi," I say, "Good Little Stars, I will never cease my efforts to clear your name."

Easter falls during the first weekend of April, and John pays us one of his sporadic visits. Sunday morning, as I prepare a leg of lamb for roasting, he comes out to the kitchen to get another cup of coffee. Seeing me in a plain calico dress and an apron, he says, "I thought you would go to church this morning."

"The church folk here have no interest in worshipping with the likes of me."

John sits at the kitchen table across from where I stand rubbing salt and pepper into the meat. "We're a fine pair, aren't we, Sarah Brown?"

I look up in surprise at hearing him use the old flirtatious gambit. "The name is Wakefield, sir," I say.

John smiles weakly, but I can see that something bothers him. "What is it?"

He runs his index finger around the rim of his coffee cup. "I may be in a spot of trouble."

"What?" My thoughts immediately run to debt or gambling.

"It's been a hard winter. We've had a lot of sickness at the camp at Fort Snelling, mostly measles, and at least two hundred have died."

His words hit me like a blow to the chest. I worry about Ina but dare not ask about her. Instead, I sit in the chair positioned catty-corner from him. "And?"

John traces the rim of his cup in the opposite direction. "Some people have accused me of negligence, and Sibley said he's going to have to investigate."

My old anger against Sibley flares up, causing me to defend John automatically. "That's ridiculous. You're a good doctor. Besides, there's no cure for measles, so how can they blame you?"

He reaches for my hand and rubs my fingers. "I wasn't very diligent about going through camp looking for cases; I only dealt with those who came to me." John looks at me, his blue eyes pleading. "I hated them so much for what they'd done that I didn't care if they got sick. But I didn't neglect patients, Sarah. When Indians came to see me, I gave the best treatment I could."

His desperate excuses make me wonder. Was his repugnance for the Sioux so strong that he was content to let them die? I can feel my face hardening with anger.

John sees it and hangs his head in a sheepish movement that reminds me of Jimmy. My bitterness starts to soften. In that moment, I realize that John is a victim of the war as much as anyone. Festering guilt that he failed to protect us, that we suffered while he was safe, has broken him. And because he is not a man who can live with the admission of failure, he has turned his rage against me, against Chaska, against the whole Sioux nation.

Just as I was once the only one who could save Chaska, I am now the only person who can offer John the forgiveness he needs. But can I do it? Do I want to?

Want to or not, I think I must. I have already decided that the only way to avoid becoming an outcast is to stay with this man. My children and I depend on him.

Sighing, I take up the burden of trying to reassure him: "Don't leap to conclusions. Sibley has a cautious nature. If I know him, he'll take his own sweet time and hope it all blows over."

"But if my medical reputation gets destroyed—"

"That isn't going to happen." I think about my husband's need to balance his warring desires for comfort and adventure, and a new idea comes to me. "If worse comes to worst, we can move. There's always California or Oregon."

John rubs beneath his nose. "You would go west with me, even after—"

I rise to my feet. "I would consider it. If I thought our marriage had a future."

He does not answer, but I don't take that as a negative sign. His pride has taken a beating, and he needs time to adjust.

I put the meat in the oven and then say, "Your coffee has gone cold." I pick up his cup, toss the coffee out the back door, and pour him some more.

"I think I'll go smoke a cigar," he says.

Nodding, I say, "I should probably check to see what the children are up to."

We walk together into the dining room, where we find our children kneeling on chairs pushed up to the table. Jimmy is drawing something for Nellie.

"What's this?" John asks, walking up behind them.

Jimmy jumps as though we caught him stealing candy. "Nothing." He flips the paper over.

"Let me see it," John says.

"It's nothing." Jimmy's voice squeaks, and I wonder why he's so afraid.

John's tone goes hard. "Let me see it, James."

The boy shoots me a pleading glance and then reluctantly turns over the drawing. John and I lean over to look at it. It features a large circle with an opening on one side. In the center is a small circle filled with zigzag lines. Around the edges of the big circle are rectangles.

As we gaze at it, Nellie pipes up, "It's a tepee!"

Of course. Jimmy has diagrammed the floor plan of Ina's tepee. I move closer in case I need to defend him from his father's anger, but John merely says, "I don't see it. I thought tepees were cone shaped."

Jimmy bites his lower lip and says, "This is inside. See, this is the door." He points at the open space on the circumference. "And the fire is in the middle."

John sets down his coffee cup and points to the rectangles. "What are these?"

"Those are our sleeping pallets. The women sleep here." Jimmy points to the side of the tepee that has three rectangles. "That was Ina's bed and Mama's and Nellie's. Over here is the men's side where Chaska and I slept."

John's mouth drops open. He picks up the paper and stares hard at it until his eyes light with discovery. Then he hands the drawing to Jimmy. "There was a men's side and a women's side?" he asks. "Did Chaska always sleep on the men's side?"

"No," Jimmy says, as he picks up his pencil and adds a few more jagged lines to the fire. "Sometimes he had to go away with the other warriors overnight."

"But he never slept on the women's side," John says. "And your mother never slept on the men's side."

I glare at him, but Jimmy is the one who slaps down his pencil and says, "No, Father. No one does so. People get in trouble if they go on the wrong side."

John turns to me with wide eyes, reminding me of his expression that day at Julia's dining table when he teetered on the edge of accepting my story. "God knows, I want to believe you," he'd said then. Can it be that all he has needed was some small piece of evidence to lay upon the scale and balance out the rumors? Something tangible he can use to answer the naysayers, if only in his mind? John blinks and says in wonder, "He was never your lover."

"Not here!" I snap. Grabbing his arm, I pull him into the hallway and out the front door to the porch. It is a chilly day, but I am too angry to go back inside for a coat. "What is wrong with you, saying that in front of the children?"

"I'm sorry. I just— So it's true. Chaska was never your lover."

I close my eyes and take a deep breath before answering for what seems like the thousandth time, "No, he wasn't. I've been telling you that for six months."

My words do nothing to erase the look of hurt from John's face. "But you loved him," he says. The words are not a question.

Sighing, I walk to the porch railing and grip it. I stare at the brown lawn, still covered with small patches of dirty snow, and recall Chaska so sharply that I almost forget John is behind me. Chaska was such a good man. For one brief moment, I will admit to myself what I have denied for so long, that I loved him, even if I could not allow myself to desire him. And he was the same with me, putting my needs ahead of his own but never straying into overfamiliarity. *A respect relationship. That's what we had.* Turning back to John, I say, "Yes. I loved him like—a *hakata.*"

"What the hell is that?"

I lean back against a porch pillar. "The Sioux have a special kind of relationship reserved for brothers and sisters. They respect each other, honor each other, and act for each other's benefit their whole life long. But they keep their distance emotionally because it is not proper for a brother and sister to become too close. That's how Chaska was with me and I was with him. We became *hakata.*"

John's gaze bores into me. "A brother. You're saying he was like a brother."

I nod. "Always."

He rubs his face as though washing it. "Oh, God, I don't know what to say. Everyone was so certain that—" John stares back at the door to the house. "And all the time, all I had to do was ask Jimmy."

Yes, I think bitterly. *Because a man's word is more credible than a woman's. Even if he's only five years old.*

John squeezes my shoulder. "I'm going to get a drink. Want one?"

I shake my head but smile to take the sting out of the refusal. My husband goes inside, but I do not follow him. In spite of the chill, I need to be by myself for a while, so I sit on the porch steps and stare out into the yard.

What do we do now? The whole time I was captive, I kept thinking, *If I can survive, if I can get back to John, I'll be able to lay down my burdens and lean on him.* But he has to use morphine and whiskey just to get through the day, and I may never be able to lean on him again.

Powerfully, I recall Chaska's voice saying, "Taŋka-Winohiŋca Waŝte, I have seen you act brave. Can you do that again?"

At first, I think it's a memory. Then I smell wood smoke and something musky like the buffalo grease Chaska used to rub in his hair.

A gust of wind blows, scattering last autumn's leaves past my feet. "Is that you?" I ask. "Wicaŋȟpi Wastedaŋpi, are you with me?"

The air grows still. Tears fill my eyes as I say, "I'm so sorry. I failed you."

The answer comes, not from the sky, but from deep within: "No matter. I have moved on."

One last gust swirls debris at my feet and sweeps it away. And then I am alone.

AUTHOR'S NOTE

Sarah Wakefield published the first edition of her memoir *Six Weeks in the Sioux Tepees* in November 1863. The following year, she published a slightly expanded edition. I believe that she was still experiencing the trauma of her captivity when she wrote her account; at times, the chronology is disordered. Events are sometimes inserted out of order, a flaw that she did not correct when she revised the narrative. The war was a time of great confusion, and Sarah lived in fear for most of it, so it is understandable that her account would not be wholly rational. She may have been suffering from what we now call post-traumatic stress disorder. As a novelist, I chose to smooth out the story, to eliminate a few unimportant incidents, and to conflate redundant ones. Despite this, the novel is essentially true to Sarah Wakefield's narrative. Readers who wish to explore the differences may want to read *Six Weeks in the Sioux Tepees.*

One enduring mystery that remains about Sarah's life is the nature of the scandal that caused churches to reject her. As far as we know, Sarah never disclosed what it was. As a novelist, I made up the backstory that I thought best fit her time period and the broader themes of my novel.

After Sarah and John Wakefield reunited in St. Paul, they continued to live together until John's death, and they patched up their relationship enough to have two more children together. A daughter, Julia, was born in 1866, and a son, John, was born in 1868.

However, most historians believe that the marriage was never happy. John continued to drink heavily. In February 1874, he suffered a brief illness. On the 17th of that month, John told Sarah that he was going to lie down and asked her to call him in an hour. Before the time was up, she heard a change in his breathing that alarmed her. She was unable to rouse him and sent for help, but it was too late. John Wakefield died at the age of fifty from an overdose of drugs. No one knows whether the death was accidental or intentional. One clue is that after John's death, Sarah learned that he had gotten the family deeply in debt. Of significance were the large sums he owed to saloon owners.

Little is known about Sarah's life after that, in part because her elder daughter burned the family's letters. Some believe, on the basis of census records, that Sarah got married again to a farmer twenty years her junior, a marriage that failed after a very short time. I think it more likely that she was working as his housekeeper and that the census taker recorded her status incorrectly. (Or perhaps, because of Sarah's track record of being the subject of sexual gossip, she lied about being married to prevent another scandal.)

Except for that brief episode, she spent the rest of her life in St. Paul. She raised her four children, and she may have run some kind of small business. Her son James preceded her in death, dying at the age of forty. When Sarah died in 1899, her obituary described her as a pioneer and a former captive of the Sioux.

DISCUSSION QUESTIONS

1 To what extent do you think Sarah's history as an abused wife influenced the choices she made during her captivity?

2 Sarah comes to recognize that Ina was the mother figure she never had and that Chaska was a better man than John. Why does she resist the idea of staying with the tribe and permanently joining their family?

3 What do you think Sarah's feelings about Chaska really were?

4 How do you think Chaska felt about Sarah? Was there ever any chance he would have taken her as his wife?

5 In what way were Sarah's racial attitudes a product of her time, and in what way was she ahead of her time?

6 How did their time in captivity affect Sarah's relationship with each of her children?

7   The question of what constitutes a good Christian is an ongoing theme of the novel. How do you evaluate Sarah in this regard?

8   What, if anything, could Sarah have done differently to save Chaska, or do you think he was doomed from the moment he decided not to leave Minnesota?

9   Why do you think Sarah stays with her husband? Could she realistically have made a different choice?

10   What do you think the long-term impact of the war will be on Sarah's children?

11   To what extent were the Dakota victims in this conflict?

12   The hanging of the thirty-eight men in Mankato was the largest mass execution in U.S. history. (Originally, thirty-nine were sentenced, but one was given a last-minute reprieve.) Do you think justice was done? Why or why not?

ACKNOWLEDGMENTS

I wish to thank the following people for helping me to obtain information and reprint permissions: Amber Bentler, Site Manager at the Fort Ridgely Historic Site; Caryl Davis, member of Christ Church, St. Paul; and Darla Gebhard, Research Librarian, Brown County Historical Society.

Much gratitude goes to my team of readers, who shared their honest reactions and made many helpful suggestions: Pat Camalliere, Ginni Davis, Susan Eisenhammer, Carol Holesha, and Barbara Melle Johnson.

I owe very special thanks to the wonderful people at Amika Press: to John Manos for allowing me to send him style questions as I wrote, to Jay Amberg and Ann Wambach for editing the book, and to Sarah Koz for creative design work.

I want to also thank Deirdre Jennings for designing the intricate war map at the beginning and Lane Brown for the stunning cover.

Last but not least, I want to thank my husband, Michael Chatlien, who traveled with me to Minnesota for research, read the complete manuscript not once but twice, listened to endless discussions about the story and characters, and reassured me over and over again, "You can do this." Michael, I love you with all my heart and will continue to love you forever.

SELECTED BIBLIOGRAPHY

Anderson, Gary Clayton and Alan R. Woolworth, editors. *Through Dakota Eyes: Narrative Accounts of the Minnesota Indian War of 1862.* St. Paul, MN: Minnesota Historical Society Press, 1988.

Beck, Paul N. "The Minnesota Volunteers and the Coming of the Dakota War of 1862." *Journal of the Indian Wars, Volume 1, Number 3: The Indians Wars' Civil War* edited by Michael Hughes, Savas Beattie, March 1, 2000

Berg, Scott W. *38 Nooses: Lincoln, Little Crow, and the Beginning of the Frontier's End.* NY: Pantheon, 2012.

"*Dakoteyah Wogdaka!* Talk Dakota!" The Native American Women's Health Education Resource Center website.

Carley, Kenneth. *The Dakota War of 1862.* 1961. St. Paul, MN: Minnesota Historical Society Press, 1976.

Deloria, Ella Cara. *The Dakota Way of Life.* Sioux Falls, SD: Mariah Press, 2007.

Derounian-Stodola, Kathryn Zabelle. "'Many persons say I am a "Mono Maniac"': Three Letters from Dakota Conflict Captive Sarah F. Wakefield to Missionary Stephen R. Riggs." *Prospects,* Oct. 2005: 1–24.

Derounian-Stodola, Kathryn Zabelle, editor. *Women's Indian Captivity Narratives.* New York: Penguin, 1998.

Hyman, Colette A. *Dakota Women's Work.* St. Paul, MN: Minnesota Historical Society Press, 2012.

Hunt, Sophia Betsworth, "Captive to the American Woods: Sarah Wakefield and Cultural Mediation." Master's Thesis, University of Tennessee, 2009. Online.

Isch, John. *The Dakota Trials: Including the Complete Transcripts and Explanatory Notes on the Military Commission Trials in Minnesota 1862–1864.* New Ulm, MN: Brown County Historical Society, 2012.

Knudson, Nicolette, Jody Snow, and Clifford Canku. *Beginning Dakota / Tokaheya Dakota Iapi Kin.* St. Paul, MN: Minnesota Historical Society Press, 2011.

LePore, Jill. *The Name of War: King Philip's War and the Origins of American Identity.* New York: Knopf, 1998.

Michno, Gregory F. *Dakota Dawn: The Decisive First Week of the Sioux Uprising, August 17–24, 1862.* NY: Savas Beatie, 2011.

Pond, Samuel W. *Dakota Life in the Upper Midwest.* 1908. St. Paul, MN: Minnesota Historical Society Press, 1986.

Renville, Mary Butler. Carrie Reber Zeman and Kathryn Zabelle Derounian-Stodola, editors. *A Thrilling Narrative of Indian Captivity: Dispatches from the Dakota War.* 1863. Lincoln, NE: U of Nebraska P, 2012.

Wakefield, Sarah F. June Namais, editor. *Six Weeks in the Sioux Tepees.* 1864. Norman, OK: U of Oklahoma P, 2002.

Wakefield, Sarah F. to Abraham Lincoln. Abraham Lincoln Papers at the Library of Congress online, March 23, 1863.

Wenger, Joanne Jahnke. "A Dead Woman's Dress: Gender and Race in Captivity During the Minnesota War of 1862." Master's thesis, University of Wisconsin–Eau Claire, Nov. 2004.

ABOUT THE AUTHOR

Ruth Hull Chatlien has been a writer and editor of educational materials for nearly thirty years, specializing in U.S. and world history. She is the author of *Modern American Indian Leaders* for middle-grade readers. Her award-winning first novel, *The Ambitious Madame Bonaparte,* portrays the tumultuous life of Elizabeth "Betsy" Patterson Bonaparte.

She lives in northeastern Illinois with her husband, Michael. When she's not writing, she can usually be found gardening, knitting, drawing, painting, or studying Swedish.

70223190R00235

Made in the USA
Lexington, KY
10 November 2017